S0-BZK-489

FALSE
ENTRY

BOOKS BY HORTENSE CALISHER

Novels

False Entry
Textures of Life
Journal from Ellipsia
The New Yorkers
Queenie
Standard Dreaming
Eagle Eye
On Keeping Women
Mysteries of Motion
The Bobby-Soxer

Novellas and Short Stories

In the Absence of Angels
Tale for the Mirror
Extreme Magic
The Railway Police and the Last Trolley Ride
The Collected Stories of Hortense Calisher
Saratoga, Hot
Age

Autobiography

Herself

FALSE ENTRY

A Novel by

HORTENSE CALISHER

WEIDENFELD & NICOLSON

New York

Copyright © 1961 by Hortense Calisher

All rights reserved. No reproduction of this book in whole
or in part or in any form may by made without written
authorization of the copyright owner.

Published by Weidenfeld & Nicolson, New York
A Division of Wheatland Corporation
10 East 53rd Street
New York, NY 10022

Originally published by Little, Brown & Company,
Boston, Toronto, 1961

Library of Congress Cataloging-in-Publication Data

Calisher, Hortense.
  False entry: a novel/ by Hortense Calisher. —
1st Weidenfeld & Nicolson ed.
     p.   cm.
  ISBN 1-555-84196-1 (pbk.)
  I. Title.
PS3553.A4F3 1988
813'.54—dc19   87–22493
                                                         CIP

*The author wishes to thank the John Simon Guggenheim Memorial
Foundation for a grant which was helpful in the writing of this
book.*

Manufactured in the United States of America
First Weidenfeld & Nicolson Edition, 1988
10 9 8 7 6 5 4 3 2 1

To C. H.

Contents

PART I
Innocence

Truth. In these days of so many trials by association, where a man **A** can show, with an infinity of fine brush strokes, how he once was an intimate of the man B, and the man B assert, with what only God might see to be craft or virtue, that he never knew the man A, I see truth as an old, hobbled unicorn limping through the forests of allegation and denial, pausing here and there to try to warm itself at some sun-foil of proof that shines for a moment through the trees. For my own strange history of third-hand listening and remembering — the history of a man formed by nature and circumstance to be the confidant, not of intimacy, but of convenience, and burdened therefore with the retentive, bruised memory of the lonely — has at least given me one bit of truth to hold for myself. It is perhaps the only such I will ever have firsthand, and it is this: I know that there are certain people in the world — two or three, for instance, that I can tick off at the moment — who either have never met me or do not even know that I exist, about whose lives I yet know enough, or so much, that I could claim entrance into their pasts with the most beautiful legalities of detail. Further, I am sure that my history in this respect is strange in emphasis only, not in kind. For I am certain that every person, even the most commonplace, if he could but search and construe his memory, holds within his orbit of power at least one other person to whom he could do the same.

False entry into another person's life, into his present by means of his past; if it does not happen oftener it must be because of lack of mal-

3

ice, whim or need. And when well accomplished, it is like the success-ful murder or the hidden masterpiece — unheralded, unsung. For this would not be that dull blackmail which deals in lost babies and old peculations discovered, but a demand of which the debtor may remain forever unaware, and for which the blackmailer, his own sole witness, is a man paid off in the currency of his need. A man perhaps who for once wants his hand on the pulse of another's life-beat, would for once see a human effect of which he is the cause — or perhaps merely an outsider who can bear no longer to stand beyond the gate.

Fancy him then, this man, standing daily, like the rest of you, in the oblique wash of conversation, rumor and murmurous fact that each night slides out to sea again like the refuse of a city. But this man is an eternal listener at the orchestrations of others, a hoarder of what others would never dream of saving, a reader of old telephone books, who never dares make the call. He saves, without reason, what a man C once said in drink about a man B; he retains gratuitously how the light fell exactly, and on what arrangements, in a house where he, long for-gotten, was once the guest of a guest; he recalls how, at a dinner table long since dropped into limbo, shadow blacked the voice of the woman on his left at the sound of a certain name. And one night, as he sits in his evening agony of non-living, listening, hand near the dead phone, to the low, mnemonic mutter of other peoples' lives, certain names, shadows, half-lights suddenly merge; all the mossy facts adhere, and he feels, formed under his hand, the stone. Shall he fling it — for if he does so, he himself will be the stone? Ahead of him, small but possible, is the entry, easy as the descent in Dante, and beyond it he hears a treble of voices, in whose singing he may join.

I know it can be done, for I have done it. First, when hardly more than a boy, in a small town in the southern part of what I still think of as *your* United States. That was when, using the chance secret left with me by Johnny Fortuna, I found out the mechanism of myself, and how it could be appeased. And later, but never again so seriously, with so many others. In a way, here in New York, I am doing it now. But here, as I know too well, it is still only the small social calisthenic that keeps one in trim for the greater risk. For here, winding myself as I have into

4

Judge Mannix's circle, and all too near his daughter's heart, still it is only like looking at stereopticons on a laughing, nostalgic evening, while all the time one craves to hear, even to be, the huge orthophonic voice. So, soon, perhaps — in some place that must be the only real place — I shall need to do it again.

Let me explain. Let me tell you about it. You being the confidant's confidant, the page to which he comes at last, carrying what could never be spoken across the dead-end bar at midnight, or whispered — as I have never dared whisper it — in the gentle hours, to the warm nipple of a woman.

Chapter I. His Birth. The Goodmans.

I WAS born, an eight-months child, on Armistice Day of the First
Great War, posthumous son of a British cavalry sergeant who had
fallen some months before (not in battle, but on home encamp-
ment, while drunk, under the heel of a horse), to his widow, a dressmaker, lying in that day not in her own poor flat in World's End, but in
a hastily prepared sitting room on the second floor of the house of her
patron, Lady Rachel Goodman — in Golder's Green. So, there it is for
what it is worth or weighs; I was born, perhaps by some already willful
act of gestation, not in World's End but in Golder's Green.

At that time my mother was past thirty, and must have looked then
as she looked most of her life — composed face, short body and stout
calves, crinkly brown hair with a look of roughness to it — one of those
sturdy, plain women who seem to age little, because nothing in the
way of beauty is ever expected of them. Her father had been in the
cavalry also, a sergeant major in the Indian army, but unlike my un-
reliable father, of whom she spoke seldom, he had been one of those
trusted noncommissioned officers who were the bone of the colonial
service; we still had — carefully framed, and carried later even to Alabama — the testimonial pamphlet, heavy with august military titles,
presented him at his retirement dinner, the picture of him as an erect,

6

mutton-chopped pensioner (his uniformed chest solid with medals and ribbons tinted to a rainbow blur by an overartistic photographer), on the lawns of the Royal Hospital in Chelsea, and the long, campaign-studded notice of his death, in the regimental gazette. And embedded in my mother's reminiscences of him, I see now what she got from him, what I never saw so clearly before. Cockney in origin, he must have mothered so many subalterns, served as *fidus Achates* to so many of them returned as ranking officers, that, like many people of his station, he had absorbed, while never presuming upon it, much of their ethic and some of their tastes — as a butler might become, in a dictionary way, and at the most respectful distance, as much of a gentleman as his master. So it was that my mother, to whom it would never have oc-curred to change either her dumpy, black habit of dress or the varnish-*cum*-lithograph mediocrity of her parlor, could judge her clients, their drawing rooms, positions and reputations, with the strictness of a con-noisseur. And, more important, lived, in her unimaginative way, as much by these judgments as in her parlor. Even by heredity, I see now, I come of a vicarious family.

Her connection with the Goodmans was a simple one. At sixteen, having shown some talent, my mother was apprenticed to a French dressmaking establishment in Lyons, with a final year in the main branch in Paris. They met there, the young Rachel Pereira, shopping for her trousseau with the old Mrs. Goodman, her generous and eccen-tric mother-in-law-to-be, and my mother (the midinette's stiff bow at her nape, but the rest of her stolid and stubby in the midst of the other apprentices with their long noses, thin, subtle French lips, and coquet-tish feet), who had been pushed forward to serve *les Anglaises*. When they returned to England, she went with them, no doubt relinquished with relief by the *maîtresse* as too lacking in presence and guile, and until the wedding, six months away, she served as seamstress and maid to the softly winning, *primavera* bride. Later, when she set up her own business, the Goodmans were her mainstay, for the plain fact of it was that my mother was not a success. She had been too long exposed to gentility to be able to summon the imitative, glacéed arrogance required by the Bond Street salons, and at the same time her sense of style, corrupted by the French, was too vivid and strange for the suburban wives who would otherwise have been her natural trade. But with the Goodmans, with their slipper-easy affections, their Phoenician love of the purple, she was at home.

From my mother's account of the day of my birth, blended with my childhood knowledge of that house, I know that day almost as if I had been present not only as a newborn wisp, but as if, under the waxed skin and sealed eyelids of my prematurely naked face, there were already working that blotting-paper power of recall which was to be the matrix of my mental life. She lay there physically hushed, my mother, anxious only because her milk had not yet come in, and there was talk that, because of the circumstances, it might not, and I lay there like a dropped doll — "Too quiet, the little man!" the housemaids hinted — at her side. The servants brought her her dinner — it would be in the covered dishes, flowered and gilded, of Carlsbad china (for although the Goodmans loved showy things, they were not the kind to use them only for show) — and the tray would be set on the lift near the stove in the kitchen and hauled up by one of the maids, who would notch the thick rope securely and then run up a flight to take the tray from the shaft that opened on every floor, to the left of the back stairs. Now and then, all through the day, young Lady Rachel herself kept coming in to see her, her auburn hair skewered in a puff high on her head — like a duchess who for some reason or other preferred to dress her hair like a char's I always thought it — one of the vast peignoirs my mother was always making for her surrounding her like cumulus, for she was almost always expecting a child.

"How wonderful to be born on this day!" she said, no doubt pausing dreamily with a hand parting the curtains, for all the Goodmans had a way of dreaming at windows that for years I thought of obscurely as the habit of a class not mine. "And, Crossie" — my mother's maiden name was Dora Cross — "too lovely of you to have had him here, for you know how I am always forgetting how to bathe a baby, from one to the other, will you trust me to practice on him? And there are all those new nappies you have run up — enough for a regiment!" They understood how to comfort, the Goodmans — it ran from them like balm.

Later, the children were brought in to see the newborn — Hannschen and Joseph of course not yet there, but Rosalind and Martin and James, younger than when I knew them, yet I can see them as they must have stood there, three pairs of wide, Goya eyes, toes curling in the gold-braided, pointed red leather slippers sent them each birthday by the uncle in Gibraltar. And after them, the grandmother herself, that marvelously muttering godmother-witch of a woman, carrying down, from the third-floor apartment that was like a crowded bibliography of Vienna, a cup of the strong coffee she brewed on her spirit-lamp — a word I have not thought of in thirty years — and served in one of the high cups that she would never let the heavy-handed serving girls touch. Last of all, just before supper, my mother said, Sir Joseph himself came. He came and stood at the door, dark-bearded orientalist amazingly down from that fourth-floor eyrie I never saw, from which he could seldom be routed, where he wrote the books for which he had been named on the King's list.

"Congratulations, Crossie!" he called. "I won't come in. I'm all over ink and dust, too grimy to meet a baby."

He wouldn't enter the room, explained my mother, with that jealous and delicate sense of pride in her betters which was the mark of her own class — which she carried with her to America, and was lost with there — he wouldn't enter the room because, although it would have been proper enough with a lady of his own sort, he knew that it would embarrass my mother.

"I'm sending you up some wine," he called. "You are to drink it, as much as you can. For you know, we shall be toasting the two of you, downstairs."

I can hear my mother saying that, her hand arrested over the old sewing machine in Fulham, or poking with contempt at the cornbread she learned to make over here. *We shall be toasting the two of you downstairs.*

The wine came, a cobwebby bottle, and she sipped it. Downstairs, there was music. Outside the window, rackety sounds and voices slipped by the night long, all the crowd-music of that night of peace, a sudden maying in November of all the young and old linking arms across the tennis courts and gardens of Golder's Green. Wrapped in the red-warmth of that wonderful household, she slept. And the next morning, her milk came in.

Chapter II. Tuscana.
He Finds Himself to Be There.

UNTIL my tenth year, then, I was in and out of that house. Do you know how it is when you are in pursuit of a woman, have reached her perhaps, but sense that she is not quite as concerned with you, how all the facts about her — whom she sees, where she is to be found at certain hours of the day — have for you a swollen intentness, how you add to and subtract from the doubled image you have of her, with the nervous madness of research? For all the years that I was intermittently in that house — the dressmaker's boy, holder of pins in boudoirs, maker of fourth or fifth at nursery games, fed with casual sweetness at the family table — for all those years I was in love; I was in love that way. I did not know this then of course, nor would the Goodmans ever have suspected how I felt about them, for their house was always full of accessory benevolences like me. And people like them, the "outgoing" ones, who spend themselves like gold motes on the air, never realize that what they dispense as generalized kindness, the singlehearted suck up as love. Silent-footed child that I was, as a boy like me had to be taught to be, on the days when I went there, claw-fingers clutching my mother's the long way out on the Underground, thinking of the second breakfast I would get and of all the coming hours of something more than food, on those days I was like a statue warmed down from its niche into living for a day, and at night, when I was returned to my corner, and until the next time, a fantasy of life remained behind my brow.

So then, I remember everything about that house. Everything. Not only its mold and feel and smell, that any child might keep, but floor by floor, leaf by leaf, the exact cinquefoil of its being. I can stand in its geography and print my track upon it, as a rabbit must sometimes stand, poised, in the lost warren he cannot hope to find again.

And, lilliputian again, I can remember the giants above. Family lore was dropped in that kitchen, glimpsed through the muddle of the cook's mind like the ring at the bottom of the Christmas custard; occasionally the older children, though usually distant, played at toss in front of me with an ornate secret or family fable. I hid it all away, the way Lady Rachel hid, in a Battersea box, under some bastings I took up to her one afternoon, the cachets she sometimes took when alone. And the thousands of conversations intoned, back and forth, back and forth above my head — I remember those — a Gregorian chant whose pattern appears slowly now down the apse of years, the lingua franca of giants, that now, giant myself, I understand. I can hear Sir Joseph's voice, the day he spoke to her about the cachets. I can see the hairs on Sir Joseph's hand.

And it was the old lady, Mrs. Goodman, who first made of me a confidant. Looking back, I see now that her eccentricity was really only a powerful refusal to have truck with the superficial, her incantatory way of talking only that ancestral harking back of the elders, which we reject to our loss. She was one of those interior monologuists who are driven by a lifelong need to see the formal design of their own lives, to fix its rubric firmly among the chapters of the world, and she ruminated best in the presence of a listener *manqué* — a servant, a stranger, or a child. Since she was also one of those blessed of the earth whose own family is the hub of their sky, it was of the Goodmans that, incessantly, I learned. She ranged her life, theirs, with the passion of a critic, and like the best of these, with a wildness of phrase and a soundness of judgment that gave me something of the method too. Listening, I knew for the first time what it was to make of oneself that gray, faceless well into which another does not dip, but pours. Not for years did I know that the services of the confidant, though apparently selfless, are never so. But it was not her fault, nor yet perhaps mine, that it was to be others' lives I ranged.

For, at ten, I was torn away. I say "torn" with reason, thinking of the ghost strength that underlies dead idiom. For, of our trek to America, the ship to Montreal, the long journey south to the town of Tuscana, even my first months in that wizened place (and even there, I gather, no one ever realized it of me), I know only by hearsay. I learned later, of course, that the Goodmans had closed the house in Golder's Green, following to Japan, with all their own bags and baggage and singsong, Sir Joseph, who held a government post there for some years. They were not the kind to leave dependents behind them like deserted cats, but my mother would never have let them know the extent of her dependence on them. And no one, not even I, knew mine. After some months, heeding the pleas of her only sister — younger than she, ailing, and married to a shrewd Birmingham millhand who had emigrated to a foreman's job in the States — she accepted the passage money they sent her, and we sailed.

Later, she always used to say that it was for me she had emigrated, but she never said why. Perhaps she could not phrase it, or would not, for hers were not the usual reasons for going to that new world for which she had a certain scorn even before she saw it; indeed, she was never to trust a country where a man, even a son, could rise so soon. I think she left England because I had already begun to look like my father. She was a plain woman who, against her own awareness of it, had let herself shine briefly in the sunny whim of a man whose handsome dash she could never have felt herself to have deserved; other women she could have borne, and probably had, but the manner of his death had disgraced her in the one milieu in which she took pride. And everyone had begun to say that I looked like him, like the specious face in the wedding picture I never saw until months after her death — one of those Burne-Jones faces the Irish produce now and then, with a hint of the spoiled angel in its sentimental modeling, in the blank, neoclassic eye. Unwillingly, that day, I marked the likeness too.

But of all that interim, of a period that must have been about four months, I remember nothing. It is the only part of my life I do not remember. Later there was no mention of illness; apparently through all that time I ate, responded in the ordinary way. When I was grown, and on a navy cruiser for the first conscious sea voyage of my life, I lay awake in my bunk all the first night out, straining for some kinetic memory of how it felt to be at sea. But none came. There is the day at Golder's Green that must have been the last day; there is the morning I awoke to myself, sitting before a breakfast bowl, in the tallow-soft heat of the house in Tuscana. There is nothing in between.

Sitting now, at the same time within the sound tape and outside it, I wake again that morning. Opposite me, someone has just said *Goodman*. I see the bowl, my hand stopped on the spoon, objects seen through a curtain of drizzle that a sudden wind parts clear. I look up into a long face with the cramp of illness on it, a face that I do not know. She speaks again, my aunt, in her thin, life-grudging voice, a voice I heard for the first time a moment ago.

Postman says a foreign package you've to go for yourself, Dora. Has to be opened at the mails by law, for fear of plants and beetles from out there. Likely from the Goodmans, eh?

Very likely. My mother's voice is muffled, heard as if from behind a door, that voice, or from under the sheets in the morning, when the dream-stuff is still cotton in the ears. My eyes slide sideways, as a horse's must feel when the blinders come off. She is there, mantelpiece figure one does not often notice but would instantly miss, on her lap the familiar flood of sewing, but the air around her has a whitish prickle to it, like the sudden, flapped blankness on a home-screen cinema. Then, as I turn, the room is normal. Only the faintest drizzle remains, always settling but unseen; until the day of the hearing nine years from then it never quite left me; it is the color of Tuscana.

The women go on talking, and I hear them, my aunt rummaging on as the chairbound do, my mother's short replies.

A fine country, says my aunt, to set itself above other nations' insects. Cockchafers here like bustards, Dora, ants like grains of sand. And at night, always the moths nosing the windows, even a frost does not stop them.

Frost. Are there frosts here? says my mother.

Silk in the package maybe, Dora; will it be that sleazy Jap stuff to be found here in the stores?

Not if it's from them, says my mother.

I listen, not knowing quite where I am, but only that I am, and knowing this because of an echo like a comfit just swallowed, a warmth in the ear, an echo on the tongue. Then my mother's hand on my shoulders: *Come along now, we'll fetch the parcel from Goodmans,* and I know what the comfit is.

I get up from the table and put my hand in hers. "Shall we be going on the Underground?" I said.

Everything in my life-to-be there is in that first walk in Tuscana. I traverse it again, inclining my head powerlessly to the right, to the left, from my useless rajah-seat in recall. We walked through the rows of company houses, a time-dirtied laundry line of houses hung once with Northern neatness and never again attended. We passed the twin-stacked mill where my uncle worked, and went along what I took to be the High street, a street too unfinished ever to know that it was one. Only the Negroes, their faces a black surprise to me, held to some invisible meridian along its length, and as they passed us, stepped aside. Down to the left was the funeral parlor from which my aunt would be buried a few years hence, across from it the church where my uncle, clinging practically to morning tea and a house kempt as it would be "at home," was to marry my mother. I passed a trio of buildings, unconscious of the unity they would one day have for me — the courthouse, the general store of Semple, the company factor, and the schoolhouse where I would go that first fall.

"If there were only a little east in the wind!" said my mother faintly. "Never thought to hear myself say that!" she added quickly, but I was already back in the bus that wound through Fulham, hearing the passengers reassure one another, with the greenish valor of the permanently cold, that the east was out of the wind. Glancing down, I saw that my knees looked unfamiliar, not red and chapped as I remembered them, and my hands too. The air sickened against my face, pluming in my nostrils like moths. A slack drugstore scent, like cheap vanillin, followed us into the post office from outside. It was the shabby-sweet odor of the South that already I was smelling, the air of a people who had to put too much sugar on their lives.

The man at the desk chatted, while we opened our parcel. I could not understand him at first, although I knew that he was joking. There were several lazy flies on his counter, and one of them lit on the pink-and-bronze kimono my mother lifted from the box.

"Nu'n but g'dole 'Mer'can bug," he said.

My mother said nothing, folding the kimono into the box, on top of the black brocaded slippers that were for me.

As we left, he nodded and grinned. "Hurry back!" he said.

Outside the door, I asked whether that meant we were to return soon for another parcel.

My mother shook her head. "It's what they say here when they mean 'good-by.' "

In our room that night, I put the slippers away. They were beautiful, but they were not what the others had had. They were not from an uncle in Gibraltar. Outside the window, from some unknown point in the hemisphere of night, a late train hooted a long sound. I did not know yet that it had a name — "the to-from Memphis train," but I knew by now that it was an American sound. As I shut the drawer, it called once more. "Hurry back!" it said. "Hurry back."

Chapter III.   Johnny Fortuna.

WHENEVER I think of Johnny Fortuna, who now, wherever he is, is a man older than myself, I see him only as he was that first autumn I knew him — a boy of fifteen, lying on his stomach in the leaves, talking into the afternoon distance. We always see the lost companions of our youth in some such way; they remain fixed for us against the scrubby haunts of our adolescence the way Icarus, in his own arabesque, remains fixed against history — at once exalted and drowned.

At the school, whose poor resources were never enough for me, where almost at once I became too enviably the best pupil, Johnny was the worst; after a while, our common exclusion drew us together. He was not dull, only dulled, and I found him because I was too. At home, except for my uncle's occasional outside evening drinking, performed as a workman's due, without geniality or social compromise, our household, mistrusting the easy fondle of the town, never became part of it; my mother gardened suspiciously among alien flowers; at six we had an immutable tea; the windows, disciplining the weather, remained closed to the heat, open to the chill. Returning "home," to England, was never mentioned; feverishly raising the flag of our isolation, we *were* at home.

And Johnny's household, one of two Polish caravanserais near the watchman's shed back of the main-line signal, was one of those that exist for a town to despise. Like me, he had only a mother, but he and his brood of younger brothers and sisters had had more than one father. Mrs. Fortuna was visited at night, and stared down on the street in the daytime, by those men whose morality kept them from the colored quarter; if she took any revenge upon them it was in that her children, no matter how indiscriminately fathered, all had the blond bullet-heads and bluet eyes of Poles, as if she too kept a national pride. At night, concertina music rose late from her chimney stack, mingled, in the pulsing red air of the signal light, with the smell of mash.

Semple was one of her regular visitors — I never knew him. I repeat it — I never knew him there, or in his store, where we happened not to trade, or in any of the chance walks of the town. There were seven thousand people in the town, and I had the matchless invisibility of my age. I saw him, of course, from time to time, as one does in a place like that, and he may have known of me as my uncle's nephew, and glancingly passed me by. Once, in the street crowd outside my aunt's funeral, we brushed, almost the closest we ever came to one another, but I never knew him. This is the point, the one that unhinges truth as people normally know it, the point I must make clear. Until the day of the hearing, I had never been made known to him; our hands had never greeted; we had never spoken; his eyes had never met mine. And now his name is a tremble to me forever. He is that mystery, the accidental man whom we unaccidentally wrong. For, the people to whom we have been something in love or in hate, whom we have discarded or been discarded by — these belong to the libretto; we can tinkle their themes over, all referent tunes. But the accidental man, who holds no meaning, holds all; his theme will never be finished, and will abide to the end. For of course I "knew" Semple — as the rememberer knows. I knew him from "around," from the air, and from Johnny. I knew him from behind.

He was a compact man, just over short, with thick, prematurely white hair, and the look of extra energy this often gives a middle-aged man. A cut above those who worked at the mill, he wore duck trousers most of the year, and these, sharply laundered below the knee but curiously rumpled and used in the region of his sex, gave the impression, as he lounged in the chair in front of his store, that his central energy came from there. He was held to be mean about money, but since his livelihood depended on how he issued credit, this may have been the verdict of those — most of the town, this would be — who could not manage their own. Johnny worked for him part-time in the store, and once, long before I was old enough to understand it, I heard it sniggered that this was the only way Semple ever paid Mrs. Fortuna. Johnny seemed to bear him no more grudge than any boy does the boss because the latter is one.

Of his own home Johnny hardly ever spoke, but I took this for granted, for neither did I of mine. By an instinctive, unphrased agreement we never went to each other's homes, never showed our friendship to the town. On certain afternoons, when my mother supposed me at the library, I did go there for a while — not to a real library, for the town had none, but to the old Victorian house, with its oddments of books, that the state maintained half as a memorial to the one notable woman whose birthplace Tuscana had been, half as an annuity for the curator, Miss Pridden, the dead woman's old niece. Miss Pridden liked me, for the accent I had retained, no doubt, that echoed a faded sojourn of her youth, for the soft way I knew how to move among the precious objects she tended and to listen to her account of them, for the fact that I came at all. It was she who later tried to maneuver for me a scholarship to a college in the North. But on those days when I knew Johnny got off early, while she prosed over the books or fumbled with the tea in the pantry, I often managed my exit and ran down toward Semple's store. Often when Johnny came out and saw me waiting, he barely nodded and moved ahead of me, kicking stones along the path we both knew we would take, and until we entered the woods, I kept my distance, for it seemed only natural to me that he should be ashamed of having no other companion than a boy, smart as he thought me, who was so much younger than he.

So then, as far as ever appeared, no one ever knew of our intimacy. In the time to come, after the hearing where, with Johnny long gone, I testified against Semple and the others, I had a shock of fear that certainly someone would come forward to bring out the old connection between Johnny and me, to say, "His testimony has no standing in law. He was never there. He is only using what belonged to a boy named Johnny Fortuna." But no one did. I thought then, with the first access of my power, that I must be unique, the only one ever to do what I had done. Experience tells me now how unlikely it is that this should be so. You ordinary people, yes; you are our constant dupes, because you cannot imagine, you will not believe what the more meditative can do with the reservoirs of recall. Wisdom tells me now that there may well have been at least one other like me in Tuscana, whose memory could skulk his world like mine, who recognized what I had done — who knew. He did not come forward then, perhaps because he did not choose to or had other fish to fry. But he may have been there. Perhaps someday he will come from behind — and enter upon me.

But now, when I return to those afternoons I waited for Johnny in the alley behind Semple's store, when, after tossing a crumb to the gamecock Semple had penned there, we made our way by back paths to the rise above the town, and lay there in the ground myrtle, peeling switches, chewing sourgrass, Johnny always the talker, I the listener — I think first of what a tender balance Johnny kept on all the things he did not tell me. For he, who had been born with the caul of the town's underside around him, who should have known of the place only what was hawked into the spittoon and raucoused after hours, never spoke to me of the town that way at all. What he used me for was as the repository of his innocence, that pitiable innocence which he could lay nowhere else. And because I was this, for a long time he kept my innocence too.

What Johnny talked about was — normality as he saw it, or dreamed it to be. For years, as paper boy and delivery boy, he had had backdoor glimpses of most of the town, and certain of these he collected the way other boys gathered the stamps that meant the aromatic distances which might someday be achieved. As he leaned over the brink of the town, the curl of smoke from a chimney spoke to him of the baking day of the woman there, the trim lines of wash that ringed his favorite houses brought forth a litany of the routines that went on inside — the church-going, the bedtime stories for kids like his brothers and sisters, the evening games — and as the fathers came out to ply the hose on these chosen yards, he could tell of the lodges they belonged to, the bright purchases they were making by thrift or installment, even the minor affiliations of the children who leagued their lawns. He was like a man studying the etiquette of banquet silver, who himself owned but a knife and a spoon.

There was one family by the name of Nellis that had once invited him in to dinner, and of this, and of a habit of theirs, he spoke often. " 'Fore dinner they say grace there, you know what grace is? Only they don't *say* nothin', just join hands around the table."

We could see that house from where we lay, and each evening, as its orange lamp popped out on the dusk, he marked it, sometimes mentioning the grace, or another of their ways, sometimes not. "Nellis's light," he would always say, though, and this was always the signal for us to go down. On the way down, once or twice in the beginning, he offered a halting excuse for why he talked so, the way a lover sometimes flaunts a practical reason for his pursuit of what others might think an inutile love. He was going into business, he said, he was going to have an automobile agency, and in business one had to know about people, how they really were.

And once, in the beginning too, when, as we descended, the light flared on in a house at the edge of niggertown, and I asked him, already half knowing, what the boys meant when they slanged the two women who lived there, he stopped on the path and hulked over me, eyes cracked close, his face suddenly wedge-shaped and Slav.

"How come you ask me that?" he said. "How come you ask *me?*"

"No reason, Johnny," I said, retreating, "no reason," and he relaxed then, thinking, as I did then, that there was not. I know now that if there is an original sin in us, it is that intuitive mischief which drives us to ask the humpbacked to discourse on humps. But that time I was learning something else — to swallow the cud of myself. I learned that day the sad second lesson of the confidant — that he may remain only so long as he collaborates in the illusion that he is not there. After that, even on the day when Johnny, breaking his illusion for my sake, let me in on his real world and told me about Semple, I held still and listened only. It was what one had to do in order to be able to stay. And somewhere along in there, I suppose, in those afternoons with Johnny, I lost forever, if I had ever had it, what might have been my own power to confide. Like those savages who bury the ashes of their own fires, hide their combings and nail parings against the magic wreakings of the possible finder, I came too to sense the sovereignty of the finder, and to resolve that no one should ever have a paring of me. Gradually I became critic enough to know that Johnny's vision of Tuscana rested like a bubble above the real one, but I never said anything. Time after time, I lay there passive on the hillside and let him spread his version of the town before us, golden as a Breughel, all its simple, wheaten actions simultaneous and side by side. And after a while, he made no more excuses. I guess by then he knew that his talking so was no more strange than my listening.

Chapter IV.   More Goodmans.   He Asks to Return.

I WAS almost fourteen and had known Johnny about three years, the summer my mother married my uncle. My aunt had died some months before. Never too much of a person, her fretful dying by inches and years had long since squeezed her smooth of that roughened human surface which is needed to draw real feeling from others, yet her death left a curious incoherence in our household. Our invalid's routine had regularized it, given it a purpose that the outside world, though avoided, might see if it cared to look; even more, the presence of the dying brings an edge of eternity into the air of a home, giving the most cramped household a bit of view. Certainly this was all my uncle and mother had shared until then, and now that the woman who had related them was removed, it must have been this, the need of some united front, more than propriety, that until the marriage was settled upon, made them uneasy with one another. It could hardly have been the fear of gossip alone that moved them, for the town would no longer have bothered to pay them even that intimacy — although my mother may have heard in her mind a lost, transatlantic echo of what would have been said and unsaid in World's End. No, it would give us all a permanency, my mother said, and my uncle would help toward my education, or find me a place in the mill.

She was sewing as usual, the evening she told me; Tuscana was one of three towns near the site of the great new dam the government was building in the river valley, and she had begun to find a small trade among the wives of the engineers from the North. The air was tight, with the binding summer heat I had never got used to, and although the evening light was still bland and I had polished the panes only the day before, there was no sparkle in them. My uncle had gone out for the one evening away a week he allowed himself. I thought of him sitting mum in the café he still called the "pub" — a sparely molded man with a dry eye and the sparse manners of those who are easier with machines than with people. He had a colorless justice about him that made him neutral to live with, but I wanted him no closer.

When she had finished speaking, I listened to the late blasting on the river, wishing that one of the thunders would crack the inferior glass, yellow the gray air behind which I lived, and lift me like a rocket away. I cast about for something dauntless to say to her, some proposal that would knock outward the underworld walls of boyhood and made me at one blow a man. I thought of reminding her of the scholarship exams I had planned on, but they were still two years away. But after a moment, I mentioned them.

"Yes, yes," she said. "We must think of those." She bent her head deeper over her sewing. "You will have a room to yourself then, to study in; that will be a help, eh?" A little time went by. Then she rose and made tea.

When she returned with the tea things, the blastings had stopped and the panes were dark. I heard a train pass, a long freight, dragging into smaller and smaller falls its long chain of sound.

"Could — could we not go home?" I said. I had never asked it.

The cups clinked as she served them. Neither of us touched the tea. After a while, sitting with her hands folded, she shook her head. "This is home," she could have said, evading, but she sat on, not denying that it was not.

"Could we not — write to *them?*" For a long time now I had not once spoken of the Goodmans; by an evasion of my own I had managed not to think of them, except in bed at night, when, with my knuckles against my knees, I had sometimes tried to walk among them, putting myself to dream.

"Them?" She raised her head in casual surprise.

I breathed fast, the way one did before heaving up the stone wheel that covered the well in the yard. "The — Goodmans."

"Oh —" My mother's soft ejaculation, light smile, plunged me down, even before she spoke further, into that gap down which the child falls, weightless, holding on to some stone of meaning which the giants have wafted aside like a feather. She was smiling, with that faint, sealing tribute people pay to the picnics of long ago, the pretty costumes they once have worn.

"Ah," she said, gently laughing, dismissing. "So you still remember."

I got up then, and moved for the first time away from her. At the age I was then, the past is our only littoral, sacred because it is all we have to go on; to minimize it, to step lightly across it and onward, to *forget*, is the treason of maturity. So I got up then and went to the window, and standing there, by an imitative act of memory, as their habit had been, I moved away from her, toward them. I saw young Martin, at the age I was now when we left them, glassy-eyed with rainy-day lethargy, rolling a marble back and forth along the sill; I saw Hannschen with her nose just above it. I put my hand on the curtain and I saw Lady Goodman, whom I always thought of as Lady Rachel, standing in one of her arrested pauses; I saw the old lady Mrs. Goodman at her window on the floor above, staring out upon Tiergartens and Königsallees melted upon Golder's Green in the faïence of the years. I saw all of them, watched by myself from behind.

I touched the curtain here in Tuscana, cut down from a patch quilt brought with us from there. The dressmaker's roster, it was made up of anonymous snippets, but down at one end there was a piece of green damask I knew and had avoided, hating the mute screw of pain that lives in all those objects which survive from one part of us to the other. I put my forefinger on it — object swum so irrelevant and far.

"That's from the dining-room curtain," I said.

I fingered the wall beside it, and I was brushing the rubbed place on the olive-drab wall where the maids eased themselves in with the trays. I bent lower, still touching.

"That's where the splash was, where Molly dropped the tureen. 'Lucky it wasn't the Nailsea, eh, Molly?' Sir Joseph said." Hung on the kitchen wall back there was an old rolling pin of whorled Nailsea glass, given to Molly by her lover, a sailor from that town, with the warning legend that if it fell it would be a sign that he was lost at sea. Sir Joseph's remark had become a catch phrase in the house, used when something broke, when a child tumbled, when a quarrel was mended.

"When I fell on the stairs, he said it," I said. I felt his arms picking me up, his hands testing my bones as he would his own childrens', his tobacco richness as he set me down. " 'Lucky it wasn't the Nailsea, eh?' he said."

And standing there, between Sir Joseph and the widened eyes of my mother, I talked on, remembering, my tongue never fast enough for what I saw. Leaving the dining room, the smell of orange bitters from the open sideboard followed one, and, transliterated, clung to the wooden pineapple on the newel post in the hall. *Have a care now,* said Molly, passing me on the stair, for I was carrying the old lady's afternoon half-bottle of Madeira. I saw myself stop on the landing to look at the light streaming through the leaded pane that showed the Knight of Malta with his white cross on his black robe, to hunt for the bit of misplaced red near his nose.

" 'Stand just so,' Martin said," I said, " 'and if the light's proper you'll see the old Hospitaler bleed from the nose.' "

"Enough! Enough!" said my mother, but I was already past her, almost among them, putting myself to dream. I passed Lady Rachel's half-closed door, that room, muffled with voile, where she endlessly wanted to be resting, and I could almost see her murmur, hand at her forehead, the way she often would at the nursery hour, *Hours to go, before good night.*

"Hours to go, before good night," I whispered, going by, seeing, as I used to, the pale blue, ladylike hours that stretched before her until she could re-enter the muffled room.

"Child! Child!" said my mother, but I was already on the third floor landing. I knocked on the door and opened it.

The old lady looked up, as if from spinning. *Da bist du!* she said, all the past in her lap, and then I was in the room with her; I was there, with them.

Here comes the handsome waiter, she said. *And what does he say?*

"Guten Tag, gnädige Frau," I said, very stiff with the tray.

Ach, such ton he has, das kleine Herrgöttle von Bieberach, she said, grinning. *You remember what that means?*

"Little Mr. God from Beeberock," I said.

Aha, she said. *I see you have not forgotten.*

No, I have not forgotten, I have never forgotten, I was about to answer, but then, wee at the small end of the telescope, my mother cried out, and came forward. She cannot reach me, I thought, for now I am with them. I opened my mouth to answer, but the long arm grew and reached me, shaking, shaking, and I dropped the tray, and all was smashed.

In bed that night, and nights after, I pressed my knuckles against my knees and waited, but I could not get back. It was because someone else knew now, I thought. Someone else had a paring of me. For now and then I caught my mother watching me. But she never spoke to me of the Goodmans again.

Chapter V.   Miss Pridden.

ON THE day of the wedding I was up early and dressed for school as usual, having all that week refused to attend the ceremony even in the serge suit they had hopefully got for me. They were leaving for Memphis immediately after; my uncle had taken a week off from the mill and had bought a second-hand car.

Now, as I went about the room that was to be mine from tonight, I was almost glad of the week alone and of their going, only wanting them to know that it was I who dispensed with them. I had grown up some in the past weeks, if growth can be said to come by stations of recognition of what one cannot have. If my mother had not come in just then to say good-by to me in just that way, in just that dress, might I never have gone to look for Johnny that evening?

But she did come, in that way, precisely minted for her eleven-o'clock business, and in that dress, with the sharpened waist, the unfamiliarly wide skirt with its assertive rustle. And for all the tender rue with which she reached for me, I saw the little raised comb of pride that hardens upon a woman, once she has a man again to show the world. I ducked her kiss.

"Do not mind the dress," she said, still reaching. And if I could bend from the sound tape now, I would bend toward her. Meeting her there, in that impossible tangent, I could explain to her that when we come of age in our own flesh we have more charity for the image of what our parents did to beget us, and after; that it is only the young who, harsh in their own straits, want to keep that image eunuch and dry. But the tape has no mercy; I answered her then.

"It looks . . . like a client's dress," I said, and ran past her out of the house.

In the yard, I reminded myself of the schoolbooks left behind in the room, but I did not go back. She did not come after me. A cardinal whistled, and other calls, still unknown to me, insinuated from bush to bush. Although it was only eight o'clock, and well on toward October, my jersey was already dark at the armpits with sweat. In the reticent, marine land I had come from, the birds were already long gone — perhaps some of them here to me. Outside the gate, the old car, heavily waxed by my uncle, sweated too, with a premarital shine. I closed the gate and went on to school.

When I got out that afternoon, the town had a Friday hum to it; it was market day, and even the steady loungers in front of the courthouse had each his paper bundle or loaded cord bag. In the long mud alley back of the main street, the tenant farmers' wives stood as usual at their slap-up stalls, behind strings of rabbits congealed in their own rust, limp fowl and garden greens, old gray cartons of dirt-flecked eggs. But beyond every turning now, raw orange in the late sun, lay the great Federal gash in the hills — its crater ready to rise. I remember now how, up on the main street, a few Negroes nudged in front of the wet red slick of a new store front, saying, "Chain store, man, chain store from the North," and how two of their women, urged from behind, walked in; how, up ahead, some of the white mill hands coming off shift hunkered up at Semple's new sign, lit ghoulish in the daylight, the town's first scribble of neon blue.

"Heavy traffic, hear tell, over to Charlotte," one muttered, and half hearing, I knew he spoke of the government hiring hall across the dam site at Charlotte, empty at first, although the rates were higher than the mill, because they were also equal for white and colored alike, but filling slowly in recent weeks, now that it was pretty certain not a nigger dared show. And looking back, I see how change comes without guns, in the sudden crater in the farmland, the silent tribune without flags in the real-estate office, the tinkle on the bourses of small towns. Years later, the historian tells himself that had he been there he would have smelled its powder. It is not so, either for a civilization or a man. The chronicler and the chronicle can never meet. But a man is both; twinned by memory, he goes on trying.

So, late downbeat always after the measure, we follow ourselves; I follow the boy who was I. I walked on down the street, slouching along in the pure cone of my own trouble, never smelling the hint that was already in the air for the town and for me — the hint of sulphur that steals up before the first tremor in the streets.

Back there in front of Semple's, craning above the shoulders of the millhands, I had caught a glimpse of Johnny's blond head above the counter, helping Semple with trade. On Fridays he had to stay until nine. I lingered on a corner, the thought of the empty house dropping down, a tear-shaped blob of solder, inside me. To the right, in what had once been the old center of town before the mill came, a few antebellum houses, most of them flats now, huddled behind their columned porticos like thumb-soiled Parthenons from a schoolboy's primer, sunken cobbles between them and the waterless, carved stone horse troughs that had sunk too, in gradual burial rite, almost to the ground. The Pridden place, painted an accusing white by the state funds from Montgomery, stood among them.

I tried the door and found it locked, but I had permission for another entry, a narrow, wistaria-hidden jalousie that folded sideways and gave on to the back hall. As I parted the roped branches, slid the shutters back, and entered, I stood still for a minute, flooded with a sudden peculiar comfort. For a moment, standing there in the flattery of secret privilege, I was washed inward, past some gate, inside. I was to have other such moments in my life, involuntary shudders of comfort great and small, and they were always to be connected with secrecy, with some hermetic privilege that was mine alone. This time, displaced in its sudden, unexpected balm, listening to its rhythm with my head cocked upwards, I told myself obscurely that it must have come because the ceiling here, high and molded with antique frivolity, had a never-before-noticed look of some in my own country, of back there. Years were to pass before I knew otherwise, before I knew for sure that the alien is not national; his drum sounds from farther below. Some are born so easy and tactile to the world's gates; others, yet so handsome and fully organed, are born without hands. I lowered my head, and the found heartbeat was gone, as it has always gone, and I was myself again, gnawing and humbly feral, outside.

The kitchen was cool, an old woman's haven, with the musty dryness the old bring to a room, dry cool of bird-bones that need flannelette, subtemperate blood that wants its tea. Miss Pridden was out marketing, no doubt, with Perry, the small colored boy who came every week to carry, to whom she always paid, with the obligation of the noble, one of her scant supply of quarters, although the going rate was a dime. Once, early in my acquaintance with her, I had been there when he came, and she had dismissed him, saying, "I think perhaps my young friend here will help me today, thank you, Perry," although I had seen the quarter change hands nevertheless. When we had returned that afternoon with the bundles, after we had stored the food away, she had offered me no money, but when tea came it was not as usual in the china pot, but in the full silver service with the urn for hot water, and on the table there was a plate of benné seed cakes. I had never seen the latter before, and did not know that they were the region's token of aristocratic friendship. " 'Tisn't the same as your seedcake, 's I recollect," she said, for, as I found out later, she was always gleeful over what she knew of my country and often even spoke to me confederately of what she called "the Continent," as if the fact of my foreign birth alone made me a qualified veteran of the Grand Tour.

Thereafter, if I happened to come by on a Friday, the ceremony was repeated, and I usually ate a cake or two for the honor I had learned was in them, as I listened to her reminiscences — because here I already knew so well what was expected of me — although I had not much taste for the flat perfume of either. For although Miss Pridden did not always descant of travel, she had, like so many I knew later, nothing to show of life but a tourist's trinkets of memorabilia, legal tender as worn as the stamped shell one buys on the *plage,* open as the postcard with the X marking the room among the hundred rooms, her only poor treasure being that the X was hers. And already I had begun to form a taste for confidences of another order. What compels me are not the common postcards of another's reminiscence, but the letters — letters from those dead emotions whose signals, faint from within the coffin, it is sometimes still possible to hear — of whose harmonics even the narrator is sometimes not aware. Or not as aware as the listener, as I.

I left the kitchen, not sorry to find it, as I supposed then, quite empty, and stole into the library. But again the machine sticks, stopping me as I watch myself leave, teaching me, twenty-five years later, that the listener too, talented arranger that he is, may sometimes be unaware. Truly, memory is God; it lets not a sparrow fall. In its foreground the main characters reanimate, their talk flashes again, but beside them, in every corner, the small still life waits, just these apples — why picked by the painter to keep this significant flame? Behind me as I left, I did not see, waiting ready on the table, a plate of benné seed cakes. She must have put them out so on many a Friday, perhaps all. Yet I never marked them, that they were already hopefully there, the times I came. There they lie, trinkets neither useful nor germane, yet if I could, as I pass by now, I would take one — Miss Pridden's X.

But I went by them without seeing, on into the library, like any of the infrequent sightseers, or the official archivists who came perhaps once a year, and if Miss Pridden had been in the kitchen she would have taken this quite as custom, preserved as she was in the stiff, museum shadow of her aunt, surviving her like the browned curator rose still to be found between the heavy pages of some volume whose owner once, for irony, pressed it there. The aunt had been a spinster scholar, one of those composite bluestocking women of nineteenth-century America, whose tripartite names ring a vague and maudlin bell, of whom one is never sure whether it was temperance they espoused or Chautauqua, bloomers or transcendentalism, homeopathy or the vote. More a transplanted citizen of Boston and New York, she had bequeathed to Tuscana only the pride of her birth and death there — and the house with the books. Not long ago I came across an old account of her — working, as I do, for an encyclopedia has, in addition to its main satisfaction for me, these minor pleasures. And when I did so, the whole flavor of those shelves came back to me — the truncated English Ovid next to the feminist homiletic, the candied-violet *Affection's Gift* hard by the pamphlet on Andersonville prison, all the balked ambience of those women whom society, seeking to destroy, first makes imperfectly male. Poor androgynous shelves, their contents bequeathed me little, but the room itself bound me forever in the opiate habit of books.

It was a perfect library. One entered by the only access — a low door under the stairs — a small, white, oval room about a story and a half high. Outside the house one saw that the flat railed roof of this room formed one of those mincing battlements known as a "widow's walk," but the inside was grave and austere, furnished only with a spindle chair and a long table whose dark leather top was ink-stained and chipped here and there to a spongy russet. The light, raying down from three clerestory openings in the wall, was poor, making the print more precious. In retrospect, I see that the room resembled a bookplate of a scholar's study, lacking only the woodcut iconographer himself bent above the inkwell with the flowing plume, but I was too ill-learned then to carp because Manfred could not have strode that battlement, or to miss, among the books, the Greek strophes that should have been there. Once inside that room, it enclosed me like an egg perfectly blown free of all but air, the shining nacre of the shelves, and myself a stray blood-fleck of life left to nourish as I could.

The nourishment, as I have said, was secondary, although this was not the fault of the trivialities to be found there. For, after half a lifetime spent with books, some of them of the purest diadem, events have made me see that books were always to remain secondary with me. I have never much respected them for the flat facts to be pecked from them, or even for those austral flights of the imagination whose unique province they claim to be. "Facts" are no more than a pox that changes its nature from man to man, from age to age, that saves in one generation and kills in another. And imagination, which speaks in dithyramb, can never equal the rough, fell syllable of memory. No,

I already went to the books then, as I did later — and as I would now, had I not a better resource — again for the frame of secret feeling in which they enclosed me.

A book too needs its confidant, as much as any man, but cannot choose its terms. In the long, suspended afternoons of childhood, that latitude which disappears with the coming of the time sense, to be counterfeited later only briefly by the first entente of love, I sat in that room for hours, turning over this or that yellowed minor page, saying to one, "This is all I want of you," to another, "This is all you may have of me," tasting, in my silent dictatorship, the terms that people would not give. And for this the minor books are best, the ones no one has read for years or will ever read again, for these are the dependent ones who seek most piteously to confide. Seated among them, I lost my servility for the duration of an afternoon. In the tricky light the room's round shape was a shaft on which I rose, a stylite on his pillar. The colorless ceiling melted before my unfocused eyes and I floated there, apprentice to that *folie de grandeur* which is most of what really goes on between a book and a man.

That afternoon I pulled down one book after another and restlessly set them aside, erecting a half-circle of discards around me, finally settling on an old miscellany called *The Rose, or Affection's Gift for 1845,* to which, for its title, I had awarded a certain reciprocal fondness. When, later, I raised my head, it was growing too dark to read.

They are in Memphis now, I thought, and bent my head again, but in that moment the tiny print had become invisible. Outside, as if on signal, the katydids began their chafing drill, the sound of the minutes scraping by. Pressing my sneakers against the chair rung, I listened, feeling smaller, for all my flight, than I had been before. On the table, strewn around me, the rejected books glimmered, pursing their blind mouths, taking that reprisal the inanimate always can on whatever living thing brushes it by. All the time I had been reading, the other part of me — the owl that sits on all our shoulders — had been waiting for Miss Pridden's step.

That (for convenience) *owl,* one knows of its existence from the

34

beginning, long before one meets up with the Freudian phrasers. It is that thing in us which is neither *super* nor *supra*, not *ego* or *tibi* or *illa*, but sits in each of us like a pocket of outer space in which all that is qualifying, human, adjectival, dies. It is what presses the wrist of the whining diarist who thought he swore not to temper the wind to his shorn self, and points his pen a compass degree nearer the skin. Back there in the library, I heard its observing, vacuum voice, telling me, as I stood on tiptoe at one of the windows and peered down into the dark tatters of the street, that I waited for the release of Miss Pridden's step, not for her company, but because then I too would have someone to leave behind.

Across the avenue, in the house opposite, a circle of boarders sat at a round dining-room table; at that distance no clatter came from them, and their heads looked as if bowed in benediction under the gaudy lotus-bell of the hanging lamp. Between us, the façade of the house, with its attached smear of cobbles, interposed like a theater scrim; forward on the trough, a cat cleaned itself to some private, arching music, tucked its paws in, and gazed. I knew the house, having more than once delivered a dress to a woman there, and now for company I revisited it in the parts I could not see, climbing the Turkey carpet that ran, a faded hemorrhage, down the stairs, padding along the straw matting of the corridor, to the smell of CN disinfectant and the drip of basins, past each madder-brown door with its card below the transom — *Reavis, Fitzwater, Smith, Mason, Dubois* . . . the last of the names eluded me, and then, zinc-sharp out of its shadow, it came to me — *Parkes*. Miss Pridden, if not returned by now, must be spending the evening with the lady-friend in Charlotte who, I had heard her say with gentle commiseration, lived in such a boardinghouse too. Straining, I pried forward to visit them there, to project my ghost between them at a similar table, but I had never been to the place or heard her describe it, and I could not get past the blank after the main street in Charlotte. I am a revenant, after all; my facility does not stretch too far beyond.

It was the hour before dinner, sweet when appointed. There in Tuscana the street was empty; here in the city it is never so. Yet it

3 5

seems to me that I have carried that particular hour with me ever since. It is the hour of other people's assignations. No matter at what o'clock it comes, its light is entr'acte, its pitch pipe the tearing softness of tires speeding forward. Useless for the grown man to tell himself that it is formed only out of the *Schwärmerei* of dusk, or from the jealous, genital wakening at midnight. I listen and wait, as I did then, and just out of hearing, I hear it — the steady pasturing of the world at its longings. It is nothing, I tell myself, except the late purchasers at the flower barrows — but the purchase is thrust by the buyer into waiting hands nearby. It is only a family leaning against its railing — but leaning ruddy against each other. And in some other street, not mine, the women merge, classic under the lamps. In those far buildings, so aerially close, the teeth of a thousand luckier diners strike against pearls.

Across the way, the lights went out on the lower floor. I went downstairs and waited outside Miss Pridden's front door, although I knew by now that she would not come. When I had been there for a time, someone came out on the porch opposite and stood there in the shadows. I took a marble from my pocket and flung it at the feet of whoever was there. It skipped into the darkness, a lost bead.

After a while, whoever was there came down the steps and along the cobbles. I moved forward, to feel the wind of his passage. He passed me, an old man with his head down, and I felt it. When he had gone, I moved on home.

Chapter VI. Ruth. The Place.

SO, THEN, that evening I went looking for Johnny. At home the house had been the way a house is when it is significantly empty. Obedient djinn, it is there when you enter, but waits for you only to turn your back for its corners to dance and confabulate, for its antihuman cabala to begin. It was a mean box of a house, like all the others in the mill section — parlor, kitchen, and two inner compartments, over all of which my mother's work baskets, the hung mementos of my grandfather, and all the other small muddle of our possessions spread only the thinnest stain of living, from which even my aunt's collection of medicine bottles was missed when we heaved it away. Yet when I came in that night, it spoke up as powerfully as any mansion — "I am here, master, waiting: see how well and quiet I wait, to make you twice alone."

On the kitchen dresser there was a big spread, set out no doubt by Mrs. Boomer, the neighbor who was to do for me — a joint and a loaf under one of my mother's best napkins, and a sweet I loved, that must have been sent out for — what the woman down the road who sold them called a "chess pie." I ate heavily, first out of hunger, then, throwing aside the napkin, with a steady vengeance, sitting a while and then returning to the pie until I was sick of it, like a dog left among the dishes of several days' feeding. Then, like a dog too, I left it and circled the rooms, picking and touching, leaning my forehead against the sour pine doorjambs, my shoulder against the tepid walls. *Take a match to it and come away,* I thought, knowing how, every season along here, two or three such houses snatched fire from their own dead heat and crumpled — not yet knowing how nothing ever burns in the past but what may still, at some later time, start up whole again, light-years away, all its corners complete.

On the kitchen table there was an envelope with some money in it, the three dollars previously agreed upon for my week's keep. My uncle, then, had no thought of wooing me with a new father's largesse; a measured man, he allowed me no margin for hate. A tea tray nearby had some small change on it, and, precious to us as water from the Jordan, the black canister of Twining's tea. This was my mother's touch, setting out those small, winning comforts with which those who will not sink all for us show us the neat limits of their love. The overhead lamp glared on me in its center; in one of those dread starts of hyper-identity my right hand clasped my left, a stranger's, and consciousness looked down on its body, saying, "This is I." I picked up the envelope of money and ran out.

Outside, I went into the privy and sat there for my needs, and a while longer. The sky, from a privy, is metaphysical; a wooden step away from the fields, one dreams oneself an animal again, crouching there in the ammoniac dark. I fingered myself, but it was not myself only that I wanted. Nor is it yet. I was passing through the strange borderland where one leaves the unconscious, tonal fugue of childhood and takes up the ceaseless, inner dialogue of oneself. I had a prescience that this black, supersonic thread of chatter would never leave me. And although I had not yet thought openly of women, I already wanted a place to lay it down.

For me love is a *place,* not a person — why did I never see that before this moment that I write it here? The why is rhetorical. Nights ago, that night after I left Ruth Mannix, and, pressed beyond endurance, sat down to commune with — whom? — I who commune with no one — I did so because I knew how the act of the pen sometimes produces the submerged idea, like the hand trailing in the minnow stream. What I must hope for is that my hand, trailing in the stream of myself, will produce me. I cannot hope to be like my old preceptor, Frau Goodman, mulling over her heraldic place in life's genealogical tree — that is for people who already have their place. And now I can no longer continue to live behind others, watching those who do. For safety alone now, I must see my own design clear. As for Ruth's safety — even in the heroin-stare of that moment when, lying beside her, I heard her say what she had guessed about me, I did not need to think of her safety — I am no murderer. Violence — my own violence — is not my métier.

No, I am in the position of a man who is his own inheritor — before I move on I must arrange my estate. And if I do not move on? If I stay for once, and marry Ruth, which is what she wants, or live with her, which is what she would accept? Then I must tell her what she would surely come to know, of which up to now not a soul has guessed as much as she. I would have to tell her the way it is with me, what it is I do, and that I no longer wholly know its meaning. Once I thought I knew; I thought I meant merely to be the manipulator behind the scene. But each time now is increasingly a rehearsal, a rehearsal for something, in a somewhere just beyond. Perhaps, in the end, with that extraordinary reed-sense of women to the timbre of whom they love, she could in the end tell me — and would that be the ultimate safety? In the end, might she come to be the place where the burden of listening is lifted, where the listener might learn to speak?

Haply I think on thee. Thus is expressed for us forever that romantic folklore of the sexual love which we are all taught to anticipate, whether we are hinted it from the cinema or the sonnet. For in the physical loves of the most uncomplicated brute of a man there is a metaphysical hunting. He hunts for something lost, or only adumbrated, in the tangled scents of his beginnings. And from the first he is taught to name it in the language of persons, as the *religieuse* is taught to name her Lord.

But if the lost quarry should be not a person, but a place? Then, even as he hangs successful on the body of his love, another part of him rises and walks away. Even as, lying loose in the after-quiet of love, I rose from Ruth. As, even while I listen, with men and women both, while I sit there storing and appraising in the familiar pattern, I walk away from them all.

Then here it is, naked on the pen point, the first piece of me. All my excursions, then, into the lives of others, from that first time in the suddenly burst air of Tuscana when, leaving the courtroom, I passed Semple's face, that beaten mask of puzzlement which dared not speak but said silently, "It wasn't you. Then — *why?*" — all, then, are not an entering, but a walking away.

Where? Some night like this one, writing along in this way, listening to that city of music which lies just below the diatonic three-o'clock silence, I shall drop the pen, hearing my own theme; I shall know.

There are two chances. There is a chance that the two languages are one — that the place may be a person. Then I need only give these pages to Ruth; she need only take them. Is that what I sometimes fancy I see between others — a person-place where, circled in safety, one need not speak at all?

Or there is the other chance — do I long for it? — that some night, raising my head to hear, I shall recognize — not whom — but *where.*

It is getting light. Hours must have gone by since I wrote that.

I do not walk away. I see that clear. I do not walk away.

I walk toward.

Bit by bit I shall drag myself up, out of the stream. Haply I think on — there.

I walk toward.

Chapter VII. The Fair. The Cars of Tuscana.

FACING me, through the warped door of the privy, a stretch of mongrel fields led behind the town, along past the Negro quarter, to the railroad line. In the half-luminous Indian summer night the weeds looked of an even height, as if they were some bearing crop. Beyond their motionless rim, over near Johnny's place, the red signal-eye burned and waned, blinking for the 8:38 freight, still a mile away.

I went outside and waited. It was a quiet night for market day; near us there were no houses close enough for me to see, but over in the black-brown jumble of niggertown, in "the backs" where they paraded in the evenings, all seemed nested down. I could hear the train coming now, but the hour must be later than I thought; this was not the slow freight, creaking along like an endless cradle, to the jerk and settle of its couplings, but an undertow that shook my belly with the ground. This was the 9:50 coming up from the South, all the way from the Gulf maybe, north to the next big city whose name I did not even know; this was the passenger-flyer, going north.

A huge white core grew toward me, splaying the dark. It rushed past, whistle mute. Under its hard breath, the weedy sidings stood up like wheat. Then it vanished, with a sound of squeezed air, and I heard it for a while far off, running on to all the other small towns ahead that burned and waned. This was the "to-from Memphis" train.

I put my head on my knees and wept. I wept for my mother, who, having let me see that I was not enough for her, had made me see that she was no longer enough for me. This is the real parting; when she died I did not need to weep.

I wept for things as they were. The stars, hanging low, crept golden into my tears, and I wept on because I might never know how things ought to be. And when I was done, I went looking for Johnny, because he knew both.

The signal light lay straight across field, but I took the long way round, delaying. As I walked, I kept touching the envelope of money in my pocket, seeing the two of us, Johnny and me, sitting almost like men together, while I treated him down at the café. As I went on, the image failed me — but I went on. This is how actionless people thrust themselves into action — first the wild image of what will never believably come to be, then the plodding, steadfast as a clerk's, to make it come to be.

Ahead, in the backs, it was dark as a cave, but I had often walked there of an evening, for the sake of the distant demi-company of the blacks. Their company — veiled glances and a soft return to their own concerns — was a kind of music to me, a negligent night music to which I need only half listen, and the short, blocked lane of their lives, blurred with oil lamps and people leaning, was a place where I need not watch. It was a painting I walked through, velvet unison of skin and dark and the candle-spurt of voices. This is the power of the ghetto for others; it releases from the friction of kin. The eye of the ghetto absolved me from being the eye; it was not possible to enter here.

But when I came to the lane it was still, so still that I stood in wonder. Here was the street that never went to bed, all of it, all the night long — tin battling paper in the yard heaps, doors flung and visiting, smells and shadows in a chutney mingle. And now it was like a space where a lane should have been. I heard the leaves scuttling like small animals, and my own breath in my throat. Then, as my eyes widened, the houses pearled toward me out of the dark, chimneys quiet, porches hanging akimbo, like people come upon in the sprawl of sleep, and all the blinds were drawn.

They are at the fair, I thought, but there was no fair that I knew of anywhere near. A street that was a fair to itself, where did such a street go?

I walked down the length of it, almost to the end. Then, behind me, I felt it, a sigh of breath relayed from house to house, a rustle like the great, parting lashes of a single eye, and I knew that they were there.

When I was almost to the last house, I heard a screen door wheeze. I stood in my tracks, behind a bush.

"Louie-lamb?" a woman's voice said. " 'at you, chile, Louie-lamb?"

A man's whisper came, rough. "Hesh, you. He sure to be in safe somewhere. Crazy, you hesh."

The door closed. And then I heard the woman's voice again, outside it, nearer, low on the same words and the same note. I hid my face from it. She came by me and went down the lane, and all the way along it I heard her interval, like a mourning dove, like bubble with a break in it, "Louie-lamb? Louie-lamb?"

Then I cut and ran, running across the remaining fields, almost up to the main line, out into the light, until I no longer felt afraid. I had never had it before, the fear that eats the South; I never had it again. But I remember well how it feels to have to cover the white face, and in justice to Semple I will set it down here. This is how it feels — I remember it yet. I felt — that a dove is a bird that should speak only by day. That, behind their drawn blinds, the demi-people doubled, and became a company of men. And that, wherever their blind was drawn, it was drawn against me.

Yonder, as people said down here, was Johnny's house; near it, the signal light, steady now until dawn. It must be pleasant, I thought, living under that unwavering glow; waking in the false damp of the mornings here one might take it for the fresh, fogbound glow of coals. I knew the outside of his house the way everyone in Tuscana knew it, all of us coins rubbing together in the same pocket. But the never-entered house of a friend is a special mystery — it is his deshabille. Whatever his truth is, it lies there.

Where I had come to was the old front of what might once have been a stationmaster's shed — it was blank and closed, all the openings boarded up with faded red planks the railroad must have put there long ago. Someone had shored up the roof with two-by-fours, cross-hatched over the huge, peeling letters of a painted hoarding for cattle feed. In the rear, in front of a number of lean-to's added on, one to the other, like dominoes, the way the Negroes did, was the yard where I had seen Johnny's blue-eyed brothers and sisters, in their Hunky pina-fores limed with fowl droppings, staring out at passers-by from coveys of dock and creeper, or chattering in their own language at the guinea hens that roosted in the trees.

I walked around the shed to the center lean-to, where light seamed around a door and came faintly through the pocked shade in a window to one side. There were no steps. Standing there, in the quiet smell of the sty, I put my hand on the door. I touched his door, and I could not knock.

I took my money out then, squeezing it for the courage in it. He had never come looking for me so; I knew well that in our afternoons together I served only as a point from which he might go looking for himself. With my fist raised and silent, I thought of how he had never once exchanged with me that precious bit of magic: "Call for me." Stroking his door with noiseless knuckles, I whispered it aloud. "Call for me." Standing there on the brink of his mystery, I wanted for once to show him mine.

The whispers we speak so intensely to ourselves, or to the un-telepathic air, do they in the end erode us with our own impotence, or sometimes, bearing us forward on the potent scent of ourselves, send us part of the way toward where we reach? When I put my hand back in my pocket, it brushed a small telephone-address book that, phoneless and with nothing to record, I had bought some months before and had carried everywhere with me since. In the pink light shining over my shoulder, I turned its bare, dog-eared pages until I came to one with a tab marked F — for Fortuna. I tore it out and wrote upon it. He might know my writing or guess who it was from. But if he did not come in answer I should never know why; I could pretend to myself that I had given nothing away. So I wrote down my whisper and left it unsigned: *Johnny. Call for me.*

There was a broken mail basket hanging by a string from a nail in the top of the window frame to the right of the door. I stepped up on the uneven sill of the window and stuck my message on the nail. And as I did so, I saw into the upper pane, where there was no shade. At a table in the foreground, old Frazer, the night watchman, in for a visit during his stint, sat over a cup and saucer. In the oil lamp light his huge, dewlapped face brooded like a hound's, but everyone knew him for a happy, fluting old man who had come to the end of a snug life with his berth assured, who leaned against the railroad hierarchy — that had brought him so safely to its bottom rung — like an old, moronic prince leaning against his ladder of kings. At the side, in the back, there were dim pallets where the children must be sleeping, and on a rag rug near the table a boy of about seven slept with his arm flung across a glinting toy.

Mrs. Fortuna came out from somewhere in the rear — the old closed-off shed it must be — accompanied by a lantern-chinned man I did not recognize as one of Semple's crowd. Her earringed moon-face looked the same as it had the times I had seen her on the street, above the same man's jersey and Mother Hubbard; her feet were bare. The man let his arm drop from her shoulder, strutted across the room in a silent buck and wing, and sat down near Frazer. She brought two more cups and the three of them sat there, sipping; once the man got up and scooped the sleeping boy from the floor, bore him into the rear, and returned with the toy, a harmonica, in his long palm. He put the harmonica to his lips, blowing it without making a sound, and sat down again, shuffling his feet and digging his head to some rhythm he carried inside. Frazer snuffled in his cup and protruded his lips in reverie.

It was the pantomine of people too easy to bother talking, and I noted, too, the easy, mindless way they all touched one another,

45

Johnny's mother leaning a hand on old Frazer's nape while she served him, Frazer staying the pot she held, and brushing her a thank-you, the second man picking up the boy or setting straight an askew comb in Mrs. Fortuna's hair. It was not just male-female touching but something else, something I remembered of Fulham, of certain neighbors there from whom my mother had schooled me away — the congruous group-touch of those so beneath class as to be only people. At home, the higher the caste the more socially untouchable, and it was toward this that people of my mother's class froze themselves, in the end even exceeding their betters, and losing the other thing forever, even in their awkward, two-by-two congruities of love.

It could not have been long, yet it seemed a long time that I stayed there, a valve in my heart opening and closing, recognizing even then something that would not remain in the picture if I entered, but was only present when seen from outside. Voyeur — that smart sneer of our nerve-triggered salons — we are all voyeurs to the limits of our talent and understanding; even my own habit is only a fortune grown out of bounds. What we see in the scene in the window frame, in the flat across the areaway, in the farmhouse ridden past at twilight, these scenes of people moving with grave, unconscious sweetness at mealtime, impermanence arrested with the holiness of a Vermeer, is the sweet kernel of the human condition — man budded domestic for a moment, on a wild planet. I rested my arms on the window frame and watched them, the reason why I had come forgotten, in this first eavesdropping of so many others to be.

"Get down from there, you!" A clout from behind knocked me into the darkness below. I fell on my ribs, the wind out of me, my cheek against the greasy earth. Somebody hulked over me, swinging a bucket. I had not caught whose voice it was, and I could not yet see his face. Then, as I raised myself on my elbow, I saw his outline — Johnny's — looming over me the way it had the day I had asked him the question on the hill. He bent over me, breathing hard.

"I told Lemon, he, any more you peepers sneak around here again —" he said, and then, peering, he knew me. His jaw fell. He stared at me, betrayed.

I could not look straight back at him, the way an animal cannot. When we are accused, guiltless of we know not what, we have still a great nameless flow of residual guilt that rushes toward the accused spot the way blood rushes toward pricked skin.

He reached down slowly and helped me to my feet. "Y' oughtn't to listen to Lemon," he said. Something, no noise, made him glance back at his own house. And when he turned again, he could not look at me.

I knew Lemon and his crowd at school, old as Johnny or older, boys who were thinly tall or stunted, who swaggered tobacco-chew between teeth still green with childish tartar, and claimed the pustules on their cheeks for a more manly disease. As I lagged behind their undercover ferment of talk, I had sometimes got a piece of what half-knowledge I had, but they had never deigned to notice me.

He bit his lip, looking down. "Don't listen to them," he said. And even I could hear what else he was saying without saying it. *Listen to me.*

"I don't go with Lemon," I said quickly.

"You mean, you come by here on your own?"

I nodded. I wanted him to ask me why now. I felt happy at his asking me anything.

He stepped back, squinting, the bucket dangling from his hand. "What you come here for?"

I didn't know what to say. I hung my head, not knowing how to say it.

"What you come for!"

"I —"

"What you come sneaking at the window for? Going to write something on it, maybe?"

I didn't want to say why I had come now. I wanted to hide it.

He stretched his neck. "Just passing by, whyn't you knock at the door?"

"I was." My voice slid higher, in the forgotten alley-tones of home. "I'd got some money, I had. I was going to knock, I was. Quite a bit of money I'd got, and I thought . . . I'd got three dollars."

His face looked so queer that I stopped. It moved like a cat's, separate on its neck. He threw the bucket of swill over me.

It was like being spat upon, although I had never been. But there are postures the spine is born knowing. Reproach for the unknown is one of them.

"Spend your money in niggertown," he said. "Like Lemon."

The sour stuff seeped down me, teaching me in one minute the nakedness of clothes. And there on the nail was the note that revealed me. I sprang for it.

I had it in my hand when he jumped me. We rolled over and over, kicking and tearing, sobbing deep in our chests with the grim joy of having found the adversary at last.

He was kneeling on my chest when he read it. I lay on my back, heaving slower, the arm that he had twisted outflung. Soft air currents in the night touched my eyelids, that all but closed in sleep. Filth from my hair trickled into my mouth, but I did not move; it had the taste of justice. It was he who bent and wiped it away.

"Stay here," he whispered, and went off into the dark. When he came back he had a bucket of water and a cloth. He stood me up and cleaned me off like a brother.

"Turn around," he said. When I had my back to him he spoke, dipping and wringing the cloth. "They been writing stuff on the windows — know what I mean?"

I nodded, head down.

"Pick times when I ain't here," he said. "Sure 'nough don't pick times when I'm here." The rag paused, continued its work. "Store closed early tonight. Semple has places 'round town I got to go for him. He let me take his car." I heard the note of pride, but more than that the way he was telling me things in the present, the way he had never done before. "Runs like a dream, she does," he said.

He mopped the back of my jeans. "Brung it back for him, walk home slow, never thinking anybody try any that stuff tonight. Ain't even been in the house yet — come round the corner, and I seen you." His hand paused again, and I felt the water run down my calf to my heel. "Nobody comes here for *me,* see," he said. "Took you for one of them, see what I mean?"

I turned so that I could look down on him as he squatted there, dangling the rag. "What I meant — about the money —"

"Forget it." He found a spot on my sneaker.

"What I —"

"I said forget it." He wet the spot down carefully. "Your maw — she in on your asking me up to your house?"

I had forgotten her. "She's gone off," I muttered.

He looked up. "For good?"

That is the way I remember his face best — when he looked up and said that. There was all his life and what he came from — in the way he said that. And it was odd how I wanted to be able to say yes to him, the way an aggrieved child sometimes tells the neighborhood that he is the adopted son of his true parents.

I hesitated, seeing the rising kinship in his face. When I lie, it is not as a fantasist, but to see if I can change life, to play with the protean gap between what is and what might be. And when I tell the truth, it is not for moral reasons, but because I am impelled to see what life does when it is left alone.

"She and my uncle — they went to Memphis for a week," I said.

"Oh." He flipped the bunched rag from hand to hand. He had not, then, been asked into a house after all, as the Nellises had once asked him — as shone always in his mind, like their evening light. Yet when he stood up, he put an arm on my shoulder, for what he presumed to be my trouble. " 'On't you fret," he said. " 'On't you fret on it."

"I've no need to fret," I said, and it was true, for the moment. We reconsider our troubles, and are helped to bear them, in proportion to their seeming like blessings to others. He had shown me the difference between us.

"They got married today," I said. "Down at the church, this morning. Maybe you heard."

"Town had bigger news this morning." He had withdrawn his arm; he was not too dull to see what I was doing. For now that I had a piece of his mystery, how quick I had been to use it against him, to do to him what I feared from others.

It made me bolder. "The money was to last me the week, but I've enough stuff to last me at home. And what I'd in mind was — you and me . . . we might go down to the café." Even as I said it, it struck me — how the image had come to be. Not as I had dreamed it — never as one dreams it. But it had come to be.

"Café's closed," he said, staring. "Won't be no trade there tonight, don't you know that? Your folks crazy, leaving you run loose tonight?"

"I walk late in the backs lots of times."

"You come through the backs?" He blew out his breath. "Reckon I better see you safe home."

"How come it's all right for you?"

He cocked his head, listening. "Shhh. Ain't that the sound of cars?"

The whistle-stop signal, where we stood, was south of where the town streets ended. The main line ran north-south on the western edge of the town. Behind us to the west were the fields across which I had come, beyond them the backs. All of Tuscana, except for niggertown, lay east of us and the main line, in a hollow bordered on the other side by the state road, four miles away. Between us and the state highway there was a curving dirt road that dead-ended here. To the north, overlooking the town, was the hill where Johnny and I spent our afternoons — one of the small moraines that marched across country here like fragments of aqueducts, marking the dry lizard-trail of some dead tributary of the wide waters farther east. Beyond the hill — in a great easterly semicircle enclosing us all: Tuscana, Charlotte and its sister town of Denoyeville — were the dam sites, breastworks that neither fought us nor defended us, and advanced without guns. On clear nights like this they rose like frozen tidal waves, darker than the sky.

We listened, and heard the sound of motors approaching up the dirt road. There was as yet no surfaced route between us and the dam site. All its exodus was from the other side. Yet, as I listened, I imagined that somehow a detachment of its trucks had overleaped its fortifications, for the sound we heard was in unison — the low humming of motors going at a slow, set pace, on work operation. Then the first car came into view, and close behind it another and another and another, until finally we could see the whole long motley string, moving in low gear, creeping toward us at parade pace — all the cars of Tuscana.

"What they come this way for?" Johnny whispered. "Weren't due to pass this way."

"What? Who?" I whispered back. He hushed me, pushing me behind him with a warning hand, then drew me with him inside one of the sheds. Its door hung askew from one hinge, an old kitchen door with a rotted tuft of curtain at its window and no pane.

All the cars were in view now, each pinpointed in the light of another, in a semicircle around us, down the road for as far as we could see. There must have been about forty of them. To own a car was still an eminence in the town at that time, and none of them was new; they were sold and acquired locally as horses had once been, each car with a personality, with a history of the fall and rise of its successive owners, with all its bloodlines clear in the mind of the town. As they rounded us, I thought I recognized farm trucks seen week after week at the Friday market, others that were a familiar sight on the streets, although I could not name their owners, and a few that I was sure I had never seen before, that might have come from Denoyeville or Charlotte. I recognized the Baptist minister's car, and the doctor's.

They came on, at a steady pace of about eight miles an hour, to the hum of the throttled engines, and there was something disturbing about the evenness with which they came. The lead car drew up and halted a few yards from us; behind it the others also halted. The lead car turned off its lights, but not its engine. One by one the others followed, and the sky came out again, with the pallor peculiar to a clear night's zenith, above the long dark line that stood stock-still in the road, its engines urgently throbbing, its gas-generated breath rising toward us like the musk of a waiting herd. Inside where we were the curtain stirred with it, the shed spread it like a sieve.

"Who they come by for?" muttered Johnny. "Nobody supposed to be here I know of. Everybody supposed to round up in town."

He dug his fist in my arm for silence, to keep me where I was, and stole outside. I peered after him through the curtain, my heart pounding with the question of who they might be, that dark, animal line. But deeper still — favoring even then the mystery of the one over the many — I brooded on how it was to be Johnny, for whom home was a place where anyone, any time, might be there.

When the gas lay so heavy on the wind that it seemed a word, a movement would spark it, the door of the main shed opened and was quickly closed. It was Frazer, the watchman, carrying his lantern, lifting it once broadly up and down, so that the whole swollen front curve of him showed, dropsical belly to crotch, making its childish, self-important "Oyez" in the dark. Behind him the other man, the long-chinned man from inside, seized the lantern and put it out.

At once all the headlights went on, paired by paired eyes springing open. In their glow I saw Johnny's face where he lay all but hidden in the long grass. He was staring at the lean figure of the second man. The man's long jaw caught the light as he handed the doused lantern to old Frazer and took out the makings of a cigarette. He shook out the tobacco and licked the paper, his feet still half strutting in their buck and wing, and now I could hear the tune they jaunted to — "Old Zip Coon" — and catch the words he hummed.

Went to the river and I couldn't get across,
Paid a silver dollar for an old bline hoss —

He lit the cigarette, laid a hand on Frazer's shoulder, and pushed past him.

Hoss wouldn't foller, so I swapped him for a coon,
Coon began to holler, so I went back home.

I watched Johnny as the long figure slouched past him unaware, almost catching his face with its heel, and slid, easy-loined, into the first car of the line. He was staring up at it with the same look that, earlier, swinging the bucket, he had bent on me.

I crept out to him and crouched at his elbow. He did not turn his head to acknowledge me. "Never knew he came up here," he whispered. "Could have sworn he never hung around with *them*."

I said nothing. I did not consider telling him what I had overseen of the man and old Frazer and his mother, of the familiar way they had been sitting at table, of how the man had replaced the round comb in her hair. Nor did I think of whispering to him, friendly helpful, friendly deceiving, that perhaps he was wrong about the man, whoever he was, the way he had been wrong about me. I knew better. Already, out of my innocence I was forming my own peculiar honesty, as each of us, not out of original sin — that I deny — but out of our innocence, is forced to do. I knew that one may only gather the threads, and be silent. I knew that nothing one says face to face avails.

We were crouched there when the lead car moved in a direction so unforeseen that we barely had time to flinch into the shadows. This was the end of the road; the line must turn around, each car in its own radius, unless it planned to go in reverse the whole four miles to the state highway from which it must have come. Behind us was the siding. Beyond it there was no road, only the rough fields across which I had run from the backs.

But the lead car moved forward, turned sharply and made for the siding. I saw the car's hood tilt up and heave ahead under the fever-shine of the signal, and I recognized it as Semple's, hearing Johnny from times past: *A Packard eight. He got it off a widow in Mobile. Hundred-forty-five-inch wheelbase, longest wheelbase made. Has a fourth gear hauls it out of a ditch like a tractor. Brewster body. Custom-built for a man six and a half feet tall.*

Behind it, each car wheeled sharply and made for the main-line crossing. As they passed, here and there I thought I recognized cars Johnny had described or pointed out to me, repeating their dossiers in longing or condemnation. It took about twenty minutes for them all to cross over. Now and then a truck moved out of line to help a weaker car over; once an old touring eight, wedged on a timber, needed the help of two. But in all the pushing and grinding no human arm appeared, no voice, no driver. It was like watching a fable of cars changed to beetles, turned masters. At the finish, shell ranged by glittering shell, they were all on the other side. Behind them the signal light, some switch tripped or wire crossed, began blinking. Then the lead car struck out alone straight across field, grinding like a tractor over hummock and stubble, making a path for the rear to follow,

53

and in a long, transverse line, single in the starlight, all the cars of Tuscana crawled forward, humming, into the backs.

When they had gone, Johnny turned to me. Under cover of the noise we had gradually been drawn to our feet, shoulder to shoulder, away from the sheds. The smell of the grass rose again, that meek smell which will inherit the earth. All was quiet now around us except for the signal light, beating on. It went on like a warning pulse, although no train would pass here until dawn.

"So you come through the backs," he said. "See anyone there." It was not a question. Then he knew I had not.

I shook my head.

"You fool," he said. "You poor dumb fool." But his eyes, shining, looked past me.

He seized my wrist suddenly and dragged me forward. "Come on! I'll see you home."

He led me north on the lane that met the first streets of the town, and all the way along he hurried me, goading me like a child on its way to be punished. We went almost at a trot down the shrubbed lane, and all the way, as I panted to match my stride with his, I could feel his anger growing, clotting.

In front of my house we stopped short, both of us winded. He faced me, breathing harder than I. I thought he was going to jump me again — me, or whomever, in his fury, I stood for. This time I held my ground, lifting my chin to look at him eye to eye. Then I saw that his eyes were full of tears.

"You — you're such a fool," he said, choking. "You'd believe anything, wouldn't you!"

Suddenly he let out a torrent of curses, words I had never heard him use, and all of them directed at me, for the fool I was. He babbled at me like a fishwife, and always for the same word, the single fault that enraged him.

"All that stuff I used to tell you about the town," he said at last, in the creaking voice of someone exhausted by crying. "Up there." He pointed up to the hill. "And you *believed* it!"

It was only two days ago that we had been up there, and he had

5 4

described for me the latest tracery in his saga of goodness. It concerned the Nellises, and it had no story really, being only an account of how, Semple having sent him there after hours with a package for Nellis, he had walked up the trim lawn, edging his feet away from the borders where the bulbs were beginning, had knocked on the door with the brass plate, so neat, that said *Treacher Nellis,* and had found them all sitting at table, clean and comely as paper cutouts; mother, father and children, all in their proper family places. And through his dim words, lame pauses, there had come, as always, the moral fragrance of how people really were.

"Didn't you!" he said.

I was silent. I would not answer him as he needed. I could not. The listener is not the friend. Few understand this.

"We'll go downtown then," he said. "Come on."

My eyes wavered shut. Too much had been expected of me. I slept standing, a column of sleep between the outer dream and the in. "But the café is closed," I said.

He shook me roughly. "We're not going to the café."

I awoke, and followed him.

Out on the main street, that I still thought of as the High, our doubled footfalls echoed. It had been paved the year before, and there were sidewalks now, one on either side, each broad enough for a man to step aside for another. We had gone on for some paces when I halted, nudged by a queerness, a difference. I was wide awake now, with the special sentience that comes like a second wind.

"What you stopping for?" said Johnny. Again I had the feeling that he already knew.

I turned, looking back at the way we had come. I turned again, holding unsure hands in front of me.

The town, I thought — it was inside out. For here on the main street, where always a certain few lights burned, municipal and lonely, we stood on a long rib of dark. And scattered like beads around us, the houses, that should have been as dark as they were silent, had each its little spore of light, those hooded lights, paler than candles, that housewives place in the window when a man is late from home.

"The town," I said. "Look at the town."

He did not answer. He waited, slow elder brother, for me to show him in my sharpness what he already knew.

"The courthouse light is out," I whispered. "And the one over the church door."

Still he waited. The wind moved, shabby-sweet.

I saw the houses, lit up for a fair.

"Johnny!" I said. I whispered it. "Who were the men in the cars?"

For answer, he led me down an alley, behind a store, where a gamecock chirred.

Chapter VIII. Semple's Store. The Hill.

SEMPLE'S store. I'll enter it again, in a moment, as the two of us did so long ago. But first, I sit here, having just reread as I do each evening the excursion of the night before. I see a change. I see a change in the method by which I record. I did not expect this so soon.

Come, come, I did not anticipate it at all. There is a dangerous arrogance in those words "so soon" — the secret pomp of the dissembler, of one all too used to being, in most company, the subtlest, the most aware. But if I begin to dissemble to myself, then I am done.

As to the change. When I began this, I counted on every resource of a memory of more than average intensity. Memory runs on of itself for most, a river always partially underground. But for me it is my harnessed "familiar" who can be focused like a camera obscura upon a chosen scene of the past. Gradually, then, within that boxlike frame, granules of light stream toward a center, and in an atmosphere dead and clear as old starlight, the color gathers again to the peach, the prussic smell to the bitten stone. Faces are the hardest, somehow foreign to that landscape, Venetian heads thrust into a *nature morte*. But even when they come they are only addenda to the once quick gesture now repeated andante, to the light word fossilized, to

the cadence of the said and the unsaid, the felt and the unfelt, all returned now in empathy to me, who will hold them like coral, forever.

Therefore, when I began this it did not occur to me to premeditate
any *discours sur la méthode.* I am the method. Nor do I forget that I
am also the critic voice, outside the scene and above it, even as Donne
was, when, in the depth of his devotions, he felt the stone beneath
his knee, the tickling straw. But I see now that the encyclopedist
cannot research his own past with the same calm as, daily, he may
do it for others, building out of the crabbed footnotes a half-column's
worth of man.

One keeps a tryst with one's own life at a certain peril. Not that my
owl, my monitor, will desert me. It is not likely that I shall lose, in the
transports of memory, what cannot be lost even in any transport of
love.

Still, there is too little of the critic voice in last night's notes; they
speak too often in the soft, mucused voice of self-immersion, in the
hypnotic voice of the child I was. "Excursion" is such a suggestive
word. I must be more careful to keep in mind that the box has a frame.

Once inside the shop, Johnny seemed to shrink, reminded, as I
thought then, of who he was. For, as he lit a lamp and brooded over
the length of its wick, I saw in his slumped shoulders only the mingy
posture of the part-time clerk, and later, when he spoke, I took the
tone of his voice for the clerk's serviceable tone. I did not yet know its
note for that dead timbre, accepting of the world's dust, which people
employ once a shock is over, already becoming absorbed in the fiber, an
already known quantity in the future catechism of days.

That night, also, I was to have my first sight of feeling gurgled up
from a heart that does not pause to know it has it, but I was too young to
recognize this, or value it for the great sight it is. Later on I would be
still young enough to recognize it and despise it. Only much later
would I come to hunt it for myself, for its intercession, as I do now.

We were in the lumber-room of the store, with no other entry but
the one through which we had come. Opposite this, a door in the wall

had been nailed up by means of two bars of hewn wood, crisscrossed over the lock. Semple's store had been let into the lower story of one of those two-decker wooden houses of the eighties, loaf-shaped, topped with a single border of crenellation, that often line the main streets of small towns here even now, receding behind their gouged fronts like faded backdrops of the vaudeville period to which they belong. The store proper lay on the other side of the nailed door, a jumble too, as I had once or twice glimpsed it, but one of cash-register brightness, filled with the unmellowed, turpentine smells of all the brisk hardware of the hour.

Here, on the other side, all the unsalable had been put to molder. One corner held a wardrobe big as a stall, made of walnut — in the South the poor man's wedding wood, the rich man's ordinary. In one of its closed panels, long as a coffin lid, the lion's mane of the burl still spumed under the dust. Elsewhere, harness hung to rot, over bladder-shapes of leather and iron and shadow, in a quiet brown of accumulation, the color of the cul-de-sac.

But in the center of the room there was a ring of chairs, twelve chairs closing a circle with exemplary neatness. And in the center of these, on one of those bent-bamboo stands which women use to set a choice plant in the sun or a nightlamp in a window, a small, clean book lay, a startle of white that held the chairs, the room. I moved toward it.

"Watch how you touch it!" came Johnny's voice from behind. "They know when you touch it."

I leaned forward on tiptoe. It was a pamphlet rather than a book. Four long pins had been driven into it, and from these white thread had been suspended, up to down, left to right, forming a hairline cross.

"Who?" I whispered. "You were going to tell me."

He turned to the wardrobe and took something out, holding it folded on his arm. "Ain't you figured that out yet?" Then he drew the thing over his head, a pointed white hood that blanked him to the shoulders, all but the pencil-holes for the eyes.

"Don't!" I said, recoiling. A chair fell over, behind me.

"Is that what they had on?" I said. "Why we couldn't see them? The men in the cars?"

"Ah-hah." His voice came blunted as a ghost's. "Better put them back their chair."

"What is it?" I said, not moving. "What's that thing for?" But deep in the acquisitive blood that learns to course with the climate it inhabits, I already knew. No one had ever breathed a word to me here of their open secret, but I breathed their oblique air. And I understood their need, being one of those born to form a hood of his own, one that would keep me a thousand times more secret than they. I looked at theirs, and felt of my cheek, that I had wanted to cover as I crouched in the backs. This was the white hood they used here, to cover the white face.

He drew the hood off. "It's all there," he said softly. "In the book there."

"What is?"

"Everything. The names," he said softly, urgently, not looking at me, so that I guessed that he had brought me here, not for myself, but for a purpose of his own. It did not occur to me that he took it for granted that I knew who "they" were in general, as the ant must assume that the nest is the organism of the world. He must have thought that I wanted to see the names, as he did, as he both wanted and feared to see, a particular name.

"You've read it?"

"I don't read so good. Not so good as you."

He is afraid, I thought, but I credited him with the wrong fear.

So I stepped into the circle, and he followed close behind me, through the gap of the fallen chair. The white threads stirred as we bent over them. The pins came out easily from the blank cover. He shivered as I laid them aside.

Under the cover, the title sheet held a single black inscription: *Klansman's Manual. 1924. Knights of the Ku Klux Klan. P.S. Etheridge — Chief of Staff and Imperial Klonsel.*

His face was near my shoulder. "Read it out."

I turned the title sheet and read out the table of contents, stumbling now and then on the one repeated letter that bird-tracked the page:

Table of Contents

The Order. Objects and Purposes. The Invisible Empire. Emperor of the Imperial Empire, the Imperial Klonvokation, the Imperial Kloncilium, the Imperial Wizard, Realms, the Initial Klorero, Provinces — the Initial Klonverse, Klans.

"That's it," said Johnny. "The K-Quad, for the three towns. Does it have the names?"

"Not here."

"Read till you come to them."

I read on, down one page after another, through all that wandering hagiolatry of pure red blood and white faces, sounding out each glyph as I could sound it now, unconscious then of the camera that stored it away. I read of the Imperial Wizard, of his Realms and Provinces, of the offices of the Kludd, the Kligrapp and the Klarogo, and the duties of those who bore them, and of the Exalted Cyclops and his twelve terrors, "a board of auditors, investigators and advisors, three of whom shall be known by the title of Klokann."

"That's Semple," said Johnny.

"The Wizard?" Outside the circle, the wardrobe door swung to, creaking. We both wheeled.

"You crazy?" he said. "That's for the whole country. Semple's the — that other."

"The Cyclops," I said. A prickle, half pleasure, ran up my forearms. "For Tuscana?"

"For the *entire* State of Alabama, some say." A flicker of triumph crossed his face — that peculiar flicker of those who live close to authority, even to one they despise. For that moment I shared it, it was

61

transmitted to me, a feeling not unlike that surge of privilege I had felt, gazing up, solitary, at Miss Pridden's ceiling, standing inside her secret, jalousied door.

"Johnny," I said. I held my hands out to him. "Can *I?* Can I belong?"

"*You?*" he said.

By such painful stages is the trade of confidant learned.

"You read what it said," he said. "You have to be born here. But maybe you could ask Lemon."

Then Lemon belonged.

"Shall *you* belong then?" I said, hating him for having asked something of him. I knew that he did not know where he had been born, or of whom.

"Most likely," he said, raising his chin. "Likely I will, sometime. But not here!" It burst from him. "Not anywhere in the State of Alabama! Not anywhere Semple is!"

"Why not?"

"Because he's rotten, that's why. He's making the whole town rotten. Anybody who hangs out with him is rotten."

Across the room, the old wardrobe creaked again, from the force of his voice. "Never you mind," he said, low. "Ain't none of your beeswax. Read out the rest of it. Go on."

So I went on reading, while he watched at my elbow through page after page, for the names. I read of the Grand Tribunal, that in organized Realms was to be composed of Hydras, Furies and Giants, and of the "Sitting of the Tribunal," of the charges involving a major offense, and of how the accused might be tried. I read of the Night Hawk, who was the special courier of the K-Quad, and of how he was also the Fiery Cross Bearer, "who shall carry the Fiery Cross in the ceremony and in all public exhibitions where same is used."

That is the only time I saw the book, that one time when I read it through. And when we came to the end of it, we found the names. A piece of thin paper, cut to the same size as the back cover, had been pasted to it, and the list, much creased and crossed out, had been slipped like a library card inside. The paste was old and dry, ready to part, and in my handling, the thin, concealing end paper fell off and fluttered to the floor. The list, left on the table, was a long one crudely typewritten, with here and there a hand-inserted name. I do not remember the names, all of them, in their proper order, for the list was almost a male roster of the town. But if a name were to be given to me now, I could still say whether or not that name was there.

And I can see exactly, as I saw it then, the twelve names that headed the list in capital letters, with their identifying offices beside them.

I did not read these out. Johnny, pushing me aside, read them for himself, his lips moving, his finger going down the page: the Cyclops, the Klaliff, the Kludd, the Kligrapp, the Klabee, the Kladd, the Klonsel, the Klarogo and the Klexter — and opposite each, a name. I saw the minister's name, and the doctor's. Semple's name was at the top: *Exalted Cyclops — E. V. Semple.* The twelfth name — the name of a man who had died recently in the town — had been crossed out, and another name had been inserted.

Night Hawk — T. Nellis. I saw it before Johnny's fist, big as a man's, crushed the list and let it drop to the floor.

"You sure sucked it in," he said. "All that stuff I told you about the town. Took you in for fair." His hand fell to his side, but I had seen where it had paused, the slow forefinger withdrawing into the fist, at the twelfth name.

"You believed it, you poor little old ninny," he said "didn't you?"

I thought back to our afternoons on the hill, to the town below, that I had always seen with the free, falcon stare of the outsider, to that other town that he had floated above it like a golden sphere — and I knew that I never had.

"Didn't you?" he said.

No, the listener is not the friend. But sometimes he smells its fragrance — friendship — a smell of roses from a garden where he stands outside.

"Yes," I said. "I believed you." It was the one good thing I ever did for him.

He pushed at the papers on the floor then with the toe of his shoe, moving one around the other, edging the crumpled list until it was dead center on the unmarked end page. Then he kicked it away. "Come on. Let's get out of here."

"Will they be coming back?"

"Uh-uh. Not tonight. They're going up to the dam. Nigger took a job there couple of days ago."

"But they went the other way," I said, "toward the backs."

He turned, halfway to the door. "Where else they gonna find him?" He waited. "You coming? Or ain't you?"

"What about these?" I pointed to the tangle of thread on the table, the papers lying on the floor.

He shrugged.

"Won't they think you did it?"

"Me? I keep watch for them in the grove. I help cut the pine and truck it down to the café. I been riding lookout for them all day." He shrugged again. "Reckon they'll figure the niggers did it. Come on. Ain't none of your beeswax."

And it wasn't of course — neither of his nor of mine. Children, coming upon the attic-hidden firearms of their fathers, do not debate the ethic of guns; to pretend that they might is only our own Lamarckian dream.

"Sure 'nough, they'll never think it was *you*," he said. "Nor your new paw, up there with your maw, in Memphis."

It was then that the idea came to me. There is an urge that arises in us when we are in hidden places — in the lumber-room, the sedile, the chancel. It is our own hidden motives, rising obscurant to hoax us. This is the attic-dream — of the enormous joke to be played.

"Let's hide it on them," I said.

He was still for a moment, but it reached him too. "Where?"

I pointed to the room — a latticework of places, of gear, and dust to cover the gear.

It was while we poked into the room's decaying niches, prying out an umbrella frame in one bin, ancient pease in another, that he told me details of the Klan meetings in the grove, of what they did there, and had done. In the end we chose a spice drawer, far up and in the farthest corner with lidded compartments that were empty except for scattered mice kernels and the dead, satin shells of roaches. We cached each article neatly in its separate hold and left them — the list, the pamphlet, the thread and the pins. In the circle of chairs the bare bamboo-stand seemed, when we turned to look back at it, the tallest thing in the room. Before we left, Johnny righted the fallen chair.

Outside, I thought at first that dawn had come, but all was still, cooler, with no birds yet, and dawn always came to Tuscana with calling trains. A vague nimbus above the dam site had tricked me, a slight, vibrating pallor, as if the sun were having trouble rising.

"Let's go up the hill," said Johnny. His face was not quite perceptible in the dark, but his voice was quiet, safe somehow, and this time I followed him as I used to do, walking behind him as if nothing had changed between us, between the hot haze of those afternoons and this dark.

Once we were among the trees, no light was visible. He took my hand, and I gave it. We climbed, peering for the path, and on the way up he talked almost as he used to do, but this time with a certain tenderness, as one might use perhaps to one who had believed. And what he spoke of, once again, was the town.

In essence what he said was that Tuscana was not like other places; it was a town gone wrong, not like other towns somewhere else. And Semple was all its evil, the corrupter who brought license with him wherever he came. Elsewhere there were towns that emerged, as he spoke of them, strong as cathedrals, resting on the holy framework he gave them — of men in their parlors with their children, with their wives in the churches, with each other in their Klans. Yes, this latter he put holy with the rest; he was not born, as this age dreams it bears its children, under liberty's caul. The horror of the list lay not in what it was, but in that any man on it was with Semple, in all Semple's other games, that he knew so well. He was only a less than fatherless boy who had placed all evil in one man, too much good in another. He had no knowledge of where to ascribe evil except singly; sometimes I think we shall not learn to do it better. He did not say all this, or know it. I say it for him, now.

So, until we reached the top, he talked on in his sweet, hopeless jesuitry, piecing together his broken sphere, floating it toward some farther hill. And as I listened, plodding along with him in an almost serene exhaustion, a curious thing happened. For the first time, Tuscana became real. As he cast it down, aside, for himself, it arose for me. I had done something in the town, to it; there was the list, ensconced secret in me, and the book I had helped to hide. Childhood is spent in the province of adults; it is only by living on in a place until the age of action, or by the action of leaving it, that, long after, one sees the province to have been one's own. In that sense, Tuscana never became mine. But as I walked that night, listening to Johnny, the path, the hill, even our house that was always so full of my sullen self, and the streets where I had walked beclouded, rose for me for the first time as Tuscana, a place of a certain geography and vegetation, that I saw almost as a boy born native to it might see it, from the receding observation car of his first train. It had become mine enough to leave.

We had come almost to the brow of the hill, climbing with heads bent to the steepness, our backs to the east. It was still black-dark, the darkest hour, but beneath us the trains now began their low, predawn stammering to one another. A piece of hanging moss brushed my hair, and it occurred to me that I knew almost none of the words for the plants and trees here. From far away across that sea over which I could not remember coming, I remembered children who had charted the sedge and the scabious with Elizabethan exactness, making dim poetry of a hundred trefoiled names, mapping their heritage in a botany of love. Here, where we were taught that each place was only a chip upon the vastness, the land-language of possession must be a different one, I thought; perhaps it was the language of trains.

"Johnny," I said. "What's the name of the next big town north?"

He never answered me, for we had come to the top of the hill.

We rounded a ledge, raised our heads, and the whole of the east struck our eyes, a black horizon with a penumbra that burned.

Before us, the great crater line of the dam site crested its silent tidal wave in an arc that took in half the world. Its four peaks rose like pediments. Each one bore a cross. Each one bore a fiery cross whose roaring current streamed backward although little wind blew — four wooden images of a man breasting the wind with his arms stretched wide, his flesh a yellow mane behind him, a running man who burned.

I watched them for a long time. In the end I held out my arms to their Biblical glory. The apocalypse reaches the eyes long before it hits the heart. Beauty bombards us from wherever it can. I watched them until they fell.

Johnny lay at my feet in the myrtle, looking down on the lights in the houses below, as they went out one by one. He looked at them steadily, chin on his folded arms. Finally only one was left, an orange lamp on a street we knew. Then it went out, the last one.

"Nellis's light," I said softly.

He did not answer.

I thought of the Night Hawk coming home, the last one, walking up the path where the bulbs were beginning, seeing his own long head, his long chin, in the brass name plate on his door.

"The man up at your mother's!" I said. "That was Nellis!"

He turned his face and looked up at me. No, that is the way I remember his face best. That way.

"Go down," he said. "*You go down.*" Then he put his head on his folded arms.

Before I left, I stood over him, remembering how he had lifted my face from the ground and had wiped the just filth away. I was of no use to him now; I had spoken; I had his paring. He would never of himself call for me now. I could never say "Call for me" again.

That same day, the dam moved forward, over the hill. Fire had crept to the wooden forms for the concrete; water and fire had cracked the heart-wall, and one whole side of the earthworks had given way. Charlotte disappeared under water, and Denoyeville, and two feet of water crawled in the streets of Tuscana, but not a man could be found who remembered a fiery cross.

And that same day, Johnny left town. At least, he was not seen there again. Some might think that he never left the hill at all, that the dam came over him with its dynamite thunder and still holds him, skeletal, inside. But I do not believe that. I think that he went on, as most of us go on in this life, as I, that night, went back down the hill, and so home.

Time does not need to murder the innocents with bloodshed. It lets them find one another.

PART II
Compromise

So ends my childhood.

We are streaked with childhood all our days, and when death finishes us with its perfect stroke we must lie like those bottles of swirled glass in the museums, whose shapes flow from the initial angle of the layers — a gadrooned column, a spread fan. Surely we do not need those latest epigraphers of the human condition to tell us this, naming for us, in numbers only as old as Greek, what we are born knowing in our pre-Hellenic bones. I know that I must already hold in these pages the gist of what some sharp-eyed scholar might well be able to point out to me, saying: "Here it is, do you not see it? And here again . . . and here!" But one cannot receive from outside what must be seized like fruit from a table. A man walks pigeon-toed through his life, looking back, up, forward at those time-spires which rise in their special way, in his way, only for him, and will sink when he does. The responsibility is mine. The chronicle is mine.

I shall meet it yet.

Chapter I. My Parents. Mr. Demuth.

O N AN afternoon some three years later, the afternoon of the day before I was to leave to take up my scholarship in the North, I went to the courthouse with my mother, for the granting of the legal paper that was to change my name.

Across from us, the lights along the flanks of the rebuilt dam, kept lit even by day, ranged the horizon in queer hypotenuses, all their constellations strictly guarded. Tuscana was a backwater now, left, with blueprint vengeance, to its mill. Alongside the other two towns, the dynamos had shouldered up again from the *tabula rasa* of the farms, and the dams' artificially calm expanses of water now seemed more elemental than the vanished hills. I went to school in the rebuilt town of Charlotte now, descending from the battered Tuscana bus, with its front seats of leather, its back benches of wood, into flocks of new buses, still built in two sections but no longer with benches, into streets whose bright, plumb store fronts, filled with the hard *r* of voices from the West and North, made the air seem suddenly cooler, the way air might be in a town on the other side of a glass mountain. Some of the ignorant in Tuscana said that the cables which carried the electric juice ran all the way from the Carolinas — "all the way from Pennsylvania, with a branch line from Massachusetts to carry bank money alongside," others said jeering, but although they were wrong, they were not so far wrong

— what they felt, relaying steadily along the cables, was the copper tic of change.

For me, those three years had been ones common to the age I then was, to that period when the young revile their own ordinariness, even while they are sure that no one has ever seen the sun-diamond on the turf, the cloud-veil on the land — the idea sunning beneath the veil — as they see it, meanwhile promising themselves they always will. Years dormant yet revolutionary, when the radices of life are never again to be seen so clear of compromise, with a violence of perception that the world tolerates in the child, begrudges the artist, meanwhile praying with some certainty for alterations in the vision of each. *Si la jeunesse savait, si la vieillesse pouvait* is, like most sentimental statements, falsely true — it is the young who have the real knowledge, age that has the real power, nullified only by what it has forgotten. It was during those years that I began telling myself that the cardinal sin, the only failure was — to forget.

Meanwhile, I saw my elders without pity and worked hard to get away from them. In that I was normal. At that age one takes even the seaming of the elder face for submission, recoiling physically aside from it, as from the circle of the corrupt. I saw how life was blunting both the inner and outer edges of my mother and uncle, and despised them for allowing it. For, although by very national temperament they were never able to accede wholly to Tuscana, shortly after their marriage they had wilted into a certain neighborliness with it, achieving, through their small outlets of the pub, the mill and my mother's trade, a modest modus vivendi. And this I saw as dishonesty. Whereas, when first in Tuscana and before, I must have craved to be wreathed in a family that in its turn would be so wreathed, now I wanted them to keep the harsh dignity of our earlier isolation, and contemned them for not having done so. Remembrance was loyalty — they had not kept it. In this, no doubt, I had merely exchanged one innocence for another — we are told that man, unlike the crustaceans, cannot regrow an appendage once it is lost, but in the physiology of our innocence it is otherwise — as fast as we lose one head of it, we regenerate a new one for the ax.

Then, also, there was the second thing I had to get away from — the sexuality of my parents. In this too I was normal. No doubt the late fact of their marriage, coincidental with my own discoveries, fantasies, made me more keenly aware of the evening door, so closed in our small house, and of my mother who, though still a plain body, and reverted now, after that one wedding excess, to her own prim constriction of dress, sometimes came home now a little silly from the pub. But the fact that my uncle was not my true father made slight difference — I was no Hamlet; his part in the drama was much the same as if he had been. The Oedipean explanation is too simple, so absolute as to make one smile; the boy and the girl, men and women, want something much more complicated than to lie with their mothers, to sleep with their fathers. Before experience, what we want is to get out of sight, out of memory of those stale conjunctions of our parents, which, by their very existence, involve us in the old cycle of generation at the very time when we feel ourselves outside the cycle, unique. Whether we are with our blood-parents or not, whether they are joined or disjoined, this is the constant for most of us. Contrarily, most of the few true bachelors and spinsters I have encountered are those who still draw upon the remote animal life of their parents as upon an annuity, trusting thereby to purchase tax-free a ticket of entry to the world. Whatever I am, of that breed I am not.

On Friday evenings, or sometimes on Sundays, those long-drawn days of the spirit that often end so excusably (as I could not know then) in wine and flesh, when my mother sometimes came back from the pub looking a trifle overmoist and red, a little too publicly fond of my uncle's arm, then it was my uncle, that neutral man saved from coarseness only by phlegm, who emerged from his sandy silences, awkward as a myna bird talking, to protect her and me from her lack of reserve. At such moments I was grateful to him, with the only kinship I ever felt for him, but I was not deceived. Later on I was able to see her lapses, his fumbling reparation, for the poor, strangulated human thing it was — to see how the vise of their class had all too well kept their loyalties for them. But on those evenings when their door finally closed, as it always did, I used to steal outside to sit on the ground with my back against the wall of the house farthest from them, sitting out the hour that, as I was learning, always passed.

The next morning my mother, half an hour late for breakfast, but more than ordinarily generous with the bacon, often said to me, "why do you squint so? Never mind the test says you've no need to wear specs. You should do." But I was squinting because the great characters of my fantasies — men like bell-towers leaning over leonine women — had stretched my eyes too wide accept these small people. And when I left Tuscana it was those two I went from — that pair, shrunk to the size of their compromises, their door.

Outwardly, I had become one of those organized young creatures who are briefly the despair of their contemporaries, of those others of equal or greater talents still softened with mischief, inertia or humility, who later go on to do more in the world than ever I have done. At the school, I had come under the notice of the new assistant principal, Mr. Demuth, a German from Wisconsin, who had fought against his ancestors in the late war, had got an honorable head wound from them — a bald cranial ridge that he sometimes tapped meaningfully, saying, "German silver, boys!" — without ever being able to tap away the mark he had got from them at birth — his Teutonic faith that *Kultur* came in catalogue, his pundit passion for drill. My ability to memorize, so quickly exposed in class, excited him deeply, and the odd miscellany of my secret reading, that I had hitherto managed to keep hidden from his less Socratic colleagues, tempted him with its disorder. At first I resisted him — although I was not yet aware of how my zealot habit of memory differed from the ordinary catechumen's, I knew instinctively that like my privates it had to be concealed. One day, however, Mr. Demuth, abroad for the afternoon on a *Wanderfahrten* of the district, which he toured as earnestly as if it had been Granada or Kuala Lumpur, walked in on me as I sat, safe as I had thought, in my egg — in the library of the Pridden house.

I remember how I watched those pedagogue hands as, sacrilegiously eager, they seized upon the books of outmoded shape — thin fifteen-inch folios of anniversary poems, sea-green atlases giving the trade routes in the time of Commodore Perry, birthday books fat and chunky as a child's Bible — that for all their cranky worthlessness were a part of me, and how, as each was set down tainted with another's touch, I had already given it up forever. More fearfully, I watched his instantaneous rapport with Miss Pridden, apprehending how the formality of each would approve and complement the other's, sensing that I seemed fated to attract the *embusqués* of this world, and that the alliance of these two would inevitably settle, as it did, on me. I discovered that I did not like people who knew me separately to meet each other, that the chameleon concessions one makes to one personality require a dangerous virtuosity in the presence of two, inviting comparisons that one cannot allow others to make without risk, oneself without pain. Above all, I knew, with that anticipation of good or bad which has rarely failed me, which the credulous call prophecy but which others like me will know for the uncontrollable *coup de main* of objectivity, that my acquaintance with Miss Pridden would be made known to my mother, and again what I wanted to keep disparate would blend.

And so it all happened. Miss Pridden, inordinately fluttered by the presence of a visitor who not only knew her aunt's name in its proper order and had read one of her pamphlets on education, but was also, as he said, "brought to his toes" by the presence of her very relict, served tea, not in the kitchen, not even in the parlor or the conservatory, but on the library table, her aunt's work table itself. I attended it all — the tray set square on the chipped leather, on that blemished map where I had so long dreamed, the light gilding down from the high windows impartially on the three of us, as once it had only on me — and I assisted as at the end of an era. I thought of running away from them before it began, but I stood fast; I parted my lips to cry, "Don't speak to each other! Don't talk of me!" — all the time helping passively with the tea things, while Mr. Demuth *sotto voce* admired my manners, my dexterity. I knew that for these two, headed for devotion to my ends as toward a missionary supper, I could do no wrong at the moment; my silence would be taken for elegance, any awkwardness — if, for instance, I dashed the tray to the floor — as the dear defect of intelligence.

"To think of finding *her* house, this, you, Miss Pridden, *here!*" said

76

Mr. Demuth. "It makes one realize the resources of this country!" He rocked back and forth in his seat; he was always carefully weighing his position in space, that man — teetering on his heels, making a rocker of every chair.

Miss Pridden, taking a responsive sip of tea, was however immediately reminded, as Americans, once tribute is paid, so often are, of her Grand Tour. They exchanged notes — with me, already their most precious trove, sitting silent between them — like two travelers who find on returning that they have purchased the same locket on the Ponte Vecchio, the very same.

"And to find the boy here," said Mr. Demuth, as if lockets had no ears. "The remarkable student: that is what one looks for in teaching. And you have done well by him. Well!" He cocked his head judiciously with a moment's pause, then went on nodding.

It was modestly revealed that I had been born in England, but this too was appropriated as one of the country's resources. "T-t-t, what one finds here! What one can find!"

When the prospect of the scholarship was mentioned, he lit to it like a candle. "We shall do it!" he said. "We shall accomplish!" And leaning back precariously, giving vent to his satisfaction in the gesture I came to know so well, that terminated every drill well done, he rubbed both palms vigorously on his "silver."

Without his help I never would have got the scholarship. Miss Pridden's humble little notes to the remnants of her aunt's circle up North — aging deans of seminaries long submerged, suffragettes huddling at eighty in some corner reserved for the espousers of causes no longer lost — must have come, even to them, more like sachets than letters. Here Mr. Demuth took over, glorying in a welter of prospectuses, recommendations and forms. And my coaching began.

Even now, in my daily round with the encyclopedias at the office, where the particular can be lost in the general like a case in chancery, where only the unsophisticated evince surprise at either the compendium of what is known or the habit of each droplet to deem itself a pond, I sometimes come across a familiar fragment of what he put me though — bits of Juvenal, Ricardo, Hobbes, Burke; lists of U.S. census figures side by side with the doctrines of Valentinus, the genealogical tree of the House of Savoy, the terms of the Pacification of Ghent and the solitary name of Eudoxus of Cnidus; fourteen pages, learned by rote, from the history of the Wars of the Roses, ten from the sixth book of the *Aeneid* and a chapter of Chateaubriand; a plate of von Helmholtz's experiments and one of the Elgin marbles — and I am once more awed at the bravado of his attempt. No learned man himself, he solicited advice on my education from a dozen authorities, and used it all. He was like a neophyte photographer unable to resist the temptation of film. His trouble was that craze for the absolute which has drawn us all, at one time or another, along its exquisite variable string; in him it took the form of a hope that knowledge might be an enclosure, that one could somewhere write *finis*.

And I resisted at first, blindly, his efforts to write it through me. I wanted my convictions — no, that is not the word — *themes* perhaps, to rise pure, of themselves. In the uncontaminated country that I could sometimes glimpse in the depth of myself, there was another kind of knowledge that sometimes turned its dark fin and disappeared again, that I must fight to keep. I did not want any help from him, or from anyone else outside. Once, only once, on an afternoon when he had persuaded me to stay for coaching after school, when I could feel him probing my mind with eager connoisseur fingers, and I, unable as yet to parry as deftly as I could now, gave him back an ox-front of stupidity, he lost control and hit my wrist hard with a book he happened to be holding. Immediately he was babbling with apology and tears came to his eyes — one rolled down his cheek on the shaved fawn stubble like a drop of beer. He was not an unkind man, but this went below kindness. He was afraid that he had damaged his machine.

Loss of control in a grown man shocked me, where now it might only intrigue, but I was not moved. It was my mother's prescience that did so. There was danger in it, from one who had my paring — even though she did not know the nature of it, nor did I. I felt that same danger the day of her death. How I should like to be able to ask her, one of these nights here, to say what she knew about me — it makes one impatient with death, with the waste of it! Although I know well that even if she could, if made to sit up in her grave with the mother-fear still stiff in her sockets, she would not. No doubt that is her immortality and ours — to live again, by slow sardonic inches, in the irreverent needs of one we have loved.

In her own country, my mother had been accustomed to steer herself by her betters, who were so both by conclusions long foregone and by some instinctive choice she would have regarded as hers. They were no star to her — often in private she had used to be sharp on them — but, rather, a handrail by means of which she had known what her rights were, who she was, and where. Her pride in them, in helping to keep them where *they* were, had thereby redounded to herself, in that fastidious balance which Americans would never understand, or countenance if they could.

Over here, all must have seemed to her a confusion — of each man steering blindfold under the onus of not yet knowing what would have been his dower at home, of people talking about their rights in the way *nouveaux riches* talk about money — and if ever she could have phrased it, her rejoinder would have been that in a country where none could be elite, all would remain parvenus. Often, during my early schooling in Tuscana, when she chanced to hear me gabbling the "all men are born equal" of my first history lessons — or any of those proud statements which sound so chauvinistic to one nation in the mouth of another — there had been a *moue* of disbelief on her face, as if she could have told me that the inequality would creep in somewhere, and had best be taken into account at the start.

Once, when someone sent her a copy of the London *Times* with an inked arrow pointing to a notice of the death by accident of a distant cousin, I found her sitting with it on her lap, folded to another page, and staring out over it, shaking her head in small, denying nods. At the time I thought she was ruminating on the death, as older persons did, but now I do not think so. When I came in she made as if to toss the paper into the grate, with an unconscious gesture I had not seen her use in years, that we had both rid ourselves of long ago — we had no grate in Tuscana. She let me see the notice, but that evening the paper disappeared. "Went out with the dustbin," she said, when I asked her for it. Perhaps she thought it might not be good for me to see it, might set me hankering — with that intractable craving which Americans called "ambition," which "spoiled" their children and which they thought so fine — after certain things at home that I would not have dared to hanker after there.

"I could have used the paper," I said. "I'd have brought it to school."

"Best turn your mind on what you bring from there," she said, not with disdain for me, for she knew I worked hard.

"I bring nothing wrong," I said.

She made no reply, bending again over her sewing, one thumb rubbing against its selvage. For she had begun to distrust my ambition. At home, safe on her own terms, she might have been braver for me, but here among these sourceless people, whom could she find to tell her what was reasonable, what was safe? And when the whole of my secrecy was revealed to her, then, sensing that my ambition, whatever it was, unknown to me as it was, might be no ordinary one even for this place, she must have begun to mistrust me.

As I had foreseen, Mr. Demuth, after our meeting at Miss Pridden's, had come almost immediately to see my mother, to tell her what a duckling she owned. I was not present when he came; he may have planned it so, but I could well imagine that interview — his surprise when he learned that my mother knew nothing of Miss Pridden (either of what the town so indifferently knew of that eminent house or of my intimacy there), and his gleeful assurance — to what portentous tilting of chairs! — that this secrecy of mine signified all the more what a prize bird, what a downy bird the two of them had. Even more clearly, I could picture my mother, her deference to the schoolmaster while judgment waited on the rest of him, and then — posed with the keenness of my grandfather, of one herself reared to be the canniest critic of who her betters were — the *judgment*, sharp as one of her own needles, that this man, born here, was no surer of his place in this country than she was.

He was no guide for her, she must have thought, this man who teetered so uncertainly on his own nativity that he could keep himself comfortable only by patronizing her for the lack of it, whose hearty miracle tale, like a drummer extolling a cure-all, of how children here always *improved* on the status of their fathers, must have reminded her the more forcibly of the surer tone of that long-gone patronage which had stood upon what it was. And when he began to prate of my abilities, of my marvelously retentive memory, then she rose suddenly and dismissed him — "Your mother does not like to hear you praised," he told me later — saying that she had to get tea ready for my uncle.

But when I came in, shortly after, nothing was readied. She stood at the window with her back to me and with the curtains wide, which was not her habit. The intrusion of the outdoors upon the in — a complexity that I loved even then — always made her uneasy; she would go out biddably enough to look at the moon when it rode beautiful and high, but always drew the curtains carefully upon it when she returned to the house.

"I did not ask him to stay for tea," she said, still with her back to me. "He didn't expect to find manners here. So I showed him none."

"Who?" I said."

"Your schoolmaster."

When she turned, her lips had the same set to them that she had awarded the history lessons. "You've no cause to worry. He didn't see the snub."

"They don't have 'tea' here, but supper," I said, aware she knew that as well as I.

"Ah, do they not!" One of her brown hair brooches fell to the floor. She bent to pick it up. "They drink tea on Pridden Street, I hear. He told me — how you play the gentleman there."

"Eh?" she said, after a moment.

I said nothing.

"Why did you let me think the scholarship was all on your own?" she said, low. "What else do you keep to your . . . what do you talk of with the old woman there?"

"We don't talk much. I go there for the books."

"Ah no," she said. "No. Else you would not have minded telling me."

"What else could there be?" I muttered it. Mothers were sibyls. I feared a real answer. And craved it.

"I cannot say," she said humbly. "I do not know."

8 1

She came forward to me eagerly. "You don't want the scholarship after all, eh? He begged me to make you let him help you; he said you would not. You were sharp there. He's no sort for that."

"I want the scholarship," I said.

"And what will you do with it?"

I bent my head in silence, dropping down into myself, as others could sometimes all too keenly make me do. Down there were my hopes. I saw them — all retreats from what I did not want, not fine parades toward what I did.

She put her hands on my shoulders, looking up, now that I was taller than she. "Then why do you not stay here? The mill is losing men to the dam every day — all to the good for your uncle. They think well of him there. He will be head foreman next year . . . or the year after. You could rise there too."

"It's not *rising* I want!"

She shook me. "*What,* then?"

I closed my eyes. I wanted to get away from what I knew too well, to a place where no one knew me. Beyond that . . . I could not see.

"Open your eyes, do not do that — open them!"

I opened them quickly, hearing the fright in her voice.

"You need friends of your own," she said huskily. "Not that silly man, nor some old woman, nor — us." She pressed her lips together. I saw her cry once. It was not then. Her hands fell to her sides. "Is there not — some boy here you would like to bring home?" She smiled at me, her lips trembling. "For — supper?"

"Nobody," I said quickly. "Nobody here."

"Here?" Her lips remained parted.

I thought of Johnny — the thought of him a dark fin too, but one no longer to be hunted. I looked at our lamp — dim here, shining orange to someone outside. "Nobody," I said, in requiem.

She crossed to the table and began quietly to set out the plates, putting them down without clatter but pressing each one hard into the cloth with the heel of her hand. "You've some plan of your own, then?"

Just then my uncle entered. He had a cough that was like a part of speech and served him almost in place of it, moving him effectively from hour to hour, from question to answer, from parting to greeting, and now he hung up his cap and coughed.

"No," I whispered. And not to them. "I have no plan."

When we sat down to table, we were a threesome. My mother leaned back and drew the curtain. She had that. My uncle had his cough. I had my whisper. The room seemed large. I had shrunk to their size.

Later that night, I climbed out of the window of my bedroom and walked the four miles to Charlotte, to the lodginghouse where Mr. Demuth had a room. Back there, I had left my door closed, my shade drawn, the study lamp burning — a composite of myself, of the half to be watched, while I trudged along the dark road, my own *Doppelgänger*, here. This was myself, I thought, this amalgam dark and solitary as the road I bore it along. I could not wait until morning to begin parting from that other.

And that night, as I thought then, all conspired to help me do so. It was about ten o'clock when I knocked at the lodginghouse door and sent in my name. I had walked all the way without stopping, without pausing until then to think of what I would say to him. But when he hurried, glowing, into the shadowy hall where I stood shuffling my sneakers, I found that my presence was statement enough — he thought I had been sent him by my mother.

"She acted quickly, eh, your mother?" he said, beaming. "Even though she does not like to hear you praised. And you walked all the way? But you are physically strong too, already bigger than me, and I am no shrimp, eh? One can make anything of a boy like you!"

I drew back.

"What was it you praised to her?" I said. "About me."

He waggled a finger at me and would not say. But I thought I knew. And I told myself, without knowing why, that I had come just in time.

He took me to his room, that room where I was to spend so many gray, abstemious hours, and over the only refreshment he kept there —

Seltzer water that he made in his own siphon, and the thin, bitter sheets of chocolate he carried with him on his intense, synoptic walks — he arranged for the afternoon and evening hours I was to come there, and for the extent of my training — which he was to be forever extending.

It was a good room to strike a bargain in, bare except for those few, glaring comforts of the solitary, which he kept scrubbed to the quick and ranged two by two in the way one so often sees them in the rooms of the single, the basin by the ewer, the razor by the strop, the shoe by the shoe. Over the desk hung an honorable discharge and a state college diploma, both issued to Hans Ulrich Demuth. His part of our bargain was in the room too, although he did not show it to me then, nor did I trouble myself over what it might be. It lay behind his shaving mirror, shoved there, the one asymmetric fact that had no contrary, to which he could find no other side. The day before school ended, when I came to say good-by to him, he let me see it. Reaching over to his dresser for a final packet of the chocolate with which he had always crowned our best lessons, his hand touched that other, brought it out in the unaccidental way truth swims up at parting.

When I saw it, I should have seen too why, of all the hundreds of facts that he had always passed on to me without preference, of all the arguments, hypotheses over whose pros and cons he always presided with the detachment of an umpire, he had given his partisanship to only one — Lamarck's theory of the inheritance of acquired characteristics — which he sometimes had propounded to me with a queer, averted passion. I should have seen this as it lay there in his hand, simple as a gem — the way the core of a life always is. But that is what the past is for — it cuts the gem.

"My son . . ." he said. And at first, squirming, I took the phrase for the *ave* that went with the chocolate. Then I saw what lay in his hand. It was a picture of a boy of about seven, gazing out at me with the non-face, the raceless all-face of the mongoloid, gazing beyond me with veiled, semifetal eyes.

"My wife stays — to be near him," he said. "She will not come to be with me. But someday yet she comes."

Then we parted quickly and as formally as usual, although because of what he happened to be holding, we did not shake hands.

I never heard that she came. He rarely stayed long in one place and left Tuscana shortly thereafter, to be rumored of more and more faintly in towns farther and farther off, like some Johnny Appleseed of the schoolroom, until he echoed no more.

But that first night, the bargain seemed all of my own making, and the clear air of that parallel room struck my nostrils with winter freshness. We would exchange nothing of ourselves, this man and I, I thought with satisfaction — only the knowledge that was in the syllabus open to all, and when we spoke and listened it would be in the Esperanto that saying all, says nothing.

When I left, again he was full of admiration for my trek to him, my impetuous energy, and pressed upon me the first of the packets of chocolate. I refused it, but he insisted, and I slipped it in my pocket. As I walked home, I wanted nothing; the night seemed mine. It was even cold, the way the smudged nights here rarely were, as if the dark, heat-modulated valley had for one night pierced the skin of its own climate. I walked along head up, exhilarated, inhaling the strange, nude smell of winter, some of the North compelled already to me.

But when I climbed into my room again, I could not bring that polar air in with me, although I held my chilled fingers to my cheeks and left the window wide. I turned out the lamp, and the sky leaped a pace inward but no farther. I leaned far out the window, and still breathed mixed air. Stepping back, I stood in the room's center, feeling for my own. From all the corners of the sleeping house there came to me the stale smell of the *status quo*, that powerful exudate which, if it conspires, does so neither for us nor against. Lying down in my clothes, I fell asleep, blaming the house.

Sometime during the middle of the night, rolling in my sleep, I felt the packet he had given me, hard against my hip. I rose up, still in my sleep, and flung it toward the window. It broke against the frame and fell inside, where I found the pieces the next morning.

Later on, I would never eat any that he gave me, always managing to leave it somewhere or let it crumble to dust in my pockets. But compromise has no taste, no muscle; one day it is merely there, in the bogged ankle, the webbed tongue. That night I had taken my first step into its dim rationale. I had wanted no help from outside on anyone's terms; I took it, on mine. One edge of myself was blunted, and by me. I had seen no way to avoid this. One rarely does. And it had come just in time. As it does.

Chapter II. In Between Reflections.

AFTER that, during the year I remained in Tuscana, I no longer went to Miss Pridden's. I was "placating providence" as we say — in reality punishing one side of myself for something done by the other. We learn very early that we have a right side and a left; one of my earliest memories — I could not have been more than three or four, for I could barely slide down from bed to floor — is of patting my left foot in consolation for having put the sock on the other one first, and of trying to remember each morning what yesterday's alternation had been, in order to change round and make amends to the neglected side. More often, I could never be sure, and was troubled by an unfairness, by a sense of having done wrong somewhere.

I no longer have that minute obsession, nor, so far as I knew, any particular one of those that swarm so significantly in the medical books, yet sometimes, when I am dressing in the morning, I remember that early flinching. We nurse that duality all our lives, and although we may no longer minister to it in such childish forms, it is with it that all our self-punishment is involved. The attempt to equate it, to solve it, in terms gropingly sensual, naïve or grotesque, is of all pursuits the most human. And the most enduring — for the pursuer is pursued, for we stretch to close that duality with hands doomed to it.

A gnomic statement! Where do they come from, these statements that crowd increasingly upon me, arriving like weather reports flagged from an unmapped country that has no season, or only one? It would be ironic if, trailing my hand in the stream of what I deem to be myself, I should bring up only what other men, in unison, have long since culled. But why else should I begin to make pronunciamentos in the name of "We," who have kicked and fought all my life to remain "I"? I must beware of falling into that soft man-trap of the larger sympathies, wherein a man stumbling along after himself suddenly discovers elegiacally that he is only another member of the human condition — and then has all the human condition to consider.

No, I must take into account that very quality of mine which I have too much admired — the vicious dexterity of a mind trained to receive everything, bent on remembering everything, in order to conceal from itself the one thing it does not want to know. These subfusc bits of some philosophy, ordered or scattered, that I did not even know I held, are at best only diversionary sops of light, algae floating in their own phosphorescence. I must remind myself again and again that the truth of a man, when once seen, is exceedingly simple, perhaps pathetically so, and is to be found not only in that underground of surrealist imagery, Argus-eyed self-refraction, which of late has so captivated the world, but *above* ground, in his simple story. It lies there — the simple gem. When I see it, its one virtue will be that I have done so. And perhaps that its face will not be the raceless all-face, but mine. Surely, even if I must learn to divest myself of other arrogances, that one I may keep?

So, then, I must learn to watch even the monitor I hold so dear, who holds back the story even as it emerges — now in a man's voice, now in a child's. For reading back over what I have written, on this the tenth night since the one when I first sat down here, I see an extraordinary thing. And in it, I see how the critic voice, exquisite *magister*, always takes something away before it gives. I thought I had recorded everything, as I must do. Yet there is one omission. I have never put down my name. Not the one I have now, whose account I must shortly give. The one I gave up.

It is an ordinary name. It would shake no worlds. If cried in the streets of London, it might wake a distant tambour in the ear of some householder who was once an urchin in Fulham, of certain servants retired to Putney or Streatham, or of two brothers and two sisters returned to spend Christmas with whatever old ones are still there in an old house. In Tuscana it would wake no one. Only the second name would sting an occasional ear, like a fly carried over from a summer more than twenty years before.

When a man changes his name, even at the prompting of others, as was the case with me, there must be, I suppose, always some equivocation of identity, some counterpoint still vibrating in the brain. Yet I, when I took up the new name, turned my head to it at once. I filled its shape at once, like those children whom legend says the *Tziganes* used to transmogrify, fattening them inside squat ampullae, until, years later, when the mold was split, there stepped forward a vase-shaped man. I never turned my head to the old name again.

This is a strange evening, still early dusk, one of those half-lit, week-end evenings when the man who has told everyone he will be away looks down onto the street, where a letter is being slipped into a pillar-box, hears a phone in an areaway honing on unanswered, unanswered, and wonders on the absurdity of his being alone. Over the East River the powerful shadow-growth begins, and the oozing timbre of the ships — gruff and choral, exchanging in German their doubled, Faustian pleas. They plead with the room — a roomful of bargains, like everyone's — where all the fine lava-dust of books and prints will not conceal other objects set impenetrably two by two.

Where so many bargains have been made, one may make one more. When the time comes, I will speak the old name. But not to a page. To someone. When I can do that, perhaps then shall I have come to the end of the story?

A strange evening, moving with strange half-thoughts. One that I have never had before. What if I too must look, not in the great, deserted honeycomb of what I remember — of circumstances piling like feathers, blanched voices, people entombed like crusaders — but in what I have forgotten?

Chapter III. My Mother and Miss Pridden.

I WAS not long missed at the Pridden house. My mother took my place there. One day, shortly after I had told her I would be studying with Mr. Demuth, she posted a letter to Miss Pridden, telling me, without other comment, that she had done so. An answer, brought by a small colored boy, came the next afternoon.

My mother saw him approach. "Who's that coming up the walk?"

"Miss Pridden's boy."

"She does not use the post, then? Or she's not on the phone?" Because of my mother's customers, we had lately had a phone installed.

"Yes, she has a phone."

My mother folded her sewing. Then, with a flick of her eyebrows, she rose and went to the sideboard, pausing there for a moment as if she recalled certain delicacies, old protocol stored there. She took out her purse.

"Let me." I stood up, stretching the height that still encumbered me. At the door, I fumbled in the tallied hoard in my pocket and gave the boy a quarter.

My mother turned over the envelope, thick and faintly yellowed, with one large, tremulous word slanting it. "What did you give him?"

"A quarter."

"A quarter? More than needful, wasn't it?"

I hesitated. "That's — what she gives him."

"Oh? So?" She gave me a curious, assessing smile, but, contrary to our usual procedure with other outlays made from my small allowance, she did not offer to repay me. She was never stingy except from circumstance — even then sometimes breaking into an intense, short-lived largesse — but she knew, as I knew from her, that an action, when paid for in whatever coin, is then and then only one's own. "And is she rich, then?"

"No. Poor, I think."

"Oh. So," she repeated. Bending over the envelope, she read out the word on it. " 'Addressed' " she said, in the ebbing tone of reminiscence. "I did not know they used that form here. 'Addressed.' "

Two days later, when I came back after school from Mr. Demuth's, I found a note saying that she had gone to tea at the Pridden house. And laid out on her bed, with its skirt spread to its full circle over the edge of its box, I saw her wedding dress, never since worn. I saw too how plain it was against either the dresses in the new stores in Charlotte or those brilliant ones on which she herself sewed, differing from her own two or three others that all seemed one, only in its breadth and its blue. It was still plumped with tissue-paper stuffing; she had looked at it perhaps but not tried it on, and had gone out in her usual black habit.

When she came back, she was flushed and bemused, but more daintily than when she came from the pub. She went past me without a word, into the bedroom, where I heard her humming, and the crackle of the paper as she put the dress away. During the next fortnight she said nothing about the visit, but after that, when it became a weekly venture, she let me understand, although she did not mention the scholarship, that my persistence with Mr. Demuth would be condoned in the light of that other patron who had been approved.

She never dreamed that I felt she had supplanted me there. I hugged bitterly this second insight of how the grown could stride briskly into a room, a relationship, into which the half-grown had preciously crept. And being already half a man, I felt too what a man often feels when two women become friends because of him — that there is always some faint risibility against him in their alliance, exploding in shameful squibs of confidence over his head. I doubt whether this was so between my mother and Miss Pridden. It was only my jealousy focused on a facet of what is always so — that the friendship between women, of women, however loyal, is never wholly substantive; the purity that some of us can give to friendship they give only to love. My mother, of course, did not know what I was feeling — either when she passed me on her way there, carrying the benné seed cakes that she had made to Miss Pridden's receipt, or some other small token — or on the evenings when, returned from there, she let fall in conversation some warm, descriptive token of the house. Several times she asked me to go with her, but I always pleaded my lessons with Demuth. Once I asked her, "Do you have tea in the library?" and her answer — "No, in the parlor" — gave me a certain painful comfort, but I never went.

I assumed that the house was her real patron, as it had been mine. But my mother had been much shifted about in the world, and never seemed gnawed by that malady which attaches itself to places, whose victims carry its Aleppo boil forever in the palm. Her attachment went to people, back to a certain complex of them that she once had known, and in Miss Pridden, for the first and only time here, she had recognized that composition once more. The dressmaker is a confidante also, and not only of the secret paddings at the breast, the bandy legs beneath the ball dress. As the vanities and the social aspirations flutter down heedlessly on the head bent to the hem, it knows mercilessly as well what other rickety lacks may be borne to the ball. It humbles itself, in hair-true snobbery, only before that *maigre* straightness of bone which, ignorant of Mendel, it calls "style." My mother had seen Miss Priddens before, in those shabby deaconesses of the genteel whose cheques came more promptly than those of the rich, who ordered a dress from her perhaps once every three years — limpid women, not overly bright or flaming with castellan ardor, who nevertheless inhabited a category for which there was no other word but the seditious one "aristocrat," a water-color world that ought to have been dead, but in whose pale depths one glimpsed, as unmentionable by them as their underwear, furtive shadows of noblesse that glided like carp in an eighteenth-century pond.

To this my mother paid tribute in the way most natural to her. She made a dress, concealing its execution over many weeks and using no fittings but the dressmaker's eye. And months later, on the evening when Mr. Demuth telephoned to tell me, almost incoherently, that I had been offered not one scholarship but two, my mother sent word to Miss Pridden, with whom she normally never communicated between visits, saying that we wished to see her that same evening. And for the first time she insisted that I accompany her there. Courtesy demanded, she said, that Miss Pridden hear the news from no one but us, and even perhaps — here her voice faltered in self-denial — that I go there alone. I would have done so, for by now I wanted to see the house again, in the same way that a man wants to encounter a girl he has once been in love with, to savor — now that the worst is over — a martyrdom on which he may safely gormandize. But when she brought out the long box for me to take, and diffidently told me what was in it, I refused. So it was after all I who accompanied her.

And so, of course, the house did not look the same. It was nether and flat, a burst secret. I could have asked to go alone into the library, but I was experiencing what the grown man does over and over and already shielding myself, as he does, from the acceptance of it — that the mystery he imputes to a house, a body, a town, that when exhausted will impute itself willfully forward to other houses, bodies, towns — is nothing but the rictus of his own mystery.

It seemed to me too, hanging behind my mother, that she presented my news and her box in almost the same moment, and that in their reception they were inextricably jumbled together. Then Miss Pridden withdrew to some inner room, and came out wearing the dress. I can see her in it now — she, the dress and the house all concluding — for during her lifetime I did not go there again.

It was a dress made of some narrow, quiet stuff in an in-between color, whose unpatterned surface my mother had worked with an infinitude of the fine ribbing she had learned in France, leaving it faintly crushed yet vertical. That is all I recall of it. Like most chefs-d'oeuvre, it left a total impression — in this case that it recognized its wearer and made her recognizable as she stood here, in her house.

"It suits me, Dora," said Miss Pridden. "See how it suits me. I can wear it to the yearly dinner. I can be buried in it." She went to a picture that hung on the wall and peered at herself in its dim, landscaped glass, although a long mirror of her aunt's hung nearby. I can still see her doing that, her epitome — not aspiring to the mirror. "I was worried about that, you know. But this is suitable to any occasion. And now I can be."

"I did not mean to put *that* into it," said my mother. But she had. Even I could see this, that attired in such a dress, any wearer it suited might go to meet either her archivists or her maker — comfortably prejudged. The dress was a triumph of class distinction. Certainly my mother never made anything like it for anyone here. Into it she had sewn her tribute, via Miss Pridden, to all those other meek curators of carp.

I saw too that my mother, in so truly taking Miss Pridden's measure, had as humbly given her own. So I slipped out and left the three of them together — my mother, Miss Pridden, and the house. They knew their place. I still had to find mine.

Chapter IV.   My Uncle.   The Name.

NOW my uncle comes forward. He moves into my life like one of those marionettes kept waiting in the wings, who come out upon the stage with jerky dutiful articulation, yet I never knew the nature of the string that dangled him. His name was George Higby. He was one of the few people about whom I never was curious. He was one of those men about whom one is incurious even when one lives with them; even long after, I can see only that now and then, stepping on some floe congealed out of passivity, he moved. There was no way to tell whether he was slow or smart, or much of anything about him, even by examining the negatives of what he was not. One could say that he did not give in particularly to drink or to abstinence, that he accepted the company either of others or of himself without distaste or relish, that he did not appear to be profoundly disinterested in life, or to bear death any grudge. He was hardy, but with the physical economy of a man whose nose never dripped, whose skin never scaled, as if he had enough marrow for circumstance, but none for waste. Originally from one of those northern counties of England where men immemorially knew about cloth — a great-granduncle had been in the Luddite riots — one could not say of him that he was northern enough to be dour, or yet that he would not riot. He had no grease-monkey gaiety with mechanisms, but sometimes, as he walked past the placidly flashing multiples of the power looms, he touched them the way the Chinese touch the abacus. Looking at him in a crowd, one would never particularly choose him as a man who had emigrated once, married twice. He was a man without effluence. What he liked, if he suffered, no man knew. Yet, sometimes, he moved.

People like him press as quietly on the lives of others as the status quo presses on us all. One never knows whether they themselves know that gravitation is on their side. He would have had what he wanted from me, except for accident. I laughed with incredulity when I first heard what he wanted, but now I do not laugh, wondering only how the image of a wish rises in the mind of such a man, a man so locked in the quotidian. As he walks steadily to and fro in the narrow environ of his needs, does he find one evening that image on his doorstep, curled like a child in a crèche? Or are they pressed too, these people so bereft of expression? Do they manage without a sound, without a sigh, in stifled breaths from day to day? He wanted me to change my name to his.

"Both?" I said. "Or would he make do with the last one!"

"Both, if you will, he says," said my mother. "But only, as he says, 'for the record.' We would not need to call you 'George' among us. But he would like it to be both, I know that."

She had nothing in her hands that day — she had come into my room without scissors, needle or selvage to guide them — and they clasped nervously. "But the last one would do beautifully." And when I laughed: "There is nothing to laugh at. I am quite happy to be known by it." And when I was silent: "Child," she said. "He asks so little. And so seldom."

Characteristically, he had not asked me, and in all those dragging months in the tight, three-cornered arena of that house, he never once mentioned it. Only after he had failed, in the brief time before I left, when it was broken to him that I had changed my name, but not to his — did we ever speak of it directly between us.

It was May when it began, and I was not due to go to the college in New York until September. There I had been offered two scholarships, one to be in residence, and if I kept up my grades, I would not need to be dependent on my family for anything. But my mother did not make it a question of money. For now she, who had always been so honorable in her home, who had always so diffidently abstained from those raw strategies with which members of a real family cheapen and flay each other, yet find relief — began to nag. She had given my uncle herself, but her short, slapped experience with my father may well have humbled her into feeling that, from her, this was not enough. There were the nights behind their door — I too know well that rush of gratitude we have, after long starvation, toward even the stranger who restores us to pleasure. In her pride at learning she had something else he wanted, she gratefully would have given him me. And tried to give *him* to me, in the way people vainly try to give those they love to one another. For she may have loved him. I must remember, when I ascribe motives to people, how chary I am of ascribing the motive of love.

And in the end she wore me down.

"What would I get out of it?" I said. "I shall want nothing from him."

She was silent. We did not speak of fathers in that household. But that day I meant to. I was cocky for more reasons than one. Escape, for one thing, was sure, and I relaxed in the prospect. My confidence was rising. It was a time when, if accident had brought the right company, I could have poured out my secrets, the small stock of them, like anyone else, and gone on to a life of conventional secrets, like anybody else. I was open to it. But accident, in the form of my uncle, and a lesson in German, inched me back along the way I had been tending. I put no blame on my uncle, poor man, so suddenly open, like me, to wasting his marrow, and as quickly closed. I merely bow to his leverage, remarking how each of us pulls his weight in this life, even when he stands still. I was *his* accident.

"And what will he get out of it?" I said. "He can't think he'll make a son out of me." Here was the other reason for my cockiness. I was eighteen now, and although I stayed clear of the girls in Tuscana, it was only because I no longer wished to know anyone there. But from the giggling whispers on the bus, the overtures the more forward ones had made, I already sensed that I would be a success with women when I chose. This was one confidence I never had to acquire — the sexual one. It was justified — in the first moment of the ballet I learned to dance. And I would choose soon, I told myself; the North held out that presto-chango magic too. Meanwhile, I permitted myself to strut like a man before I was one, deriding my uncle as I had heard men deride each other, even themselves, for wanting a son and being without.

"I don't look like him," I said. "Nobody will be fooled."

"Nor do you look like me." She was cutting a collar out of some thick mustard-colored stuff, and the scissors went evenly round the curve.

"No I don't, do I." My eyes followed the scissors, and I was suddenly dead sick of all the sewing that driveled through the house and every conversation, matting every table with the undersides of femininity, with the clear tale of how any woman, fat or thin, was basted together. I wanted to be in a room with men, talking, as I had read they did, of *princesses lointaines*. "No," I said, "I must look like my father," and saw the scissors halt in their curve and slash the collar half through.

"Tell me about him." My voice was strong. These last months I had lost the habit I had had so long, of talking low, chin tucked in the neck of my shirt.

"I knew him for a year. I've told you — all I knew of him." She had, and I had always thought her ashamed only of the way he died — a cavalryman kicked by one of his own charges, drunk when kicked. Now I saw that she might have been ashamed of not knowing much more, much more than I.

"Have you a picture of him? You must have. Show it to me."

She shook her head, her hands piecing the ruined collar together, but she was staring at me as if I were new to her, and not new. Then I was sure.

"Come to the mirror," I said. It was the first time I had ever commanded her, used such a voice, and she obeyed me. She let me take her by the arms and raise her up, showing me the first of those small graces of submission with which a mother gives her son his masculinity, without which gift — if she does not — no woman will easily be able to give it to him later on.

We stood side by side in front of the mirror. Anyone judging us for the proportion of secrecy in our temperaments would have given the palm to her at once — to the purple-brown lights in her hair and eyes, to the drooping inclination of that small, round head, all its draughtsmanship in a few tight lines, to the hooded eyelids, convex as a bird's. Yet, reticent as she was, quiet as she was, anyone who knew her well could see clearly almost every thought she had. I looked into the mirror, that box of gray gleams collected by some impossible asymmetric trick that escaped me no matter how many times Demuth coached me on the basic law of refraction, and I endeavored to look at my face, alongside hers, as a stranger would look at it.

I had been flaxen as a child, and was darkening somewhat, as many such do — my brows had changed most and were now black — but I had kept, as I still do, that aureole of frankness which surrounds the fair. My features were straight but would not be delicate; there was already a man's thickness in the nose and chin. The mouth was less heavy, closing evenly. In repose its corners turned up, and — but only to the more than casual physiognomist — in. But it is the eyes that, more than anything, give my face its extraordinary — only because it is mine — front of frankness. They are eyes that occur more often among the Irish, very blue, the whites of which, when struck by light from the side, give it back slightly doubled, as if refracted from a thick crystal, and at some angles the eye looks as if it had a light behind the cornea itself. Such eyes are not uncommon, as I say, and when the other features are regular, their effect is to give the face the open look of a face on a calendar, an almost dull lack of concealment. Often they occur among the rather dull. Looking at me, even those who knew me might think that they could see clearly every thought I had.

99

I looked at myself as a dog looks at himself in the glass, seeing a possible enemy, possible friend. I put my hand under my mother's chin as we stared at our images. "No, I don't look like you, do I."

"Yet you are mine."

I put my forefinger on the glass at the center of where it reflected me. "There. There he is, isn't he?" I said. "Why should I not keep his name?"

Her eyes stared into mine. "He died before you were born," she said, and left the mirror.

Bending over the table, she began smoothing the yellow material in order to cut a new collar. I picked up the ruined one.

"Nasty color," I said. "Color of turd."

Once or twice, recently, she had chid me for using the kind of language we did not use. But this time, unexpectedly, she smiled. "Mrs. Thwaites," she said. "Some women try to match their complexions. Always the wrong ones." She glanced up at me, sideways, almost flirting, a faint flush rallying her cheek. "Mind you pick a girl with no green to her skin. Else you'll have to live with such colors the year round."

She had never spoken to me like that before, acknowledging my growth. Through me, she bridled at the memory of having been chosen by a man who, though he may have deceived her, had been sought by women. And taking sides against her own sex, as women will for their sons, she found a sly satisfaction in thinking that I too would be good with the girls.

But after that, in the sessions that went on day after day, she took warning and would not allow me the privilege of argument. She became the exhorter and I once again the listening child. Moral issues flew round my head like succubi, and I learned what dialecticians parents can become, what evangels, when they want a child's salvation for the sake of their own. She took every advantage except one. And that was the one which overcame me.

Whenever she spoke of my uncle now — yes, she must have loved him, for how could anyone sense the inner drama of such a man except in love? — the phrase she had first used of him recurred: "He asks so little. And so seldom." And one day, just after she had left the room in angry misery, with those words upon her lips, I heard in them the reverberation of the one word she had not used. "I ask so little." That night, tossing, I heard the phrase in all its variations — *She asks so seldom. She asks so little.* And the next day I gave in.

Assuming a new name is not as difficult as some might think it. For the innocent, it is made easy. If I remember the law correctly, it is necessary only to declare that one has no debts that would vanish with the old name, no fraudulent purpose, and those of us who feel pure enough in heart to say this now, or to confront the possible burden of proving it later, need not even seek the comforting acquiescence of the courts. My mother, however, knew of course that my uncle would want things as legal as possible, needed to hold, hot and neat in his hand, the intangible — that is what people go to lawyers for.

The one lawyer in town was also the judge, a man whose name — Hannibal Fourchette — I somehow produced effortlessly for my mother when she asked it, conscious that it had some familiarity for me connected neither with the fact that it was current, or odd. Mr. Fourchette — as we learned he was addressed during his attorney hours — was a black-haired Creole in his seventies (some said the hair was dyed), who ran his office without a permanent secretary, with the aid of a fifty-year-old son who looked almost contemporary with his father, but, unlike him, was always red, and breathing of anise by noon. The senior Fourchette was one of those men, neither broken nor bent, who nevertheless give the impression of having descended. One felt that just as he seemed more than his son, so he must have slipped from fathers who had been more than he. Their breath was still on him, the way anise was always on his son's, and one could imagine that it had long since dictated his place in life, causing him to settle in some place where he could still command from his inferiors an authority that he had not quite been able to retain with his peers. Later on, when I knew a little more about the hierarchies of the South, I understood better the possible nature of a descent from Louisiana to Tuscana.

We learned from him that the business at hand was cursory. We must petition the court for the change, offering the proper statements of no intent to deceive, my mother to make the petition in my name.

We must offer some corroboration, birth certificates or the like, in token that I was the person I purported to be. He inquired whether we had them. We did, but when he heard that I was an alien, he deliberated for a moment, passed his hand vaguely over the backs of some thick, calfbound books on a short shelf behind him, opened and shut a drawer in a wooden filing case. There was some legal exemption concerning name changes for aliens, he thought he recalled — possibly it pertained only to translation, or at the time of entrance into the country. But in any case, it would be wiser for us to take due process, he said, meanwhile covering a yawn with two fingers of a ringed hand. It was plain that our doing so would save him from having to trace what the technicality was. I never found out what it was, or needed to, but at the time I wondered why an alien was exempted from the procedure for natives, whether it was because he was considered to be nobody when he came and only somebody thereafter — or vice versa. Meanwhile my mother kept nodding, and when he had finished, asked about the fee. Seventy-five dollars — she could pay that? He called her "ma'am." Fifteen pounds, she said to herself, and nodded. She meant, I knew, to pay it out of her own savings.

That would be all then, said Mr. Fourchette. His office would frame the petition and send it along to us for signing. "In due course" — we never knew whether this was the legal interval or the sauntering routine of that office — we would receive notice to present the petition, with ourselves, before the judge. Once granted, notice of same should be published in the local newspaper, Denoyeville's, since Tuscana had none. That was all.

He passed a clean handkerchief over his forehead — he wore a coat, although the dog days were already beginning — stretched an arm, forcing the stiff shirt cuff almost to his knuckles, and dismissed us as a lawyer should, leaving us with the conviction that the law was still arcane, and our problem almost too humble for it. Only later did we realize that since he was also the judge, he was in effect petitioning himself.

I had decided to let them give me the full name, George Higby. Any admixture with my own seemed to me specious, confusing, shiftier somehow than the full change. Somehow I knew furtively that I would never assume it; it was like one of those rubber stamps whose print would not cling to the skin. Providence would take care of how this would come about; as I have said, I knew uneasily early that providence was the other side of ourselves. At worst, I could drop the name in the North, averring some hitch with the scholarship, or even flinging it rebelliously back to them, over the distance between us.

Distance has a special import for me, of whose significance I am not quite sure. It is not the idea of travel that haunts me, the romantic dispensation with the daily, although I know as well as any man with closer ties how the departure, the tour, the "time out," relaxes the moral bonds with others and heightens the tie with oneself. In travel we all browse upon ourselves. Nor am I much struck with the rapidity with which distance can be melted. In an age of air travel, I am still an eighteenth-century man, in a bent universe still a Euclidean. I can never believe that increased speed between two points, even the speed of light, can ever annihilate the gap between them.

The place of departure . . . the place of arrival, and their simultaneity on a point of time, that is what hypnotizes me — the simultaneity that no speed can outwit. I feel this on a bus shuttling between two villages, in the same city between two hills — the gap between "here" and "there" that no shuttle can close. And when I look down on a map of the world, it is not the nervously dotted lines of communication that compel me, nor the hemi-demi-semiquaverings of the transoceanic wires — but the incurable coexistence of places. I am not alone in this. My whole century suffers from it, now that it can truly survey its heterogeneous world. But a man with two names itches more than most to be in two places at once. Or in one that is all.

But in Tuscana, of course, I still thought that there was a permanent alchemy in leaving. The petition came and I watched my mother sign it, pursing her lips over the shoddy typing, the erasures, knitting her brows over the circuitous phrases, in whose designation I appeared as the "infant." The long envelope was given me to leave at the Fourchettes' office, a small wooden annex attached nepotically to one wall of the courthouse itself. It was in front of the courthouse that, each morning, I took the bus for school, and was deposited by the return bus from Charlotte, in the early dusk.

The first afternoon when I went there, the office was closed. The second day it was open, but there was no one there. A fan was on, idling just enough to scatter the flies. I sat down and waited for some minutes, watching the flies as they lighted on the desk, struggled in the swath of the fan, flew off to a corner and circled the desk again, returning to the vortex as if it were honey. No one came. I do not mind waiting for someone in a quiet corner. It is like the travel time in which one regains oneself, in which one can watch the time of day that no one else appears to be watching, as it sinks toward the earth. At last I put the envelope on the desk. The envelope was thick, but the breeze of the fan lifted a corner and would end by inching it on the floor. Just as it reached the edge, I retrieved it. I centered it again, and weighted it down with a large conch shell that I found near a typewriter on a second desk beneath a window. Still I sat on, listening to the loud flies. It was the last time that I was to be fully myself, although I was never to be "George Higby." No man knows the date of his death. Or the ovum the exact hour of its birth. Then the mill siren blew its long, swelling cry for six o'clock, and I left, closing the door on the hush-hush of the fan, and when I arrived home and my mother asked if I had delivered the letter, I said I had.

Chapter V. The German Lesson.

IT WAS the next day that I had the German lesson, the fourth or fifth in a series that Demuth had instituted about a fortnight before. Once the scholarships had come in, he had advanced one reason after another for continuing the coaching: I had been lucky in the examination questions, in being the only candidate from my region; up North the standards were severer, and I would be competing against boys who had been prepared by many masters for years, in the way he alone had had to do in one. Would I like to start calculus, for instance? We both knew that he had kept abreast of me best in mathematics. In Latin, the only language of which he had a smattering, I had outstripped him once we got past Cicero to Virgil, and in Horace and Catullus, where the understanding moves as much by elision as grammar, he had been utterly lost. No, I said cruelly, if anything I would rather do a new language, perhaps Greek.

He looked down at his hands. We should have to wait for the books, he said, and of course he would have to check on what was required. But he was an honest man. "I realize," he said, "that as a mentor for you now, I have certain . . . certain —" he paused. "Certain . . . *lacunae*," he said, and irrepressibly he brightened. "You know what that means?"

I had not the heart to tell him so. He revived, in explanation. "Come tomorrow at four!" he said then, plopping his hands excitedly together. "Maybe I have a surprise. Yes, we shall have a surprise!"

And the next day we began on German. He had already sent away for a dictionary and a grammar. Meanwhile he brought out a German Baedeker and an old brown-paper edition of *Struwwelpeter,* whose flyleaf, flaking off as I touched it, was inscribed *Herzlichster Geburtstagwunsche. Mutterchen.* He had never once mentioned knowing German. It must have come hard for him to reveal it.

He knew German as a man knows his earliest language, one rejected before he had learned the colorless abstractions needed to cope with trouble and fear. We began with what he knew, and in the bread-and-milk words as he remembered them, in his excited asides as he disinterred a nursery rhyme, a family aphorism, I could almost see that simple, fundamentalist household emerging. As he recovered the forgotten nuances, his English inverted.

"Bitte," he would say, "how can I explain to you what means *bitte!* It means 'if you please,' and 'you're welcome' if it comes after the *danke schön* . . . it is so much more convenient than anything you . . . And *gemütlich* — how am I to explain to the boy what means *gemütlich!"* He sighed with pleasure. "You have nothing like . . . it is so much more *convenient!"* he said. He flushed suddenly and touched a furtive finger to his crown. But in a moment he was off again. *"Rahm!"* he said. "You know the skin that forms on boiled milk or hot cocoa, that is what we used to call it — *Rahm!"* And from there he might go on to the bits of Goethe or Heine that he had been taught to "speak" for company — *Über allen Gipfeln* or *Du bist wie eine Blume,* that he taught me too, until the grammar books, of which Tuscana had none, should arrive by mail. Occasionally he would hum under his breath a song that he sometimes identified — "Rose in the Heather" or *"Die Lorelei,"* and once by accident one that he cut short and never repeated; later I knew it as *Die Wacht am Rhein.*

It was a queer way to learn a language, lisping it in the numbers of another man's childhood, and I suppose it helped to project me back into mine. What happened that next afternoon, the day after I had left the letter, was only as predestined as any ordinary event is — and that, within certain terms, is considerable. It is the terms that are fresh and personal to each life; the process is always the same. We live by the blind collision of what we are, or have come to be, with events that after a time seem to strain toward us because of what we are. This interplay is no less occult for the most humdrum life than it was for mine. I was already predisposed to live by remembering; Demuth was not strong enough, as few are, to live by forgetting. One wonders, to no profit, whether things would have occurred any differently if the grammar books had arrived on time. This is what did occur.

The Baedeker had proved too difficult, the *Struwwelpeter* too foolish. Demuth, who was unsure of his conjugations and had never learned script, had ended by teaching me altogether orally, repeating the names of objects as he himself recalled them, rehearsing me on how to enter a room and leave, greet my elders and bid them adieu, coaching me in all the formal, scraping little phrases with which a German childhood begins.

"No," he said this afternoon, "the books are not yet here. I have written them a second letter. *Also, sitzt du!*"

I sat down.

"And how would you say that to me?"

"*Setzen Sie sich, Herr Demuth.*"

"*Richtig!* I say *du* not because you are a child — you, a young man with two scholarships — but because we are friends, intimate, *verstehts du?* Still, it would not yet be *nett* for you to say *du* to me. When you have your degree, perhaps, when you come back to Tuscana."

Through his window I could see his landlady's washline, the dishclouts hanging rigid in the flat haze of the sun, and beyond it, on one of the dun back porches, two women slumped on a torn parlor settee, their boneless voices blurring toward us through the sweaty air.

"I shan't come back here."

He shrugged. "And if you did, maybe, maybe I would not be here either." He pursed his lips and looked down, his hand going out automatically to the siphon that stood on the desk, on the tray with its one glass. I was sitting low enough to see, almost at eye level, the red frizz on his knuckles, the creases and spots that life had dealt one of those rounded, middle-aged hands that are like a worn boy's. Physical nearness to a person, no matter of which sex, often makes one think suddenly and sharply of the physical contexts that may be theirs, and I wondered suddenly whether he did as other men did about women, whether he went without, if his slight tinge of the ridiculous clung to him when he was with them, whether that hand would lie uncertain on a breast, or sure. Then the thought faded, and perhaps because of the low stool and the language that reduced me to a child, I had a vague sense of having sat so once, seeing, long ago, the black hairs on another man's hand, I did not know whose. Then the sensation passed, and Demuth's hand offered me the glass of Seltzer. As was customary, I refused it.

"Speak in German!"

"*Nein, danke schön.*"

"*Bitte*. You are no quicker than many I have had. But you retain." He drank. "Yes, you retain. And this is anyway not such a bad way to learn a language. Very modern. And very ancient. *Der Vater spricht. Das Kind antwortet.* The father speaks. The child answers." His voice died to a whisper, as if he were retelling himself a fond tale. His eyelids pinkened. "The father sneezes. And the child answers — *Gesundheit!*" He got up and stood at the window.

"*Gesundheit.*" I imitated him without difficulty. "Does that mean . . . 'God bless!'?"

"No," he said, his back to me. "It means . . . 'health.' And the word for sickness, when a child is sick for instance, that is *Krankheit*. And the word for a smart-head like you I do not know, we will look it up when the books come. But the word for 'stupid' I know. It is *dumm . . . Dummkopf.*"

" 'God bless,' " I said. "Is that . . . *Gott . . . Gott schütze dich?*"

" 'God keep you,' that means." He turned around. "I did not teach you that. Where did you pick that up?"

"I don't know . . . somewhere. I must have read it."

"Not when you can make the *ü* like that, like a parrot. You have heard it somewhere." He brightened. "What a sponge you are, eh . . . we will look that word up too. *Also, komm!* To work! Enter the room! You are me, Hans Ulrich, and the ladies and gentlemen are here for coffee."

I lingered, looking at the desk. *Gott schütze dich.* There was a voice connected with it, a sexless old voice, the voice of memory itself, at times meandering, at times hard. A wine glass stood beside it, not thick like Demuth's tumbler, but an etched bell, on an amber stem that joined the wine as it was poured. I could see no more than this, hear nothing more, but I could feel one powerful thing. I could feel myself — back there. There was another receptacle back there, besides the glass with its wine, and it was I. I was the glass, open as a bell to the voice as it poured verse and chapter, chapter and verse into me. I had no face other than the face of the wine, another's wine as it poured into me. I heard the impersonal sound of the wine-voice, listen-listen, as it poured. I had no face of my own. I was the glass. "Madeira . . ." I said. "There is a wine called . . . Madeira?"

He nodded. "I have never tasted it. *Warum?*"

I shook my head "I don't know. Let's begin."

"*Also* — I give you the English words, you give them in German, and answer." He perched on the edge of the desk, screwing up his eyes with pleasure. "I am — whomever. You are Hans Ulrich, you answer." He began. "Hans! The door!"

"*Hans, der Tür,*" I repeated. "*Ja, ich geh.*" And so the lesson went. I greeted *Damen und Herren,* brought chairs, passed cakes to uncles and aunts, all as Hans Ulrich Demuth had long ago. I said *Milch?* and *Zucker?,* brought a Fräulein Schmidt her *Handtasche* and replied that no, I was not at school today because *heute* was *Sonntag.*

Now and then his landlady, going up and down the stairs, passed our door, ajar because of the heat, but she ignored us, used to the droning of our catechisms, and in any case would not have noticed, as he no longer did himself, how often he repeated, with hypnotic insistence, "You are Hans Ulrich." I did not much notice it myself, habituated as I was to the way people inclined their image of me to their own uses — as Miss Pridden had done, and Johnny, and returning to me now, another old voice that had begun it all.

"And when do you go?" said Demuth.

"Go?" I said in English. I could hear that other voice struggling toward me. "Go where?" And the voice said, through the phlegm of the past: *So this is the last time, eh, handsome waiter. You go in the morning.*

"To school, *Dummkopf*," said Demuth. "Where else? The lady asks when you go."

"*Morgen*," I said mechanically. You go in the morning.

"*Korrekt!* And what do you say to the teacher?"

Through the window I could see one of the women on the porch, alone now, rocking and nodding.

"What do you say?" said Demuth. And the voice said it also. *What do you say?*

"*Guten . . . guten Tag . . .*" I said, and dreaming, my hand stole toward the tray.

"*Nein, guten Morgen!*" said Demuth, but I had already lifted the tray. And as it lifted, I remembered. Across the way the woman was still rocking, and holding the tray stiffly against my chest, I remembered it all.

"No . . . *guten Tag* it was," I said. "*Guten Tag, gnädige Frau* . . . that is what it was. Now I remember."

"You *remember?*" he said.

Aha, said the voice, *I see you have not forgotten.*

"No, I have not forgotten," I said. I was grown now. I knew I could never get back. The gap was permanent between "here" and "there." I put down the tray, Demuth's tray, and nothing was smashed. But I could still remember, with the harsh breath one draws to cover the gap.

"She would say *Wer kommt hier? Wie heisst er?*" I said. "That means 'Who comes? What is his name?' Doesn't it?" He nodded mutely. "And I would say . . . "*Das kleine Herrgöttle von Bie-*

berach. Little Mr. God from Beeberock. It was some sort of joke . . . it didn't mean anything."

"Who?" he said. "*Who* would say?"

"It was — before I came here. To America."

"So. So someone has taught you. So you knew German already, you rascal."

"No," I said. What had she taught me? Or had I been born to it? To listen. To be the glass. "That was all I ever learned to say. But that last day, when she found out I didn't know it was the last one, that no one had told me, she gave me some of the wine to drink and taught me a German prayer. And when I left the room, that was when she called out after me — *Gott schütze dich!*"

"And you were how old?"

"When?"

"When you knew . . . whoever it was . . . this person, these people?"

I was born there, I thought. When does one begin to know the people among whom one was born? But I saw him looking at me with that semiofficial interest he always had in my mind — "the mind," as he was fond of referring to it, and I thought: Ha, no, that is not for you, that is mine, it is for no one.

"I was ten when I came here," I said. Back there I had asked her something; what was it? She had shaken her head sadly, the old godmother, everyone's godmother but mine, and whatever it was, she had refused me. For once I had asked something of someone; the glass had assumed a face of its own, a mouth, and had spoken. I had gone down on my knees to her, to ask it. I remembered it well, how it felt to speak for oneself at last. But she had refused me whatever it was, fending me off with the wine and the prayer. Four short phrases the prayer had had, but I had refused to repeat them after her, to learn it, so that, as she had said, I could always remember. I had refused her, as she had refused me, and I had closed my mouth. I had closed it.

"But you remember before that, *natürlich?*" said Demuth.

Then I had taken up the tray and gone out without a word. And standing at the top of the dark stairwell, I had heard the *Gott schütze dich,* the blessing, trailing after me like a scarf — with the sound that words have which when spoken are already part of the past.

"Everyone remembers," I said. *"You* remember your German."

I saw him flinch. Then he answered me in kind, as people will. They turn the other cheek, but not their own. The mind is not Christian yet, nor ever was. "But you —" he said. He squinted at me shrewdly. "You, my fine friend — you seem to remember *everything.* Is it not so?"

I had stood at the top of the stairs. And then I had done it. I had not dropped the tray. I had thrown it. I had sent it hurtling to the landing far below, all of it — the tray, the bottle and the thin, beautiful upstanding glass. And such had been the force of my arm that I had toppled after it to the bottom of the stair. Voices had opened out then from all levels, from the scullery to the fourth-floor eyrie, and had come toward me, marveling at how I had remained uninjured, hovering over me where I lay for a minute in the welter of wine and shards, with my mouth closed. All was smashed. And that was the end of the last day.

"No . . ." I said. "Not everything." I recognized this with fear. For to remember is to be in possession, to be safe, and although I remembered much, more than most, it was not all. I could forego the blank lapse between that last day and Tuscana — it had been merely the gap between. But there was something more. I could not recall, try as I might, what I had asked Frau Goodman and she had refused me. I could remember with all my being how it felt to trust, to ask. I knew the taste of the Madeira after she had refused me; I could have told him that it had the taste of justice. And I could remember how it felt to learn for the first time that the listener is not the friend. But I could not remember what I had asked.

"Nun?" said Demuth. "Then let us proceed." He settled in a chair, head thrown back, smiling, eyes half closed.

I looked at him. He had slapped my wrist once; then had come the easy, abject tear. *You are Hans Ulrich,* he had said to me, returning to himself through me. I thought of Johnny, accusing me of believing, when he could no longer believe. Even Miss Pridden, who would not dare her own image in her aunt's mirror, had not been too timid to dangle her faded trinkets, her postcard X before me, to see herself — not me — in me. And now my uncle. If I attracted the ambuscaded ones of this world, was it because they felt safe with me, already seeing that I was fated to be one of them? Or was it because they saw that I, only the listener, was nothing, was already less than they?

"*Mach schnell*," said Demuth. "The *Kaffee-klatsch* is almost over. Stand up. *Steh auf!* Recite now the poem."

I stood up. For some time now I had been taller than he. This was the first time I felt it. "I am not Hans Ulrich," I said. "I am *not* Hans Ulrich!"

He looked up, eyes wide, shaken back into focusing on me, shaken out of that inward stare they all have, the confiders — the self-lost look of a man threading a needle a mile and a half away. "But of co — I did not mean . . ." He stared at his lap. "I am tedious, hmmm. I have bored you. I am sorry . . . Perhaps you are right to feel . . . this is a stupid way to learn." He smoothed one hand, its aging plumpness, over the crown of his head in the familiar gesture, but this time it was slow, wandering, and lingered doubtfully on the ridge that he was so proud of, as if he wondered how the ridge came there. "Perhaps you are right . . . one should remember only for oneself, hmmm?" He shrugged, and with it his face lightened. A gesture could always lift him. Perhaps it was bravery. Or the incurable optimism of those who can cure their spirits with long walks. "So we will manage without him, hmmm? And soon anyway, the books . . ."

"Send them back," I said.

"Back?" He blinked.

"When the books come. Send them back."

"You . . . do not wish any longer to . . . ?"

"No."

He said nothing, but leaned forward, staring intently, as if he saw something. Dusk was settling in the room, in first one corner, then the other, like a returning old hound dog lapsing down with a sigh, recording its master with steady, faithful eyes.

"I must be going," I said. "There's no late bus in summer."

"You will not come tomorrow?" He was still hunched in his chair.

I shifted my feet, not answering. I was to be asked that question often later on, often by women. I could never explain to them that my leaving had nothing to do with them as women.

"Listen!" he said. "I have to tell you the truth. You have been beyond me for a long time now. With the books. But we could still talk. There are things —" He bit his lip. "I have lived longer. That should count for something."

This is what the old always say, I thought. For their own good, not ours. He had already told me otherwise. Each man remembers for himself.

"All right then," he said. "*I* am Hans Ulrich! And I remember many things. I could tell you . . . a life is worth something. Then you would be ahead of the gamble, hmmm . . . why should you have to wait to acquire?" He glanced at the dresser, at the thin packets of chocolate stacked there like a gambler's cards.

"I will come again . . . sometime," I said. This is the lie that no one believes.

"*Moment!*" he said. "Listen, for instance . . ." He began to talk very rapidly. "At home we were from Schwaben — the grandfather and the grandmother. *Schwäbisch,* that is the comic dialect of Germany. No matter what you say, how serious, it sounds *annh-annh,* like sheep talking. My mother was not their daughter — she was a *Norddeutscher,* from Hanover — and she was ashamed of them. They were a funny couple to look at too, he very small and she very tall and bony — *der Spazierstock und der Kloss,* my mother used to say — the walking stick and the dumpling. And they were not very smart, but they were very fond of one another, and always talking in their old *Schwäbisch* sayings, *annh-annh* together. When Americans came to the house, my mother would hide the two of them, or not introduce them. They always kept very still — they knew how they were and what was required."

He stopped for a moment, swallowed, then went on. "At my graduation party they were in the kitchen; I was ashamed too, and the principal was coming. But in the middle of it, the parlor door opens, and there is my grandmother. She does not want to come in, but my grandfather pushes her. She is wearing a hat with a feather. He is in his striped suit from the boat. He goes up to the American principal and says in German, "This is the grandmother, Herr Direktor." My mother comes up behind them, very red, but before she can say anything, my grandfather screws up his eyes, opens his mouth wide in her face, and there comes out *baa-aa* like a sheep, in his *Schwäbisch.*" Demuth took a deep breath, leaning forward. *"Jederma-ann ist etwas von jedem Ma-ann!"* he bawled suddenly, and the words sprang from his mouth as if they had been waiting for years on his tongue, in a long, yeasty cry — a sheep's bawl.

He looked at me then, startled, the way one person looks at another when a faraway cry is heard late at night. *"Verstehts du?"* he whispered, glancing guiltily at the open door. "Did you understand? 'Everybody is a little bit every —'? You understood what he said?" He shrugged. "But it was altogether so funny . . . no one could help laughing." He was silent for a minute. Then one hand crept toward his crown, stopped halfway. "But the funniest of all . . . *nicht?*" he said. "That now I, Hans Ulrich . . . am the principal?"

It was getting dark outside his window. In the shadowy room each corner had its faithful hound. Through the window came the mnemonic odor of night, dark river carrying its pearls to the diver, stealing forward even to this backwater room, to him, waiting outside his window for me.

"I must go," I said.

He sat hunched in his chair, not moving. I had never seen him so still, palms on knees, head bent on rigid torso, all his seesawing suspended, as if he were tired of weighing himself at last. *"Listen,"* he said. "Only listen . . ."

No, I thought. To none of you, any longer. I must remember for myself. And if I listened to others, it would be for my own ends, reminding myself always that if ever I were to speak, that is the way others would listen to me. This was the lesson that was not in

German. Out of all that he thought he had taught me, this remained. Perhaps I should have told him so. A life is worth something. But I moved toward the door.

"*Moment!*" he said. "I think . . . now would be the time . . . yes, now . . ." He had not stirred. So people sit sometimes, holding themselves down in space, when they know how little their weight is. "If you would like now . . . to call me *du?*" he whispered.

But I was already outside the door.

Chapter VI. Ruth Telephones. Pierre.

RUTH telephoned tonight. That likelihood has always been in the back of my mind these three weeks, or the chance that we might meet on the long daily walks I have been taking, partly in preparation for the evening's task — movement, either in a vehicle or on my own two legs always stimulates thought, reminiscence — and partly because I am physically neither sedentary nor a solitary. All has been silent here. I am supposed to be away. But I miss exertion and I miss people, who are the food of thought. And since she and I live so near, I have formed the habit of taking a bus first to some other part of the town and walking there, often to the West Side, along the Hudson's mock-regal streets, once or twice to Harlem, and once — on a Sunday so sun-calmed and sociable that I came almost to the point of breaking off my evening's tryst — to the empty, lavender caverns of Trinity and Wall.

The East Side is no use to me; it is the present, and it contains Ruth, that gentle woman who is nevertheless my present danger. Even on those other odd streets, I often look behind me now, something I have never done before, although I of necessity know well the attraction of watching others from behind. Curious, I suppose, that although I have never ruled out the eventuality that one of my own ilk, someone who had accumulated knowledge of me elsewhere, might use it to enter my life, I have never feared it. I should recognize the breed at once. And our way is not literally to shadow but to knit hearsay with accident.

With Ruth it is different. It is not for nothing that the lover is called the follower. Even the world knows, laughing and condoning, the fantastic research of which the lover is capable, the wildly unfortuitous meetings on a corner, the hegiras that some have made halfway across the earth in order to be able to say to a certain face in a hotel vestibule, or to a voice on a blessedly local telephone exchange, "Fancy both of us being here!" So, now and then in my walks, I look behind me, although I know that if she follows me, she does it with love.

In her eyes, the way I have acted toward her must be unforgivable. Or almost so, for I know well their endless forgiveness — women. They all have it, not only those like Ruth, warm and intelligent and chaste in the mind, where chastity should be, but the slut also, as the sentimentalists know, and even, as they often overlook, the woman enameled by money or eroded by a profession. Even the spinster has it, waiting for some man who has not yet arrived. If they are women they have it, a deep, self-paralyzing sea of trust, an endless remission for some man's sins. And one seeks them for it almost as much as for their sex, although one may say this only privately in this country, where the sexual emotion must not deviate too far into any other, lest one fail to recognize what it is, or of which sex it is. I have therefore never enjoyed conscious brutality toward them. I have been guilty only of that other sort, committed by either side — the inescapable brutality of loving less than one is loved. And aware of this, have been even more careful to be kind, to observe that ritual tenderness which often reassures them more than love. But with Ruth I did not do this. For the first time I was brutal in the other sense. What I did was to sleep with her and not see her again.

It has been a year now since I first walked into the Mannix household, armed as usual with my store of references. I came there not to know the Judge, although anyone would want to know him, but to know the household *entière,* one of those nucleal households that attract by virtue of their own warm enclosures, whose auras I can always recognize even from afar or second-hand, even as I recognized it in this one when Walter Stern, years back, used to tell me about it. By the time I came to know it actually, Mrs. Mannix was dead, and David, the son whom I was supposed to have known, dead too, but the household still had that *vertu* which does not die until the last arc of such a circle is gone. And Ruth, who must have been half grown when Stern — one of the accessory benevolences that such homes maintain — had first known them, was grown. A year, and for the last months of it, between Ruth and me, that familiar slow affair begun by a man and woman in the name of friendship, the friendship that steals its name from Plato and waits for it to be stolen by Psyche.

She knew this before I did — I do not have to be gallant here. I was unalert to it because I had not come to that household for her. I had entered it, become its intimate under the usual false references, with the usual preknowledge, and, as for some time now, only the slight social risk. For some time now I had risked nothing more serious — a pickpocket keeping his fingers lithe. It might have been thought that I was growing toward society, warming myself down from my cold niche on its fringe. At times I almost persuaded myself that this was so, but in my heart I knew it was not. For, until now, the people I had chosen to enter upon were flotsam, people well out of tone with my daily life or beneath it — people like those in Tuscana that day of the hearing. But this time I had chosen not the random ones from whom one could easily abscond, but persons who belonged to the stratum of my life in New York, who were, as it were, contemporary with what I was now. Why, now, did I choose such a household, something I had never done before? What I came for was the same as always, the same inexplicable sensation. The control that comes from foreknowledge — that is part of it. Detachment — I take my place, specious as it is, in their midst. And in the possession of both these things, a covert sense that although I do no evil, I nevertheless strike a blow. But above all, a sense of the utter secrecy of myself. For when one is among people on false terms, then no matter what emotion one gives them, one really gives nothing away.

Women love the inaccessible in a man; often I have seen them attribute it when it is not there. In any success I have had with them, I have always known this to be its deeper cause, although it is the last thing I would consciously use. When a man gives you his confidence, he does not necessarily ask for a token return; oddly, often he assumes that in giving you his intimacy, he has yours. But with a woman, confidences are the signal for love, and love asks a return. It craves a return in kind, applying endlessly for it, but it will settle for less — as I had often found. For I find it hard to believe that some men are frightened of sexuality. For me it is the one closeness I dare. For me, in the act of love, even without love, dissimulation is at rest, or in reflex. In that profound dissimulation there is a moment of trust.

But this time I dared too close. In my sorties into other people's lives, it had sometimes happened that I had had relations with women I found there, but they were always, like the others around them, persons of unmeditative mind. Once, in a situation that involved no women, I had however found myself dealing with a person of intelligence equal, probably superior to my own — Belden, the Communist bookseller. But that world, though the obverse of random, is as fixed in its own distortions as a world under water; itself an aberrant, it has little time to ruminate on personal aberrations, and in it even such a mind as Belden's loses its percipience of people as they are — although I often suspected, beneath his conscious motives, a devious pattern that came near to resembling my own.

But with Ruth I was dealing, first, with a world whose norms were my own surface norms. And I was dealing with a woman. The male imagination is more often extensive, galactic, flings itself robustly abroad. Women are miniaturists. They can imagine anything as possible, whorl within whorl, but they more often focus their flights on their own small field of space. And, finally, I was dealing with the delicate, ciliated intelligence of love.

And now I will let myself remember. It was afterwards, when we were lying together in the small room they call the library in her father's house. Although I had often had women in my flat, I had never asked her there. Often, recently, she had been waiting to be asked. I did not examine my reluctance to let her see it, or see me there. I ignored the warning — my own alertness muffled, trying to tell me that she was a person to be feared.

I had already, as I see now, ignored another warning. When she first began giving me her small confidences, telling me of her brief marriage, referring lightly to her first jejune experiences of girlhood, mentioning here and there some man she had known, I understood it at once — the old, old sexual plea saying, "This is the way it was. We look back on it together. And now I look to you. We look to each other." It is the oldest gauntlet, and I responded at once, as most would to a woman like her. As a companion I had already begun to hold her dear. And this was not unique for me either with men or with women; always before, my will and need to be secret had told me when it was time to leave. But this time, simple as her confidences were, I found myself reluctant to hear them. I am never bored with another's revelations, with the occult thrill that comes from listening. I was not likely to use what she told me; I had richer stores. And yet I wanted to seal her mouth. I did not want to listen to her confessions. I wanted to warn *her* — that I was a person to be feared.

So we approached each other, the guileful and the guileless, and we met. Neither of us said a word.

Lying together, palm to palm, after love, is like lying in another country that some Dives has allotted for ten minutes or more. The voices that speak there are already the voices of paradise lost. I remember what I thought when I withdrew my palm. I thought — I could love her, if it were not for myself. We spoke then, or she did, of how we had met, of all the stages that had brought us to this night, in the way women love to do, exactly as children ask again for a story, secure in the fairy-tale end. Her hair was across my forehead. I was only half listening. The moment, with its treble of voices, was over. I watched it as it sped away, pluming into the gathering distance, leaving one of its voices behind. If it were not for myself, I could love her.

She was speaking of the circumstance that had brought us together, the encyclopedia soliciting her father for an article, the discovery that I had known David after the war, when he was serving with the American Friends in Germany, before the crash of the commercial transport in which he went down. I have of course never been in Germany. The war took me to the Far East, then home. It was Walter Stern who had been there with him, who used to speak to me endlessly of "Diddy" as he called him and of his friends the Mannixes, their house, their habits, meanwhile handing me, across our adjacent beds in the orthopaedic ward, the letters he was editing as a memorial, sitting up to read them to me — I with a leg in traction after a ski spill, he preoperatively spry, with his hump clinging between his shoulders, the night-light hollowing his eager face — that racked, Ancient Mariner face which all such people have. I had done him no wrong, merely appropriated him, what he knew, after his death, as people often must do with the dead, who, if they could, might prefer that to nothing at all.

"You are not listening," she whispered. I drew her hair over my face. I thought of all those whom we leave for dead, either in the grave or in the past, who grow again between our shoulder blades. I thought of the great hump of memory I had made for myself, of such a shape that I could never hope to lay it down. And then I made the accidental slip. I spoke unaware; I was listening, but not to her. And I found myself with the enemy lying beside me, in the flesh still quivering in communication with mine. I discovered why I had never looked behind me. The real danger walks toward.

When I came back here that night I sat down here at my desk. All she knew was that there was something to be known, but I saw the thinness of the membrane I had always kept posed between myself and others. I wrote her a note full of evasions, another saying I was going away, tore them both up and sent none. "Tell me," she had said, her mouth at my breastbone. My words until now. The words of the confidant. What I had to tell depended on a long chain of causation, from the beginning. I needed a place to lay it down. And the only safe confidant was myself.

But often, afterwards, in the nights here since then, after I have written and am returned to the present, I think of her, and then I imagine her as still lying naked and vulnerable under the blanket I crept from — immobilized there, as I am here — and I wonder over the nature of my fear. I might have gone on as I was. There must be many who live on with effrontery under strange private burdens. The ordinary, advancing like lichen, protects us all. Yet I did not, because of whatever it is that spins its filament between us, as she lies there, as I sit here. Often, after being with a woman, the pattern of that connection lies like a tracery in the muscles for days; one carries the other person about with one, a silent companion, certain that one's own impress is being carried also. This is like that — if fear can be like that. I sit here, remembering what I must no longer dare.

I sat so last evening. It is a strange process, this alternation between the present and the past, in which I have deliberately made the present as null and stationary as I can, in order that the past may fill it to the brim. As I approach what I am after, I feel that it approaches me.

Last night, I was thinking of the people called "accident-prone," those who need to injure themselves. There could be others, I thought, who sought the good accident. And if so, they would fear it as well. Then the phone rang, so late, so unaccustomed in the dead room that I knew, unless it was a wrong number, it would be she. I looked at the clock, almost four, and I understood, as well as if I had lived it, the evening she had lived through, that had brought her naked along the filament, here.

I picked up the phone and listened. If I answer, I thought, I may learn what my fear is.

"Yes?" I said, and our voices collided.

She spoke again.

"Pierre?" she said, and I drew in my breath at the collision of the present with the past. For in the memoir I have not yet come to that name.

Chapter VII. The Fourchette Office. The Shell. The Namesake.

THAT was the name I chose. At the time it did not seem to me in the least odd that I, of English and Irish heritage, living in America, should suddenly choose to be known henceforward by the name of a half-French Viennese who had once shown me a brief, putative uncleship, letting me creep into the knee-high circle around him, long ago, on a few brilliant, lost afternoons. Nor that in doing so, in assuming my name, I meant contrarily somehow to preserve my identity, my singularity from the depredations of others. The young act from a pure, breathless logic still ignorant of the conventional barrier between dream and possibility. When a man begins to *act* logically according to others, to try to impose their kind of order on what the worm already whispers to him is an irrational world, then he has left his youth behind. As he begins to concede to the reality of the majority, the instinctual power of fantasy recedes. So, little by little, we bargain our youth away, and can no more quarrel with this inevitable than we can with the slow exchange of life for death. Some do, of course, pushing that earlier logic to the extremities of martyrdom or art, and history is made by them for a time. But I had neither their strength nor their luck. I am only unable to forget it, to let go of the *Heimweh* that remembers what it was once like to have.

I still had it that evening. When I left Demuth, I already knew what I meant to do, with an intent as hot and cleansing as anger. I was going to the courthouse, to Fourchette, to take back — to seize if need be — the petition, and destroy it. Underlying that was another, a new satisfaction that for the moment I thrust aside. It was akin to the satisfaction that comes from leaving, from leaving anywhere when there are others left behind, but it was more complex. Later on I would recognize it often — the faintly corrupt serenity that comes when we have turned somebody down. It too was a sign that I was growing. A child's hatred exudes, natural as honey, toward those who refuse him, who do unto him. As he is civilized, he learns in his turn to hate others for what he has done to them. Going down Demuth's stairs was, I think, the moment when I changed sides.

I had dropped another simplicity by the wayside. It glitters back there like a bit of mirror in a hedge. But I had more.

Outside, it was not much more than six o'clock; the night had not really come. It was the long, stationary dusk that at this season held the land for hours in a spider-colored void. Half a mile down the road to Tuscana, I caught a ride on a truck whose driver had picked me up once in a while before. We rode on through the pall as if it were a thicket, seeming to get nowhere except where we were, unless we glanced back at the huge, glazed waves of the dams.

"Sure is some combine," said the driver. "Sure is some combine." Ahead of us, on the state road, the wet streaks of the mirages skimmed one after the other under the wheels. Now and then we passed through a pocket of gnats frizzling in the air. Same specks came in the eyes just before the sun hit you, said the driver; one time he had to park by the side of the road for an hour before he was sure which.

"Dead town for sure, ain't it?" he said, as we drove into Tuscana. In front of the courthouse he set me down. "Hitch along sometime, kid — I'll carry you to Memphis."

I told him I was going north. "Uh-*uh!*" he said. "Get there, send me down a satchelful that ice." He tipped two fingers at me when I thanked him. "Hurry back!" he said, and drove off.

The courthouse square was deserted. This was the hour when people lay about wherever they could, letting the day press from their pores. If the office was closed, I thought, I would even go to the Fourchette house, but the door was open, and on it a note: *Ticely — you want that writ Pa promised, look in around nine.* Ticely was the name of the sheriff — a sharp reminder that the office, for all its slackness, was the precinct of county business, of adult affairs. But the note was signed *Junior,* by the fumbling, heavy-breathing hulk of a man who was the son. Thus my luck followed me. I should not have got away with what I did, under the rubbed-stone eyes, denatured yet sober, of the elder Fourchette.

Inside the office the fan was blowing, going on just as I had left it, under the wheeling generations of flies. That other day I had been here was "there"; this was "here," with the fan between them, a weaving "now." Only I, a patchwork of all three, a being continuously repaired and accreting, had changed. I could still hear, as I did just then, the to-from Memphis train spreading its cloudy horn along the land, but now I had the beginning, the necessary deafness. I could still listen to the voice of memory, but from now on, even to this voice, with calculation. I was almost ready to begin the exchange of unpremeditated feeling for the privilege of knowing at all times who and where I was, for that absence of pain which I would learn to confuse with joy. And I knew the name of the next town north.

I smiled to myself, remembering how once, to know that had seemed the sesame to everything. How enormously more I knew now, and how much less likely I was to be diddled — the proof being that I sat here, ready to defend my name, my selfhood, like any knight-at-arms. I felt the presence of all my appetites, huge to know more, and the possession of them gave me, even as now, the conviction of health. In my knapsack there were still two sandwiches and I hunted them out with sharp pleasure and ate them in great bites. On a stand near the desk there was a dish of pears under a netting, and with a brigand's look over my shoulder, I lifted the netting and stole one. I felt all the excellence of growing up, the bravery that opened like a door in oneself, the privilege that arrived in mysterious, due course, and no one at the moment could have persuaded me but that growing older was a quantitative affair. In my pocket there was still one brown-papered bar of Demuth's chocolate, and putting aside childish things, I ate it with a knowing cannibal twinge. My "themes" had not left me; if intent upon it, I could still summon them at will from the uncontaminated country that was still most truly I. That inward country was only more richly textured than I had dreamed, more deeply situated than a child's. But I could still draw from it a deep surge of innocence — though it came now only at will, preceded by the faintest tinge of injury, and from slightly farther off.

At the window, in the hallucinated lavender that hung just before dark, even Tuscana's stingy shapes took on the weak lyrism of a town that, though hated, was shortly to be left. It was my duty to cherish that hatred for all that it had meant to me, to hold to the real substance beneath those dim porches, so ingénue and soft now in their evening summer. It would never, I swore, become my province — that Cloud-Cuckoo-Land of youth which other people, sometimes even my mother, saw in the teacup, the time-cup, brooding over it with a bemused smile. But now that I was leaving Tuscana, I could afford at last to admit that I was in it, that this was America and I was in it, here.

Back there, during the years when my mother used to mention, halfheartedly, the ridiculous idea of coming here, "America" had had the comfortable shape of some leviathan humping so far behind the horizon that one could talk of it without ever fearing to see it. For a long time I had not even understood that it and "the States," as it was called in Fulham, were for the most part the same. "America" was what my mother had always called it, and from her silent head-shakings over the letters from her sister, I had come to regard it as another part of the ill chance that dogged my aunt, that had dogged her also with a mortal disease. So too it had dropped occasionally from the old grandmother's accented tongue — *Amerika* — sounding down the endless, travertine corridors of her family whenever she spoke of Pierre, her favorite brother who, though a great traveler, had settled permanently there. And on her lips too it had the rap of some uncomfortable destiny that a man less feckless or obstinate than he would have had the sense to avoid. For all her spa acquaintance with Europe, she was a provincial, reconciled to England only because *die Familie*, all the core of it except Pierre and a ragbag of auxiliary cousins, was gathered there. She had, too, all the European woman's deification (in her case Germanic and Hebraic as well) of the males of the family. And for this brother, the Goodman children's distaff great-uncle, she had the special matriarchal passion that often extends itself to the adventurer.

Actually, he may have seemed an adventurer only to her. To others he must have seemed merely that natural dilettante which all such mercantile families inevitably acquire on their way from money to taste. He had his business interests along with the artistic. Although she never said precisely what he did or was, showing at times an irritation with him because she could not, it appeared that he dabbled in export-import, always in some charming currency — Carrara marble, sometimes the finished statuary, terrazzo, wine. Apparently he hovered between his taste and his money, casually augmenting one with the other, and this, although it was not solid enough for her to approve, she could understand. What troubled her was that he did it "over there." She was the family's recorder, its central repository, tending, in the continuous brew of her incantations, what she clearly regarded as the family soul. But like the true duennas, the best witches, she had little imagination. Pottering over her memorial fires, she could evoke that concentric family, its panoply of death, birth, banns, houses, taxes and long uneventfulness, in all her known sulphurs and blues, making for herself and them — and for me — such a family as was never anywhere else. But Pierre's life was lost to her, a blank patch somewhere in the North Atlantic mists across the world. She could not weave him in. It was not his change of country she objected to, or his far journeys. The family, since Egypt perhaps, had had many such — but always together. If Sir Joseph had taken the family to *Amerika* on the morrow she would have gone with him, as later she surely went along to

Japan, no doubt settling down devotedly at once to weave that in too. But Pierre was alone. It was not that she thought of him — although she may have — as wandering over savannahs she would have been at a loss to describe. Nor that he never corresponded, except by presents — sending a constant stream of curiosa from everywhere, America as well — and came to see her only every four or five years. Without the family she could not imagine him at all. He was therefore the sole denizen of her lamentations; to death and other scourges she gave only a token *sabacthani,* revering these as the natural enemies against which a family circle was formed. Meanwhile she saw him — and made me see him (soon, she said, to be seen on one of his visits, in the flesh) — as a Merlin of talents that could conquer anything except his own waste of them. On her elegiac days as I listened to her, I saw him in *"Amayrika,"* held fast in the laocoön coils of its central dark. At other times — on the days when, chatteringly gay, she talked at me as to some elegant crony of the Ringstrasse — America appeared merely as something he had somehow contracted and would one day abjure — like an absurd *mésalliance.*

He was of course also the "uncle from Gibraltar." I had not yet reasoned that out on the day I went to the old lady's apartments as usual and found him there, having just discovered his presence in the house from Molly, who had called me back as I was bearing off the tray at the usual hour, saying, "Hoi there, hold it a tick, the uncle is with her!" — and carefully replacing its glass with two others, pale red with dots of white on them, that I had never before seen. "Can the boy manage?" I heard the cook say, low. "The Eye-talian ones those are, sent her Easter last," and Molly's answering whisper: "Fair treat to watch him. Can he not!"

"Ach, so it is *your* day is it?" said the old lady as I entered. "Here comes the handsome waiter. And here *he* is," she said proudly, clapping her knuckles together and nodding toward the dapper, mustached gentleman who sat next her on the sofa, "the naughty wanderer we speak of so often, at last. Here is my brother Pierre." She turned to him with glee. "And you, *Brüderlein,* wait."

Then she put me through our little routine, and he tossed back his head and laughed, smoothing his short gray curls and the mustache that matched them, slapping his sharp, silken knee.

" 'Here comes the handsome waiter,' eh? My God, Franziska, how you remember! I can hear our dear mother saying that to me now." I knew that he was really the old lady's stepbrother, younger and of a different father. It was strange to hear him name the old grandmother, for although she often referred to herself thus in her recitals, I had never heard anyone in the house say it aloud.

"And who is this?" he said, turning to me. "Not another nephew-once-removed I have lost track of?"

"*Ach!*" she said. "Although you — you are capable of it. Of course not. It is Dora's boy. You remember Rachel's Dora." I made as if to go then, reminded of who I was, but she motioned me to stay. "The others are always off somewhere. We have long conversations together, he and I." I was too young then to remark, even to myself, that in reality I never said a word, but I remember thinking: Those are "conversations," then — we have "conversations."

He fixed his eyes on me, brown plush instead of his sister's black but with the same mottled keenness. The lids were paper-thin, under brows that bristled and curled at the tips like secondary mustaches. " 'Handsome waiter,' eh? Would you believe it, that's what they used to call me. Hmmm? Can you believe it? What do you say?"

It was a warm June, and he was wearing a vanilla-colored suit of the silk my mother called "pongee." His hat lay beside him, a rolled-brim panama of the same tinge, and next it a smooth, yellow cane. In his tie, pale as the rest of him, something twinkled — a horse with its pinhead hooves stretched to an extension no bigger than the nail of a man's thumb. "Eh?" he said.

"Not — not the waiter part," I said, and again he tossed back his head and roared, ending up with a sip of the wine.

"Mmm," he said, "that's the stuff I sent you. Must make a note to send you some more next time I go there." He turned to me. "You're a canny one, you are." He had no accent that I had ever, or have ever, heard. Neutral of itself, it seemed to shift with whomever he talked. "What you really like about me is my horse. That's what all the children like — what I keep in my pockets, and the horse. Here, take a look at it, but don't prick yourself, its edges are sharp." He slipped it from his tie and handed it to me. It was made of minute diamonds set so close that one could not see the gold, with a saddle of green stones, and a single, wild red eye that was infinitely laughable yet made the thing move. I held it, looking at the eye and wondering what other marvels he kept in his pockets.

"It is wonderful wine, Pierre," said Frau Goodman. "I drink every day a toast to you, and my thanks for all the things you send me. I am beginning not to have room for them." She waved a hand at shelves lined with goblets and preciosities, over every one of which I had seen her crow and adore. "But I must remind you, one can get all these things even here. I would rather have you."

He whistled under his breath. "Why do you not come with me, then?"

"Leave the family! *Du bist verrückt!*"

His eyes crinkled. "Or for a visit, at least."

"And what home do you have, that I could visit it!"

"Right now a beautiful one in the *Vieux Carré*. Really now, Franziska, you do not think I inhabit the savage parts of the country? And after that, perhaps San Francisco. Why are you not more pioneer?"

"The winter here is enough pioneer. Like an aquarium nobody cleans. And the maids! Even the boy here dusts better. What would I not give for a *Dienstmädchen* from home!"

He laughed. "I'll send you that too."

"Always you *send*." She shrugged.

He reached in a pocket. "Here. Something for this young man. Something he could not get here, even at Fortnum's." He opened the packet for me, exposing three immense tan, nut-studded ovals, one of them crumbled, each as large as his palm. "Taste it." He watched me. "Good, eh? New Orleans pralines. And now perhaps, if I am going to meet my new grandnieces, I must have my horse again."

I gave it back, holding it by the stickpin guard at the end. It was indeed very sharp. "You like it, eh?" I nodded. "Better than the candy?" he said. I flushed, my mouth still full. "Don't answer," he said quickly, "that was not fair. Besides, I know the answer. But tell me, what is it you like best about the horse? Best, mind you!"

I smiled at him. He was the easiest man to smile at I ever saw. "The eye!" I said.

He raised the brows. "Hmm. Not many say that. And he can dust too. And he has conversation. I could use a boy like that, eh, Franziska? Perhaps I ought to take him along with me."

"Where?" I said. He was the only person I had ever met for whom I would have deserted that house.

"Have pity, Pierre," muttered his sister. "Indeed you have not changed an inch. Do you not see he believes you?" She had forgotten, or never knew, as often the charmers refuse to know, how far she had already taken me herself.

I flushed again, understanding now that he had not meant it. This time when I turned to go, neither of them stopped me.

"See?" he said. "She will not let anybody pioneer." He held out the packet that I had left on the table. "Here, don't forget these. And be sure to attend tonight; there will be a grand giving-out of presents, and I shall find one for you too."

When I had closed the door behind me, I leaned against it. I had never listened at doors in that house, and I was not aware that I was doing so now. I yearned merely to be in his company.

"And how is my nephew?" I heard him say.

"Well. He works hard; my God, how hard he works, one never sees him once he gets to that top floor. Today is the day he goes to the museum. He would of course be here to greet you — if you did not always come like the birds. *Ach* . . . Pierre."

"And Rachel?"

"She is sleeping. You will see her at dinner."

There was a short silence. "Another child?" Again a silence.

"Always sleeping," he said. "The last time also. And at dinner, I suppose, those big, pale eyes . . . Do you not think she sleeps too much . . . my God . . . she is not yet thirty-five."

There was no answer that I could hear, but he must have been walking around the room, for I could hear the well-known clink of certain pieces of bric-a-brac as he handled them, the wooden shove of others. "You are right. I send too much. But this time I have brought small things. For you — a little French box . . . so . . . with nothing in it. You could keep an angel's tear in it. Point lace — I do not even know the name of it. And a lavaliere . . . you would be surprised what washes up over there. Some of the pieces I have brought — I have never seen anything like, even in Mamma's time."

"I go out so much? I should wear them?"

"You will hoard them then. *Für die Familie* . . . you think I don't know you? There was another silence. "Of course . . . I could always sell them . . . at Sotheby's." And then they burst out laughing together.

"Be now serious for a little," she said. "What must I do . . . to keep you here? They need us downstairs, you know, even if they do not notice it. The old ones are still needed . . . even if only to quarrel with . . . to keep a house together. The day comes maybe I would need you, and not for a visit — *eins-zwei-drei* and away again . . . Here, have some more wine, dinner is not until eight." I heard the shifting of chairs, and after the bottle was set down, a long pause.

"And I," she said, "I am getting younger, yes? There was Minna Faber, you remember . . . she used to come like clockwork every afternoon. She is gone. And both the Kleebergs — the wife, and Emil too. I go out now only to funerals . . . Last week, even the old Weil's daughter, you remember that rascal's stupid Rosa, she comes to us for years yet, always with her hand out, and we support her, because what else can one do, because her father stole from Papa in eighty-nine . . . Even that old stupid . . . even she."

"*Ach*, Franzie, Franzie." His accent had thickened. "The devil is not so choosy."

"Not he. Your sister neither. Nowadays I talk to anybody . . . One has to have *somebody* to remember with, you will see for yourself someday."

For what seemed endless minutes, neither of them spoke. Then her

133

voice came, with the warmer timbre it sometimes took on with the wine. "Wonderful to have you here. Wonderful. What must I do to keep you, hmmm? Maybe I should steal from you that horse."

He laughed. It was his voice I listened for. Hers, so available, I scarcely heard. "I have to make them like me — children. I don't know why. I cannot bear it if they do not." He laughed again, on a different tone. I did not know him well enough to know whether he was teasing — perhaps no one ever did. "I have been thinking . . . perhaps I must marry, hmm? Before it is too late."

Someone's footsteps came up the stairs then, and I could not stay. Through the door as I left, I heard her cry — "Pierre! You would not . . . you have not been thinking — from *over there!*"

Afterwards, after he had left London again, she spoke less of him, at first not mentioning him at all, and if he did marry, or when he came again, I never heard, for within the year we ourselves had gone.

But for that night and days after, he reigned in the house, with his saturnalia of gifts, his amnesty — for children — of all ukases. He knew how to use the treasure-scent to set the demurest of them very near to riot, as if he had brought back with him a renewed sense of how close the scalping-party lurked beneath the skin. There were hunts on the stairs, caches tumbling from corners, under napkins and pillows, and just as they had begun to tire of what Martin, the oldest, called "geographical" presents — the water flowers, butterfly kites, anomalous belts, birchbark canoes and papier-mâché masks that he took more pleasure in perhaps than they — there would be a round of real thumpers from the stores, like the polar-bear-on-wheels that stood alongside Hannschen's bed one morning, and James's inflatable raft.

That night the grandmother, who always took her meals alone, came down for dinner, and when my mother brought me in as requested, after the savory, Frau Goodman was there between her son and her brother, her eagle face curving beneath lace pinned with a jewel to the flyaway hair that one of the maids had marcelled. I was afraid that she might embarrass me before the others, the circle of children, with our private greeting, but she had no eyes for anyone but Pierre as he gave my mother her present — a bit of lace that she told me later was Honiton, that she laundered yearly thereafter with sugar water, and laid away. I did not notice what he had brought Lady Goodman, but his present to his nephew was extraordinary — a long cape of quilted harlequin feathers that Sir Joseph, his sallow face tinted, said was literally a prince's, was archaeological, and must have a glass case or be lent to the museum, but that tonight, sitting outside the circle of his children around the uncle, he wore. For me there were other presents later, store-bought and forgotten, but that night he gave me a conch shell of the kind that used to be kept in drawing rooms, a large one with the water sheen still on it and colors like the cloak's in its nacre — a prince too among shells.

It was while he clasped me to his knee, showing me how to listen, with the shell to my ear, for the sea, that I noticed the other children's feet, all pointed toward the hub of the circle, all clad in beaded moccasins now instead of sharp-toed red leather, and understood then that he was the "uncle from Gibraltar." I pointed my foot in too, and he saw me, bending down half to me, half to the others, with a brilliant air. "We must have your measure, and send you a pair too," he said, and the promise lodged in my heart long after I could have used the slippers had he ever sent them, like the invisible stitch, ultimately melted, that the surgeon does not remove.

Just then I caught the look on Sir Joseph's face, turned on his uncle, a quizzical look almost of censure, but he was outside the circle, and I, though standing awkwardly, was inside it, left by the uncle for its center, where he was acting out the tale that was to be our favorite — the story of Alphonse and the pig who spoke Creole.

"So the judge say to Alphonse: 'Alphonse, for why you steal ze leetle peeg?' And Alphonse, he say, 'Oh no, *m'sieu le juge,* I no steal ze leetle peeg. I say to ze leetle peeg: Peeg! You weesh to come home wiz me? And ze leetle pig, she answer *Oui!*' "

He squealed it, and all the children gave a delighted shout, except me.

" 'And I ask ze leetle peeg: Peeg! S'all we run? And ze leetle peeg, she say *Oui!* So I take ze leetle peeg zat speak such good Creole, and she say to me *Oui! Oui! Oui!* all ze way home.' "

Each time he made the squealing noise all the children made it in concert with him, and only I stood silent, mystified, my eyes hot, for I had not spent holidays in France, and I did not know what the joke was. As I stood there, I felt a bit of paper slide into the hand I held behind me, and glancing round, I saw Sir Joseph tucking his scholar's pencil back into his waistcoat under the cape. On the paper he had written in precise script: *The pig said "Oui," which is the French for Yes, and sounds just like what a pig does say — Wee.* When I looked up again, his chair was empty except for the long bright blur of the cape. But later, when we came to go, we found that a cot had been ordered set up in the nursery, and that night, with the shell beside me, I slept again in the house in which I had been born.

And here, on the untidy work desk beneath Mr. Fourchette's cramped window, was the shell, although it was not mine. Mine — overlooked in the packing and buried since in those archives whose key I myself had thrown away — had never been carried here. But here was its brother, its thousandth cousin, resting silky pink and serene on the scrabbled mess of Junior Fourchette's papers, the same regal pearl thrown up again by the ceaseless repetition of the sea. I picked it up and held it to my ear. The sound was the same hollow, super-sonic sigh, the monster sigh of some being with an infinite supply of breath, but the burden had changed. In the interval, life — mine — had secreted there. I could still hear the Goodman household, but now I could hear the restless undertones beneath the solid C major, the single haven-note I had heard as a child. I saw the family's genitive impatience with what it must love, for husband for wife, for brother for sister, for Pierre, the flitting inciter of children, and I thought of how canny a dilettante one had to be if one could not trust oneself to be loved or saw its limits too clearly — how careful, just in time, to move on. All that next week of his visit, I remembered, I had been the one to laugh loudest at the story of the pig, but he had never noticed it, never again preferred me after that brief election of our first meeting. I had waited in vain for him to give me the horse to hold again, vowing that when he did I would prick my finger with it, secretly leaving him some of my blood to carry away. He had never done so, and I could smile at myself for that now. And at him too, I found with surprise, for it seemed that although he had carried away no blood of mine, I, with the long prong of memory, had drawn his. I smiled at him in triumph, the smile with which we decorate the graves of those who have escaped us, and I put down the shell.

As I did so, Junior Fourchette came in the door. Seeing him around the courthouse, in the wake of his father, one thought instantly that he must have had a blonde mother, and then forgot him. On the streets of the town one sometimes saw him lumbering alone, always bent forward with the puzzled, side-to-side heave of a behemoth following a whip-tease too low for his bulk to catch. Here in the office he swayed too, standing still, blinking at me as if I traveled an orbit that would not settle down. He wore no jacket or tie, but his shirt was sharply laundered, fine-seamed, and the odor that walked with him was deep, overpleasant, like a barber's essence. Years later I knew other drunks like him, gin or whisky drinkers to his Pernod, who kept themselves in the same way assertively clean and shaven, holding themselves up in the vertical, mannerly world by the strength of their shirt fronts, the sight of their cuff links, while their secret life evaporated steadily from them in that deep cologne.

"Truly sorry to keep you waiting," he said, peering humbly into the room's general shadow. "Truly sorry." And looking back at him in the light of those others, I can see what comfort he must have taken in the excessive graces of Southern convention, through which he could spend the endless fund of apology, of placation, that was his own.

Resting against the door, his shoulder rustled against the note pinned there. He bent to read it, nodding. "Recollected I was to be here, but the time escaped my mind." His drawl was like his father's, clearer than the glottal, cotton-candy speech of the region, but with a curious added stammer to it, not of consonants but in the vowels. Between its pauses his voice came surprisingly soft and golden, the way the voice of the stammerer often does. He nodded again. "Ticely!" he said softly to himself. "Yes sir — ee. You wait now. Recollect I changed that writ this forenoon."

"I'm not from Ticely," I said. "I'm not your appointment. I came for something else."

He moved past me with a peculiar lightness of foot, a heavy man stepping across brinks with a special adroitness, and stood over the desk, puzzling on the papers there. "Had it in mind it was somewhere here. I do beg your pardon."

"You didn't keep me waiting," I said. "I came for something else — for the petition."

"Saw you through the window," he said, still fumbling. "Occupying yourself with that shell. Thought to myself — no telling how long I've kept him." He looked up. His eyes were yellow-brown, large and full-lashed, his nose and mouth shapely above a square chin well clefted. If one could have torn from him the bruin haze of his humility, he would have been a handsome man.

"Petition?" His hand trembled over the papers. "I surely had it in mind it was a writ."

I explained. It was like squaring a circle that submitted mutely and yet remained gently evasive. But I got through to him in a way.

"Change your name?" he said. "That's a wise move. If you young enough. Recollect handling that petition. Thought — only eighteen, too; he's a wise one. Thought that to myself at that time." His hand, in passing over his forehead, trembled so violently that his other hand, in a movement of which he seemed unaware, reached up for it and guided it into his pocket. He sat down at the small desk that held the typewriter. The tremor was still visible in his upper arm.

"Made some mistakes on it, did I?" He reminded me of a shop-keeper taking back an article he well knows had a flaw when sold. "Tell you what. Give it here; I'll do it over. Then you come round for it some morning. Morning's my time. Or tell you what. Some evening. Around nine."

Sweat stood out on his forehead. Then, as quickly, for he had been a damp white, his face revived to its usual freckled bronze-red. His eyes brimmed. It was painful to watch him, a man-baby naked to the ebb and flow of thought. "Got the name wrong, maybe?" Laughter racked him silently. A profound gravity replaced it. "I can fix it; you give it here." The hand in his pocket emerged, fingers protruding, managed to close round the shell and held itself there, violently still. He regarded it. "Truly sorry," he said. "Can't oblige you at the moment. Morning's my time."

I explained that the petition had been signed and returned the day before. He shook his head. "Not here then," he said. "In there." He pointed to the wall that joined the office to the courthouse. "Gone into the file. For the court." Off his feet, he seemed to regain a certain sobriety, almost more intense than the real, as if his balance, reaching for the norm, had slipped past it. His eyes, large on me, were not for me. " 'Twas a bad job, eh?"

I spoke across him, an overreacher too. At the moment our logic was not unlike. "How do we get it back?"

"Pa has the key. And he's gone to Montgomery."

"When will he return?" My courage sank, not of itself, but of my sad knowledge that it was my first and that I did not yet know how to maintain it for long.

His answer was at once monstrous and infinitely believable. For answer he pulled open the bottom drawer of the desk and slowly fingered, counting, the bottles there — tall white ones with a French label. "Three," he said. "Left me three. Three days."

Confused as I was by what I could not quite interpret, I could still follow him. The shifting, the thin-skinned are myself — I move as they move. With those who are all one dense fabric I cannot engage. "Doesn't he leave the key too?" I said. "Somewhere . . . somewhere you could find it?"

His eyes, sly now, were on me for me. He entered now and drew me after him, into that opposite atmosphere of the drinker, in which all that is revealed is to be avoided also. Tact was all around us now in a cat's-cradle of invisible string. He put his finger to his lips. We were trapeze artists, he indicated — hanging by our toes. There was a universe, there in a corner, to be sidestepped, to say nothing of all those conniving by many paths to meet us — among them a son who bore so humbly the name of his father, and a father with such a special consideration for his son.

Walking on the balls of his feet with a delicate lurching, he went toward a cupboard and opened it. Umbrellas and jackets hung there, and a monkey-black cape too small to be his own. From the folds of this he removed, using his left hand, a flat key. It was not for the door. This opened noiselessly into the courtroom, no doubt to allow the elder Fourchette to doff or assume whichever half of him suited the calendar. His son went through it silently in his ring-nosed gait, slipping across the bare, oiled floor to a row of filing cabinets lined up against the far wall, most of them old wooden ones like those in the office, a few of them, at the end, new and gray. He used the key to open a drawer in one of these.

"What name's it under?" He had put on a pair of glasses with dark-tinted lenses that, with his pleated shirt front, gave him the look of a man who chose to be at once dandified and blind.

"It's under Higby," I said. My courage returned with the sound, although the room was eerie under the single lamp over the entrance outside. "Had you better have a light?"

He muttered that he had forgot his flash, and pointed to a switch behind me. Six polished white domes sprang to light above us, far up against the high ceiling, attached to the brackets of a fixture that splayed far above us like a daddy longlegs. I cannot now remember whether I thought of the resemblance that night, or later. This was the first time I had been inside the courthouse. It is like the school building when school is out, I thought, recognizing that same hush of institutional guilt suspended. But the school had a different smell, the cheerful stink of bad children busy being weighed. Here, later on, they came to be found wanting.

But I cannot fragmentize what I knew later, saw then. I know that he had trouble finding the paper and that I stood there a long time.

This then is the courtroom as it was then and later, as it no doubt always is. It is a large room with an audience of chairs that sit in an immanent threat of waiting — when empty, for people; when crowded, to be cleared. Its spectrum is brown — tobacco, urine, disinfectant and the battered wood that holds them, porous flesh of the state, waiting to be replaced by stone. Here official cleanliness covers human dirtiness; some argue it other ways round. The final admixture is the judgment.

I heard him grunt when he found the paper. He stood over it, his head weary on his chest, moving to its counter-breath side to side. He took off the glasses and screwed up his eyes. I crept nearer behind him, near enough to catch his essence, blended with the faint, criminal flavor of the room. There would have been time to snatch the petition, seize it and tear it, be gone. Note that I did not.

"Turn off the light, would you?" he muttered. "Would you kindly?" I went to obey him, walking across the big room between the chairs. I heard the swift padding behind me. When I turned, he had vanished. He had had time to close the door to the hall and the office door. I could hear a thin clinking. When I entered, he was sitting at the typewriter, just closing the drawer. He lowered his eyes, covering his mouth with the back of his hand.

I was angered enough then at his tricks, his slowness, to stoop over him without speaking and take the petition from the muddled pile in front of him, delaying only to check that it was the right one. But when he stammered out what was I doing, where was I going, I stopped to answer him. Note that I did.

For his answer, he held out the key. By hint and suggestion, never saying an explicit word, but lapping me in the strengthless flow of his "tell-you-whats," his "sorries," he made me see what he skirted: that if the petition were missing without explanation, his father would come to know how often clients made him do the work over, how he concealed it by stealing the key. Once again I listened. And this time I spoke. Old Fourchette, I thought, so clever at leaving bottles, would be as subtle on keys.

"I'll bet he does know," I said. "How can you think he doesn't?"

His son said nothing; only the red of his cheek merged deeper, as if I had committed a solecism we must both ignore. He opened the cabinet without a further word and replaced the key in the cape. He is

1 4 1

like that fabled giant made of water, I thought, with his politeness, into whose form one's fist plunges meeting nothing, against whose bulk one cannot move. His right hand began to tremble. I gave the petition back into the other.

Later on, excusing myself, I told myself that one must never parley with the weak, for while you do so, they give you their weakness to hold. That is a fine bit of wisdom. But the hall of apothegms is made of mirrors; it is unlikely that we can pursue there even one image to its end. While they give you their weakness, you take time out for yours. And even this may not be the close.

At the moment, I promised myself that I would come back to see old Fourchette on Monday. I could still see that act, a tiny flare of action yet to occur, in the distance, only a few days away. I did not want to go home, thinking of it. The clock said eight. I would leave him to Ticely. I turned to go.

But he meant to thank me in his way. "Join me in a little refreshment," he said. "Always keep some on hand." He reached, not into the drawer as I had expected, but behind his father's chair, into a space behind two of the leather volumes, from which he drew a whisky bottle and two glasses. I had my growth, looked older than I was, and it is probable that he did not remember, had it mattered to him in that region where boys were men at my age, that I was eighteen. He must long since have reached the stage where he carried little over from minute to minute except the burden he carried always. And in that too, the drinker is compelling to those who, as he forces them to see, merely frivol on the norm. His bleared eye, fixed on the important, shamed me; I could not keep my own from that hand, so tremulous, that seemed to be held in flame.

He served me from the whisky bottle, then, turning his back to me, shielding what he was doing, he downed a quick shot from one of the bottles in the drawer, served himself another and turned around again, holding his glass, paler than mine, ostentatiously in front of him, like a child who takes two nickels from a drawer and comes forward saying, "Look! I took this," holding out one. I marveled that such a behemoth of a man could seem like a child, that such a huge child should persist at times in reminding one of a man. At these stealthy moments he was a naked man. And at others (as when I had challenged him about his father) he seemed suddenly to reveal that he knew this, and humbly inclining a forehead that had its patch of Mosaic wrinkles, to exact of me only the covenant that it not be admitted between us that he knew. Sitting opposite him in the small, hard chair reserved for clients, with his typewriter between us, a heavy old desk model shaped like a pew, I had a curious thought. I thought of the Romans, who read their augurs in the guts of fowl, and I wondered whether, if they had used men instead for this purpose, they would not have chosen to read their mysteries, their augurs, in the entrails of such a man as he.

Meanwhile he sat there, comforted, in the bit of social peace garnered from being able to do what he must within the public frame. I took my whisky with the testing sips of the novice. It had a wet-ashes flavor much stronger than the treasured Scotch that once or twice a year took the place of beer at home, but it did not make me drunk. I had eaten the sandwiches and chocolate, and although I was not yet aware of it, I had the steady head of the man whose plight is to loosen control, not to keep it. But I was mortally tired and stressed, and it was the hour of the day that for me often brings apperception.

For a fleeting minute I thought of Johnny — of our lost tryst together at the café. Even as a grown man, sharing a drink with another in some "local," the thin, surviving shadow of that sometimes dips by, in spite of all else that his memory meant to me later. What does not happen we keep forever green.

Fourchette had forgotten me, except perhaps that if anyone entered, my glass excused his glass. These ruminative, interim pauses that fall between men at such times, when the cup is held suspended, the knuckles absently rub the chin, the rain suddenly begins outside the room and is listened to and no one speaks although all hear, or someone says "the rain" and all nod and are silent — these are the most powerful moments in life, when its fathomless current is distinctly heard. The chair says, "Lo, I am the chair — in a museum a hundred years hence if I last"; the grate says, "I shall be gone, but now I am here"; the rain says, "I shall be the same then, though not for you, but tonight I am for you," and the silent room is filled with their thunder. On my deathbed I shall be thinking of such a moment if I am able, yearning for that old order where the drama is stilled and all that rich, anonymous current prevails.

"Where did you get the shell from?" I said.

He raised his head, bemused. "Lots of them, down home. Came in on the ships, I reckon. Don't rightly know from where. Used to have us one for a night-light. In the vestibule." He suddenly snapped on the desk light and held the shell over it, flushing the rosy epithelium that lay concealed. It glowed in the room's darkness like a great ear. "Hear the Gulf in it," he said, and set it down.

For a while we sat silent. His hand remained on the shell, his fingers closing on it, their muscles almost still. I thought of home, of how it would have been if I were entering there now with the petition torn in two, my mother and uncle sitting at our table, the two severed halves placed triumphantly before them, in the bitter charade I had planned. And now I could see that imagined action as a child's tantrum that changed nothing, that merely retreated from what it did not want, that had no argument of its own, that struck no blow. It was the tantrum of the dressmaker's son, reared among the minor contretemps of that trade — the awkward slash of scissors, the fabric that incontinently tore. It was a revolt scaled meekly to the world of my mother, to the reverberations of a dropped pot, a smashed plate, to all those petty mishaps with which women obscured the face of the serious, that they mustered so loudly against the real. It was this I should be fighting — not my uncle. He and I, in our male dreams, were allied. It was my mother I should be bitter against, who was using my uncle's dream to limit me, who, whether she knew it or not, was the natural, the female guardian of all the philistine. My heart contracted for a moment in piety; she had left that needle inside it. But it was she I should be withstanding, for refusing to reverence the other half of me, for fearing all the sore, imaginative life that was mine. If a blow was to be struck, it must be at her. And it must come from there.

"Meant to thank you," said Junior Fourchette. "Thank you kindly. Had it in mind." I heard his humbleness. It made me shiver in fear of my own.

"Can you change the name for me now?" I said. Shamelessly I used what I knew of him. "The name you got wrong?"

His hand stole toward his pocket. "Now?"

"If I wait," I said, "I might not keep my nerve."

He nodded slowly, intimately, as if we exchanged a professional secret. His eyes, steadied with sympathy, were almost sober. And in me, from some inner fount, the sense of how to manipulate my brothers rose like wine. To do it, you joined a little of your truth with theirs.

I thrust the petition under his glance, and pointed. "They want to give me that name — my stepfather's. But I'll have one of my own. I'll have any, before I have that one."

He bent to read. Alcohol coarsens only the coarse. To others, like him, it gives a fumbling clairvoyance. They receive what one has to say on the fine edge of their own trouble. One can speak to them as one might to some poor, spoiled priest who is the more safe because he will not remember, all the more catholic because he has been defrocked. He shook his head, reading where I pointed. "George Higby, Junior." A corner of his mouth pulled down. His hand came from his pocket. "No, not that one," he said. "No."

I helped him put the paper into the machine, but I could go no further. The machine, an ancient one, bristled with clumsy spools and spacers, and at that time I had not yet learned to type. The paper he used was thin as tracing sheets and lined, perhaps to guide him, in the same bluish purple as the lead in indelible pencils — a kind of paper I have never since seen. Any erasure tore it. "No, I'll do it over and then insert," he said. "We can keep the last page." This was the page with my mother's signature.

His face turned damp and pale again as he labored, and the sweat stood out on it in viscous beads. I had time to notice again the square patch of wrinkles in the center of his forehead, oddly autonomous in the wide, smooth expanse, as if the Lord had at the last moment ceded this much complexity to a child. Once he reached for the drawer by rote, hesitated and closed it again. When he came to the last page of the three to be recopied, he stopped, and remained for some seconds with his eyes half shut, head sunk on his chest. I had seen sick animals remain like that, motionless, harboring their illness. Twice he stayed his right wrist, that had begun to shake again, with his left hand. Then he took out a large handkerchief, folded it into a narrow sling, looped it around the trembling member, and held the two ends of the handkerchief tightly, creating a torsion, in his other hand. He did this with dispassion, like a man bandaging his own wound. And managing himself so, typing with the one hand in the sling, he finished the page. When he had done so, he looked up, the patch working in his forehead. "Hurry," he said, as if he had been running. "Now give me the name."

I gave it to him almost absently, in the way that, thinking of other things — a pinprick that did or did not occur a long time back — one gives one's own. The sound of my own voice startled me. He was still looking at me. I repeated it. "Pierre."

Still he waited. I stared back at him. His face was exhausted but clear. And the petition, what I could see of it in the machine, was perfect copy, typed for a brother.

When he spoke again, at first I did not understand him. "What's — what's rest of it?" he said. And there was my logic, exposed.

A last name. I had simply not thought of it. As for the second name of that other uncle, the distaff uncle, the stepbrother — I had never even known what it was. I cannot explain now, looking back down the long groove of more than time, of qualitative change, how this was — how it could be that I had not considered it at all. It is easier for the rich man to enter heaven than for any man to stand again inside the frame of those pristine days before he was conscripted to the practical world.

A curious blankness took possession of me, a whiteness of the mind. In after years, I have often since had a dream in which I find myself being examined in a language I have not learned, yet recall. I look down on an examination paper couched in words that are warped, yet familiar, algebraic symbols braiding almost to sense, musical notation that just evades a tune. And always there is an unfilterable whiteness interposed between the paper and me. Yet in my student life I never feared examinations. I think now that in those dreams I look down again on my lost logic, to which I can no more return than a ray of light, once chromatic, can go back again through the prism, to the single beam on the other side.

"Hurry!" whispered Fourchette. Even he, absurd in his patch and his tourniquet, had been able to show me the flaw. Even he, poor accomplice, was on the other side of that complicitous fog.

I reached out for the shell, and held it to my face. Its cheek was warm against mine. Turning it over, I listened to its endless respiring. Help me, I prayed. For I am still innocent. Give me a sign out of the current that prevails.

My own voice answered me. It came cracked but human, the sound of feeling gurgled up from a heart that did not pause to know it had it.

"Goodman," I said. It came up like a gout of salt blood, the secret I had not known I had. "Put down — Goodman."

Chapter VIII. Life Meets the Memoir. The Mannixes.

S O THE memoir and my life come together, only much sooner than I had planned. "Pierre." Said by me over twenty years ago in the Fourchette office, and written down here. But before I had done so, the voice had already come to me over the telephone, saying "Pierre." I had meant to keep her — life external — stationary, until I had completed the most difficult entry of all — into myself. Difficult because, as becomes increasingly clearer, the whole gradual process of my life has been one of using the truth falsely, meanwhile never lying to myself along the way. In memory I have always been painfully honest, indeed more honest than others need be. For if I should once lose the line of demarcation, then I should go down in confusion. Not to lose it, but to keep it, to be both true and false and to keep within myself the distinction — that has been the triumph until now. And when I sat down here, how many nights ago — fifteen — it was to be for the purpose, dangerously new to me, of using that honesty no longer as a mere bookkeeper to memory but as its surgeon, going one by one through the tissues accreted over some piece of truth that had been unaccountably lost but never, I could swear it, willfully perverted, and which now I myself, unaided, would lay bare. Then my outer life might start up again; I should know then which door to open, even if it should be disclosed to be mine.

But the present, moving to its own rough theorem, does not keep in strict equilibration with the past, as in the calculable old algebraic lunacies of Smith and Brown, who in the primers used so comfortably to navigate the world. "If Smith" (who is the present) "starts at a given point, traveling at the rate the earth goes round the sun, and Brown" (who is the past) "goes from the same point, at the same rate, in the opposite direction, the circumference of the earth being known, at what point are they likely to meet, or is Smith standing still in relation to Brown?" And what is the answer if a man, who is x, is in himself both Smith and Brown?

The answer is — that the phone rings. The answer is that bit by bit the arrogance of memory is being taken from me, the safety crumb by crumb. Up to now I have told myself that at least I am the taker, and that this is in its way a triumph. That no one can bear too long the bleat of his childhood, the blind, glaucous voice of his youth, without shame. And that I must get on to the trial, where, if the perversion began, so did the man.

But the phone rang, and I chose to listen. I will listen, I thought, long enough to find out why, of all the many there might have been to fear, I chose her.

"Pierre," she said again, but this time there was no question in her voice, and I, who had said "Yes," said nothing. The silence fell between us like a rest in music; we plumbed it and rested there. Then my inner dialogue began again, its shorn fugue mending. If I let the present in now, I shall never be sure where safety lies. But is that what I fear? Meanwhile I said to her, "Yes. This is Pierre."

"I know," she said, scarcely forming the words. I heard her breathing, hard but slowing, the *râles* of a child run a long way to fling itself inside a door and lean back, pressed against it, to breathe. I remembered how, long ago, claw-fingers clutching my mother's the long way out on the Underground, my breath would go faster and faster with the wheels until it seemed as if the suction of my love would draw out of me the necessary air — until I was inside that door again, the terrible angina of absence was over, and I could breathe. And I thought how odd it was that this, on which I had never allowed myself to dwell in tenderness for myself, I remembered now in pity for her.

Before I spoke — I do not know what I would have said — she spoke.

"I am not ashamed," she said. So she told me again what she had already said in a hundred pleading, oblique acts of submission, of favor, and what, in that one night's grappling, she had shown me in all its nuances, shrinking and bold — but had never said in so many words. There are women from whose lips, true as any, the three simple words — the declaration — break continuously, like three golden bubbles, as if they had a fountain of such constantly forming, springing golden from inside. And there are others, like her, who can do everything but speak them, who have tongues witty and easy for all but this. Who send instead mute gifts selected with the perfect stroke of adoration, letters built in the careful, flat planes of friendship, as cunningly as a house of cards which the breeze from that one triplet of words would make fall. And who, when they give someone the strange, mute gift of themselves, do so with lovely simplicity, feeding him with their fingers, opening their nudity to him with quiet laughter, pressing their faces against his secret flesh, his against theirs, in a streaming abandonment of mouths and hands and hair. But for whom, as for some men, as for me, nothing of the flesh is as bare as the certain nudity of words.

"I am not ashamed," she said to me, with the sadness of declaration. Not, she was saying to me, of that night either because it had been or had been only one, nor of letting me see what all the nights between had been, nor of coming to me, along the filament, here. And I thought that her face, if I could see it, would have the *triste* dignity of a woman who lets a last garment slip to the ground.

"I am the one to be ashamed," I said, thinking that even if she had come, not across the wire, but taking up her blanket instead, barefoot through the four-o'clock streets, even the street-corner churls must have bowed their heads to her trouble, turning their eyes, shamed for me or themselves, aside.

"That's all right," she said brusquely. And as quickly, she was clothed. No, I thought to tell her, stay as you were. Else you will never approach me. And is that what I fear?

"And you?" she said. "I didn't wake you?"

"No. I was awake."

"I had a feeling you were. And — I couldn't sleep. I kept hearing the boats."

Their house, my flat, are ten blocks apart north-south, and almost the same short distance west of the East River. At times, as old houses will, they vibrate like decks to the river traffic's gliding calls. And now and then, in the foolish telephone interchange bred between incipient lovers, she and I had stopped to hear one of those long, humid blue notes simultaneously, entranced at the viability of sound, that made it possible for us to squabble metaphysically over who heard it first, and by what blended aural image of ear on phone, on phone.

"I've been working here nights." I did not know how to begin. Nor, for the first time, how to leave.

"Oh. Then you aren't . . . at the office these days?" Her voice was timid. Then she had not called there. Or pretends she has not, I thought, but could not persuade myself that she lied. I knew the spoor of honesty too well. If it were I, I would have called and concealed it. If she were more like me, I thought, I should have nothing to fear.

"No. I'd arranged for time off." The next day, not before. But my tongue had already twisted the tense, reminding me how well it knew how to give nothing away. "If you called — they think I'm out of the city."

"I — did not call." Her words came after a pause, and I imagined her mouth as she said them, its frank lines that always expected the same of others, even of me — and I could not bear not to be honorable with it too. In the small things, I thought. That do not matter.

"I arranged for it the next day," I said. "I've been doing something of my own. Something I've had to be alone for. I tried writing you a letter — but I couldn't explain." I waited for her protest but none came.

"It had nothing to do with you," I said. Lies breed lies, I thought. But for me, the truth does it as well. Which part of me will she believe, the truth or the lie? That is part of the fear. Which.

"Then I was wrong. I thought it had. That's why — I could call." Her words came in a rush. "I thought — I think now I have for a long time . . . there's . . . some part of your life you have to keep to yourself. And because we'd made love, I thought I could trespass. But I was going to tell you now . . . that I could . . . that I would — manage not to."

The phone trembled in my hand, at my lips.

"But if I was wrong, then —" Her voice altered, retreated to the promised distance. "Then I should not have called. Then I am ashamed."

"No. Never." I was grateful to the mask of the phone, that let me say it, that kept her from me, from the helpless cycle of touch that would have begun again had she been here. And again there was a rest, a silence.

"Listen!" she said suddenly. And I thought — now the thread will break. And I can leave.

"Yes?" I answered. I should warn you. Only for myself.

"Not to me," she said, as if she had heard me. "The boats. They're beginning."

They had begun all around us, pushing the city up toward morning, the island voices. We listened on our peculiar electronic island, on which, from a safe distance, we could breathe in unison, almost as in love. Heard by each of us through our separate windows, and doubled again through phone on phone, the chorale of the river pierced and tremored, until it seemed as if all around us sleepers must awake and join us, or must be held by the island breath of the water in a legend that endlessly lulled.

"It's getting light here," she said, and from a depth almost of sleep

152

I answered, "Here too." My head bowed against my hand, and I must have dreamed off a little, into a legend where the two of us listened neither for ourselves nor for the other, but, acutely together, to the rich current as it came.

Then I awoke, but still in the spell, like someone started up from a dream of drowning, who leans back, before he opens his eyes, on his deep urge to be drowned. Perhaps, I thought, in my sleep I told her everything. From the beginning.

"Have you gone?" I said.

"No. But I can sleep now. Keep — keep well."

The light was paling, reassembling the room. In a moment I should have to wake to it. The boats were still.

"I lied," I said. "I was avoiding you."

"It doesn't matter. I've watched you. I know how you are."

Of course she watches. How easily I forget that others do.

"How?" I said. "What do you know?" That I never knew your brother. That I was not always Pierre, and now am never wholly who I say I am. That I, who meant to be so undispersed, so single, have played for so long with the protean gap between what is and what might be that I am almost no one at all. "What do you think I am?"

This was the longest silence. Her answer prolonged it. "Honest."

Innocence, I thought. Beyond belief, this innocence. Can one believe it? From far below in myself, from farther off than it had ever come before, I felt a flicker of mine.

And this was what I feared. The receiver slipped from my hand to the desk, hanging soundlessly on the thick manuscript pile. How had it come about; how had it ever come about? After the first compromise, I thought, all others follow. I learned to accept that long ago. No man, after a certain age, can fail either to know this or to marvel, like a man breathing under an avalanche, that under its numb, insidious powder-weight he is still — though not the same — alive. But how does it ever come about that the return of what his maturity mourned, his youth meant to keep so savagely pure, is the one further weight he cannot bear? That I tremble in fear of what, if ever it quickened again, harsh and lovely, up from the impossible dead, I meant to greet with joy?

From the desk, the phone spoke. A broad blue stained the room, assembled now in sanity, all its bargains plain. In spite of them, in the face of them, I picked up the phone. "I lied," I said into it. "From the beginning. I lied."

I waited for her answer, but none came. The return is not that verbal, that easy. And perhaps before I said it, I had made sure that she was gone.

For I know now what I fear. I fear that I may trust her.

Chapter IX. A Day in 1936.
Morning in Tuscana. The Courtroom.
Evening at Home. He Leaves Tuscana.

ON AN afternoon, then, late in the August of 1936, a young man and his mother could have been seen walking down the main street of a small town in Alabama, on their way to the courthouse for the granting of the petition that was to change his name. If you were a stranger in town and had idly chanced to ask who they were, either because, together in their dark clothes, they made such a clear print on the hazel afternoon, or because you, your informant and they were the only ones foolish enough to be out on the heat-stunned street at this hour, you would have been told that it was the wife of George Higby, the second foreman at Rhine's, and her son. Rhine's is the mill that you see for yourself, without being told, must once have drawn in every man around, but looks now like a collection of old cigar boxes at the base of a pyramid. The latter is one flank of the five-mile stretch you can see of the dams, about which you know a good deal, since this is probably the reason, via the overflow of the Denoyeville boardinghouses, that you are here at all.

It is possible that you will not even be told that the couple verging toward you are not natives of the region, for your informant, a courthouse loafer by the smell and the stubble of him, has a curious eclecticism toward out-of-the-country foreigners, for such an ill-educated man. In his long residence here, a matter of almost two hundred years now in one version of him or another, he has seen all kinds of trade and tackle — Dutchmen to Huguenots, odd Pole tailors, even a coastal seeping of Spanish — and except for an infrequent rabbling of zeal against the infidel, he has neglected all of them almost to the point of tolerance. He has little energy to spare against that kind of alien; he is a xenophobe of skin, of the special foreigners who for the last hundred years have been on his neck, outnumbering him, burrowing in his groin and making cheese of his brain, ready at any time, he is sure, to hang their bone-chant on him, doubtless stirring his soup at this moment with the white clavicles of girls. Therefore the Higbys, here only eight or nine years and a quiet sort who keep to themselves, are in a way his colleagues, though never his kin, even as you are, and he is pleased to join you both in the affable custom of the place, which is to retail, even to a stranger, the secondary gossip that will make him feel at home.

George Higby, he tells you, is expected to be chief foreman when old Blankenship steps down. The wife does high-class dressmaking on the side; the boy is hers. Neat-looking woman, he adds, as the two pass on the other side of the street, the woman plump and convex in dark blue, with her hair coifed tight over her ears, the son heads taller than she, man-size ankles jutting out of his serge "best," walking beside her as young men do with their mothers at that age — hanging back, hands in his pockets, blond head cast down.

As they cross in front of you where you stand, in front of Semple's store, your informer gives her a respectful nod, his eye straying to the pavement at the corner, where a sunken horse trough bears a whitewashed street name, for the exchange of cake plates is an *Almanach de Gotha* in the town, and he has remembered with whom she takes tea. Son's a real scholar, they say; old Miss Pridden at the museum has got him a scholarship to New York. And here, if your accent is cooler and drier than his own, he will suddenly rein in. He has done all that politeness, to your sort, requires of him, and besides, he has noticed that Mrs. Higby and her son have not turned the corner to Pridden Street but have paused at the foot of the courthouse stairs.

"Ah-hah, New York," he says with a spit to the side, and he waits, with a tucked-in grin, for you to declare yourself, your station, which he doubts you can do as well as he. He knows, the grin says, views supposedly held up there of certain matters down here, but excuse him if it just won't hold water with him that under that skin you don't secretly feel the same. In which case, his squint says, your case is pitiful, for he has seen before the unease of your sort when "they" step aside for you, or worse still, poke Uncle Tom fun at you in a way that under his hot eye and lazy nether lip they would never dare — except that they know it pleasures him to see what they think of you — a sort not born, as he is, to command. No fine talk, he knows, can give you what he has — the rested psyche of a man who from birth has had somebody handy to despise. At the moment, however, a little current of interest blows toward him from the courthouse, and he is reminded of a spectacle there that will engage him, though not, by any invitation of his, you. This is Tuscana's business and hence his, down here where the pursuit of what happens to people is a serious and open entertainment. He ambles off to attend to it. As the proverb says, his glass is small but he drinks from his glass.

But if your accent is within even a few hundred miles of being as soft and spatulate as his, then things are quite otherwise; the conversation begins and ends differently all the way around. Been boarding in Memphis, have you; by God, he's known a thing or two about Memphis in his time. He sends you a look from beneath his lashes, and either from your response or from what he sees, the set of your haunches or the fleshy fold under your eyelids, he feels free to name a street that used to be wide open, a particular place, the damnedest, you'd never notice it in passing, back of a livery stable. You have been there too, and this does it — what closer fealty between strangers than the fact of having been to the same one of those? Used to be a Polish woman here, no longer; still, he's able to give you a street and a number, even some encouraging gossip about Mrs. Emerson, with whom you currently board. And when the couple, mother and son, pass before you in their slow, dark swath along the street, he answers your idle question with information more intimately slanted. Boy looks as if he'd like to be anywhere but where he is, at his mother's elbow; from Alabama to Timbuctoo a widow mama is the same. Saw him do right well, though, in the Kid Gloves match in the new Charlotte school gym last year. Stood up against Jack Lemon's boy, who's old enough to vote and had no call to be there at all.

When Mrs. Higby crosses he gives her the same modest greeting, but when she is out of hearing he adds that she was Higby's dead wife's sister, something in the Bible about that, he isn't sure whether for or against. Anyway, there's been no issue of either marriage, and poor Higby is going to do the next best thing, adopt the son. Expect that this, maybe, or something akin to it, is what they're heading to the courthouse for now. He keeps an eye on them, but you, being your kind of stranger, might prove to be even better entertainment, and he is convinced of this when you offer him a cigar. Ever see any cockfights in Memphis? If you have a little time on your hands this evening, you might notice some activity not too far from where you're standing, in fact in back of the store. Store is kept by E. V. Semple, a man prominent in several fields. You think you have heard of him, you can't exactly say where. As your informant strikes his match, he momentarily holds one thumb against the other in a peculiar way, the bent knuckle of the right at the joint of the stiffly extended left, forming an angle that might be nothing — or a letter easy to read. He squints when your eyes meet his, as your thumbs do the same. It is when the two of you look elaborately away from each other, down the street, that the woman and her son again come to mind. The pair at the courthouse door seem to have been having one of the low, intense exchanges of persons who do not make scenes. Then the woman turns suddenly, her wide skirt belling with the force of it, and goes in. Whether the young man will follow seems to be in question. Then, as if he knew he would all the time, he goes in.

"Court in session this afternoon," says your new companion. "Judge just back from Montgomery. Every time he's fresh from there, it's a rip-snorter. Say he goes down there to get himself an injection of the law."

By instinct the two of you, hands at ease with cigars now, turn slowly and regard the courthouse. The street is as motionless as a strip of desert sand. Heat oscillating above it makes a pattern, light running up watered silk, that you have known since a child. It will be different inside there; the climate of law is always opposite. In the winter cold snaps it will be musty with steam and hard as snuff to breathe. It will be dark as an old bruise inside there now, if not cool. On the way your informant, known to you now by name as you are to him, tells you that no one minds if the judge hogs both sides of the law here, people are kind of proud of it; besides, he always gives you your money's worth, always puts on a good show. Gossip was, when he first came here, before the speaker's time, long before, that he never finished his law study in Louisiana, never finished it anywhere at all. But nobody bothers about that nor ever did, figuring a thing done often enough and common enough is surely legal. By now, if it wasn't, half the leases and liens in the county wouldn't hold, say nothing of the jails. You nod agreeably; down here people are comfortable about such things; to you nothing of this sort has to be explained.

As you enter you are both quiet before today's matter of interest, the natural spectacle always provided a man who keeps himself healthy in mind. Up North they may believe what they like, but this is a country of humanists, where the deepest theater is what happens to people. You have been bred to it, as you have been bred — not as they have — to know that life cannot be passed without violence, without resignation, and that a man who has no time to watch has no time at all. Forward, in the mauve shadow of the rostrum, are the judge, the mother and the son. The day has provided. Slouch and take your ease.

There were two such men at the back of the courtroom that day.

And the gist of that day is that I let my mother come to it, to its rostrum, unaware that anything had changed. As I look back there, I know that I have never done any one thing more irreparable than what I did by doing that, nor any more natural. If by "natural" one means not merely that red sequence of tooth and claw which drops hunter on hawk, hawk on mole, but the feral, inner sequence of a man. That red sequence in which we are sent first against ourselves, then, as we grow cleverer at eluding, against others we can use in place of ourselves. And in the order of things, those we use are the nearest to hand.

As I walked home that night from Fourchette's, what had happened there seemed to me already almost a fantasy, the enactment of a daydream I had never before so fully admitted I had. The next morning I tried to forget it, almost to persuade myself that it had never been. I could do neither. I was never able to deceive myself as openly as some. And memory, that was to keep me so faithful, was already beginning to take from me the strength that knows how to put what is done with aside. I was already of the persuasion, as I remain, that what we do is never really done with. I had yet to learn that with what I failed to do it would be the same.

And so the days, not many of them, in which I could have willed things otherwise, went by — days of grace we like to fancy them, contra the facts that tell us that if the precious interim of our inaction could come again, it would come again in the same terms of ourselves — again the constricted lover would not will himself to kiss, again the man on the beach would move just too late to lift the lost face from the wave. Days during which, if I could have brought myself to tell my mother what I had done, much might have been different — and during which I vengefully did nothing.

I told myself that I was afraid to reveal what I had done to her hopes, to see her rage, that I had never yet seen. And this was true, and foresighted. I was afraid, and her rage, when it came, though not as I had envisioned it, was dreadful. I reasoned also that in the "due process" peculiar to the Fourchette office — even I could see that this was like a coil of rope payed out as needed, sometimes hawser-thick with ceremony, at others thin and neglected as old tatting thread — there was a good chance that the petition might not come to light again for months, by which time I would be far away. And this was reasonably true. But beneath all that I told myself was the deeper truth — that I longed to see the rage, to strike the blow. So I let myself swing in the lap of things-as-they-were, and "did" — as I persuaded myself — "nothing." And I was not disappointed. No wonder we ultimately adore the *status quo*, hating the sense of it only in our tragic moments, or as good boys to the preceptors who tell us that it is too low a form of mental life for creatures risen to the distinction of a future and a past. For meanwhile it creeps for us, doing our good work and our dirty, giving us a pale respite in that Eden of the animals from which we are barred.

Once during those days a particular chance came; it had no number on it; it was not that illusory "second" one to which we limit ourselves; it was merely a particular one of the infinite train, offered us with the precision of minutes on a dial, whose progression, in order to live sanely, one ignores. On the Friday after the Monday on which Mr. Fourchette Senior had been due to return home, newly swollen with law and order, from Montgomery, I came home late in the evening after my weekly job of loading and unloading trucks at the market. Summer market days were thronged now, even in Tuscana, and went on until midnight. Our house had no hall, no hall table, but on my way through the kitchen I passed the shelf on which our scanty mail was always laid. A long envelope lay there, Fourchette stationery, addressed to my mother. It had been opened, I saw, and for a moment my breath bounded with relief — the secret was out; my need to decide, that I had pretended did not exist, was over. All sorts of hazards crossed my mind — that the petition, bearing one new name or the other, had somehow been granted *in absentia*, or else that Mr. Fourchette Senior was communicating with my mother, having discovered his son's fraud. I unfolded the enclosure. It was not the petition but its forerunner, gazing up at me with the same neuter, conscious lack of blame with which the messenger gives the tidings that open the Greek play. It asked all please to take notice that such and such a petition would be presented on such and such a date — a week hence — at the opening of court on that day or as soon thereafter as counsel could be heard, that an application would then and there be made for an order of the court directing a change of name of said infant, pursuant to the civil rights law of the State of Alabama, and that said petitioner would then and there "apply for such other incidental relief as the court may deem just and proper." Signed *Hannibal Fourchette, Attorney for the petitioner,* and dated the previous day. Although a projected name should probably have been incorporated in the notice, none appeared there; the form of Mr. Fourchette's legal notices, like so much of his law, was his own.

Through the kitchen door I could see almost all the rest of the house: the nearer end of the sitting room, then my door, closed although I kept no concrete secrets behind it, and theirs, closed with the same habit of reserve. They might be here, already behind it, or since it was Friday, not yet returned home from the café. I could knock at the door or wait up for them.

In the sitting room, dimmed with shades both night and day, my aunt's old parlor suite stood at attention on cabriole legs, its fabric, never renewed, holding the remote look of winter cloth in a warm season, each claw-footed leg clutching its ball. I felt as clenched around the immovable as these. I could not let go of what I meant to let happen. Beneath the periphery of my glance I could see the envelope lying where I had dropped it, on the table next to the canister of tea. Long ago, on the night they left for Memphis, another envelope had lain there. The old canister, years since emptied of its original hoard, had been purged too of that mute twinge of remembrance which it had once held for my mother as well as for me. But I would keep all the fidelities that others seemed almost

162

intent to lose. If I recalled how once she had set out the bit of money, of Twining's tea for me, I would also counterbalance it; I would tally too how I had wept for her in the privy, with the wry gape of the child who first learns, left behind, that someday he too will want to leave. Over the years I had almost been persuaded to forget this, until that night in Fourchette's office when, as I sat glass to glass with his son, that poor squeezing-vessel who drank liquor and sweated truth, some inner guardian had risen to remind me that leaving, unless it had its own argument, changed nothing. And straightaway, up like a djinn from a dust heap, an argument, strangely my own, had been provided. I could well marvel now with Demuth over "the mind," seeing without mysticism its literal power over matter, wreaked daily, ignored and repeated in the perpetual associative hum that tossed up people like analogies, names like truths, truths like shells. To live daily with that marvel, its surprises, even its hurts and horrors, to be logged with a history of my own to interpret, perhaps at the end of life, luckily so far away, to understand — seemed to me all the meaning that one would ever crave. Voicelessly I repeated to myself the new name, signal from that part of myself I meant to preserve.

And still I stood there in the silent house, wondering whether she, they, were behind the door there, at its core. From old habit my muscles motioned me toward the outside, to seek out that accustomed seat with my back against the farthest wall. In another part of my brain a fantasy that I knew to be such slunk back and forth like a ghost hoping to be relieved of its round — the image of myself tearing the envelope across, waiting up to tell them my secret, or bearing it forward through that door, inside.

By an effort of will I kept myself where I was, staring out through the window at the landscape I had lived with for so long. It was moonlit now to a pure absence of color — but in those days, in any case, I rarely saw the colors of the world. The world was black, white or gray in those days, in such tones, one is told, as might be recorded if one could use the eye of an animal as a camera. But one need not go to the animals for such; one need go only to the inner eye of the utterly self-contained. There the world rose for me as always, a backdrop, in its center tonight the dam, clear as a Nuremberg mountain around which my wishes, my judgments flew like angels out of Dürer, in moral striation, untouched by the error of pity, in a wooden perfectibility of wing.

If I had had some mentor to whom I could have said, "Save me from what I shall do!" I might have wavered, but she was the only such mentor I had ever had. I told myself the filial truth that one comes to, that a parent forgets what one is like or has never known it, that whether or not she had a history of her own she was only an actor in mine. I turned from the window and looked at her door. Even if she was behind it, it was closed. So I moved away from her and gave to memory the blame which should have been given to the ancient grudge that antecedes it, to the bias that comes through the archway of birth with us as we are born. So I left the envelope on the table and "did," as I persuaded myself, "nothing."

The day came, as none fails to. In answer to a telephone call that my mother, all agog, had made on the eve of it, we had learned that the judge would be busy at other affairs in the morning; we need not present ourselves until the afternoon session. Later I heard her awkwardly trying to coax my uncle; it was never her habit to coax, and the sound of her voice, alternately its stolid self and the tiny voice that some women make when they wheedle, made me blush for her, and against her. She wanted him to take the day off from work and accompany us.

"No, Dora," I heard him say. "Let it be." He would by nature of course stiffen away from any public parade of his feelings, but he would be constricted too, I assumed, by that vulgarity of class which held it vulgar to feel. My mother, on the contrary, was in an access of the same delight that moves the grave Jew to get tiddly at his son's circumcision, that sends the whore to strut austerely a step behind the little daughter who goes before her through the cheap streets, crimped head under cotton Communion veil, on her way to partake for the first time of her Lord.

"And let the boy be," I heard him add.

I came in just then and joined them at table, wondering if he had any doubts of me, of my conduct tomorrow. I had nothing against him; I was glad that he was not coming.

Although we seldom said grace, I bowed my head as if ready for it to be spoken. Extraordinary, in what detail that last scene, last supper, comes back to me. I see the cloth with its pattern of dulled blue-and-white daisies, a frayed thread hanging from the collar point of the shirt my uncle had just changed to, my mother's pricked hands and my own, poreless and young — all the stray facts of that room convened now in space as if they had been rubies. Powerless, a god outside the machine, I look down on our three bowed heads from above.

"Just think," said my mother, glancing from one to the other of us in her fool's joy, "by this time tomorrow there'll be two George Higbys!"

She could have said nothing better to show me how gladly she hurried to annul forever my father and all the heritage of that other life, hers too, that went with him; how eager she was to clip the foreskin, veil the eyes, to gain for me — for her own salvation — the great enclosure of the norm.

My uncle gave his cough and did not look at me. Was he less self-deceiving than she? He bent his head over his plate. "Let him be."

The next morning I woke early, a pulse thudding in my throat, my eyes wide. In that tinder-paper house one could hear every domestic sound, but this was not always an irritant; often I listened gratefully to the chirruped signs of the family unit encamped with me, in whatever bondage, against our mutual wilderness, the world. My uncle, on his way to shave, cleared his throat on the same modest, middling note he made every morning — impossible to say whether he greeted the day or deplored it. My mother could be heard up and about but did not knock as usual to awaken me; did she think, in the generous overflow of last night's glee, to allow me, as myself, a largesse of dream? Or was she thinking to keep me as safe as possible until that great moment when I should be hatched anew? I could not convince myself that she suspected anything.

Through the window as I dressed, I saw my uncle departing. Seeing him from behind, I noticed for the first time the long, good shape of his head, his fine square posture. I knew well that the latter had nothing to do with this special morning, with me. It was merely that I was seeing him as a passer-by might, instead of at the looming range which makes the intimate invisible. So slight was the silhouette that he made on any nearer awareness, so lacking in the antitheses with which others roughened the vision, that I was surprised to discover, as I watched him recede, how much I respected him. He must have earned it at the rate he did everything, imperceptibly. It came to me too late that through him I could have approached my mother. He would have acceded, and I could have asked him, I did not know why, any more than I knew what had moved him to attach his name to me. As I thought of last night it occurred to me, with the first shiver of interest I had ever felt for him, that of the three of us he might be the least self-deceiving. Perhaps that was all the mystery there was behind a man who seemed to live from modulation to modulation, undisrupted by central song. "Let it be; let him be," he had said to my mother. And he had bowed his head to hide from her, not from himself, his foreknowledge that there would never be in any real sense two George Higbys.

With that thought I forgot him, turning to regard the cramped room that I was leaving. I should never quite hate it as I meant to hate the rest of Tuscana; it had been mine. As this last morning was mine. My wallet was on the dresser behind me, holding the small remainder of my last week's earnings. I took it up and was halfway out the window — only three feet from the ground and in an angle concealed from the rest of the house — when by a sudden stricture of the eye I saw the room as it would look, without me, to my mother. This would happen to me often later on, this inner flick that put me without warning in another's place, and I learned to accept its advent as I might that of an old crony who audited but never advised. I took a bit of paper from the wallet, a pencil from the cleared desk, wrote a line and tossed the note on the pillow: *Back in time.*

I could have left her to fears that I would be late or even had decamped, to any number of facets of that anxious doubt she always had of me, that I presumed all mothers had of their children — the formless worry in which she kept disaster warm for me, seeming to hold me already foredoomed. But I was no longer a child, with the simple brutality of a child. She was the first woman I left, as she is for most men, and she herself had taught me that a few ritual comforts left behind could ease the mind of the leaver, that there was a certain neat kindness in which the collapse of trust might be enclosed.

And all that morning I walked about Tuscana, my eyes prying out its ugliness and weaknesses, storing them up to remember. Most of the middle-aged will no longer understand what I intended by this, but some — quite ordinary people, but still joined to their youth by an umbilicus of sensibility, meditation or suffering — will know. Years later, a man told me the story of how he and two friends, on the eve of their graduation from a harsh school that each had mastered but loathed, swore a joint pact that no one of them in times to come would ever refer to his youth as "golden." In the same way, bathetic and alone on that valedictory morning in Tuscana, I meant never to gloss mine.

Gray to the eye as the town was, calloused with its own desuetude, it was not these physical attributes only whose print I meant to keep. There was another attrition always felt, never phrased, a deep circulatory lack, more of the brain than the heart, that pervaded the land as invisibly as did the shabby-sweet aura of some cheap, anonymous vegetation that I had never learned to identify. If there had once been a land-language here, green or otherwise, it had now been translated into terms of the dams, and Tuscana had been shunted away from these. The vegetation I knew was its people, their faces and voices, the cat's-cradle patterns of their mornings and evenings, the tenor of their ways projected on their streets.

Therefore, as I walked in and out of these, I observed how, on their slack filth, the ingenuous, lemon coolness of the early day deepened to a dirty yellow, hot and barred as the zoo-pelt of a lion. I noted without charity certain tribal concavities of face often to be found here, narrownesses between eyes, of jaws, a certain reddish-haired skin — never browning in the men and crumpling early in the women — of a fairness almost nasty, as if the very theory of the place had bred this phosphorescence. And as with any grand in-quisitor, my step seeded the ground as I walked it, and what I looked for sprang up to be found.

There were three places I turned away from. I did not go down Pridden Street, and I did not follow to its dead end a path that now led nowhere, that once had led to the hill, now entombed, from whose myrtle Johnny and I had looked down. And when I came to the edge of niggertown, I stopped on its border line, remembering my walks there on those fermenting evenings of adolescence — when to be up late, to walk late anywhere is still an act of pride, savage and emancipatory — and how the night music of these people, their nearness, had rested me as well. What I felt about them, then or later, was never egalitarian; I was a neutral here as I was every-where else. But no one can live near the ghetto without feeling its instruction, even if only as we feel the presence of those orders of nuns who pray for us against our wishes, interceding for us un-ceasingly with a heaven in which we do not believe. I looked down the lanes at their yard heaps, always reactive, always changing; through the flung doors I smelled the close odors bred of fealty, heard its steady, contralto drone. This was worthy, I told myself, but it was not Tuscana; this was that city of tribulation which is bed-ouin, which is anywhere, and I turned aside from it and went on.

The town was a small one; in two or three hours I had can-vassed it, up one street and down another, and if I found any nook or face that flowered, I ignored them and went on. I had no intentions of justice toward it. No one but the years ahead could inform me that as a man adores or despises what he comes from, so is he invested with grace or malformed.

And when I came home, not stepping in through the window this time, but walking through the front door, I found my mother in that state of apprehension which levitates its harborer above the heads, voices, company of others, making him literally a wire-walker, an *exalté*. She had not found the note; blown by a breeze from the window, it had floated to the floor and lodged under the bed. Kneeling, I saw it, too far back for my arm but not for my eye, lodged in that dim plane of quiet like an old inhabitant. My head felt too heavy for my neck, and for a minute I could have wished to stay there, my eye growing rounder as it had as a child, watching what had escaped the broom to trouble or supply this lilliput country, a penny as big as a table, a dust curl that must be a dune to them, two steel girders of pins. When I got up off my knees I found that she had followed me and was standing there behind me, her hands tranced from her sides. Although it was not yet noon, she was already dressed in her best, with a towel pinned round her waist, and this — the towel and her distraught, faraway manner — put me in mind of the poor girl who had lived downstairs of us in World's End, a girl either deserted or dreaming of it, who, until she had been taken away, rose each morning, donned the same party satin and spent the day so, a towel always around its gradual soil and her arms a little out from her sides, as if, if she only could keep uncracked the enamel of her preparation, everything would yet come true. My mother's face, its fixity not for me but above me, had not moved one jot from its neatness, yet seemed blurred. Was I mistaken, was it the weight on my own neck, or had her head taken on an imperceptible tremor? Or was it the nimbus of the terrible heat that mazed us all? I noted, perhaps because I had been noting faces all morning, a blanched flatness above her mouth; who would ever have thought she had so much space there, stiff and white, between her upper lip and nose? Her hands moved toward me in two jerks and her lower teeth came out to worry a puffed place in the upper lip that I had never noticed before, just over the right eyetooth, a small hanging unevenness of the lip line.

"I thought you were gone," she said again, not talking to me but about me, as if — having no friend of that sort here, no confidante whom she could call up as women do, to whom she could say without preamble, handing over her desolation, "he is gone" — she were handing it, the news, to me.

"For good?" I said. There was an echo there. Someone else had once said it.

She did not even nod. Her fixity answered me.

"Why would you think that?" I said, but that was for cover, for time, that was for so much talk, and she did not answer it either. Because when I went, it would be for good, and she knew it. Because she had forced me, made me to do something against my nature, and deep down she awaited from me before I left a reply that would make her answer for it, hurt her somewhere. In the same way a man walking in the dark, expecting a friend's knife from behind, will wheel suddenly on no one, his fist already clapped to his chest at the spot where the point will appear. She shook her head, not in denial but as if she were trying to shake something from it, and put her finger tips to her temples.

"I seem to be shivering," she said. "I've done so all morning. In this heat. How can that be?" Then she squared her shoulders, tucked in her chin, brought her hands to their customary clasp under her breast. "I'll make us a pot of tea," she said, her voice once again in its notch like the rest of her, and turned her back to me as if she had nothing to fear from me, as if to do this were the most natural thing in the world.

Thousands of times she had brought in the tea and I had not heard the small jangles and clinkings incidental to its making as I heard them now, with sharpened breath, with the pitch of acuity which comes to us in the midst of our own dramas, freezing every gesture — an outburst of a hand, a down-sealing eyelid — into bas-relief in the rear galleries of the brain. I had heard them in the same way on the evening she had told me she and my uncle were to marry. Now it was I who had something to tell her.

Obediently I had sat down to the teapot, as from time immemorial, at her bidding. Now I got up suddenly, left the table and went to the window, standing there, looking out. This habit at least I had not got from her. Yet as I stood there, words pressed against my teeth and I held them in forcibly with my lips, without knowing what they would be when they came, what they were.

"Don't go today," I said then, almost inaudibly. "Don't go to court."

"You have to go when the calendar says you do." I heard the strength return to her voice at the thought of an authority beyond us, at her first swallow of tea.

I turned. "Let me go. Let me go there alone."

She was drinking from the cup with both shivering hands clasped around it to warm themselves, as she had used to do on the fog-bound winter afternoons of my childhood. She saw me watching their tremor.

"It's nothing. Nothing but what I should have recognized the signs of before." She rubbed one knee, her left. "Why . . . mind now . . . only last week at a fitting my leg trembled so it wouldn't bear my weight, and I had to sit down." My heart sank, suddenly recalling the obscure disease, never defined to me, that had bound my aunt. But her voice was not tragic, only musing and a little self-mocking. "I suppose it takes some women one way, some another." She veiled her face with the teacup. "Nothing . . . but what . . . comes to women of my age."

I had never thought of her age; she had always been there. Even to eyes other than mine she must have been then in that middle plateau where many persons, particularly the unpretentious, having weathered so far, seem interminably to stay. She was about fifty now, no, past that, although except for her hands she could have been taken for much less. My uncle was five years younger.

Through the steam from the cup her face appeared both sad and coy. And even to me, her son, her voice had held the tone, half fated, half smug, of women when they speak of their bodily mystery, that even in its decline bloods them to the universe, making a man only a step above the drone with its single, discontinuous sting.

"Besides," she said — and now I was included in her mockery — "how could you go alone? I am the petitioner."

So she was, and now that the tea had warmed the whiteness away from her mouth, letting me hear too that voice sleeked with the midwife's purr, half seminal, half Eumenidean, I could remember again how powerful a one she was.

She brooded across at me, smiling, and I had a sense of how in her, always until now so much the same for me, there must be multiples that she could bring out if she wished it, if she dared it, one after the other like a *diseuse,* like a conjurer, one by one.

"Great booby that you are," she said. "All six feet of it, and its beard showing. Go and shave." She leaned forward, the puffed place on her lip accenting the gleam of the tooth beneath, and lending her something of the mien (although I did not know enough to think it then, and know too well the significance of that askew lip now) that women have, softly battered, after love. "In the petition you are still 'the infant,' " she said. "Remember?"

She looked at me through her lashes, and across the death-distance that annuls the filial I can return that look now, glimpsing what my father must have seen in her, my uncle found — the deep coquetry of a woman uncertain of her powers, who, in the rare hour that she is made certain, is more daring than a beauty, than a whore. "Eh?" she said. "Eh . . . George?"

Yes, she was the petitioner, the promiser who had already forgotten what earlier she had said to me — "We would not need to call you that name among us" — who, if I let her, would lead me from stone to stone over promises that sank behind us as we left them, not because this was her way, but because this was the way of the world, and to bewitch me along it was her role. If I let her I would learn how to accede, how to step so far into the center of the dim web that I would no longer see it around me. I would learn how to smear the possible over the impossible, how to forsake the pursuit of who I was for the practice of what I could. And if I came along gently and gave no trouble, one day I should find, with a sob of safety, that at the last the membrane of myself had broken, that I had forgotten the uncommunicable word I hunted, that at last I had lost what I needed to lose in order to be gathered into the enclosure where so many others already were.

I did not answer then, but plodded off to shave. There was no answer I could make, except one. She herself had forced it upon me. She was the petitioner, and she herself had made me see how much she asked.

Later we came out of the house together, the door scraping shut in its swollen frame with the comment that the usual makes beneath an occasion. "I am the same," it says; other things are not. Inside the house the heat, domesticated, melted the wax in the furniture grooves and dried the shadows to paper shams, striping a brazen seam around the shades, but outside it struck once at the optic nerve and enclosed us, a column that walked as we walked, hung from a blur invisibly above us in the great stare. It was a day bearable only if one walked with it toward a sea. Gorgon images assailed eyes too lax for them; light flowed in a mane up from the pavement; down at the end of that waving plait each of the two men in front of Semple's store had a face as dark as a negative, in a nimbus of iridescent hair. And all around us the dams held, a bracelet of steel lakes hoarding their cordial, in which, if we could have slit our way toward it, we could have lolled like tongues. My mother breathed with economy, her pupils strained forward as if they strove to sweat, a band of white circled her mouth again and there was not a bead of wet upon it. I came a pace or two behind her; she was ahead of me as she had always been, but this would not be for much longer, for I lagged behind to a new rhythm. Now that authority drew us in due process toward the courthouse, the name, the one I intended, beat up out of hiding, inserting its irregular notation in my ear — one, two-three, one, two-three — involving my heartbeat, the animal shrink and dilation of my skin against its box of clothes. The name throbbed without timbre, waiting to be filled with mine; I saw it as still halved and blind, as if still expurgated on the page: P——e G——n, heard it, not as a name that rippled or came firmly down but as one with a hesitation between its parts that suited me, an interrupted name. And so we came along, each on his own leading string, to the courthouse, and stopped there.

I stopped there.

"What . . . what?" muttered my mother. "Come along . . . it's time." Although she had halted with me, all of her still strove forward from the breastbone, like those caryatids which both move and stay. She leaned toward a picture ahead of her, and I was there in its center, not behind. "Eh?" she said, breathing short.

I was the one who looked back. There was nothing to see — a street, quiet as a dune, that had no power to hold me, the high dust curls of the dam, two lilliput men. "Don't go in," I said. "Come away."

"What are you say — what can you be . . . ?" She put her fist on my forearm. I felt it grind on the muscle. "What . . ." she said and stopped. If she had any prescience, she saved herself from it; she refused it. Her fist dropped from my arm. Mine, unclenching, fell to my side. "You welsh then," she said, and now her voice had all the breath she needed, a long, alto breath sliding in at the spine. "You go back on your word — you go back . . ."

The light mottled what she said, suspended it. Back. Where was it? Who went there? My lips framed nothing.

"Then I will go on with it. It can be done without you. I'll go in alone."

"Do not."

"Yes."

She wheeled, her skirt belling with the force of it. I had time to see again that it was her marriage dress, no symbol, present here in that subtler poetic of accident by which objects litter emotion to the end of life, their presence never escaped, never solved. Then she went in.

But I could tell that she waited; one corner of the dress remained motionless, just inside the door. I inched forward until I could see her face, immobile, drowsy with its own fate, in that moment surely resembling mine. A binding of love went between us that would never be again; the whelming sadness of those who are victims of one another. Then I followed her.

When the two men entered the courtroom through the side door and seated themselves, their entry, seen through the corner of my eye, settled on us like the arrival of latecomers just before curtain, the final, premonitory click of the *mise en scène*. As we ourselves were met at the door by the guard who tended it, a group of people just heard had filed past us — one of them a small, thin girl of about fifteen with the long corkscrew curls that some of the girls here kept with them through the movie-land dream period between pubescence and sex, who held a minute cuddle of blanket, no more than a palmful, slacked at her chest, its sealed face upturned. An older woman, fat, sullen and vindicated, walked between her and a boy of about the same age whose face alone of the three was tear-stained, under a cap of bird-colored hair that tufted over ears and collar — the putative father perhaps, looking younger than his babe. A wake trailed them — Coke, soil and a faint milk-sour overlay — detritus of moisty afternoons and gawky evening scuffles, already composting what would be from what had. Then the door-tender motioned us into central chairs in the first row and left us.

At first I assumed that we were alone. On the wall to the right, above the door that led to the law office, rolled-down maps, varnished and aged to vellum, showed county and township divisions in the thin, black scrolls of a past era of mapmaking; beyond them, in a vast framed work of one of the tinted litho-techniques of the turn of the century, blurred figures grouped round a conference table on some last military or judicial eve. In the corner joining the front wall, a silk ceremonial flag, corded and fringed, hung on its stanchion like a flag in a museum, in a stiff central point toward the ground. Back of us, at the long windows, twelve or fourteen feet high, that faced the square, the outer shutters had been swung to, and the long, muddy inner shades drawn, making a gloom that swarmed with after-images like those on the inside lid of the closed eye. The chairs waited behind us. Light came down from a pair of open squares near the ceiling in the left-hand wall, in two hot, gold patches that blinded at first, one of them gilt and blue, the trembling moss of a Byzantine mosaic — then I saw that this was the massed yellow leafage, shifting a hairbreadth, of a tree that looked in upon us from outside. I fixed my mind on it, on a tree I could not place stirred by a non-existent wind, on a cool limbo whose beings, flying smoothly through ozone, left a breeze on leaves. Facing us, the wall was wooden, paneled in dimness; between us and it the oak lectern reared up like its antler, its prong. On this, forward and above our heads, there was a round hole of darkness — a draped Bible perhaps, for the dark cloth hung down on either side. Then, as I studied it, the hole lifted, resolved itself into the youthful ebony of Mr. Fourchette's seal-cap of hair. His face looked at us between arms spread out under a cape or gown, then bent to the desk and was again concealed, as if a bat, pasted unnoticed to the wall, had for a moment lifted its visor to reveal the white face of a man.

Beside me, my mother let out a small sigh of assent, of recognition, her bargain, her fifteen pounds' worth, well in train now, well on its way. She settled back, head bent, as if she were in church. She seemed to find nothing unusual in his keeping us waiting so for minutes on end, himself unmoving, studying some incunabula we could not see. Once she stole a glance at me, a mother checking a child new to a ritual that is home to her, lowering her lids consciously again, as if she understood fully this silent sermon from above. She must have visited courts before, I thought, no doubt at home in England. It was then, at the thought of this, that I was truly frightened at what I had done. Professionalism, parched and venally weak though its face might be, had stared out at me from under that visor, and it was against this that I dared to pose my amateur hand. This was the one courtroom I had even been in, and I had trusted too much to the benevolent house-pride the town gossip took in its crankiness, its one-man audacity — to what I myself had seen, that one night, of its careless underside. Now I felt what I had not foreseen — that even it would subscribe to a conventicle that powerfully supported its oddest prelates; that even through that head bent upon us now in the personal ritual of the half-mad vain, this court partook of a wafer that went round the world. I caught again the room's faint flavor, the odor not of justice but of practice. In front of us the lectern reared like a cenotaph around whose base one could breathe the odor of the bodies on which it had been raised. Here it pointed only to the ceiling of the courthouse in Banks County, Alabama, but behind its crude, country carving there was a huge alter ego that could divide and assign the crowd with the force of the finger that parted the Red Sea, or, with a more delicate action, press one man into his grave. Possibly I was too small for its notice — at the moment. There was the gamble that my bit of self-assertion, first minute essay against it, was by chance at the edge of its orbit — that this time I would get by.

At the thought my breath expelled, and fright with it, replaced by another, long with excitement, indrawn. This was the gamble. It had begun. But the most potent fact was that the gamble *was* — wherewithal of interest enough for the lifetime of any man. The owl tapped, objectivity revealing itself on my shoulder, alluding with its beak to all that one could watch, to the great spectacle — chance forever doubling on certainty — of all that was. In its release, I forgot my mother now, as later I would forget any person by my side.

For if before, on that day for instance when I left the envelope in Fourchette's office, I had felt the swelling of appetites huge to know more, but indefinite, now I began to know what that "more" was. It included all the roaring diapason of sex, ego, ambition that went with my age, but it went beyond it, hovered above it. What I had, what I was beginning to discover, was an appetite for alternatives. I saw opening slowly before me a horizon of watching and experiment at all the shapes of life — life mutated by lie and direction, life when it was left alone — in all the combinations and permutations thereof, hand over hand over hand. And if this is what is called the sense of wonder, fiery and common to the mind of the young, then I had — and still have — my share.

Meanwhile, I peered hard at that blot of dark on the rostrum, the wig-smooth crown of Mr. Justice Fourchette, as a man might stare at a contender against whom he bets himself. I leaned forward so far, so unaware, that my mother, signaling decorum, touched my hand. It was then that the two men entered, on the balls of their feet, heads obeisant, the way people enter a ceremony they are no part of, tiptoed to the rear, and sat down. Mr. Fourchette raised his face again and looked at us, the case before him, and, with a trouper's faint lift of the chin, at his audience — tardy, but arrived. One arm, short and matchstick in the sleeve of his gown, less imperial without its show of linen, beckoned to the doorkeeper. The latter, a tall emaciated man with great discs under his eyes and the kindly stoop of those whom a protracted inner disease allows to remain upright, left his post and came forward. Apparently he acted also as the clerk; in this court, perhaps more openly than in most, no one was himself alone. A rap of the gavel; then the judge put it sharply aside, brooding over it for a moment, seamed and sour, as if what should have been a rod of serpents that rolled away of itself was seen to be a nothing, a nondescript out of any kitchen drawer. But his face, when it looked up, was still charged with the greed that remembered the port-wine taste of the law in Montgomery, the eagerness that, at seventy, still dyed its hair for hope. His voice when it came was not leathern, without bellows, as it had been in his office, but easily heard in the farthest corner — a clear Southern reed, still golden, that he might have stolen, without the stammer, from his son — and staring out over the five of us as if we were a multitude, he said, "Next! Higby!"

We stood up, my mother and I. The old clerk, taking over what should have been his from the beginning, cleared his throat and informed us that we were convened in the matter of the application of Dora Cross Higby, petitioner, for leave to change the name of the said infant, myself. And at that moment, one half of our audience in the rear snickered. My back was turned to them; therefore I had no way of knowing whether or not it was the half from Tuscana, although I suspected it — the visiting stranger being more likely to have a guest's humility — but I thought I knew why he laughed. I, the infant, was already six foot three at the time, all hocks and wrists, grown out of my clothes but not yet into bones that appeared formed of a long taffy that nature was still incredibly pulling. I seemed even taller than a man of the same height would, than I would myself ten years hence, and my mother, the crest of her head stretched to its highest, was more than a foot below the shoulder of her infant. The laugh was to me merely part of the daily silliness the young must accept politely from elders who "could not get over" what my bones each day literally taught me — that things changed. It did not occur to me that there might be a tickle of the sexual in the snicker, over the gross possibility that this great infant was a bastard brought in belatedly, come at last to be legalized. No doubt it had occurred to the judge, to any of the town who knew of it, and now to my mother, although she gave no sign, but it was not this public poke at it over which the judge now took umbrage, or seemed to. He was not defending my mother, whose three-minute bit of office trade he had seen fit to make a pother over; indeed, he seemed to have forgotten her, and kept her standing through all that ensued. It was his court, all courts and their language, that he now undertook to defend against this polyp of ridicule coughed up by the *hoi polloi*. Outrage, a pretense of it, puffed his sunk cheek, but he could scarcely repress the smirk of the man who has been proffered the excuse he has been looking for. One hand crept toward the gavel and rejected it, came down on the desk instead with a slap that must have reddened its palm.

"Order!" he said. "Some clarification seems needed. For the uninitiate." He inclined his head, squinting toward the rear row of chairs. "In order that they may fully understand that nothing derogatory is here intended. That there is a fixed nomenclature by which an entity or entities — *vide* objects or persons —" here he bent his glance on my mother and me and we lowered ours under it — "by which an entity, its limitations and its essence, is defined in court. In accordance with which this young man, entering here for such special purpose as shall in due course be revealed —" here he paused, and we felt the notice of all, an extra heat on our bent necks — "is hereby designated 'infant.' " This time no one snickered.

"A short exposition, then," he said. "By your leave." In the silence that overcomes a classroom of mocked children, the old clerk polished a pen with a saw-toothed cloth penwiper as big as a handkerchief, set both down, and with the tolerance of a saint for his ordeal, folded his hands. And we, standing like turkeys at market under the auctioneer's impenetrable spiel, listened to Fourchette's "clarification." It came in that same voice, clean and mellow but circling and never centering, the words distinct of themselves but the meaning in almost unreportable periphrasis. Once there was an interval, restfully blunt, in which he listed, in the patient voice one uses to children, certain legal terms that did not mean what they meant to the laity — the "curtesy" that did not signify courtesy, the "escheat" that had no connection as we knew it with "cheat." And once he said without preamble in a negligent, fatigued nasal that I knew, without ever having heard such before, must be perfection: "Montesquieu. *Esprit des Lois.*" Thereafter the outpouring continued so majestic in pace and confidence that minutes passed while the ear fuzzed, eyes squeezed closed in concentration, the head stretched from side to side, before the key came to me — as it does to the identity of a foreign language — in one surmise.

What I was hearing was the near-sense that was not nonsense but hovered, fearfully grandiloquent, between — the antic of a brain contorting against itself, toward others, in the spirals of its prides, its vanities, its need, and so cannily touching now and then at the sensible that only the spiral itself, encoiling the speaker ceaselessly in the one manifestation he could not control, had given me the key. I closed my ears to all but the sound of it. This was no more, surely, than — in the large, magnified to the third power so that the cracks in the reasoning showed — what all men did in their private moments at one time or another: the child singing his ego-song at stool, the young man orating his future at the mirror, old men of

Fourchette's age haranguing themselves. But the town, a public macrocosm, accepted it publicly. Therefore, if there was mania here, it was the town's. I was too young to take this as usual or to understand, as I do now, that no man when he thinks with a group is wholly sane. As Johnny had once, I assumed that Tuscana must be different from other places elsewhere. Meanwhile I was here in its coil, tasting for the first time the knowledge that once one put one's private affairs in the public domain, one was already in the prisoner's dock. Fourchette's voice returned to my ear in the dying fall of peroration, and I recognized a foreign language I knew.

"*Respiciendum,*" he said and cleared his throat. "On the functions of a judge: '*Respiciendum est judicanti ne quid aut durius aut remissus constituatur quam causa deposcit; nec enim aut severitas aut clementiae gloria affectanda est.*'" It was a different Latin from the classical pronunciation I had been taught — Italianate, Jesuit perhaps, with the soft *ch* of its *respiciendum,* its hard *j* and *v*. He was translating: "The judge must see that no order be made or judgment given or sentence passed either more harshly or more mildly than sentence requires; he must not seek renown as a severe or tender-hearted judge."

Residual guilt rushed to my head like blood; I thought myself indicated already for intent, already called to account for what had not yet occurred. Then I recognized the tone, falsely humble, that ministers use when, referring to themselves as the instruments of God, they wish nevertheless to call some slight attention — "*Ecce homo*" — to themselves. "Therefore, for the judge of true vocation," he said, "no matter is too small. And for the true court."

Upon this, the clerk, as if he knew this place in the service, took up his pen. At my side my mother swayed, but would not sit down, and instead gripped my arm. The judge looked vaguely on us, catching movement, but it was plain that he did not see us except as those entities which he had been defining. We were, I thought, like those "clots in consciousness" spoken of in the mechanistic philosophers Demuth had once set me to reading, and the consciousness was Fourchette's; until he snapped the tension we could not move.

181

"In accordance with which," said Fourchette, "in the matter before us, we shall see what is set down here in the matter of names." Drawing closer to him a loaf-shaped book concealed until now by the black folds of his sleeves, he began puttering at its pages. *"Nomen collectivum . . . generale . . ."* he muttered to himself, and for what seemed minutes, fell still. Silence covered us, the long, shared public silence, a canopy upheld by participants who dare not, until the signal, lower their arms.

"Ah," said Fourchette. He pushed the book from him and at the same time snapped on the light in the lectern. In its arc the eye of the clerk blinked, patient and uncynical, the farthest figure in a holy picture, but still drawn in along the master painter's invisible radial line.

"Names are mutable; things immovable," said Fourchette. He poked a finger over the rostrum, not at my mother and me but at his audience, those two in the rear whose faces I should have liked to turn to see — chapfallen and won, were they, or like touts watching the barker, or — heads back — catching flies?

"Nomen mutabilia sunt," he said, enunciating the text for them in the delicate accent slipped down to him from no dame's school, from sugar-tongued grandfather, father or uncle gracefully tagging the postprandial brandy, or from the tutorial knuckle-lash of priests, *"res autem immobilis."* He fell silent again before he gave out the reference, head drooping, eyes veiled. In the mauve light the eyeballs showed almost spherical in their sunken hollows, the long cheeks august in their furrowed decline; for a moment one saw the whole, fine heirloom skull under the Mardi Gras wig of hair. Then he raised his head, and I saw the quizzical seam of the mouth, the eyeballs — looking at me and beyond me — of a soul that in the midst of its own *blagues* remained undeceived, an immovable pinpoint within the spiral, and I was filled again with bewilderment and wonder at all the permutations of the world. Waving an arm at the clerk, he gave out the reference. "Six, Coke, sixty-six."

And at once the clerk fell to, like a suddenly whirring clock. The pen, poised in abeyance, dropped like a pendulum to follow lines whose bluish purple I recognized, to trace his place down each page of a sheaf of papers — one, two, three — that he held up now to the arc light and gabbled from in a rote voice that ran on indistinguishably over syllables, a merged prayer heard from a stall, in which he raced his breath, his disease perhaps, flinging out to us now and then the clear pebble of a phrase, not that we might know where we were, but that we might know his speed. And as he gabbled, traveled, flew, the room relaxed to his voice as if it were a breeze; in the background the two spectators stirred, scuffing knee over knee, and one of them — which? — cleared his throat; Fourchette touched a handkerchief to his forehead, then sank his chin in its folds in the attitude some assume when they listen to music; up at the high window the leaves spangled, tossing lightly. Outside a shutter banged, then another, then no more. And still the clerk raced on. Only I felt nothing but the hot pulse of my own breath as it listened, and the weight of my mother, still upright in the proud torture-case of her own will, but hanging heavier, heavier on my arm.

"In the Matter of . . ." said the clerk, beginning. "I . . . hereby state . . . am the son of petitioner herein . . . reside with her at . . . I was born in . . . on . . . emigrated with mother to . . . on . . . have duly registered . . . Alien Registration Act . . . received number. . . ." I have a number, I thought; he said it too quickly; where did they get it? — I never knew.

"I have read the annexed petition," said the clerk, "know the contents thereof . . . do hereby consent to granting of the relief prayed . . . signed . . . dated . . . Tuscana . . . 1936. . . ." He must stop for a breath, I thought, but he was too quick for me.

"On the day of . . . appeared before me . . . known to me to be the person described . . . executed the foregoing . . . duly acknowledged . . . that he executed same . . . signed . . . Notary Public." The notary was the druggist; I had never gone before him to execute such a form; it must have been drawn up without me. And here the clerk rested. In the lull we could hear a swishing of the upper air, no spatter in the streets. At the high window the tree, moving sidewise in steady motion, and seen now to be a single branch plumed upward and bent at the crown, nodded in on us, a portion of the natural world nosing in at the human. My mother shifted her weight on my arm. The clerk turned his page. And this ended the first paper.

"In the Matter of . . ." said the clerk, "application of . . . an infant . . . by . . . his mother to the . . . Court . . . County of . . . your petitioner resides . . . is the mother of the above . . . Father of said . . . to wit, one . . . deceased having died a resident of . . . on or about . . . said infant resides at . . . with . . . mother . . . and . . . who is the stepfather of. . . . Said infant is of the age of . . . having been born in . . . annexed hereto is a certificate of . . . he is not employed . . . not a member of armed forces or inducted for . . . single and has never been married . . . never convicted of any crime. . . ." Why must he pause there, I thought, aware again of the sneaking aura of the room, a room from which even a man judged innocent might emerge sensing the underground taint of other crimes for which he had long since judged himself. Fourchette had not moved. Outside a wind was certainly brewing, pulling sullenly at the walls.

"Break the heat maybe." From behind us, an intended whisper creaked in the sudden pocket left by the air. As if on signal, to demonstrate that no failure of breath had stopped him, the clerk resumed:

". . . no judgment or liens against said infant . . . no action or proceeding . . . never been adjudicated bankrupt . . . no claims, demands, liabilities . . . to which said infant is party . . . no creditors. . . ." A door in the corridor slammed. The clerk, raising his voice, answered with a sentence in entirety, loud and unelided. "And no person will be adversely affected or prejudiced in any way by the proposed change of name."

Farther away, another door reported. The window shades swelled inward in unison, were sucked flat. An increasing silver lashing came from outside, the sound of a hard wind rising in groves of foliage, although there were only two trees, tall and sparse, in the square. "Present name of said infant . . ." said the clerk, his voice

the faster as its content was snatched away, "name proposed . . .
that shall assume . . . grounds of application are . . . as aforesaid
. . . also as aforesaid. . . ."

My mother rose on my arm, breathing almost soundlessly. "What
is he saying? Does he get it right? There's a noise in my ears. I did
not hear." Nor had I. I moved my head in a nod or a shake, I did
not know which, but away from my mother's face, taut against my
shoulder, cupped upward to mine. But again I was forced to look
down at her, turning with the slowness in which one moves against
the iron of dreams. Her eyes were glaring wide at me, in anger I
thought at first; then I saw that her jaw was trembling. Tears, I
thought. This must be the way she cries. In the lowest part of me
a thought flickered like an adder: "Is this all she will do then —
cry?" Heavier still, her weight bore down on my cramped arm in
such a way now that I was almost unable to withstand it; raising
her, I motioned toward the chair. Shaking her head a hairsbreadth,
she remained locked where she was. Then, stealing almost imperceptibly along the side of her that was pressed against me, I felt the
tremor, a continuous tremoring that shook her from ankle to thigh.
This was no ordinary trembling, but one that did not seem to belong
to her, a drumming in which the leg went on of itself. Slowly she
lowered her chin to look down at her foot. Because of holding her
I could not see it, but in a gap in the wind I heard its heel rat-tat-tat-
ting on the floor. Under the halo of light from the lectern, the
clerk filed away inaudibly at the record, while one by one, in a
steady chording from cellar to ogive, all the draughts of the old building
answered each other. Suddenly I felt her stiffen, draw a long breath, a
second. Then the heel came down hard, and was still. Her eyes were half
closed. On the third breath she opened them, half smiled at me, lifted
her weight from my arm, and stood alone. The clerk turned over a page
and put it down. And that was the end of the second paper.

"At a Special Term of . . . Court, State of . . . County of . . .
at the Courthouse . . . Street . . . City of . . . Alabama, on the . . .
day of . . . nineteen-hundred and thirty-six," said the clerk with a
flourish. "Present: Honorable Hannibal Fourchette, Justice." He paused,

in a backwash of quiet. Noises inside and out had stopped, leaving a hollow that pressed the ears. The electric light weakened in the sudden sulphur gloom, fluttering once in the familiar pearl of my mother's breastpin, given her — I recalled now, after all the years between, by whom and when — at my birth. I thieve nothing, I told myself; it is an accidental name that I may never use — interrupted, patched in halves.

"Go on, Clarence," said Fourchette. His voice was absent, fading too in the gloom.

"Beg pardon, it's the order itself, sir," the clerk whispered. "You usually read the order. . . ."

"Ah, yes, yes, thank you, Mr. Whitlock," said the judge, rousing quickly in a voice intended to cover, raising his chin from his hand with a large look at the rear of the room. He reached down over the lectern and took the paper. A smile of terror parted my lips. My arm, released from my mother's weight, felt as light as air.

"On reading and filing the petition of Dora Cross Higby, verified the twenty-eighth day of July, 1936 . . ." Fourchette's voice was flat, an old man's office tones now, enunciating every word. He stopped now to verify the two of us, his court, his audience, with a glance, cleared of its mist, that knew us for what we were. ". . . praying for a change of name of the above infant, it being requested that he be permitted to assume the name of Pierre Goodman in the place of his present name and the court being satisfied that said petition is true and it appearing from the said petition and the court being satisfied that there is no reasonable objection to the change of name proposed —"

I did not move, turn an inch to look at my mother, from whom there had come a sound, a motion like a muffled wing-beat, but no word.

"Now on motion of . . . hmmm . . . *attorney* for the said petitioner it is Ordered —" Here he paused. It seemed to me, staring, that I fed him with my breath. "— that the said infant, born on November 11th, 1918, be and hereby is authorized to assume the name of

Pierre Goodman in place and stead of his present name upon complying with the provisions of this order, namely . . ."

I must not look at her, I thought. I will not look at her, for it seemed to me that if I did so everything would fall away, all the counterpoises that held us up, together — the family illusion shared of shared days, the illusion of love and the fabric, not of hate, but of anti-love revenging itself for what it is. The word "turn" swung in my mind like a compass needle. It is her turn now for one thing, yours for the other. Only turn now and see what you wished for arrived. The room will fall away, you will fall away from each other — all as you wished — you will be two nothings on a plain. Why is there no sound from her, I thought, no cry? Yet I could not turn.

"That this order be entered and the said petition upon which it is granted be filed within ten days from the date hereof in the office of this court in the County of Banks, that within ten days from the date of entry hereof, a copy of this order shall be published in the *Denoyeville Dealer,* a newspaper published in the County of Banks, Alabama; and that, within forty days after the making of this order, proof of such publication by affidavit shall be filed with the clerk of the Supreme Court in the County of . . ."

I am innocent, I said to the rostrum, my lips dry over my teeth in what I could not be sure was a snarl or a smile, for it seemed to me truly that I held a part of myself to myself, as the young mother had held her child. And now I heard it again, the tic, the drumming spasm of the heel on the floor. Save me from what I shall have done, I thought; who brought us here? We bring ourselves, we brought ourselves, we came to this dock together. Let me remember that when I turn.

". . . that, following the due filing of the said petition and entry of said order as hereinbefore directed, the publication of such an order and the filing of proof of publication thereof, said infant shall be known as and by the name of Pierre Goodman . . ."

And then I heard the sound. And I turned.

"— which he is hereby authorized to assume and by no other name:

(and it is further ordered, that a certified copy of this order shall not be issued until proof of compliance with the above provisions has been duly filed with the clerk of this court.)

"Enter.

"Hannibal Fourchette . . . Justice Supreme Court."

My mother stood upright, her hand clapped to her mouth. It was a posture seen at once to be physical; this was no hand holding back a cry but the cramp of agony in which the hand presses back the actual knife in the throat, the burst in the breast, the clutch in the bowels. Her heel was still now, the foot clamped to the floor by the rod of the leg — stiffened to the hip — on which she appeared transfixed. As my arms went out to her she bent from the waist, looking down on the alien rod that would not let her fall; then, as I touched her, she straightened, and as I caught her she fell.

The chairs next us had arms to them and she was not to be bent; on my knees I held the upper part of her from the floor. Above the hand that concealed her mouth, her eyes looked into mine, not a cloud between us, lens into lens. They were wide and bright, stricken with knowledge, not with death.

"You . . . are —" she said, and the third word, the glottal echo I ponder yet, escaped me except for its vowel. *Lost* I thought it was once, then *false* — I was sure of it — then for a while that it was surely *gone*; I have risen up at night and struck the wall above my bed with my fist, saying, "The word was *wrong*," and believed it for the span of a cigarette, and I have halted, as to a gong, on a street corner, thinking *all*; what she said was *all*. Each is a facet of the central stone. The glossary goes down the years and will never be done. It is the word — suckled, lost, hunted — that is written at birth on the wall. It was my paring, and I thought then that she spoke it, behind the hand that slid down then and showed to the sudden cluster of faces above her the puckered seam of her lip, dragged downwards, smeared to the side.

"Sunstroke," whispered one of the men. "Hits you worst in hurricane weather."

"Not the sun kind," the other said low. "My father — I know the look of it"; and the old clerk, hunched over his own chancre of mortality, said nothing. I searched for gospel in any face that would give it.

"Phone the doctor from here, Clarence," said Fourchette from the rostrum, "and get her home in my car." He had not moved; there was no need for him to, although a lesser man would have. Authority, stepping forward from him like the ghost of all that he had slipped from, dictated to us precise details of what to do.

The two men lifted her up and from me, their faces goblin-near to hers, as in a deposition. They refused my help as I got up from my knees. "Stay here a minute, son," said one, "and pull yourself together. We'll meet you outside." As they steadied her between them, the old clerk reached over, his head humbly averted, lifted the portion of her skirt that hung between her legs and folded it across them, and I saw that it dripped wet from a wide dark circle at the groin.

Then I was alone. Fourchette was there, and yet it still was so. To the right of one of the pictures a clock that I had not seen, expected clock of public rooms, assumed and seldom noticed, showed its hands at three o'clock; three hours more before my uncle would come off shift; less than an hour since we had come here. It asserted the day, joined me to it, yet I had more than enough time to note with pedantic care that its frame was yellow mission oak like such clocks everywhere, that its scraped gilt name was "Seminole." I had time, as one does when alone, to feel an air current pure on my hands, to turn them over in it, examining their scars, the faintly begun script of the years, their pores. I stood in one of those yawns of identity when alternatives lock, where one can only wait and be. In a minute I would live, move again, live forward; meanwhile I idled there in the languid horror of the human when it first sees the web, when it first knows that what it will fight to the death to keep and what it will fight to the death to lose are the same.

Above me, over the lectern, the waiting hole of darkness had returned — Fourchette's head, sunk over its next case, or its own. As I turned to leave, its visor lifted again and the white face looked out at me. I thought of what I secretly knew of it — devious leaver of keys, doler-out of bottles to its son. Contender or collaborator, we were together and alone. It was no wonder the town kept him on as the world keeps Hamlet — lucid immovable who knew us each for what we were, and whom we could then call mad. Outside, on the courthouse steps, my legs wavered like a convalescent's, but they carried me forward to the waiting car.

Our cortege passed slowly through streets still darkened by the tail of the wind that had brushed them seasonally and veered off, leaving behind it for some hours yet a sound as of a train riding in the air six feet or so above us, the declining hurricane's characteristic roar. The car was an old touring eight, its shape vaguely familiar; the men had placed my mother on the long rear seat, themselves on the two jump seats facing her, and had shunted me up front with the clerk, who drove. I felt nothing. I was a nothing on a plain. But I was alone.

My uncle opened the door to us. He had seen us from the parlor window where, all against custom, he had been sitting, unaware of what had occurred. He did not explain to us, then or after, what had brought him home at that hour — later I saw the ceremonial bottle out on the sideboard and the white stain on my aunt's walnut table where the small glass, its modest ration slopped over in the moment of drinking, had left a ring. Mr. Whitlock's telephone call to the mill had missed him; the doctor had not yet arrived.

He received us, our bedraggled procession, our circumstance, full in the face, while this side information dribbled from us and him in the crosshatched babble that attends such a blow. His face did not change when he saw us, but no one who watched it could ever again misunderstand the plight of a face that could not. At the moment when the two men, walking directly to the bedroom with the surety with which everyone in the region knew these houses, were about to put down their burden, my uncle, who had been following numbly behind, intervened. Arms upthrust, in a sudden motion that staggered all three men, he scooped her from the other two, held her for a moment over the bed, defying gravity and them as if this were his privilege, and gently lowered her down. My mother's eyes, still wide, remained so; her crooked lip said "George," and one hand, the unaffected left one, scrabbled at her shamed dress, as if she asked his help to conceal it. My uncle nodded, then his face changed at last; his lips turned in upon themselves, and bending, he rested them for a minute over the stain, on the hand. Watching, I felt my throat distend, not for myself, but as any bystander outside the life and accident of this house might feel the salt hurt, salt surprise of his first sight of what intimacy was.

One of the men, the stranger, clearing his throat, mentioned hot applications and spoke again of his father. Just then a neighborhood slattern, a Mrs. Jebb, who had never before been in our house, walked in among us, upborne by the righteous eagerness of those quick to adopt the minor role that disaster allows. When she saw we were all men there, she pushed through us with disdain, stood at the bedside in her fat slippers, then waved us aside. Grouped toward my uncle by her entry, the two men offered him the embarrassed shoptalk of tragedy. "Doc ought to be here soon now . . . reckon the storm passed us over . . . heat in that place was terrible . . . know how the air gets, all tight, before one of those Gulf winds." One of the men stepped forward.

"Reckon I ought to take this opportunity — name's Mount, Dabney Mount." It was not the stranger, who might have, who introduced himself, but the courthouse lounger, the sight of whom, dabbled by the seasons as a park statue is by pigeon dirt, had been silently known to us for years. Generations back, an ancestor had endowed him with a powerful nose that slacker heredities and a single-track diet had perverted at the eyes and the chin, adding the dull roguery of gapped teeth, making of his face a kind of Punch without the intelligence, around its mouth the great, humorous brackets carved by bad feeding, its hatchet shape not entirely guileless of harm.

"Dabney Mount," he repeated, offering me the serious hush of a man greeting the bereaved. Not a derelict quite, but a man long unused in the ordinary way of things to being in family houses, a life —

fed out of paper bags, in no time frame, in flophouse random — that would seek out the public wedding, public funeral where, exhaling its carious, short-order breath, it would find the excitation of kinship almost as satisfying as a sit-down meal. A giggle spurted from him. "Have to give this boy time to recollect which, hey, young fella? Right fancy name you got yourself down there today."

My uncle heard him with lowered eyes. Excusing himself, he stepped back to listen at the bedroom door, which Mrs. Jebb had half closed.

"Don't try to raise yourself, honey," we heard Mrs. Jebb whisper. "That's it now. There."

Mount shook his head; his eyelids even pinkened. The stranger — a heavy man with flat white cheeks and an urban taste in linen and haircuts, one of the well-heeled boarders of whom the dam had brought us dozens, family men often, with fringe tastes for the cheap company brought on by their manner of living — cast him a look of disavowal and murmured firmly that they must go, brushing aside my uncle's brusque thanks. Mount nodded in solemn, side-kick agreement. But my uncle's terse handshake unnerved him, admitting him so without prejudice to the company of men who by normal process participated in each other daily, jumped to the emergency, rode in the judge's car, were detailed to carry a sick woman home. It was too much to ask him as well so suddenly to leave the stage.

"Fine woman," he said, "everybody knows it. Stood up under the judge's sermon like she felt her business was her own." His eyes, roving my uncle's face, seemed at the same time to near each other; his mouth pursed like a valve. Sensing the intent, though not the direction of what was coming, I thought that the circumstance that had removed this man from the center of men might know better than our pity, that there was a force which knew what it was about when it swept him aside from the mainstream. "Stood up under the heat well enough; recollect she wouldn't even hang on this boy here's arm. Funny thing — how it was only when the judge gave out the name that it struck her."

My uncle raised his eyes and looked at me. I avoided them. But I was rescued. I was no longer a nothing.

"Thought of that when I was carrying her," Mount continued, his pleasure dwelling on that past role. "Thought to myself — the family will want to know that. Case anything happens, the family will want to know it looked like she repented just before she was struck down." His tongue protruded slowly from his lips, and his companion moved away from him with an indefinable grimace. It extruded like a tongue from an anus, a dirty reminder of the sore red tissue of which we all were made.

"She had nothing to repent," said my uncle, flanking him toward the door the way a broom urges over the threshold a piece of ordure that ought not to be touched. "And now get out, man. One job doesn't excuse the other."

But to Mr. Mount, moved to hysteria by sudden affinity with his kind, this was yet another reminder. "Got your mind on jobs, hey, after this morning, and shouldn't wonder — heard the news about it at Semple's this noon." He fumbled in a crevice in his clothing, took out the smallest size paper bag, from which he extracted the pinched half of a cigar, and inserted this in the wet, restless round under his nose. "Tip you off — crowd down there ain't too sweet on you, sum totally. Happens I'm sponsoring this gentleman there this evening. Glad to do the same for you any time." It was the remnant nose, after all, that made for travesty. Watching that bleared cockscomb above what crowed beneath, I understood how a flock might peck to death one of its kind — because he was.

"Come along," said the stranger. "This gentleman has no time for that now."

"Coming." Mount made a jaunty half-salute with the hand that held the cigar. He winked. "Promised I'd take him to Semple's by way of the Three Sisters." The other hand cradled the near elbow of the stranger, who this time seemed unable to flinch from it.

Behind us, Mrs. Jebb came out, finger to lips. "Maybe she'll drop off, now, you all be quiet."

"Tuh, Jesus!" Mount bent almost double, pantomiming his remorse over forgetting about noise. He was almost over the threshold now, but again he halted, blinking his scanty lashes. Perhaps he felt our triple enmity, triple disgust radiating toward him, accepting it as the return of that element in which he normally moved. His hand moved to my shoulder.

"You recollect it, don't you though, young fella. Tell 'em how it was the way I said it was. Wasn't till the very moment the judge give out the new name, skips my mind what it is. But it was right then and there that your mamma fell down." His hand, with its sickening, ancient slug-smell, nudged me, pleading. I could not flinch under it either. What I had done, what the stranger would do, linked us to it.

My uncle's clear, sandy glance took us both in; there was no telling what it had received. At the moment, as the stranger had said, he had no time for us. He turned to Mrs. Jebb, sleazy concierge of the bedside, for any message she might have. And as he did so, the doctor arrived.

She had had a stroke, though a light one; the history of such cases was that all her faculties, but slightly impeded now, would return. It was true also, to be sure, that the same history predicted the return, far ahead but inevitable, of another and another of death's strokings until the final one — each to be preceded by the visible spasm peculiar to such cases, that strumming whose end appearance was muscular but undoubtedly began hours or days before in the great banyan trunks of the nerves. And this in itself was encouraging, since these very symptoms, always premonitory, when once felt by a patient were henceforth unmistakable and with prompt medication could be controlled, postponed time and time again before they reached their ultimate — although of course the real ultimate could never be postponed. But was not this latter, said the doctor's bonhomie, the same sentence as lay in wait for all of us? Mrs. Higby's case was no different from the rest of us, except perhaps in that she had been given an insight — always alarming at first but soon tolerable — into the special terms under which she might expect the tap that comes for us all. Merely a warning, an inkling of the kind of death he would pick for himself had he the choice of one; here followed a light listing of the morning's pitiables, although how he had consoled these gangrenous amputees, terminal cancers, was not revealed. As to the time limit, let her not think of it — time enough, like the rest of us, to be in an automobile accident or have a flowerpot fall on her head. Years of it. Years and years.

After he had gone, his sentences burned curatively behind him, and through the crack of the doorjamb at which I had been listening, the sickroom glowed in the spiritual blue shed by the one lamp, around which Mrs. Jebb, before leaving, had pinned a twist of the paper from a roll of surgical cotton. It was an aniline light I recalled from the sickrooms of childhood, falsely peaceful and removed, on the edge of nightmare. In its coal-gleam shadow my mother, raised on pillows, her braided hair on her shoulders, appeared freakishly young, a dwarf-woman with the lined face of a pseudo child. The sedative given her had not yet taken effect. Eyes brooding past the horizon of the room, hands upcurled on the coverlet, she lay immured on the raft of her bed like those women whom one glimpsed from the hospital corridor at visiting hour, women cleansed for exhibit, from whom the drama of illness had been taken — Mrs. Jebb had even bound ribbon in her braids.

"What are you mooning there for, lad, she's going to be fine. No need to pussyfoot behind doors!" My uncle, returning from "just a few words" outside with the departing doctor, had brought back some of the latter's manner with him — he had never in his life called me "lad." Genially he dragged me forward to the bedside; she raised her drowsing eyes; I looked down. The glance we had exchanged on the courthouse steps was equal — this was also. It was a glance from which each of us tried to break away, to which each returned. My arms, heavy as if they still had her weight on them, hung at my sides. And she looked away and back again, as the mother does who, never having held her child free of foreboding, now has that nameless worry confirmed. Who can tell how all this begins between those equilibrists fated to each other, parents and children? I never see them together at a playground but I think of it, watching the child, always at least one, of whom ill is already subtly expected, who can but grow up to fulfil what is asked of him, by and by. She tried to speak now, straining until the neck cords showed, her lips stiff and parted, but only a gurgle escaped them.

"Don't! Don't do that, Dora, don't try. You heard what he said just now. It will come back to you." My uncle stood by the side of the bed. "It's something you want, isn't it?" She nodded, rolled her head from side to side. "I tell you what — close your eyes." She had already closed them, but her face lacked the sweet, open nudity of faces in repose; the twisted mouth guarded it, satirizing my uncle, his game. I tried to slip out of the room, but he held me fast with his hard hand on my wrist, and again this broke the usual form between us, for always he had been careful to be the uncle, the stepfather; he had never laid a hand on me, never touched me before. "No," he said, "you might guess it quicker than I."

He began his litany — was it food, warmth or drink she wanted, was it the bedpan? One by one he enumerated the bread-and-meat facts of a household, of an illness, of existence, and as he uttered them with bowed head a poetry issued about them, from this man whom I had once compared to a myna bird talking. One by one he dealt with them — animal, vegetable, mineral — in a voice whose justness I had never seen to be tenderness, under whose careful phlegm I had never suspected the ultimate poise. I remembered now how one might see him at the mill, his head inclined as if he were listening to certain multiples, his hand going out to, never touching, the looms. Was it the wireless? He could put it on the nighttable. Was it the household? He could provision it and as she well knew there was enough money. If it was the clients, he would phone them. Was it the stained dress? He would put it to soak. He had already thought of how she might manage tea — there was one of those bent glass tubes she might drink from. One recalled then how many years he had lived with another invalid, but he had never been like this with my aunt. There seemed no corner of my mother's needs, of her longings that he did not anticipate, con over again in that dry voice so willing to run for them — the drink, the blanket, the pillow — that uttered them like endearments, as if he said *darling darling darling* out loud in the increasing shadows of the room. Animal, vegetable, mineral. But above that mocking lip-seam, her eyes remained closed. The voice faltered, failed. "Not — not the pan?"

All that time through that listing, that lesson, his hard fingers, unconsciously clasping, had nursed mine. And I had no response I could make, except to guide them to the one circle of her needs he stood outside of, had forgotten.

"Ask her," I said, "if it is something about me." And before he could ask her, the lids flew open, her eyes stared.

He dropped my arm. "Ah, yes," he said. "Will you ask her then?"

"Let me go," I said low. "Let me go."

On the pillow the gurgling began again, the head tolling from side to side.

"Don't! Don't!" cried my uncle, almost shouting. "Let me see, let me see," he said, muting his voice. "Perhaps a pencil, no, you couldn't manage it, could you." He nursed her hand as he had mine, bent his lips to it absently. "Wait," he said, "I have it." He sat on the side of the bed. "Hold on." He took a pencil and a bit of paper from his breast pocket, reached for a book that always lay on the night table — the pocket Bible given my mother by her father when she went to France. Resting the paper on this, he took my mother's left hand, placed it against his. "You know how the deaf-and-dumb talk to each other," he said. "With their fingers. You do it that way, eh? Trace the letters one at a time, in my hand. And I'll write each down. And show it you as I do."

That was the way her rage fell upon me, not as I had envisioned it — (never as one envisions it) — transcribed silently from her hand to his to the paper, while I cringed, stiffened, remained. Regret is not wild. It is a silence hung between two masks, in which we lay our foreheads first against one, against the other, knowing that if given the magic return to the moment before choice, we must choose as before.

My uncle finished, read what he had transcribed. The paper crumpled slowly in his hand. "Then . . . what that nasty . . ." He got up from the bedside and led me from the room, closing the door behind him. We stood in the hallway, hearing each other's breath in a savage mingling that all the years of to-and-fro in that narrow passage, narrow house had not achieved. Over his shoulder, the sitting room, not three feet away from us, the bottle on its table, the clenched chairs, appeared like the distant edge of the civilized world.

"What have you done?" he said. "Back there in court. What can you have done to her?" He reached upward, in back of him, but only to turn on the hall bulb. Its glare made us blink, a light in limbo, that no one had ever bothered to shade. Did I hope, in the moment while his arm went up, that he meant to strike me? I know that I moved closer, not away.

On the floor between us lay the dropped paper. I touched it with my shoe.

"Never mind that. Answer me!"

"I took another name. But — not yours."

"You took —"

I nodded.

"And without her?"

Yes.

"How did you manage it?"

I told him.

He swore, so far under his breath that I could not hear the words, although I thought I caught one — "town." After that he was silent for a moment. Neither of us moved. "She should have known," he said then. "She should have known."

"What?"

He raised his head. "You."

Does he not see then, I thought? Even now? That if what happened to her befell her because of me — it is because she *knows* me? He is blind, I thought, staring into his eyes, and there is no need to tell him.

"I should have told her," he said. "That it could never be."

Timidly, for the first time, I touched his arm, perhaps because one did not needlessly hurt the blind. And perhaps not. "I did not do it — against you."

He did not shrink from me. But I found that when one tells the truth out of pity, that is often the way one gets it back.

"You poor . . . poor . . ." he said. And because he said it without patronage, in a quiet marvel over all of us, I could feel that I was. I know now that he was a man from whom, if ever he had touched me, I would have learned; if ever he had spoken, I would have heard. And I know now why he moved so carefully, spoke so seldom. He was a man so undeceived about others that he could say little that would not hurt or repel them, who in his own life dared move only from modulation to modulation because he had so little self-deception on which to depend. But that clear inner eye from which he suffered was not, as Fourchette's was, disengaged. For all his outer evenness he was still immersed in the current, still mortally capable of pain, and of more.

"What did you think, then?" he said roughly. "Did you think I thought I could get a son by letting her scribble my name down for him? I did it for her!" Then he struck his fist against his forehead, a single blow, not distracted, almost grave, that might have been anything, a reproof for forgetting her now or the sharp "to heel" of a man returning himself to himself; and pushing me aside, he went into the bedroom again and shut the door.

I picked up the paper from the floor and held it, still crumpled, in my hand. What more could it teach me that I had not already learned? I had not even thought to impute that — that he did it for her.

Just then the door, ill-hung, ill-fitted like every part of that house, swung silently wide as was its habit to swing, back and forth in the draft from the passage, unless it had been latched. Raised on her pillows, my mother faced me. She was still awake; her eyes gleamed in the light cast from behind me; to her I must have appeared as the men on the street had that afternoon with the sun behind them — a dark face with a bright nimbus of hair. My uncle was oblivious; he was kneeling at the side of the bed with his back to me, one arm flung across her knees.

"He did it against me," he was saying. "Not you. He did it against me."

Lying there under the blue lamp, she said nothing, made no move.

He would not know why she could never believe him — he was child-less. But she would know that I did what the child must do — hunt for the quick of the parent, and pierce there.

"Please believe it," he said. "He did it against me."

He does this for her too, I thought. How chary I have been to admit it — the real motive. But this, that he tells her now, she surely cannot believe.

Then, as I watched them, as the door inched slowly toward me in its reverse arc, her arm came up around him. I saw her head nod, not in sleep, her eyes close and reopen, and still nodding, she held him, kneading his bowed shoulders with her good left hand. The door came between us like a curtain, leaving me outside it, outside them. Once more I had forgotten to impute the motive of love.

Three days later, on the evening of the third day, I left Tuscana. I had no need to spend the intervening hours in arrangements. My effects were few and I had always planned to take less; I was going where abundance was. In a great city, personality itself is to be had for the making; this is the deep, real reason that carries a clever provincial there. And in my summertime dreams of my arrival there — fantasies bred while I worked at the market, never seeing the hawker's colors of that evening bourse already undergoing its own fatal change — I saw myself arriving in a dawn whose steel-flushed outlines and avenues I had already studied, saw myself facing that chemically rising light with nothing but the brain that had got me there. I could have wished to have awakened like a foundling on one of its paving stones, naked even of swaddling clothes, or to have rubbed my eyes open to those complex rays like some gay stripling who has slept all night in a doorway, and now finds himself hungry, powerful and healthily amnesiac, remembering only his name. Now, instead, I found myself in a strange preamble of nakedness, under edict in Tuscana, here.

The words on the piece of paper had been these: *I want him away. Tell him I do not hold it against him. But I want him away.* Nothing further was said, nor was the paper itself mentioned by my uncle again. The paper had vanished; he seemed to assume that I had seen it, that I would do the right thing — and that I would know what the right thing was. Only in retrospect does the simplicity of that last seem extravagant. For I did know.

I knew that my mother wanted me to leave at once, and without seeing her, without her having to see me again. One learns from the hurt one inflicts as well as from the hurt one suffers — this is a lesson elided in the popular self-help primers of love. And at my mother's bedside I had learned that it is not the victim in us that needs to turn away.

My uncle, when I told him I was leaving, said little. At first he merely registered a cough — that dry, aphysical trade-mark of a man who collected neither crotchets nor colds — a cough without ponder, a mere punctuation. I think now of how long I lived with it, despising it as the tic of an inner aridity — that sound which instead marked time for him while he chose from his heavy store of honesty the least gnomic reply, the answer that would least trouble others with the weight of themselves.

"Best," he said then, "best for all of us." And then, before he had time to warn himself, cough again quickly: "I knew you would know to do that."

This was the first he had addressed me since our exchange in the hall. "She should have known," he had said then, and now — "I knew." His blunt expectation, even at this late date, of the best from me, was something new and astringent, masculine, making me suspect what I might have lost by having been reared by women. How strangely he was making me feel, with his assumptions — was it he or I who had changed? Confused, I waited for more. I did not ask him, as I ask myself now, how he knew.

But he required, gave, nothing further. Thereafter, while he absented himself from the mill until a nurse should be found, and spent all his hours with my mother, I was left to my vacuum. Except for the fact of going, I was already gone, disposed of as the consciousness must of necessity do with those, good or bad, who are about to be removed from our sufficiently complicated scene. There was no malice here; it was character — of the twenty-twenty-visioned eye that, strive as it may not to make a show of anticipating the purblind, cannot always keep from anticipating itself. It was the perfect ostracism, one that did not even turn aside. And the perfect punishment — for which others are never more than agents — the nudge, not of dogma, but of life. I had wished for freedom from all ties; now I was left to find out what that freedom was.

Friday had been the day in court, Saturday the day I had told him my decision too late for the schedule; Sunday there were only local trains. I would leave on Monday evening — a short interim, but more than enough time to explore the vacuum that has no clock. I often think of that solitary bout — it was my first. It was my first step into the sinkhole of identity. Every man, even the most coherent, the strongest, has moments when his foot sinks suddenly in that abyss — a voice asking, "Who am I?" To which echo answers, "Am I?" Loneliness is a mere wavelet on that surface, a kitchenmaid's word for a crater whose term of definition, if there is one, must lie among the philosophical — perhaps some black neologism that compounds them all. For these are moments that come by seeming vagary, uncoupled with ordinary loss. Ordinary misery — loss of a woman, of a child, of a friend in war, of any appendage of the heart or the body — is no vacuum. The sundered body is a bowl that fills with dark. But in the vacuum one comes, *pas seul,* to that farther edge of ego where, if one does not whirl away quickly in some *pas de deux* of activity, one might feel what only the dying should feel — the loss of loss.

As everyone must, I was to find my own ways of dealing with this; under the aspect of eternity all methods are no doubt equally absurd. But at that time I had none. Three feet away from me was the edge of the civilized world, but as far from my grasp as the far shore in a binocular lens. Meanwhile, flowers came for my mother from Miss Pridden; some of them had time to fade. In my room I had already had for some days now Demuth's parting gift, parting shot, never to be acknowledged, a German grammar on whose flyleaf *"Forsan et haec olim meminisse iuvabit"* had been elaborately inscribed. "Perhaps some-day you will be glad to remember this." What I remembered instead when I saw it was that other tag, truism from the *Schwäbisch* of his fathers, that other untranslatable, all-translatable sheep's bawl. But that too came from a distant shore. I had meant to rise hand over hand on the single rope of myself; now, without the asseveration of others, the rope disappeared. And meanwhile my uncle passed and repassed me in the hall.

On Monday evening he drove me to the train with my parcel of books, my one bag. I had expected to walk; his offer came to me as a surprise, a rescue. It was again one of the long dusks, the air cotton-warm and clogged, but I felt the wonderful, cool renewal of doing, as if I had been ticking away under a bell glass that now was removed. The traveler is crisp with organization, his very flesh hardens forward; to his futurist eye those who are staying on behind seem soft and idle in their lack of schedule, safely placed folk but fainthearted, already receding. Seated beside me in the car, my uncle as he drove looked so to me.

At the main-line stop, although we were well ahead of time, the red signal was already blinking. The old huddle of sheds and lean-to's, once piled against each other like domino counters, had long since been cleared away, leaving the ancient ticket office with its iron-rib-banded eaves, although one still had to buy one's ticket elsewhere. There was no platform; we would still have to cross to the track from the cindery siding on which a few other travelers were already stand-ing, well back from the huge rush of air that would come with the train. The train stopped regularly now; there were eighteen thousand people in Charlotte and Denoyeville, and more coming. But Tuscana still had the main line.

A light summer rain began falling, welcome on the cheek, smelling of the reviving grass. Here and there a traveler lifted his face to it, re-garded the sky and spoke of the night, that after such a rain might be clear. Voices were single in note but joined in portent, as they are in the open air and when speaking of weather. A bit of crushed bird's egg lay pale green in the cinders near my shoe, and I felt the foolish softness, weak happiness of someone long housebound who is admitted again to the range of the seasons, under whose passing in his absence people have maintained themselves like sturdy blooms. From a distance a man wearing a hat and carrying a briefcase waved to my uncle, who nodded back, fumbling at his collar. He had lost formality, even neatness, in his nursing; he had come out without a tie, and his shirt collar was soiled. Between its limp tips his throat seemed newly meager, and the underline of the chin descended in that aging tautness so particularly human when, as with my uncle, the jawbone kept its youth. Far off, communicated not yet through the ground or any shimmer in the air, but in the hardening curve of the group waiting, we sensed the oncoming train.

My uncle took out his watch. "Four minutes yet." He held the watch overlong, warmed it in his hand, hesitated, ran his thumb over the chain, before he slipped it back in his vest pocket. Sometimes I fancy now that he meant to give it to me, tried to, failed. "We'd have had time for a short one," he said. "For luck. I had the bottle out . . . but I forgot it." Forgetting that Mrs. Jebb had come over to stay in the house while we were gone, he had run back, just as we were leaving, to answer the tinkle of my mother's bell. "Well . . . God bless," he said, and gave me his hand.

"When we came home that day —" I said. "You were home before your time, before us. And you had the bottle out that day." It was never out, as we both knew, except for celebration.

"Ah . . . yes." Although the track was still quiet, his answer was almost inaudible. "You will not have heard." Red tinged his cheek. "Blankenship has stepped down."

The train shuddered in then. We fell back in the smacked air. He is head foreman then at last, I thought, as I lugged my bag up the iron steps to the coach car. I remembered the bottle and pushed-back chair in the sitting-room window, on my aunt's table the whisky's slopped ring. Blankenship has stepped down. He had had it ready to greet her with when we greeted him with her. I turned to catch sight of him at the window and found him behind me. He had followed me into the car.

"She will want news of you," he said hurriedly.

I nodded without speaking.

"She will want to write to you . . . after a while. But at first, you understand, I shall have to do it for her." He coughed. "Tell me then — under what name?"

I looked down at the seat, at my bag. "The new one."

"Yes, of course. But I must not ask her. What is it?"

I stared, then gave it to him. Why did I not know him before, I thought? Neither will he speak, neither will he press others to.

He repeated it, spelled it out, tested it. "Pierre Goodman," he said, not a hint on his face, and nodded. This was the first time I had heard it spoken aloud outside the court. It half felt as if I received it from him, as if in the moment of parting he for better or worse dubbed me with it. The train lurched and he turned. I followed him to the end of the car. There was something I ought to say, but I had no idea of what it was. For a minute, while the train paused again, he clung to the iron handhold of the coach. "Well, God bless," he said, and swung himself down.

The train grooved a few yards down the track and stopped again. Other travelers in the car were leaning out of their windows in the superstitious concentration of the leaver, exchanging with their people on the siding the nods and smiles with which each reassured each that he would be brooded upon until perspective bodily removed him, that not until then would either lean back, even in sorrow secretly relieved. I leaned out with them, though not as far as the rest. He was still standing there among the others, our opposites back there on the cinder path, but his face was hidden by a taller man. Timidly, half hoping I too was hidden, I waved. The tall man moved aside. An exclamation, some formless syllable, came from me, one of those sounds, mysterious to their makers, that unnerve us with the sudden sense of our still uncalculated selves. But the distance was too far for speech, and I saw that my uncle was not looking at me. He had remained, perhaps out of that inflexible, median courtesy of his that would not allow even the offender to leave town unspeeded, but he was looking, not idly, at others around him who, absorbed in their ave's, were not noticing him. It seemed to me that his face that could not change had changed. Distance, much more swiftly than I had expected, was showing me its alchemy, teaching me how little apart one needed to move from a man. I thought of the map of the world, of those nervously dotted lines of communication between two places whose simultaneity no speed could outwit, of how two men, dotted next to each other, were not unlike these; and for the first time in my young life I ascended to that grim cliché from whose height all philosophers, lovers, friends before me had gazed down. For the first time since I did not know when (since those listening afternoons with Johnny, since that last day when Frau Goodman had refused me what I could not even remember, since I had been born, perhaps), I thought of it not as my safety but as my prison — that all of us, man beside man, friend beside friend, should so incurably coexist.

The train moved again, pulling me backward, forward, away. I could see my uncle clearly. He was looking at me now. Surely his face had changed. He was waving at me. Good-by. I leaned out with the rest, as far as the rest, but in the moment that I might have, I forgot to wave. For in the moment that the train, gathering speed, suddenly bore me away with a centrifugal lurching, I had recognized him. Then, like a pinpoint scooped from behind, he vanished, a man of whom I could have asked, whom I could have trusted never to ask — the confidant I could have had, the last man on earth to say "Listen . . ."

A mile or two ahead we stopped again. I had had no time to do more than sit stiffly within my new name, revelation, the way a boy sits in a new set of clothes, half reluctant to disturb or discover the unfamiliar seams of his housing. Then the lights went on and the two conductors came down the aisle in their grave, ticket-taking antiphonal, one repeating the passenger's destination to the other, the other sticking the proper replacement ticket up above.

"No, ma'am," I heard the forward one say, "dining car stays on until Memphis. Just taking coal on here." Then they came to me. "New York," said the one in front to the one behind, scrutinized my sheaf of tickets, tore off one and returned it, while his aide placed a long red ticket in the slit before me. "Forward cars only going past Memphis," said the first one. "Pretty crowded up ahead now, though. You better off shifting when we get there." Then they passed on, the talker and his mute, carrying on the craft-ceremony that from then on in all the travel-years ahead never failed to confound and amuse me — to require two of them, and for such solemnity, there surely must be more to what they did than met the eye.

I watched them in the first of these fascinated puzzlements; the only other great train I had been on had been the one that must have carried us from Montreal to wherever we had made connections for Tuscana, and all that belonged to that period of hearsay, which I had never yet been able to recall. At the end of the coach they turned and came back. This was the last car. I felt a thrill of confirmation that it should be; in my reveries "leaving" had always begun just that way. This was my luck beginning, I told myself, my peculiar, personal brand of luck, and indeed it was — the chance, fledgling move of an imagination unorthodox but always earthbound to the possible, as objectively chill to itself as to others, that in foreshadowing events in its way half compelled them. I walked to the rear of the coach and let myself out into the open, onto the short platform of what in my ignorance I thought of as the "observation car." We were carrying no freight; there was no caboose. I could look back unobstructed. This was the way I had always imagined leaving — looking back from the observation car of my first great train.

Behind me the lights went out in the coach and all along the train, blotted out now to a dark serpentine curving far ahead and to the right, between the end where I stood and the engine, uglily knobbed and pygmy-attended, appearing now and again in occasional flashes of red and white, like a magic-lantern slide of a hippo being fed and watered. I knew where we were now, although since the place was approachable otherwise only by roads under construction, I had never seen it. We were in the uncompleted railroad yard that had laid waste a wide territory behind the dams — holdings of farmers who had for years plumed themselves on their safe escape from the dams, then had scattered agitatedly before the maw of the dragon called "eminent domain," then had settled back fatly to advising less fortunate ones to sell out now, even if they had to sell off to niggers, and join them in their newly industrialized lives. The yard was to be an enormous catch basin for the toppling traffic of freight sluiced in because of the dam. It was the first such expansion of the railroad in the memory of any local ancient, in this queer new kind of pioneering in which steam no longer opened up a country but followed humbly after more demonic powers, in which townsmen who had moribund rail stock certificates in their bureaus raised their heads again at the thought that the trains might still be the land-language of the nation, and no one, under quiet skies where a steel wing still drew upturned faces, could conceive that the next language to die for us might be the land. For the change, plain to be seen now by everyone, bulldozed into the geography, energized into the pocket, was still thought to be only in the terrain; those riparian banks, convoluted to the heavens, edged by dainty lines of light that outshone day and at night made them look like impenetrably risen Atlantises of the air, were still the land.

We must have remained there for as much as twenty minutes. Trainmen ran past us with the special lanterns that as a boy I had always wanted to examine, hold in my own hand. Here and there along sets of track that fanned in every direction, others probed and swabbed at the undercarriages of coaches strewn like huge building blocks between drums of wire, concrete mixers covered for the night, and holes that sent up the strong troll-smell of freshly excavated earth. Farther back, away from the incessant shunting of the front lines, in the dead, starlit aisles of the freight cars, yardsmen slunk suddenly from them like huntsmen from blinds and stooped over cupped cigarettes, over their shoulders the long, faded mottoes on the car sides streaming almost as if heard, only silence needed to melt their Munchausen horns. I watched, spread below me the vast, smudged final impression of a Biblical woodcut in which I, raised and imperially hidden on my platform, was like the presence concealed in the cloud. "Hotbox," said one of two men going past me with lanterns, and I envied them the pygmy lore of their black trade and wished to penetrate it, as in the cobbler's shop I had sometimes wished my fingers tanned or emeried close to his tallowy secrets, or on waterfronts would one day wander past the ship chandlers and wish myself initiate to the creakings and joists of the sea. Yet it was not any of these simple apprenticeships I wanted; what was it I would ask for if, as in the Bible pictures, there were an angelic being, its cheek puffed with prophecy, in the upper right-hand corner of the heavens — a demanding voice rayed from a cloud?

Above us, the night was clear, as the travelers had predicted. Under the milky light of the nebulae only two of the four peaks of the dam site were visible; I was north of them now, they no longer enclosed the world. On each of the two a searchlight of a candle power that erased the humble thought of candles swept toward us at a minute's interval and disappeared again, passing its pale field upward over the motionless cirrus-sheep that ranged the blue. In that pale federal light even the heavens were neutral; nothing might ignite there without being seen. Beneath it, on the crest it protected, I could see the fine, suave sodium air of a no-man's country. There no men ran like burning crosses, no crosses stood like running men who burned. Back of it lay Tuscana, whose little collection of spore-lights I could just see through the divide. But there, on that one strip, the swinging alternate had annihilated the bitter and personal dark. If by a like alternation I could annul the bitter personal of my boyhood, then was that what I should ask of my angel? To be apprenticed from now on only to the protean; to acquire the gift of tongues but never choose one. To make a no-man's country of the past. Ahead of me lay all the variorum of living, into which, if I was to step freely, I must do as the parvenu does, who halts only to drop behind him in some crevice his old bundle of the past. For back of me too still lay Tuscana. To hate it would still be to choose it. To hate it would be to stay.

So, standing there on my platform, that is what I prayed to the angel. If memory is what keeps us, what saves us from neutrality, then allow me, who cannot forget, to forget. For it is memory that keeps us where we are, what we are. If to forget is the cardinal sin, the only failure, then for once let me commit it. For once help me to fail as others do. Allow me to forget. Make this fade.

When I raised my head we were moving, but only inching, as if the train too could not quite decide. Then we gained speed. As we swung north, northeast in a wide arc, I saw the little collection of spore-

209

lights slip from view. Next the dams faded, showing me how even the four corners of a world could recede. Ahead of me the train gave tongue, as if it had at last made up its mind. It was the long wail, half resigned, half triumphant, that I had heard every night there of my boyhood, the sound of the to-from Memphis train.

After a while it was silent. We were running through all those small towns ahead that night after night briefly shone toward it, briefly waned. Above us, in relative motion, the cirrus clouds streamed backward, away from us, yet stayed. And in a dark patch in their center, there was Tuscana; I saw Tuscana, keeping time with us too. I leaned backward from it as if drawn by the hair, but it leaned forward with me, both of us drawn by an angel through a stratum so thin that perspective vanished, and I could see it now as never before. It rode lightly with me, that bitter and personal dark. Desire and injustice were there, and people flowing toward me like analogues, and feelings rubbing together like knives, all the shapes of life at their game — *he did it for her, she did it for me, and I did this, and I did nothing* — hand over hand over hand. It was there that I had found others were necessary even to me, the listener, where I had begun to imagine how people might even hoard trouble in order to feel. Where I had come to the resolve that even if people should be for me always too late or too soon, too open or closed, too near or far, then living itself was the privilege, and interest alone would carry me through.

I looked back at it for a long time. Now that I was truly leaving it I could see it most clearly. I closed my eyes. Now I was leaving. Now I had left it. I opened my eyes. I looked back at Tuscana and it was beautiful in memory, as are the faces of all those we leave.

PART III
False Entry

So I shouldered memory, and set out to be a man. Since, like the young everywhere, I had been bred by preceptors who wanted me to believe that life was conducted by choices, I still believed them — out of the wonderful disorder that confronted me, no doubt a retributive god would one day demand that order be made. But, like all my fellow-pupils before me, I secretly assured myself that that day receded dimly ahead — dim as my own death. Our mentors either did not see for themselves or could not bear to say that with each move we would make or that would be made for us — and with each permutation thereof — the choice was already being formed.

So it would happen to me — as to all of us who, whatever else we were, were unreconciled to living unexamined — that memory would become not nostalgia but necessity. Out of the continuum in which we found ourselves to be floating, it would come to seem the one autonomy we might still retrieve.

So, between what I have done and what I have not done, I have come this far. And I begin to see how the chronicle is made. What we do not do persists, classic and perfect, beneath what we do. The final admixture is the judgment.

Chapter I. The Upstairs World. Maartens.
Mrs. Papp.

AND so — I have written to Ruth.

Very morning-clear, that small, lower-case "so," after the pneumatic, midnight three struck chordally down the preceding page. I use "pneumatic" as one might expect the part-time pedant would, in the old theological sense of having to do with the spirit or soul (*pneuma* — the Greek "breath"), and yet with a chuckle for its modern usage too — "filled with air." Not that I decry those three others; they have produced the fourth. Where will it take me, that sudden cap to the winds, that small "so"?

How it came about is after all quite simple — amazing that the switch had not taken place before. For I have been sojourning down there for a long time now, on that long skin-dive into the nether regions of myself, learning to move about in that intense, direct element of motive which underlies the upper atmosphere of acts. Most men shift about in partial glee, discomfort, behind the façades they see themselves presenting to others; I differ only in always having been able to reach a minim or two more accessibly behind the façade I present to myself. But one finds — or rather, the exquisite, reflexive sanity of instinct finds for one — that one can parlay that accessibility only so far. Time up for air. The foray is over, not forever, but for now. For in whatever way I am aberrant from the average, I am not, any more than most, a Jekyll-Hyde. My "split" — that cocktail party profundity — is no more than the next one's, and the halves, if there are such, are quite, quite aware of each other. I have never indulged in much thumb-twiddling over my basic sanity, either in parlor games or in private. Even in adolescence, when the very elasticity of any decent brain — its almost felt growing — is often a wonder and a worry to its owner, I seldom teased myself with that semidelicious question, "Am I mad?" Within the unreasonable limits of my species, and the quanta peculiar to this hour in its history, I am sane. Man is a schizoid animal. And Socrates is a man.

What has happened is that I have been returned to what, for want of a better term, one must call the daytime mind. A misnomer of course — it is rather that part of the mind which moves, according to its own style and accomplishment, at any hour of the twenty-four. Daytime is, however, its quality. It is the part of us that can mock — if it does not wholly mistrust — the midnight phase. I do not mistrust. If a djinn should smoke suddenly from a bottle, offering me two forked paths to the absolute — one bushy with exaggeration, stalked by the hypertrophic banditti of midnight, and one in which the serious is minced down to the companionable, birds in their nests disagree with jurisprudent irony, and melodrama is put out of countenance by the clear humors of morning — I know which I should still have to choose. But for the moment I am removed to the satiric distance. And from it I can see that I am still bound by that insensate word "choose." As if one could choose between the parts of the whole blood, between the red and the serum, decreeing that only the one shall flow in the vein! Yes, Socrates is a man. And no one seeing only the "I" of these pages might suspect how antic and buoyant he can be on occasion, how reasonable a citizen of the lower-case world.

When I awoke this morning it was, as usual for these past weeks, somewhere before noon. I had been going to bed night after night at about four, stretching out each time in the quiet, sweated relief of a man who is at last at grips with the contretemps which has hovered for years. Each night I had experienced the same seven hours of intense sleep. Normally I dream the good citizen's mumbo jumbo of the day's palaver and anxieties, mixed with whatever hints from the vesicles are at hand. But on these nights I slept as if clasped around some chalice that led me from one night's pages to the next, even the sexual abated in that process, profounder than any autoeroticism, by which I hoped to be regenerating myself. Mornings I awoke into the alert, whole faculty of childhood. City walks by day were no more than sanative plunges from desk to garden, in which passers-by exchanged their dioxides with me as impersonally as flowers and I took my meditation among them as the philosopher takes his to the company of the phlox. Each night, reading back on the work of the previous one, I learned to scan what I found there with surgical joy. And each night found the continuity preserved. .

But this morning, awaking with the start of the malingerer, ears uneasy against the practical echoes of the street, I bounded upright, like a man on holiday who hears the business clock give a sudden, loud tick in the heart of sloth. When I stretched my cheek at the shaving mirror I did it intently; I was preparing this face for people, and I drank my coffee in the citizen's modest twinge of retreat from a not too pedestrian dream. Only half awake, as on the groggy mornings before this account began, I could already feel the lack of that deep supportive reverie on which I had floated for so many days. Being gone, its loss is already difficult to describe. It is a sensation known to the good swimmer, drugged almost to the point of no return from his own amphibian ease, bobbed suddenly to the vertical by his ruthlessly mortal lung. His ear drumming with the depth that has nearly murdered him, he still mourns it; the heavy water of the present drags his garment, and he meets with a shock of sadness the warm, terrestrial pull at his heel. Gravitation warmed me; I felt saved, but empty of what had been snatched away.

Now I felt the familiar urge to lampoon myself, the rising barrage of acrid comment by which a clever man reminds himself he is not a fool. Reaching for the *Times,* nonexistent on the kitchen threshold, I marveled at how many days there had been, almost a month, since I had canceled it, asking myself now if a man of this time, this place, this ilk could be said to exist without. If the *Times* says it isn't going to rain, this can't be rain. It was not raining, however, but a brilliant morning, the sun spreading like butter on the front of the house opposite, whose flat, limestone-clay color has always obscurely pleased me. A sound truck went by, braying some exhortation — to the cinema, to the spirit, perhaps, but not to vote — one knows very well that this is not November but April. And it is Tuesday. I ran a finger along the morning's deposit on the sill; yes, this has the look of Tuesday grit. You know very well who, when, and where you are. Day for the cleaning woman — no, cleaning *lady*, one of the trusty serf-shadows who flit city-wide and only for bachelors, leaving Mehitabel notes useful for breaking the ice at your parties — a shadow vaguely Czech, dimly sixty, whom you have not met in the flesh for years — was it for her that you shaved?

Outside, in the back garden of the house next door, the superintendent, a richly oily Italian, hitched his brigand stomach, chirked at his dog *bac bac bac Baccaloni*, and shook his lovelocks *don don don Giovanni* at the sky — all against your private knowledge that he has a Scottish wife, a red-nosed stick of a child always screaming for "swayties," and was himself born in Throg's Neck. Despite which, when you glimpse him from the shower, you often switch from "*Freude! Freude!*" to "*Là ci darem la mano.*" Yes, this is the morning mind. It has its own diapason. By its wry self-apostrophe a man convinces himself that he holds the reins; with a thousand surface iridescences it lures him back to the representational world. Do not belittle its powers. It too is "the mind." And its chief power is to deny its own matrix, to laugh at the demiurge.

"Listen," it says in its cranky, comedian rattle, "we're not alone. Always somebody under the bed. Whoever told you we were?" "My dear sir," it says in a clear, eighteenth-century ratiocinative, "may I present my allies — and yours — the city, roaring so gently; the *Times*, always so ready to fill a gentleman's empty mind with the issues proper to his station; and that entrancing garrulity of your era, the telephone. All at your gate, ready to explode their petards. Let it be a philological joke between us that *pétarder* means 'to break wind.' " And so to its French. *"Solipsiste!"* it screamed, with the same rancor with which it might have said, *"Sodome!"* And then, in softer, chemise-colored tones, *"Pauvre solitaire."* Last came the blunt croak of the sportsman it is — "Look 'ere, what's that pogostick you're 'oppin' abaht on, call it your singularity? Picked it to place or show?" And then I stopped, or tried to, for who can hope to prestidigitate as *it* does? As well try to duet with the world's best harpsichordist, with Chinese back-scratchers tied to one's hands, and from three feet away. Let it play; you follow. Most manage that way most of their lives. I drew an experimental breath, and yes, the quondam depth I had come from seemed sunk almost to the nonsense distance — all the doggerel of sense dropping lightly to my aid.

"Demiurge" was a word I had borrowed from my painter friend Maartens. Looking through the kitchen doorway, I could see down this long room — the old ballroom of the house, with a musk of conversation still in its linenfold and a ceiling high enough to accommodate the *fin de siècle*. In the dimmest corner — farthest away from the oasis of gaiety in the bay, where drink, music and shadow screens interpenetrate their boxes behind a previous occupant's sofa (dropped on their modern manner like a Crébillon joke) — is this desk, shyly battlemented beneath the books. On it I could see these pages, arrested — by some silently sliding safety door of the will — before they had come to the incriminating matter. Nothing much was in them as yet except that *peccavi*, common enough since Rousseau, by which a man might subtly work himself over to the demonstrably good side in the course of revealing his bad. Should I burn them then, as Maartens, in an access of overcritical rage, disgust, or fear — whose terms no one could understand but himself — sometimes burned a painting? Or should I do as he, get away before the destruction and take a therapeutic turn with what he calls "people outside"? Of whom, to him, I am one. Those periods are when I see him.

I imagine that there are many outside the arts to whom Maartens is "my painter friend," kept much as a doge might have his dwarf, a cultivated Philistine "my poet," an alert politician "my Jew." He brings the dark, dye-pot range of his artistic difference just near enough for them to dip their fingers in its fascination and congratulate themselves against its dangers. When he tells them — with seeming naïveté and actual insolence — that he seeks their company because of *their* difference, they are flattered to find themselves in possession of what they never knew they had. And finally, he reassures them, since he happens to be an exceedingly ugly man. Maartens, I'm certain, has only a callous, professional interest in his own tints and composition. But as they observe orange hair vying with pink, bladdery nether lip and exophthalmic eyes (whose red-lit brown I once heard him call, in his precise Dutch voice, as he sat for himself, "the exact color of a bedbug who has just eaten"), they are comfortably reminded once again that beneath any exaggerated effort to compose the world in order or beauty, the specific neurosis is plain.

Maartens rests me. I made his acquaintance without guile and he has none, having as little façade, beyond the skin, as is possible. This is in part because words have no aura for him outside their use; he uses them for whatever, by the usual covenants, they can perform. Magic lies elsewhere for him; although he is not physically nervous, I've grown accustomed to seeing him wander a room not his own, aligning objects and colors, or cavalierly shutting them away, and except in those periods when he can't work and is seeking the company of the Philistines for that obverse service he hopes they will do him, I'm rather sure that he sees the human only as another kind of "arrangement." Nevertheless, it's at those times, when his power "to make," as he calls it, deserts him, that he develops a certain uncanny ability to plumb its habit for others, the way a countryman, in the city and sick for home, can speak of it like Theocritus, for an afternoon.

"Yesterday," he tells me, "I was at work." Then we sit a while in memoriam, as if he had just said, "Yesterday I was alive." Fairly soon he will begin to tell me how it happened, but only in order to be able to dwell afterwards on what he has been exiled from, the way an Israelite, to whom Canaan is as much remembered as promised, might haughtily map its milk-and-honey rivers, not to a kinsman, but to some Gentile stranger who has no hope of it at all.

He sighs. "Did you happen to notice what it was like, the day *before* yesterday?" he asks.

I remark that it was thus and so — last time, that it was nice.

"Nice!" he will say. "Superb! Baked by a pastry cook who put on another flourish every half hour. *Cordon bleu. I* noticed," he says with a certain emphasis. "Wind, girls, buses, everything. I spent the whole day at it."

Earlier in our friendship, when he first sought me out at such a time, I would have asked "Why not!" receiving the answer reserved for fools: "Not with the upstairs eye!" But now I know that old saw of his and I nod. Suddenly he smiles — Maartens is not witty as we verbal ones class wit, but he has the broad humor of those who, lash about as they may, have an ultimate faith in themselves.

"Cecile says" (she is his wife) "that I always act just the way women do about their monthly — let them cry at a cheap movie, or feel the whole world in the small of their back, or see the pimple in the mirror; still, twelve times a year they will say to themselves, 'I wonder why.' And I'm the same — I never see it coming."

And the next morning or the one after, his lapse comes. In the studio, he does not go as usual at once to the canvas, always faced to the wall, away from all eyes but his own, and turn it about, as one uncovers a child. The room's happy confusion, ignored these six months, worries him. He spends the morning leafing through what judgment has abandoned or completed, roaming his lifework with a housewife's sour, prophylactic stare. When he can no longer avoid it, he goes to the last canvas and turns it around. And now, shrugging at me, he throws up his hands.

"Bad?" I unwisely ask, and he gives me another of the looks he reserves for the people outside. Bad would be hopeful. It is nothing, neither one way or the other.

And now he begins what he has come for — to describe, with the sweet roweling of memory, what he has lost. The canvas is the eye, he said once, the eye on a string from the navel. The string one can drop and pick up again. But what he has lost lies behind. Stretching his lips around words, he brings them forth like a dog that, howling for its master, develops human speech. And like the dog, dangling his slack leash, he noses me back to the studio, snuffling at the fled footprint, saying "here" and "here."

"Did you burn it this time?" I cast a glance at a small work of his, hung over my mantel, that I bought last year. No, he answers, not this time. He has locked the door on all that order, given the key to Cecile, who cries, "Oh, not again! But I knew!" gone down the stair, and come here. Inside the closed studio, as he makes me see it, the wind streams under the sash like a continuous peal of laughter, bearing in that pointillist surface which none can ever hope to abstract or diffuse. Somewhere back there too is that lost land, lost depth from which he has tried. He falls silent, despairing of its description, that pure, angry country from which a man can presume to pose a four-by-four canvas against the Augean confusion of the world.

"Demiurge, Number Three," I say. That is the title of the picture over the mantel.

"Oh, for God's sake, Pierre," he says, "that's a dealer's word. The dealer insisted on names and we got it out of the dictionary at random. I like the words that come before and after just as well," he says, grinning — "demitasse, demirep." Already his voice is a little more arrogant; in my obverse way I have helped him. I know why he comes. "No," he says. "To *make*. That's as far as I'll go with you word-mongers. To *make*."

"Only an auxiliary," I say. "Make peace. Make money."

"Basic," he says, getting up to go. "Make water. Make love." I watch him go down my staircase and stop at the landing.

"You know what Cecile shouted after me when I left," he says, looking up. " 'Burn it, why didn't you,' she says, 'you *flâneur*, the ones that are left will only be worth all the more.' "

I laugh, and he joins me, for since he is already being collected by both bankers and museums, that is probably true. "What will you be doing now?" I call after him, but he has not heard me.

On his febrilely merry "Be seeing you," the door slams.

As, for the months of his dry season, I shall. For what Maartens will do now will be to bury himself, at first desperate, then with calculating fervor, in the nonvisual world. He may be heard of as attending a music school six hours a day five times a week — he is a fair cellist; on another of his "tours," as he calls them, he will earn his certificate at a cooking school — two uncles were chefs, on the Swiss mother's side.

On his afternoon visits to me, he becomes less and less expository; he is forming his secrets again, nursing up his slow, fruitful anger against "the people outside." It is at that stage that one meets him, as I did first, at their parties, drinking in as if it were elixir the heliumated gabble of those who do everything but make. He listens with interest to their version of him, how to one he is a primitive, to another an artist made healthy by his "hobbies," to all a House and Garden version of the Renaissance man. "Ah, Maartens," says a lady lay psychiatrist, summing him up, "he *lives* everything out" — and she gives him the smile with which the viviparous are regarded by those who have learned, like Jove, to give birth only from the brow. Maartens says nothing but one hand nurses his stomach — he has rather a tidy pot — the way pregnant women do, and I amuse myself with the surmise that he is congratulating himself on having a navel, in the specious presence of so many who might almost be imagined to have none. For what is he doing there if not using them, by night, as by day he uses modes of expression that are foreign to his, as he would haunt even the world of the blind in order to be sent back with force on his own?

And on one of these nights one meets him in that gay-dreary little backroom cloaca of all such parties. He is looking down at the bed and there is pity on his face for the mink and polo cloth exploded so hopefully on the counterpane, for that touching pile of pupa-cases left in the back room by those who expect so faithfully to find themselves angels, breathing the *Zeitgeist,* in the front. As he tugs on his muffler, however, he is muttering expletive in one of his languages — dirty Marseillaise lingo maybe, or outhouse Flemish, or perhaps only the universal guttural of nausea. Be seeing you, he says with some embarrassment, for we both know that now he will not. He has got it back again, that hard and temporary country of his dominion. Will he remember from there that I have listened and half understood him, being halfway between him and those others outside? Of course not.

Were I to call the next day, Cecile would tell me that he is at work. And the messages he sends from there are indiscriminately for all.

No, I thought this morning, one does not call upon Maartens. He does what he can by doing what he must — while the rest of us have only the chronicle of ourselves. I walked over to the desk and looked down at these pages. Through the open sash the greening wind of April riffled them, turning up on page after page the same watermark — footprint of the self up from its own depth and pacing its own cubicle — I, I; I, I. I gathered them up roughly and held them over the grate. They trod a circle, but until they crossed its center could I burn them? Or would they plague me forever, bringing me round again to the dead-end bar at midnight, to the point at which I sat down here and began? No, until they bore up their trophy they would not burn. Yet even the most doting autobiographer must feel the shame of the ceaseless monotone that to others is only "he." Was that why the morning wind had brought me Maartens? The satiric distance has its uses even for him, I thought, and on an impulse to dramatize it, I put down the papers and went round the room snapping up every blind, meanwhile smiling at the thought of the cleaning woman who, imposing her Grundy code, would tour the room again pulling them severely halfway down. Then I flung open the window, leaned on the sill, feeling the hot purr of the sun, and regarded the world.

From where I was, am now, one can see only the back gardens of these brownstones. No one was in them at this hour. The superintendent had gone, and I regretted him. My own voice must be a croak; for weeks I had used it only when buying food. Behind me, the pages shifted under the breeze, and turning, I gathered them up and slid them into a drawer. One of the heavy spring-binders knocked against the telephone, loosing the steady dial tone. I let it whine on for a moment, then replaced the handset. That tone must be immediately annulled with a number; it is not bearable company. In the silence I had an urge to hear a voice, any voice. Urban children, I gather, have a game in which they dip like jackdaws into the wondrous rags-and-diamond bag of the directory and hold surrealist conversations with strangers — I knew who had told me that, her arms clasped around her knees as she rode that charming hobbyhorse of hers, the peculiar delights of a city childhood. We did it as much out of wonder as mischief, she had said — we could choose from a multitude and spell one of them into the hollow of our ear. As if we were all together, she had said, in a kind of synagogue of the air. In the city a child is never far away from his fellows, from the vastness of man, she had added with a musing tenderness, and I had not answered, thinking that, daughter of such a father, such a home, she would not have been — but of how many there must have been who were. And I had thought of my own game, and of how close it was to that other.

"Tell me some different things you did as a child," I had said, trying to forget in her presence what I did as a man. Now I looked down at the phone, in which hers and mine had been the last voices, and it seemed to me that it still held that residuum, sending up its bouquet of fear. I fear that I may trust. I knew the look of the page on which I had written that, and I had an impulse to lock the drawer. Lifting the phone again, I let the dial tone whine on. There should be a listening service, I thought — a mechanical presence that would record nothing, merely registering its attention now and then in suitable syllables. Thousands would use it the first day. And after due survey, it would be found that the same syllables were appropriate to all. Then I reminded myself of a safe number, ME 7, and dialed it, with a grin for the animism still lurking for us savages in our most inorganic contraptions — for what Plato would deny soul to an instrument on which, in certain places, one might dial ME? For a few seconds I listened to the time signal, tiny ant-voice always climbing toward infinity. When you hear the signal the time will be . . . 12:59. And always falling back again. No, I will do first as Maartens does, I thought, and closing the door without a look behind me, I went down the stair.

Outside on the doorstep I shivered in my jacket, blinking at the house opposite like an animal up from its hibernation, then started walking. The air was cooler than it had looked from above, a pre-spring mixture of capricious sun and cool already passing its zenith and on its long afternoon trend downward to the winter ultramarine that was the New York color above all others — a blue hour, I had read somewhere,

224

of a purity to be found nowhere else in the world, in a city, except Lisbon. I did not know whether this was true, but I flattered myself that I knew all the prototypes of day bred by this city between its waters and its ether. If I had time, I thought, I could construct a semicelestial gloss, a new-sided kind of Diurnal or Hours in which those to whom a day was an entity still evasive behind the weather reports could find the "days of New York" numbered to the closest tolerance, weighed and named perhaps as the elements are in the international table, from actinium through curium, gadolinium, krypton, palladium, tantalum, wolfram, yttrium, and all the others that Demuth had made me learn, down to zirconium. It would be a listing like that one, susceptible to addition but rarely to change, and with no more poetic than is natural. Take the sidereal hour, I thought: angle unit of right ascension equaling 15° measured along the equinoctial circle. Let the standard atomic weight be oxygen at 16. (*According to such measurements and others, herein this book is described, with addenda for industrial precipitations and all others short of cataclysm, a day for instance of such a blend of color, texture, mood, and other qualities as might be called the Interim or Jade: medium, nonseasonal, opaque rather than overcast, from the air dull over the cardboard Flushing flats and perhaps faintly Brontëesque over the Rocklands, but in the sea-level midtown streets of a caressing, mutton-fat dampness as perceptibly pleasant and undemanding as a held-back, happy tear. Colors without penumbra in that atmosphere. Green especially rises to viridian. Ladies should not wear bluish-reds. Day without edema, good for the purchasing of shoes. No sunset. Evening will impinge without drama, dishes with some condiment recommended, a little fugitive poetry among friends, or the milder forms of conjugal love. No stars.*)*

This is the intensity of the convert, I told myself, as I waited for the long light at Park, teetering on my heels with a certain bland assurance at knowing how much longer that particular light was. Always a tendency to press on the natives those evidentials to which the latter were so informally born. That summer I had arrived here, a month before school began, I had tossed my clothes in the dormitory room and never been in it from dawn to dusk and sometimes not from dusk to dawn, roving the streets with the same magpie acquisitiveness I had hitherto given to books, learning the city strata with a voyeur scholarship that had soon outstripped the obvious, until remarkably soon, thanks to youth, shanks' mare and subway, I could botanize any neighborhood — until in time I could dispense his own heritage to the native, telling, for instance, a third-generation New York Jew, *genus German, habitat East Eighties,* of the Ankarese Sephardim in New Lots, of a street, not far from Hester, not quite Mott, where pariah Galitzianer had mingled with Eurasian Chinese. Even now, that punditry, though relaxed, is the only one I am not averse to displaying — for though an encyclopedist, like members of some other professions, is, after the American habit, much buttonholed for free in the parlor, I prefer not to draw too much attention to a mnemonic talent outside the routine.

The light changed and I crossed, thinking meanwhile what a dull street Park was, a hallmark; even at Christmas, with its evenly illuminated trees equidistant along the stream of cabs, it had only a barely standarized faërie, like a hotel salon trimmed once a year for the chambermaids' ball. One might felicitate oneself, of course; it was not every provincial who had learned to despise Park. Still, I thought, I was forever convincing myself into the city, mentally possessing and repossessing it; for all the years I had been here I could never see its towers without a disquieting sense that I must regrow them for myself each day. This was not man's universal reaction to cities, I told myself; this was the parvenu's trouble — always trying to forget what he must not remember. Or always refusing to remember what he must not forget? How agile of you, dear harpsichordist, I thought, and how unworthy of both you and the old professor in the course you were so proud of taking in your first year here — "Metaphysics of Vitalism and Pragmatism," and his name was Phillips — who was forever pressing his young gentlemen to note how little grist was ground by paradox.

I turned a corner down a street of embassies, one of them painted the same buff, yellowish cream, slightly grimed, as the house opposite

226

mine. I stopped in front of it. Answer me this, then, I thought, still apostrophizing my bright morning musician, there aren't many such houses in New York, and I don't find any connection — why do I find the sight of this one so pleasant? — answer me, you who know so well that free association is never free. Ah, it answered, if one could travel the whole world, know every recondite cave and the tops of all the topless towers — as should soon become possible, even laughable, as men find their own planet only a miserable insectarium in the garden of the sky — then to such a traveler all places will be analogues of one another. From the boundless store of his impressions he will turn up a bit of yellow Mississippi mud on the Irrawaddy, on Second Avenue a dusk that was Portugal's, in the Himalayas, cornered perfect in its monastery, a day out of your gloss. With that terrible weight on his shoulders, any Canaan of place will be lost to him forever. To the man without further hills, who can see on both sides of the horizon, all places will become less dear, none final. No, I will not admit that, I answered, and staring again at the house front, I thought — perhaps it reminds me of hers. But that was absurd; hers was the old brownstone like mine, which, when sanded back to its quarry color, as the Mannix house had been, has a henna-violet tint in the evening and in the last flash from the west almost a carnelian — one can imagine a row of them then in their heyday, inflamed by the late-century sun. For a moment I stood there and imagined them. I have always preferred their era to the skinny-shanked nineteen-twenties so favored by this one; it was an era of *embonpoint* in women, in sofas, in time. They too had been all but eaten by the time signal, I thought; then, how absurd to take flight, as I had done each day, from this neighborhood of their ghosts. Under that aspect, what could it matter, the conjunction of a soon-to-be-ghost woman with a similar man? No, I answered myself, one does not go down to that subcellar and pull the centuries over one's head. Between one's appetites and one's dangers, one moves on.

Down the block a few stragglers waited for the bus. When it came I pressed forward with them and sat down on one of the long front seats that faced in. I knew the strata of the buses also, on these cross-town routes always more mixed and original, with people less sluggishly in context than they were on the avenues, men whose self-priming touches to hat or collar suggested that their confidence was out of its district, women who worried at each signpost and clutched their purses like women abroad in a foreign land. I stared absently at my *vis-à-vis* and they vacantly back, no doubt registering the facts of me according to their own lights and preoccupation. Surely the nature of a crowd is that everyone in it thinks himself the godly observer — the others are always the crowd. But in the subway and elsewhere when men are disposed *en face*, it has always seemed to me as if, for the purposes of travel, each man subsides, in truce, to the homunculus. Here, in a subserving silence so remarkably without overseer, a man may examine his opposite as if the latter were a bit of jeweled dirt, and for this no gauntlet is ever thrown down. And suddenly I was reminded of what my years here had made me forget, of how in those first weeks of wandering the city, what had surprised me, awed me most of all, was this great conspiracy of silence. In towns such as I had come from the streets are a constant ripple of nods and tipped greetings, a bath of human acknowledgment. And before that, in London, I had been a child, to whom all elders are a single, high sentry mouth from which one takes as scripture the handed-down distinction between the seen and the heard.

But as I had first walked the streets of New York I had been filled with amazement. Here and there on the tenement stoops there were clusters, and the bicker of children. Yet even these people put their necks in the yoke when they went on the main streets, abroad; a chance encounter with a known had a tinge of embarrassment at its edges, as if one had been surprised incognito; even lovers and families fell proudly silent in a kind of disownment, and only the inanimate, unleashed and braying its triumph, gave tongue. It's this, I thought — as the bus came to the end of the line, the driver said nothing, and we all disembarked — that makes the countryman say he cannot bear the noise of the city. What he finds unbearable is the non-noise of the human.

A clump of schoolgirls came toward us, all shoots of arm, gawk and hair. They were speaking to each other but really to "the gallery" hung in each heart like a collective valentine just opened that morning. They rolled past us like a huge sweetmeat ball sugared with giggles, leaving an eddy of smiles or annoyance behind. We dispersed around them, each of us taking his way alone, and as I stood looking down the long street with its busy rodent-fringe of shops, I could see perhaps fifty or more like us, a congress of fifty human beings passing each other as silently as if under edict, like people who walk about under some mutual concept that all assent to and none has authored, under a ban of tyranny or war.

I turned westward with some of the others, toward the Hudson. How sunshine muddies the thinking I thought; the absurdity is mine. The city merely makes demonstrable, in broad daylight and in numbers, the final distance between psyche and psyche, between C sharp and D flat, between one and one. A distance to be yearned over occasionally in private, but sensibly welcomed — as the naked bum blesses its trousers — when abroad. The city is nothing more than anonym on the avenue, in place of anonym at home in double bed or at family table, at his analytical desk or on his painfully self-examining knees. This is the feverish sensibility of the truant still tied to his memoir, I thought — now it's time to go home. Nevertheless, I continued walking.

Ahead of me on the broad thoroughfare, two or three of my compatriots on the bus were still with me going my way — and perhaps one or two behind. Did I really wish to know them, and why? Ego, no doubt, in part — the concatenation of thirty-five persons and Mr. P. Goodman on an east-west bus on a particular afternoon in the year of our Lord, April, either has a significance toward which all their past lives have tended them, or none — in which case neither has he. In which case neither *is* he. Or *who*? But the whole of it was that I was still in fact greedy to know them all, not themselves but their single story in all its variable, in each of which perhaps there was a chip of mine. And if I could, I should have wished to know not only theirs but all the street's and the city's, like some emperor, sadder and less satiable than Alexander, who knew that the world to be conquered never ends, being round.

Behind me the footsteps dropped off. Up ahead, only one of the crowd on the bus still led me, a small, elderly woman hobbling along with jerky neatness, as if her long skirts concealed an endless wheel of paper-doll feet that one after the other came down. I trailed her, if only because I have always had a hard time making myself let go of the casual, knowing how subtly afterwards it may be seen to have woven itself into the choice. Then too, we were approaching the university neighborhood and this gave me a practical reason — I have always been adroit at finding them. For I still meant to keep my evening appointment with myself. If I cannot approach through the depth, I thought, then I shall probe downward through the surface — even if it means doing as the encyclopedist does in the office, even if I should have to record the "I" as if it were another's, as if it were "he." And these blocks, though not for long, were the next environ in the memoir.

The woman ahead, eyes bent, was covering the ground with the tortoise intentness of the elderly. She turned into the doorway of one of the large apartment houses that front the river there, her slow pace allowing me time to make my direction nonchalantly hers. This too was the impersonal advantage of the city. We stood together inside, in front of an elevator that descended somewhere above us with a servile sighing, like an omen that had to please everybody. I knew these old lobbies well, their ochered Ionic plaster and dirty marble from which the corporation had long since removed the Oriental rugs and Queen Anne thrones of their prime, leaving behind only what could not be removed and was valueless — their echoing, anachronistic space. Above, the middle middle class lived with its pretensions and its roomers, the professor housing the student, the salesman hanging on to his debts by his expense account, while their wives, hunching their collars through the Puerto Rican side streets, protested "the river, the park for the children," meanwhile keeping up an elegy in tune with the elevator — "running down, everything running down."

The old lady, about seventy, had the classless neatness peculiar to some elderly women, flesh faded serviceably toward soap, past *crème*, long since pensioned off into its black. I had a fancy that she lived here; this neighborhood, as I knew from my college days, was among other things the habitat of the in-between relict of indeterminate age, ancestry, and bundles. One passed them so constantly, each under her artifact, a black hat, shaped like a pot or a dusty meringue which changed its shelf perhaps but never its season, that after a while they became the same one, recurring like a figure on a willow plate of blurred, indefinable pattern, or on some humble karma wheel.

The elevator was a long time in coming. I studied my lady as one might a shell plucked from a beachful; her eyes were cast down. Faint iodine stains on the white hair told of blondeness fifty years before. A long nose, patient with its own length, a Hapsburg lip, slightly trembling, one Manila paper bag — was she dispensing or receiving? — on which thick leather gloves with a gift shine to them firmed themselves now and again to a crackling in time with the lip. Her cheap scarf caught my eye; there was always something. Printed with clowns and balloons in the crudely coy dime-store art intended for children — chosen by a child perhaps, or borrowed from one. She might be academe's widow or salesman's mother-in-law. She might be anybody. This was her mystery.

To the left of the elevator there was a tenant directory; from it I picked an imaginary destination — Gerber, 10A, on the top floor, from which I might then walk down, taking a survey perhaps, hunting a room — I had no plan. It seemed odd to have none, after so many years of meeting, as strangers, those with whose dossiers I actually was so often secretly armed. But here, of course, I had no intent to enter her life past her door. Madam, I am investigating accident. Specifically, the accident toward which all our lives may have tended us, and, except for my action, veered us away. I intrude no personal acquaintance; I crave merely a bit of cosmic gossip — what history it was sat so silently next to mine. Doubtless there is no connection other than the slight fortuity of existence. Pardon this amateur philosophizing — I attended school in this neighborhood, at the innocent age when such problems had force.

The elevator door opened and I followed her inside, stepping to the rear, although, except for the operator, an old Negro whose hat was his uniform, we were alone. Her form, bowed in front of me, had the simple, touching curve, drawn by a master, that comes with age. Perhaps I might hurt a fly, I thought, but toward you, rest assured, I intend none. Nevertheless, as we rose slowly together, I felt a heavy sadness. Probing, I recognized it for the familiar, sad portent that comes to us when we are about to enter a relationship; the shiver that comes even on the brink of love — as we descend knowingly toward what will change us — and will have its attendant crimes.

As it happened, no plan was necessary. We stopped at the third floor. The old woman fumbled in her purse, then turned to the operator. "You know whether she's home still? I forget my keys."

"I dunno," he said. "I don' take nobody down from there since I get back from lunch. I seen the kid walk down."

"They let him go out like that," she muttered. "A baby." She put her glove on the old man's sleeve. "You wait, yes? I give you a quarter anyway."

"Dunno if the super's around," he answered. "And he never give me no passkey." But he waited.

She rang a bell at a door down to the left in the dark hall. After a long interval it opened, to a muffled exclamation. We heard the old woman's whisper, "I forget my keys to that place. I have to come back."

"Oh, for God's sake, Ma," said a voice, "that's the second day you've lost this week."

"You won't lose, you won't lose," said the old woman. "I go back tomorrow. They don't care."

"All right, all right. Well, come on in, what you standing —?"

"I'll go down again. I'll go sit in the park by Johnny."

"Now listen. How many times I got to —" The voice jammed, then went on. "The kid don't *want*. He's gone on eight years old." There was another pause. "Well," said the voice, "out or in?" After a moment the door closed.

The old man peered out of the elevator, then shook his head. "How do you like that?" he said. "How do you like that! She do that to me two-three times already. Ain't never seen no quarter yet." He put his hand on the starter. "Where to?"

"What's her name?" I said. "I see her around now and then, but I don't know her name."

"Don't know, sir. She ain't a tenant."

"But she lives here."

"Eyuh. Come last month. Six-seven bags I tote in for her, that th' oney quarter I seen yet." He chuckled. "But she ain't a tenant," he added fretfully. "Forty-eight tenants here. Got enough on my hands keeping track those."

"Oh, she rooms then."

"Eyuh, she rooms," he said. "Got her a room in her daughter-in-law-'s house." A buzzer rang sharply. "Coming," he muttered, and looked at me again, inquiring.

"Ten," I said. "Ten." We rode up slowly, the cables sighing. How easy it was to follow, I thought. Got her a room in her daughter-in-law's house. On the way out, I slipped him a dollar. He looked at me, mouth open.

"Some of her quarters," I said, and I heard his "Yessuh, yes*suh!*" break into chuckles as the door clanged and he went down.

There was a window wide open in the hallway, and I leaned on its sill for a few moments, looking down at a court, a side street, and the riverside park. Up here the wind brought in a steady precipitation, settling on my arm, grinding like carborundum between the tiled floor and my heel. I knew this day too at this hour, the long, straight shadows peculiar to an island rectangular, as if the side streets, in dark, animal file, advanced on the avenues, and at one strike of the lights fell back and fawned. I still felt the portent. The lone history I had forced my way upon had not slaked it. Down below, the crowd moving on looked speciously joined. Ten flights up, however, need not be mistaken for the aspect of eternity, I thought, and walking on tiptoe, but taking my time about it like a reluctant conspirator, I went down.

Outside, I walked downriver. The western sky was peachblow. Under its drag of light, over the seal-colored palisades, one could almost believe in a chariot descending the other side. Above us the welkin was forming, a blue that steadily accreted toward the dome, toward that mythological center which never leaves our hearts, born as we are of a race of whom each must believe, against all acquired knowledge, that wherever he stands is under the apex of the sky.

Once more it was the hour of other people's assignations. One grows to know, sometimes very late, that the private phenomenon one has nurtured so secretly in the breast is common to all. This hour that had grown along with me, up, up from my childhood, that I had brought along with me from Tuscana, had long since come to seem to me especially identified with the multifarious city — the hour when the lights went up willy-nilly in every breast and the unlucky held their breath at the sight of the lucky ones streaming by car, on foot, by wire toward their love or even their hate, their ambition, their piety — somewhere. I turned my back on the river that doubled its plangent depths on the other side of the low wall as suggestively as a sky, and walked rapidly eastward through the blocks that led toward Central Park. The streets were mediumly soiled here with a living, neither high nor low, that lacked the black, bituminous drama of impoverishment, and people moved on them still in the convention of silence, but under the pre-lamp, powdery air of evening, one could find a rhythm in that susurrus, as if they came forward in coda, subscribing toward a silent tune. The phlox were moving. They came forward singly, in pairs, and single again as I was — the vicious, the sweet, the broken and the indomitable, all intermixed, as who knew better than I? But my back was to the light and their faces touched to unison by the sunset compline. The ordinary were advancing; this was the ordinary thing. Once more I looked in at their window frame, this time holding the old woman's history in my hand like a bit of jeweled dirt that had begged for notice, like a visa thrust into my palm. They bloomed quietly toward me and past me, face linked to domestic face in that temporary gilding, each moving patiently under the small arc of its personal death, pitting its slight shadow against the interplanetary sky, shadow to shadow, speciously joined. I walked hopelessly faster to annul them, like a man pacing his hitherto perfectly controlled garden and caught there by a sudden hallucination in which bushes burn

2 3 4

voices, corollas clap their tongues and the power of the inanimate pollinates the air. Shadow pressed to classless shadow, they surrounded me and passed me, and I hurried through them as if I were in danger of being snatched into the orbit of the wheel they turned on, drawn forward into the blur of the willow plate. Then the street lamps glanced on, spreading a garish light even more reasonable than day, and I escaped.

Through the park I met almost no one — a late mother wheeling one child and hurrying another, two mounted police, their heads and their horses' eyes front, like monuments that moved, lastly five or six high-school boys with the slouch and sidewise peer of the slums, who shrank together, hands ganged in their pockets, conspired in excited whispers, and ran off in the self-induced paranoia of some imaginary, adolescent chase. After that I was alone until I reached the exit. There I turned and looked behind me, where there was no one. I listened for him, in the dark hollow of the archway. For him, for them, for whoever it should be. It comes so quietly, the counterstroke hidden in ourselves. I had never feared to be followed. Now I wished it.

Three blocks over eastward, I hunted up a stationery store where I might buy my paper. Nowadays a real stationer's is a rarity in New York, except near the business districts. These crannies are something else again. Tucked in some narrow nook lopped off a larger one and soon to have their trade lopped off altogether by the drugstore and the supermarket, they survive like the last crazy-corners of the off moment, of the few beleaguered notion-needs that will not fit into bars. Small people necessarily keep them, sweatered old men and women, emerging from the mouse-life behind the rear partition, wiping the mouth with the back of the hand. As with a bar, they cater much to the intermediate; Charon perhaps must keep such a place, purveying the late news and the final, obsessive bit of tobacco, the envelope to catch the midnight mail and the last telephone.

There was no one behind the counter, but all its news wares lay disposed in front of it — these must be among the last stores in the city to dispense anything at all on neighborly trust. No doubt this is because of the article they vend; few who followed the news these days would not feel a grim, citizenly obligation to pay for it. I set down my coin, passed over the evening paper and took up a copy of the morning's *Times*, feeling at the same time the dull, required guilt — dull because it was so abstract — that any conscientious man felt nowadays when, even once, he let the daily communiqués of cataclysm slide by without him. It was a hopeless guilt, the newsprint conscience, formed in him by being forced to attend the vast panoply of struggle, crimes international and small passional ones, at which he could not assist. He must be present at every agony in the garden, able meanwhile to bleed with only a few.

I folded the paper under my arm, thinking of how many such days I had let pass by unsifted through this strange, frustrate bookkeeping. Yet I had been no anchorite — at least outwardly; from my undergraduate days on I had made the average social gestures of my generation. In a mild way I had campaigned for certain of its enlightened causes that still seemed to have a center to be left of; later I had fought its war as every young man does, singlehanded even in the absence of single combat. Afterwards I had tried earnestly to catch hold of any discernible prong reared up now and then from the hetero-homogeneous mass of cause that remained. Along with most, I had learned to pay my bit of money, fealty or action; in a modest way my name was available to certain rosters, my voice to certain committees and salons; I had shouldered my share of those compromises by which the modern man of good will deluded himself that he was *engagé*. Except for my bachelorhood and my somewhat unusual version of the subterranean departure that is in each of us, I could be the very model of the average cenobite, the community man. And I knew that under the mass of evidence accumulated daily against him, tuned in as he was to an enormous rack of sufferings of which he could at best anoint only a few, no medieval man had ever had to be as calloused as he. This was the daytime world. Actually he was absconding from it. Deep down under its superficially hale crust, each of us was keeping what nucleus he could. One might begin to suspect that there had never been such a race of anchorites in the history of the globe. One might imagine a host of us, driven back upon the memoir.

In the rear of the store a man stepped halfway out of the one telephone booth, holding the coin returned to him by the coin box, then reconsidered and stepped back inside. He was a short man with a neat fringe of clipped, gray hair, a good suit that ciphered all of him except the wrinkled network of anxiety around his eyes. The booth had a seat in it and he sat there — after doggedly dialing what I fancied to be the same number — as if he had been tailored for it, gazing absently out the door, his free hand vacant on his knee. Suddenly he hung up and tried again. I could hear the signal, not the "busy" but the "don't answer," and I understood his compulsion; "not at home" but one dials again, persuaded that one has dialed in error; in lieu of that one dials someone else one owes a call to (if necessary going down the list of those one has neglected for years) — unwilling to accept the ultimate rejection from the air itself, by a machine. I held back an impulse to pass him the directory. Here, phone anyone — here's a Mr. James Sugrue — no, that's a forbidding name and a Maiden Lane number, won't answer at this hour; here's a more sympathetic one, Mrs. Anamaria Perez. Watching the hand on his knee, so open, patently waiting to be listened to, I all but addressed it. If all else fails, here's my number; I'll be home in ten minutes, and I understand this brand of telephonitis. Try this number in ten minutes, and at least for a moment there will be an answer, the blessed gap when the receiver is lifted. No harm in these surrealistic conversations with one another. In ten minutes, try me.

I was about to turn away when the man in the booth got up and left it, went by me with a tip of the hand that said "It's all yours now," and out of the store. The proprietor's idle eye was on me. I am not always so craven to the conventional. But it is human to alternate, and at times the very fear of my own strangeness will as suddenly make me bow to what is expected of me. I went in. And once inside, I felt the satisfaction, both fierce and submissive, of one on whom circumstance has forced what he had not courage enough to do on his own.

Taking out my address book, I riffled through it in careful pantomime. Some of the names were almost lost even to me, burning in the faintest of recollection. Others belonged to distant cities, although that was no drawback now in a world where the rictus of communication had been perfected, stretching all our mouths agape. Some were dead, except to address books like mine. I had never been able to erase any of them; I kept them all. Still others, fresh and unrubbed, belonged to the present, in various levels: "How nice to hear from you!" it would be, or "Well, you're a fine one!" And spotted among them were numbers, not many, belonging to certain sorties of the past, through each of which I had drawn a line. Hers was among these, still uncrossed. I studied them, sedulously avoiding the one.

I'll call Maartens, I thought suddenly, and putting in my dime, I dialed. He and Cecile were old hands; my wish to remain incognito in the city would be received without inquiry; no sudden conundrum in a friend's nature could surprise them. The very bourgeois steadiness of the life they led made their place a beacon for certain tremulous acolytes of bohemia, less steady than they, whom one met there sometimes at dinner or of an evening — raw-eyed creatures ("a very fine sculptor," Maartens might whisper) just getting over the drink, the dope, the breakdown, the girl. And like so many of my friends, they had never met any of the others. I grinned with relief as I waited, imagining Maartens' huge laugh if I should take it in my head to say to him, with the proper wryness, "What do you think, eh? Yesterday I was at work." All I needed was an interim away from the incessant scraping of my own awareness. Without a bit of company, the strongest of us sank into *Schwärmerei*. There was a certain justice in this day's ending in a bit of his. Then I realized how long I had been listening without an answer. There was no one in.

Calm deserted me then, and I too began calling — first the Maartenses again, then a succession of numbers from my address book, at random. Hysteria forms, I suppose, at some point of refusal between ourselves and what we at last take to be implacable. And for me — as, I suspect, for many — a special hysteria resides in the machine, to which we have come to attach that final implacability which used to be reserved, with more dignity, for death itself. For the machine is still speciously half ourselves. And when we rage against it as I did then, we rage against this. For, as I can remind myself now, I did not really choose numbers at random. I chose numbers belonging to people not quite vanished but superannuated: a faddish man I had once worked with and had dropped for overpressing me socially toward his "circles"; two jolly, free-talking magazine spinsters of whom age, plainness and lack of much sexual impulse had made substitute aunts to the general; one or two former girls of mine who had lived in the Village, the village of chancy, evanescent numbers owned by a floating population of such girls. They belonged, all of them, to that useful company in whose members one would never dream of confiding. At this hour, if existing still as I had left them, they would all be drink-hazy, drink-valiant — if they were home at all. None was. As I hung up on the last of them, several customers, off some bus perhaps, came in, deposited their coins for papers and went out, leaving the store empty again of trade. Through the glass panels of the booth I could see the front windows, faintly barred with neon that cast a fakir's light on the pens and ink-bottles beneath. Night air came through the doorway, soft and remote as an animal's pad on the palm. At his counter the proprietor rang up a sum on the register, then subsided again on his high stool in a semi-alert drowse, his fingers poised on the glass over his wares like a man seated at a planchette. Once more I put in my dime and listened. For my own ends, I thought. And at last I dialed.

Three rings only, but already relief, alien as a blush, crept over me; because of her father in his wheelchair it was a household where there was always somebody there. And now that rescue was on its way I could afford, like most of us, to be contemptuous of it. The truth shamed me: that in this moment I would settle for anybody — only to be able to spell anyone, for a moment, into the hollow of my ear. Even my past sorties into a life here, a life there, had been more straightforward. They had kept the line of demarcation; they had come from choice. All that this day had brought me was what classically attacked the anchorite in his desert, the desperate itch toward the mirage of others. I could almost have hung up now, understanding Maartens in fraternal sadness, itching for the more honorable dominion of the nights when I searched for myself.

It was Anna, the housekeeper, who answered. The Mannixes are a family of a type that still persists in New York, finding its servitors early, while its own members are young, and keeping them on, often only one and for life, in a manner more steadfast and personal than that of the rich. One recognizes at once in such households the odor of stability, compounded of furniture polish and the other smells of good service, all blended with a faithfulness responsibly returned. Anna had come to them, a greenhorn fresh from Czechoslovakia, in the nineteen-twenties along with their own children; the brief interim of her own marriage and widowhood, long since quenched almost from conversation, had not changed her — certainly not her conviction that nothing which happened to her would ever be as important as what happened to them. When she answered, I had an impulse to hang up — it was almost enough that the machine at last had listened — but I had already said "Hello." I did not identify myself but I could tell that she knew me, as I knew the waxy cool of the niche in which she stood — in the probable aura of one of the meals that unfolded as regularly from her as if she concealed a cornucopia of them in the wide, starched store-house of her bosom.

No, she said, Miss Ruth and her father were not at home. He had gone to a convention in London, and she with him, about a week ago. That must have been when she phoned me, I thought, perhaps the night before she left. I too was familiar with those restless eves of travel when, brave with going, one plucked at the string one was to leave behind.

They would return in about a week, said Anna coldly, making it clear that any really loyal intimate of the household would know this. Only two months ago she would have teased at me like an auntie, her warmth guided, as all of her was, by what she saw on her mistress's face.

I saw the two faces as I had last seen them together. Honesty impelled me toward the one in the absence of the other. In the small things, I thought, that do not matter. "This is Mr. Goodman, Anna," I said. "This is Pierre."

"Well, my hosh," said Anna accusingly, dropping all pretense. "Well, my hosh!" Her glottal, Czech version of "gosh" was a familiar expletive, long since affectionately adopted by both the Mannixes; I could hear them exchanging it over a book, a letter, across the back of a chair.

Yes, I had been away, I said. No, there was no message; I would get in touch with them when they returned.

"Come on to dinner," said Anna, crafty duenna. "I got nobody to cook for meanwhile."

I was tempted, as I am always tempted to that house. Then I recalled where years ago I had first heard that "my hosh!" — Walter Stern saying it absently from his hospital bed, then, cheeks flushed, eagerly, giving its derivation.

No, I was going away again, I said quickly, and thanking her, repeating that there was no message, I rang off. Other humps — like his — I thought, were inoperable too. Just then a jet plane soughed over the city, taking us all up for a second in its suction, and dropping us back again, each on his own mote of concern, each absurd pea. But it came too late to down me now; I had already had my bit of conversation, my balance, and striding out of the store without a backward glance, I walked rapidly home, exempted at last from the day.

This flat is four flights up, on the top floor. Years ago, when I first rented it, the old mansion, newly renovated, stood empty, and I could have had my choice of the garden floor or any, but, still the stylite on his pillar, I chose the top. An elevator has long since been installed, but there is a small spiral of stairs in the rear that I often prefer to use. During these weeks I have done so. Ritual has mildly obsessive uses for the solitary; as I climbed the steps on these evenings I liked to imagine that each one advanced me as it were backwards, into the relative composure of the past. And this time I leaned as carefully on habit as on a trusted arm. Night was here again, returning us once again to the illusion of a hiatus in which the world stopped moving and we could judge ourselves; over the chimney stacks of the city one could imagine seeing, if one had the proper ray for it, thousand upon thousand ellipses of memory circling like single birds. I am just on the crux of it — like a man bending over his own headstone — I thought; I cannot stop now. And walking up the last flight I visualized the shades half drawn and even, the desk cleared, the lamp set burning in the way invisible entities managed the task in a fairy tale.

But when I opened the door the flat was dark. I snapped on the kitchen light; there was my morning cup on the table. In the big room the shades were still up, the curtains wide on the floor-length windows through whose blue-black oblongs the lighted panes of my neighbors crowded interestedly, before this transgression of city etiquette, as if at any moment hundreds of inquiring rounds of faces might start up over their orange sills. Down the long room I saw the neglected stubs and ashes of the week's living — books disarranged here, a jacket lying there, the fallen pile of spring-binders — all sending up the odd sense of oneself departed. No one had been in the place since morning.

I turned on the sharp arc-light over the desk, leaving the windows as they were. A city flat is the thinnest of aquariums, whose element, half out, half in, I still perversely love. On the desk there was no usually propped note from the cleaning woman, large pencil script always written savingly on a grocery bag. As I ransacked for a quick meal and ate it voraciously, calculating that my walk, deceptive as such often are in New York, must have been six or seven miles, I felt a flicker of orderly habit outraged. This was the second time Mrs. Papp had done this, after an unblemished record of three years. No doubt she would arrive tomorrow without explanation, as she had done once before. Yet it was not so much that she had lost her character as that I had lost hers — in the city one tended to set special store by even the faintest remnant of the feudal. There were the notes she left — the last one posed months ago here to a cocktail party: *Tal lenlo. Aints oner cink.* I smiled, recalling the girl who had read it aloud, one of the researchers from the office, the sudden ferret brightening on her face, our laughter. Of course, she had said, with the authority of the best pupil in the class: Middle European accent, just take it phonetically. "Tell landlord. Ants under sink." Later that evening, after a restaurant dinner with the remnants of the party, I had taken the girl home, since no other man had volunteered and on the lees of the drinks, had kissed her mildly at her door. She had misread the kiss as the long-awaited amorous tribute to that intelligence which would someday be so requited, and for weeks after, whenever she had managed to bring her copy herself to my office, her lame, grinding joke, "No aints under the sink, hope I hope," had accompanied it too. So Mrs. Papp's note, like everything else, had had a place, small though it was, in the event-chain.

And still my mind went ticking along in exhausting clarity; they say the brain itself never tires but sits like a punkah set in the center of a house at the inception, eternally waving in its own sensoria, eternally clearing them, until the subject sleeps, until he dreams, until he dies.

I looked down on the body that fed it, oddly matched, some would say, to its humors — the long, heavy-boned body of my grandfather and his farmer forbears, not the desk body of the natural desk man. I was pacing the room now, but each time that I passed the desk I avoided it — I, I; I, I. There must be thousands of such journals, I thought — self-tender, scared of the present as it approaches, shut away. Stopping at the window, I stared across at the people outside. I had had my turn with them — all day long I had been thinking in thousands like some ruddy philanthropist with a pile of stage money, knowing all the time, as Maartens did, that the minute one ceased to defend the self — *en garde!* — from the general, the importance of the picture, of the diary, ends. No, I will get on with it somehow, I told myself, and then if I must, move on. And breaking the circuit, I went to the desk and pulled out the drawer so violently that it sagged in my hand, spilling the manuscript in a wide fan on the floor. Cursing, I bent to retrieve it. The thin pages slid as I reached for them, and I trundled after on my haunches, damning my own clumsiness but relieved by it. And it was just then, as I squatted goose-fashion, that it came to me — snapped from anode to cathode quite without warning — that the old woman I had followed might have been Mrs. Papp.

I must have remained squatting there on my haunches for some minutes. It is the ultimate position of self-ridicule, taking us dimly back perhaps to our preprimate days, or to our childish days at stool — either way it is not one in which a man can deify himself. And during all these solitary nights here, that is what I have been doing — in memory we all deify ourselves. I sat down on the floor, spotlighted there in my circle of scattered paper for anyone who cared to look, and after a while I began to laugh quietly to myself; if I had done so aloud it would not have alarmed me now. It was the present, bubbling up in me, humorous and healing, after so long, and it came to me now that I had been scared of the present all my life.

I picked up an odd page and regarded it. What tunnels we breed for ourselves, I thought, when at any moment might come the assault from outside — death, sickness, and all the other taxes, including the ordinary that crept like lichen, Mrs. Papp. There was irony in that I, for years such a self-fancying authority on the variable, had forgotten this. I glanced up at the windows, unshaded as I had left them for her that morning. Let them all look, I thought — the others — and let me look too, to be reminded that the satiric distance is not one we impose on ourselves.

Was it she, had it not been she? But what did it matter? I thought of Semple, toward whom in this welter of pages I had always been progressing, and had never yet put down. While I approached him, old dead accident that he was, all that time his counterpart, counterstroke might be approaching me. Memory, though still the powerful vehicle I could not desert, was not safety, and had never been. The present, stealing along my veins even now like some analgesic midnight sun, was the reverse of the medal. This was the variable, and I would no longer deny it. I began picking up these papers. Even if I had left their true element forever, I meant to go on with them, even if I had to write by daylight, as one wrote the biographies of other men; even if in them I might no longer be "I," but "he." In whatever way it had to be done, I would put Semple down.

Gathering the pages, I put them into one of the spring-binders, where they looked — perhaps as they should — much like any man's. Now that I had done so, I let myself fancy, glancing through the thin windows, that the opposite windows no longer stared back at me quite so unitedly, but came at me each humbled into itself, one by one, one and one, and one. I leaned out to look at the house across the way, a foreground floating separate from the crammed pearls of light around it on every side. Unlit itself, the façade moved forward from its nimbus, brooding at me with the clued familiarity of a repeated thing. London, I thought; she is there. Peering, I wondered whether all these years here I had been living in sight of an image of another house, subtly remanded here, but in the same moment that other, oldest house came out to me, clear in its own cincture — a cobbled brown-and-blackish brick that any taste but memory's would call ugly — not this pale evocation of Portland stone. The term had slipped in of itself — Portland cement, commonly called Portland stone. No, it was not that house nor any particular one, but merely one of the great colors of London, whose semblance opposite, faded by the diamond winters, summer meltage of a harsher city, still remained to obscure and please. I remembered them now, long crescents of such houses, laid like gray scythes along the interchangeable dusks, dullish streets of childhood that quake in a man's mind and are still sickened for as a boy does for a lost, bad home. But I had not thought of them until I had thought of her there. The brain never tired, but we could never foredoom how memory would seed the future except to know that as we advance, erect, upon the body of the new, we hold up the body-ghost of the old.

I bent my head on my arms. At last I went to the desk and sat down. It took me long minutes to put the pages in order, several hours to read them slowly, as for the first time I did, from the beginning. The confidant's confidant, I saw how he had arrogated beginnings and conclusions that might be either, good assaults and bad. I heard him refuse to listen except for his own ends — and doom himself eternally to listen. "Nothing one says face to face avails," he had said - - and I watched him look, from his hiding place, at every face that passed.

When I looked up, it was the city hour that I have come to know so well — the hour of minor horns and major silence, and the constant expectancy of a theme. Absolutist that I am, I still awaited it.

The hour passed while I sat; in London, where she dreamed, it was break of day. In my window panes the dots of light went on and off in the darkness, one ellipse of memory resting, the next waking. There they are, I thought: I, they, she — we who so incurably coexist. Tiring, tireless, until the subject sleeps, until he dreams, until he dies. Until, before dying, he wakes. Is that what she dreams? I heard her voice again, across the three thousand miles of air that I could annul in a moment, over the distance between us that no speed could outwit. "It's getting light here," she said, and I answered, "Here too." "Have you gone?" I said again, and she answered, "No, but I can sleep now. Keep — keep well." I knew what she dreamed, and that it was more than the dreams of women, and that other apostles had had it too. That we may wake in time to cure one another. That this is all the conversation we have.

Time passes, I thought, invisible fluid, rosy and bitter, through which we suspend, can never return. It is the bystander. As is the natural world. When Darwin first made us look at our history, it was not the facts of our descent that set our teeth on edge but the anguish of our final separation from what once had been ours. From the green insentience of the plant risen and reaped with its brothers, from the unpuzzled face of the animal living inseparable and dying back into it, from all that unconsciously waxes and wanes outside and beyond us — slow cactus, piled cloud — all saved from the knowledge that they are as impermanent as ourselves. For which we have exchanged this lambent perpetual in the skull, this responsible, ticktock, weeping flame.

I looked behind me. Nothing was there except the blank page in the machine, the white, cataracted eye of the present, visible from every corner of the room. I sat down and wrote her the letter upon it. *When you return,* I wrote, *I may have something to show you.*

The key word is "may." No one, except his twin, can divine the hesitance of him to whom others have always seemed less important than he to them. Nevertheless, she watches, I thought — how easily I forget that others do.

Downstairs at the pillar-box, its iron flange, wet with early dew, creaked as I tipped it and held it. She watches, I thought, and was comforted. She is the present, I thought, holding the letter, and I am afraid of them both.

A car passed quietly, a second and a third, with the softly attentive sound that tires make on a damp pavement. The citizens were moving again. Then dream as they do, I thought, as she does, as perhaps you dreamed this morning. That we all belong to the same city, the city which is bedouin, which is anywhere.

Letting go the flange, I heard the letter fall, with the brush of paper on paper, on the others inside.

Today, as I sit at the desk here, I face the sign, that reminder which, when I returned, I pinned on the wall in front of me, where it cannot fail to meet the eye. In the encyclopedia office, where the seven and seventy of us sweep our mops against the sands of knowledge, the wall over every desk is covered with such reminders — clippings in type and in galley proof, in every print from Caslon to Goudy, not excluding that weakened but still tenacious imprimatur, the personal hand. Mine here is in pencil, in the large block letters with which we begin our rubric and end it. FALSE ENTRY. And now to Semple. From now on I shall not read back.

Chapter II. Pierre at College.

IN COLLEGE Pierre Goodman learned above all, as so many do, how to handle his humiliations. All around him others were picking up those surface convergences to the center which would help them to live more dexterously with their fellows — the poor boy learning to sport his leather elbow patches with the same worn chic as the quietly moneyed, the rich boy learning to pretend, at week's end, that he was broke. And Pierre, surrounded by so many who were at that temporarily protean period of their lives when a change of pose was as normal as a change of shirt, learned to bear his own façade more lightsomely, at times almost to the point of forgetting that it was there. It was a happy period, the lovely swaddling time in a company so sharply defined by age, so busy cultivating an intramural difference from the world, that his sense of a personal one could decline. Looking back on it in later years, he often found himself wondering whether even many an Oneida, Brook Farm, utopian blundering in the wilderness, had not really been harking back to this same shorter experiment of youth dormitoried against its enemy elders, swapping clothing as freely as ideas, self-boundaries almost as freely as clothing — to that springtime of communism which comes only to the young.

Meanwhile, in his own curious way he was learning what the rest of them were — how to estimate, reserve, and refine his own public impression. He learned, as actors do, that a simulacrum of passion, displayed with taste, is more acceptable to the world than the incautious gaucherie of the real, also that it was more comfortable to himself. He was confounded to discover (and quick to use it) that in those very arenas where the world advised against pretense — the acquisition of learning, of honors, of love — the natural pretender often had a handicap advantage. Luckily, if he was saved from venality, it was by other endowments that also seemed to him specious — his appearance, of which he had never been vain, and his memory, that he still took pains to hide.

His appearance was good enough for vanity; under the currying of the city it improved even more. What he had never counted on in his rare boyish broodings on mundane success (one remembers that it was not "rising" he wanted) was the value of a conventional exterior. Except for his unusual height, which became less noticeable as he consorted increasingly with the well-fed and the racially intermixed, his looks, he began at last to surmise, were of that healthy "regular" sort — too sound to conceal the lacerations of too much intelligence — which inspired confidence in both sexes. Most people assigned certain physical configurations to certain psyches; it was the median that most inspired trust. That his inner self didn't match their conception of his outer gave him a disguise which otherwise he might have been troubled to seek. And in the end this no doubt kept him more median than he thought he was.

As to his memory, it seemed now to have found an environment ideally suited to its excesses, if — as he sometimes began to doubt — such these were. The university was after all a temple to memory, often its Babel. Pierre, concealed in his own *expertise* like a priest inside the confession box, began to recognize all the devices of others and forgive his own. He came to know the amusement of watching the unoriginal steal their opinions from authority; he grew accustomed to the confrere sadness of listening without protest to a radical intelligence forced to claim authority for opinions that were its own. From time to time he did both himself and benefited accordingly. By hiding what he owed to the spadework of memory, he could sometimes persuade the brilliant that he was of their company; by openly averring it, soothe the second-rate into the surety that he belonged to theirs. He was becoming that exemplary scholar who is suitable to each side and discountable by both. And being so, he found that each often sought him out privately. No warning musk of ambition seemed to emanate from him — people were safe in telling him the story of theirs.

Socially too — and for much the same reasons — he became unobtrusively successful, never becoming violently partisan to one group, mildly ingested into the pattern of many. Being of the age he was, in the environment he was, it is to be feared that for the first and only time in his life he even preached. "Values" were being examined all around him by those still young enough to be convinced that they must do so, by elder instructors pretending that they still were. Later on in life he formed the habit of destroying personal papers as quickly as possible, on the grounds that they detracted from the power of memory rather than aiding it, but there was extant at one time a philosophical essay, written in his third year, whose thesis was that values were only the momentary "clotting" of alternatives. It brought him a second prize, a taste of the terrors of exposure, plus a number of inconvenient confidences from those who are always waiting for some such signal to fall. Later on too he could recall that no such signal on his part had ever been needed — that if the bleating of the lamb excited the tiger, then perhaps even as a child he must have had the reverse power — a silent cub, unaware of his own stripings, whose orange aura drew forth the lambs. But at this ebullient period of his life he no longer resented his portion, even pursued it. As with most young men, and young civilizations, the technique of anything attracted him. If, then (as he told himself intoxicatedly at this silliest, most ordinary period of his life) he was perhaps destined to be an *éminence grise* to someone or some section of society as yet unidentified, he might as well perfect himself now. So, reminding himself that self-interest was the most palatable compromise of any, he accustomed himself to listen once again without rancor. Certain tonalities of confidence became as familiar to him as finger exercises — the stop in a man's voice — like the musical hold in a measure — that preceded a tale of love, the moist phrasing that shaped a woman's lips confessing it.

Women especially liked and trusted him, against any obscure warnings about himself that he at first might have felt romantically bound to give them. Early on he discovered, like many an intentional blackguard, which he was not, that such warnings only attracted them the more. Given the basic attraction — and the range of his seemed to include both the woman of parts and the frivolous — it seemed that he had only to assure a woman that he could not be permanently counted upon in order to have her hang on all the harder, first in order to suffer the consequences, then to deny them. If in an affair he made it plain that he wasn't serious, his partner tended at once to be convinced that he was — and of his honor as well. No, the pose of the frank disclaimer wasn't practicable — besides, though he'd felt all his life that he had something to disclaim, he had not yet found out what it was. Altogether, his natural inaccessibility did him extremely well, allowing women to assume in him a lovable "difference" that they could tout to others and to themselves, without ever having to come to terms with it. An ideal lover for most women, he concluded, was one conventionally well enough endowed to excite public envy, coupled with some exciting but tractable variation from the norm — such as a revolutionary not averse to wearing a dinner jacket, and carrying it well.

But now let us put an end to such reflections, always darted so easily, with twisted, avuncular lip, at our younger selves, and pick up our hero some two and a half years after his arrival in the city, in June Week, say — though of course we do not choose this week at random — end-of-term week of . . . it would be 1939. We are sitting, with the dearly bought privilege of retrospect, gazing down at the young man from the rafters of his own future. Augustly situated as we are, he still has the advantage, for we shall not be able to change by one minim what we shall see. But this time — very early morning but already broadly past dawn in the way that summer days open — no spectator would wish a change here, for as our gaze spirals down, down, it rests on a scene always fair to the benevolent — we find him in bed with a young woman who is still sleeping by his side. Indeed, as he leans on an elbow, just awake, wishing idly for the coffee that, if she does not rouse soon (and she will not), he will get up and make himself, he would be happy to be so found, prideful over his membership, not absolutely new but recent, in the ranks of those of whom this sort of thing must be expected. And with some reason. It is June Week, end-of-exam week — the best of those sectors of time which the academic year offers, conveniently docketed, to lucky recipients who then may know, without the slightest further personal effort, who they are and where.

He is a junior. For another year he will be heir apparent, a year away from exile into a life lacking such markers. Outside, the moist blue morning is turning itself with noises once as sudden as brickbats, still exciting because no longer strange. A bus heaves by, with a characteristic groan the girl beside him had once mocked him for cherishing — as part of a glossary, so welcome to him, that she was born to; an ash can clangs down and he knows, without stirring, how the afflatus of dust follows after, settling a moment's visible rhythm on the air. Charming, gritty noises, if one has no pressure to heed them, but can lean on one's elbow staring into the kernel of this week, the slowly expanding summer, the future, the ages, meanwhile nestling one's backside. Backside is one of a category of good old English words that his inhibited share of his heritage had hitherto denied him, mildest of a number that he has learned to use, although not with the insistence of some around him. In the same way he is not much given to other typical excesses; on occasion he has been drunk, but seldom as a steady member of that undergraduate virility cult which many will maintain long after graduation, and when he exercises that long muscle on which, smiling backward now at the girl and a bit of Balzac, he thinks that he might play her a tune if she would only awaken, he does so with a modicum of the demonic self-consciousness of his time. Something has kept him median here also. We in the gallery can shift in our seats if we wish, remembering certain more intense demons he thinks he has left behind. He shifts too, but only to cuddle into the softness back of him, while our movement has foreshortened our range.

We are in the room with him now, silent and invisible, looking at him eye to eye.

His are veiled and he is still smiling, though more practicably than before. He is thinking of the summer job that awaits him in ten days or so and will keep him up North quite excusably, just as other jobs have the two preceding years. This year he will have one of the university plums, equivalent to the editorship of the *Law Review* for a law student, and like it ordinarily given to a graduate student. Pierre's major is philosophy. Hindered in his choice of one by his almost too various equipment, he has been helped to it by one of the university's real notables, Sanford Serlin, a man whose antennae are always alert for the protégé, whose motives for this even the more scurrilous campus gossips do not impugn. Serlin is not the department's head, having no patience with this factitious distinction, his being more worldly, but the college tolerates this as it will for the few whose reputations will thereby redound. Other scholars of this stamp often keep salons; Serlin's is more in the nature of a symposium. For although his large apartment, more like a family place than a bachelor's, is always running over with *Kaffee-klatsches* and small dinners (presided over by a housekeeper of whom Pierre will one day be reminded by the Mannixes' Anna), Serlin is the kind of professor who goes down onto the hustings and can be found, more afternoons than not, at one of the lowly zinc tables in the soda shop or drugstore currently favored for dawdling. Found there, he looks more like an undergraduate than any of the long-necked goslings to whom he is modestly listening — a small man whose head, though haired, has the startling all-over pallor of a blanched almond, for he is an albino — a former child prodigy who will resemble one to the end of his life. His coloring is the key perhaps, for he is one of those whose flaw has not crippled but become a kindly *Sesame* to the flaws of others. And perhaps too, his name, with its odd, Judaeo-Germanic echo of Merlin, the "Sanford" a mother's vanity obscuring what might otherwise have been "Solomon." Not a feminine man, probably never a sexual one, he is one of the rare neuters who make the world's arch-appreciators, which is what he is in his field.

The most that the gossips can say of him is that his foible is always for the young, the worst that he tempts these to — a bachelordom of scholarship like his own. Each summer he takes two students, chosen as much from the drugstore as the classroom, up to his mountain home, there to assist him with his edition of the classic philosophers, to which he adds a volume every other year. Two young men so tapped will have a chance to meet the really elect on the easy terms of the campfire and the outhouse, will have their names attached to a preface, are already, like their predecessors, marked for observation themselves. And Pierre will be one of these.

As he stretches himself, the cathedral tower equidistant between the college and this vulgarly cozy apartment sounds the quarter of an hour he does not know, and strikes him back with it, adding its fillip to the planes of idleness in the room. It is June Week, tune-week of a year, it is true, when Hitler has already entered the Sudetenland, but there has never been a year in the history of undergraduates ivoried safe from history, of which this kind of *post hoc* elegy could not have been made. It is youth who has the power. And he is here, in a city that gives most of its celebratedly hard heart, much of its preferment, to the young; a city so great for anonymity that it puts a cathedral in a slap-up back street. He is here, far away from what he once knew too well, in a place where no one, even himself, need know him — here in the city of coffee-drinkers, where he will seldom even need to refuse the tea which, even when it is pressed on him, is not tea. A truck, rumbling by, dislodges a flake of calcimine from the ceiling, and as it wafts down he waits for it as for an augur to see whether it will anoint him or the girl. It comes to rest on her cheek like a beauty patch. Never mind. The patch is half his, or will be shortly. And he is heir to the ages. Coffee is all he needs.

Once he has set it to making, according to her recipe, in the kitchen whose glisten and completeness is part of the whole comfortable sphere of her attractions, he returns to look down at her. It had all come true; in the first steps of the ballet he had learned to dance, although that was a long way back, and not with the girl lying here. He seldom thinks of this, except in some popinjay moment when he counts on his

254

fingers — of which he still has more than enough to spare. Already he knows how healthily a present woman will expunge prior ones, how obligingly memory will abscond for him there. There all the world and poetry, as well as the funny paper, will conspire to reassure him that men are separate creatures; here he need not feel himself in the least unique. But this is his first affair, and though come to him in terms as ideal as any young man could wish for — *ménage tout compris* by a woman, the reverse of fly-by-night, whose permanent plans do not however include him — "What a setup!" as a coarse friend has commented — he sees no reason to abolish sentiment because of it. Impermanence breeds its own sentiment, tenderness not precluded. Subsequent women will hate him for this and say so, but — how lucky he is — not she. We who are in the room with him can doubt his luck — and even doubt her. Of her we will never know for sure. Watch him is all we can, while, wearing an air of experience as consciously as a turban, he bends to her cheek and blows on it.

Really, a woman who is all comfort can be too much so; she is sleeping on like one whose every dream is habitable. He kisses her, knowing better. Nevertheless, at twenty-six, lying there with all her chunky prettiness exposed — round face and waist, snub breasts whose cocoa-pink tips match her unpainted mouth, short legs, feet that are unbeautiful in shoes but look, when walking naked and even-toed, as if gravitation were something they awarded the floor — she has the matter-of-fact aura, even in dream, of a woman who, promising no more nor less than she has, knows that these promises will be fulfilled. Any man who gets her for good shall have permanence exfoliate round him like a rose made of stuff sterner than roses, house and board more extravagant than he needs but always solid and in the end a bargain, bed as is good for him, and children like the one she already has, all chub demispheres of herself. For this, such a man must give her the means — which is money — but she will not take money unaccompanied by other worth. In return, gravitation will be awarded him daily.

"Mmm." He blows again and she answers, eyes closed. Born Leah Appelbaum, she has been known all her life as Lovey, a name that no one has ever thought to decry. The telephone listing here, however, remains under the name of Jerome Donegan, Irish jewelry salesman, dead four years ago in a car crash, while on business upstate "for the firm." The car, a gray coupé scarcely battered, she noncommittally still drives. They used to drive up the parkways on weekends — and they were still paying for it on time. Crazy to buy a brand-new one, even on the fine salary of the job she has returned to (secretary to Bijur, the head of the firm); and the large sum from the insurance she had made Jerry buy before they were married — "After all, he was top salesman; he could afford" — is doled out only for the weekday nurse for the child. Besides, the car is needed every Saturday to drive the child to its grandparents in Brooklyn — "You ever been on the New Lots train Saturday morning?" — where the little girl, a lovely Irish-Jewish mutation, is the idolized excuse, along with tragedy, for reconciliation with a daughter who has married a *goy*. And besides, as she will say without a quiver, she still likes to drive the parkways. Like her figure are her reasons, a maddening ooze of the soft into the sensible, that only an ingrate, or perhaps a non-Jew, will attempt to divide. One wonders whether Jerry, handsome top salesman, ever wondered which category he belonged to, or cared. For — as to the listing — "This single-girl stuff, in the telephone book, it don't look good, ever" — and before Pierre can speak — "Doesn't!" she says, flashing him a smile, for she encourages him to correct her English — this too has value — and he seldom has to mention the same error twice. It would be his error to think that she values only the tangible. From the cabinet photo, large almost as life, sole object allowed on the immense, polished surface of her proudest and quite good investment — "You mean to say you don't know what a credenza is!" — Pierre knows that he markedly resembles Jerry. In any case, for whatever reason, the telephone listing remains unchanged.

"Love that bell." Her eyelids droop, but are open. "Specially on Sundays." Now she is staring at the ceiling. Remembering? Or reminding herself that she is a working girl — she never has denied that she has loved going back to work. Never to deny what is for what has been — is this the way tragedy, not annulled, for that can't be, vanishes rather like the dry rot under the housewife's new season?

"West Side bell."

She giggles when he says that, teasing reminder of her ingenuous confidence at their first meeting (in the park, over the child and a ball) — "Don't you just love the West Side?" She is inordinately proud of living here. Yes, he "does"; he is as touchingly vain of his new status as she — "her nurse is off for the day" — is of hers. Bijur himself, the head of the firm, lives here, though of course "a lot further down." A prince to work for, widower at only fifty, but the whole firm is his family, one son who don't like the business — a college man like you. That's a Jewish name, Goodman, but not you. Oh, don't ask her how she knows. Ingenuously or not, she soon tells him.

As he kneels over her on the bed, he thinks of all he could tell the world and the firm, Bijur, Jerry. A lover always knows more about a woman — we see that he is still wearing his turban — than all the rest of them combined. Particularly a lover she conceals. He could tell her world, so cynically used to the devices of the garment district, that these breasts are real. He could tell the firm, well aware of whom its hard-headed little secretary has her eye on, that she, who quite honestly disapproves of certain girls as "fast," obstinately keeps a secret that, if once rumored, would burst all her plans. He could tell her boss, in whose office she dresses like all the others — satined and teazled as show girls two steps from bed — that this one perversely slicks back her hair, washes the paint from her face before she goes to bed with a man. And he could tell him, Bijur, who keeps a mistress but is uncomfortable about it now that he is on the board of Temple Emanuel, that this girl, if allowed to requite permanence with the same, will give up her secret at once, and never have another. Never deny what is — or will be — for what was. Bijur is the man she has her eye on.

And he could tell him, he adds to himself, as he places his hand deeply, that this is the way she best likes to begin love.

"Coffee first." She grins and rolls away from him, and he laughs. At himself — give him his due. Then he brings her the coffee. Two apiece, then the cups clink in their saucers, the spoons idle; anybody can see that this is intermission. There is a scuffle, but anybody, too, knows it for a mock one, can see that the young man in the room here — back there — is the true heir apparent. He stretches his arms to it, to

257

the coffee, the week, the bell, to the age and its summer. Then he plays her the tune.

Just before she lets him, she does what she sometimes does — often on Sundays. She reaches up and tugs his hair, dangling so close on her forehead. "Irisher!" she says, eyes closed. Then nothing more.

This is what he could have told Jerry.

These were Pierre's "passionate salad days" — a phase he had delightedly discovered himself to be in while reading, with his usual fondness for the passé, in old Edmund Gosse — and no man nearing forty, least of all his biographer, will pass up the chance to linger again briefly those arc-lit byways. We shall not, for instance, see Lovey, that girl so vivid even in arc-light, ever again after that day. For to date, neither has he. But we have seen what he was, or thought he was, in his twenty-first year. And as indicated, the day is not chosen at random.

They drove to Palisades Park that day, swam in the pool and did the funhouses; she had a bouncing fondness for these places, as if she thought of herself as soon to outgrow them — always roved the chance booths with a rube's faith and could never resist anything eatable from a stall. In the car on the ferry trundling them eastward across the Hudson, she leaned, full of near-beer, on his shoulder, and dreamed aloud of the Bermuda trip with which any groom must make her his down payment, wondering whether she was a good sailor — was he? "I don't know," he remembers answering truly, abandoned to his first vision of the city from the river — at this hour a city seen through seven veils, unapproachable from the Jersey side or any other. There was no need to be guarded with her; like everyone up here she knew of him only as a Southerner, and was provincially all but deaf to any accent except her own. Indeed, like his namesake, he had come to have an accent, neutral of itself, that shifted with whomever he talked. But he had touched unwittingly — he had been aboard ship once but could not remember it — on that uncertain bridge leading to all from which he guarded himself. And the city, seen at the widest angle and just before sundown, before its own lights spring it back to merely an electric marvel, an incredibly soaring funhouse, looks long, blue and Himalayan —

258

a cloudland from whose trajectories any man will slide. In that light, as he has often seen it since, it sometimes looks like its own ruin, an Angkor Vat of itself seen centuries on, monument to its own or any man's self-assertion. He shivered, as once in the courtroom, feeling all the magnitude of his. Then the old ferry, more a piece of land creaked loose from its moorings, grazed its dock again, shivering with him like a sympathetic old lap, and he set the car in motion, rolling carefully between the ferrymen — chewing, noncommittal welcomers hawsering him safely onto the streets of an ordinary evening.

In front of his house she changed into the driver's seat and left him, to meet the grandparents he must never meet, and the child — who was getting too bright and talkative to meet him often. He was rooming that year in a former frat house whose delinquent exchequer had finally been bought in by the university management. Two terms of this had not yet quite dulled its sybaritic arrangements — the cordovan lounge chairs, bequest of the outgoing brothers of 1927, the pine paneling, gift of a razor manufacturer's son. At fine French windows opened to the sunset, musing in those chairs on a square of the river framed like a patron's commission, one could well end the day making the grand tour of one's expectations. But at this season the place was a scramble of trunks and all the catcalls of farewell, a boardinghouse being evacuated by a yearly plague. He turned away and instead walked westward up the hill along the city cross street that bisected the campus, was in fact privately owned by the college. To renew this privilege in New York, such a street must be closed to public use once a year for twenty-four hours; this was the night when the corporation, not quite disinterestedly, declared a Campus Night, barricading the termini with guards and a few garlands through which anyone with a bursar's receipt might pass in order to dance on asphalt that, until midnight, was his own.

Tonight hundreds had done so. On the library steps the university band, its ranks already decimated, lumbered along by drumbeat, the brass melody snatched away by the city's roar. Couples surrounded him, yards from each other but each barely moving on its dime's worth in the decorous hunch chicly impassive above the knees. Someone had placed the ritual insult, whatever it was, on the head of the statue of Alma Mater. Her dignity, blind and verdigrised in the starlight, had survived it. A tug of war had just died aborning. A few urchins, squeaked in from somewhere, gazed up devotionally at its stragglers, hoping for a football star. But most of the hundreds here came from the vast enrollment of the accessory schools that now all but smothered the austere nucleus of the old liberal arts college — boys from the declining school of pharmacy, men and women from the thickening weed-growth of the "education" courses, theological students holding their beaver-faced dates at arm's length — Pierre saw scarcely anyone he knew. It was a dull saturnalia, to the sound of bluchers working enthusiastically on stone. But like so much of what he had extracurricularly learned here, it was a social lesson on the hierarchies — so vigorously denied by the country and the college — that persisted here and would be met again outside. One could pretty well tell a man's status, brought here or projected, by what he did or did not do during June Week. Only the most earnest would attend Baccalaureate Day — these were the future layers of wreaths, setters of cornerstones, along with the prudently early subscribers to the national habit of public joining. To these would be added, at the Senior Dance, men who were desperately engaging themselves to a girl or leaving one, plus a few late recruits from the fraternity house celebrants, more of whom would never get to the main dance. Most of the "intellectuals" (except for those who must blush for arriving family) would abstain from Graduation Day, none of them mount their sheepskins in walnut. At the very top were the men who had attended the university, city-vitiated though it was, because their fathers had, plus a scattering of girls either filling out their postdeb hours or representing the new social consciousness of the old rich. None of these, by now long since off to summer homes or Europe, had ever attended a college function at all. Life made its divisions early, no matter what the Constitution proposed.

Still, as he stood in front of his door again, he was not wholly immune to the mood of the season, feeling the loneliness of one who knew too much too soon, yearning, as precocity does, for some more comfortable division than that encased in itself. The sight of the river could always affect him, and did so now. Circling the city, indeed its primary vein of *extra*-human, by day it thrust the streets back upon their own mortality, miserable or effete. At night it ennobled them. Like any great configuration of landscape, it persuaded the spectator that the stretched dimension was in himself. From where he stood on the embankment the shuffling up on the hill, intermittent blurts of the band, traveled down to him like echoes of some midsummer whirligig, carrying the enviable mystery of the party to which one is not bidden. He let himself luxuriate in the self-pity that was always so fine as long as it was baseless, telling himself that he would have gone back up that hill if he could have taken his regular girl like the rest of them — even while he felt his limbs still suppled with the morning's lovemaking, the skin of his face and shoulders pleasantly burned with afternoon. A little angry, a little sad, and quite happy, he let himself mourn the circumstance that kept him secret where others could be open, meanwhile preening at the drama of it, descended so early on him, still so young.

As he opened the house door with his special key — there were only twenty-five of them — that outdoors-indoors blend which always excited him followed him in like the heady admixture of life itself, and held him poised. In the swath cast by the hall light the sky looked at once wilder, more blue and shy, visitant piece of that natural world which was the invisible guest outside the most civilized habitation and would end by being the host. Even the weak bulb in the hall, faced with that spectral blue, had gathered to itself the wigwam glow that was the core of all habitation. Life had never been more instant, more real; he was here, floated in on that current of marvel ceaselessly offered to him, the instrument — neither existent without the other. The present suffused him like whisky, as it did in those moments when, reading in some philosopher who strove dubiously to prove the real, he flung the book down, stood up and stretched, conscious of teeth strong enough to chew every appetite, loins ready to swell, a mind, dancing in its own essences, that had no need to prove. He stretched like a cock now, ready to stay up all night if necessary, in order that the world might continue. Not at all sleepy, he would lull himself over some book forgotten by all but him and the faded listing in the catalogue. Generous pity flowed in him for all such, for old Gosse and all those whose salads were over, all philosophers, majestic or piddling, from whom reality, not waiting for definition, had decamped.

As he passed the hall table, he ran his fingers lightly over it; it held no threat for him; the monthly letter from his uncle, arriving always on the first, like a statement and almost as noncommittal, had come the week before, and he had not yet attained the eminence of bills.

His hand stopped. *Rhines Brothers & Comp* — He saw the old-fashioned letterhead tip at once, half concealed by mail for other tenants — the factory stationery on which his uncle always wrote. *Your mother has partially regained the use of her hand,* he had written over two years ago. *She sews at the machine again, and at Rollins' suggestion has taken on a few clients. One of the blacks — a woman who has been to the French convent in Memphis, does the finishing. Any small motion of the fingers still tires them. So for the moment I shall continue.* It had been kind of him to explain it so, Pierre had thought at the time. But he forgets that I am a dressmaker's son. Who does the cutting? She would entrust that to no one. There had followed, in that letter and subsequent ones, messages of love from her, and at intervals shirts whose workmanship was unmistakable. But the pretense had been kept up and she had never written. He knew why.

Still he did not move to take up the letter. Whatever it contained was untoward — no one could think otherwise knowing its author, that gradual man. Whatever it held would take him away from here. Something untoward. He would not let himself phrase it further. Pierre raised his head and listened. Except for the caretaker, far off in the basement where his own trunk was already in place with those of the others who would be returning, he was the sole occupant of the house; he and this pile of deserted mail. He knew what he listened for and what he heard — his biographer hears it yet. He was listening to that blind undertow of self which he had been taught to call selfishness, whose instinct is often surer, more cleansing in the end than the gentle, sacrificial waters that overlie. It told him to leave at once, take off for Serlin's early, abscond as if he had never seen the letter, let it be lost or pursue him too late. Few of us are strong enough to obey that voice. Thetis, when she dips us in the Styx to make us invulnerable, always holds us cannily by the heel. One by one he picked up the envelopes that covered his own, envying the other addressees this flotsam — a few bright throwaways from haberdasheries, a letter, delayed for postage, from Warren Brown's girl, whom he had married in chapel yesterday morning, several warning library notices to gay defaulters who were gone for good. There it was: *Pierre Goodman*. He stared at the name finally come to terms with by the sender. The envelope was written in his mother's hand.

Six hours later, he left for Tuscana. There was no need for this kind of hurry, but after sending his telegram, he had spent the last four hours sitting on his bed, his packed bags between his ankles, and arrived at the One Hundred Twenty-fifth Street Station an hour and three quarters before train time. The station was deserted, as if only his being awake maintained it. Dawn came while he sat, misnomer here for a stir of air the color of bird droppings. Above the disordered sea bottom of these streets, houses appeared marine and wavering, as if already obscuring, liming with his absence, his banishment, in a beginning rain of invisible ash. Not yet aboard the train, he was already looking back with the paranoid glance of departure, in which cities crumple as we leave them, and the scenes of destination precede us into being one moment before we arrive. Already his was coming out to meet him along thread after thread, respun at a touch, that he had thought destroyed. Down there the house waited to puff into being at his presence, the smell of tea, arrack sweated from a thousand pots, in all its corners; from one of them his uncle coughed his exact and maddening interval; in another his mother waited with marionette patience, opening and closing her convex eye.

In the train speeding away from Grand Central, he told himself that he could still get off at the next station, but when it arrived there he did not move except to take out the letter, grasping it unreopened, as if it were an amulet to hold him down. As the car filled, he wondered how many others, in all trains, were consigning themselves by their own hand toward destinations which their very cells refused. Places

263

were not upheld by sand and girders finally, but by the heart — that sometimes faltered — beyond that, to the last trump, by the memory that sometimes tricked but never faltered, that was the heart of life.

To know this beforehand was the worst precocity of all.

Chapter III.   Pierre Returns to Tuscana.
The Grand Jury Prepares.
Lucine.   The Jebbs.

A T THE last ditch few of us have time for salutations. "You got my letter?" said his uncle, meeting him at the train, and he nodded, not knowing what else to do, because of what his mother had said in hers. *Later on I shall have to be in hospital, and would rather see you before. Rollins was wrong. The clinic in Denoye-ville gives me about three months at the outside. George knows, but is not sure that I do, so we do not speak of it. Mind you do not. Better so for now.* God bless, she had said at the end, but no salutation. And as his uncle clasped his hand and looked into his face, he had his first sense of how people, huddled cipher to cipher on the embankment under the great, overarching span of death, might have no immediate use for names.

"You'll find her changed," said his uncle, and Pierre nodded again, unable to speak, finding his uncle so changed. His uncle's face, even-featured to the point of anonymity, never in his remembrance sweated or flushed with drama, still persisted, but now it looked as if some gross amateur stagecraft had been at it, puttying at the cheeks, scoring lampblack under the eyes, making of it an anomaly beneath whose exaggerations the median man of fifty had disappeared, leaving the beholder in the wings to choose for himself whether this was an old man or a young. When last seen at this same train, his uncle, in a soiled shirt and tieless, nevertheless had had the air of a man caught short by a disaster with which he still felt able to deal. Now, in a dark suit and collar pin, his dress had the same excessive, finicky neatness of those houses, swept clean of every mortal odor, that wait for bereavement.

The car too, the same one, shone in the dark as they crossed the siding to it; she was still able to take a drive in it afternoons. There were no other cars waiting. Tuscana was no longer the main line. Eastward over the ridge there was a faint palpitation in the heavens that real newcomers might mistake for heat lightning, never suspecting, if arrived from the west instead of the north, the tremendous kingdom of light that lay beyond the hump of this one remaining hill. Once out on the main street, it would surround them, crowd them to the center of its fixed swarm, but here, on the old siding, Tuscana had remained to itself as it had in him, a pocket of darkness that had resisted everything but eternity. The car started painfully, needing to be coaxed. While they sat in it as it warmed up, his uncle fallen momentarily silent, crouched in the tender alertness toward mechanism that was his bond with the new world, every sluggish throb of gas-tinctured air breathed him, Pierre, back into his boyhood — if he loosed memory by one inch from its halter he would see, to the left, a line of cars advancing single in the starlight . . . careful, he must remember that he had seen them going, not returning . . . he would hear a boy's voice exclaim, "You come through the backs?" As he had now. He had come through the backs of the present, always accumulating behind one; the place of arrival, the place of departure were reversed. He was here. Then the old engine caught firmly, with a powerful rejuvenated purr in which one could clearly hear the tappets, sounding louder, more capable than the quiet, city-serviced motor of the car he had driven only two days ago — ready to roll him once again along the streets of his valedictory walk. He waited, flinching. Instead, his uncle took his foot off the gas, letting the engine die to a pulse, remained for some seconds with his hands forgetful on the wheel, then turned and placed one hard palm on Pierre's knee. The red signal blinked, reflected, a manic point of red in his still steady eye.

"I curse Rollins," said his uncle. "I curse him eternally." That was his confidence. Then he removed the hand.

There had been no stroke, he said, at least not one detached and causative in itself. She had a growth on the spine, now inoperable, that must momentarily have encroached on the neuromuscular systems back there three years ago, then receded, and was now dexterously busy impairing one vital function, releasing it to pursue another, on its ultimately single-minded path. These last weeks, in a miraculous recrudescence of strength, she had risen from her bed and taken over the household, but the clinic had warned him that this kind of change often occurred in such cases, where the heart and other organs were strong; he was not to hope. It was the last flare-up, in which the body, dominating its damaged parts, held its shape together for one bright image of itself before it fell; she was being consumed.

I curse Rollins. His uncle, rousing the car again, drove them off without repeating the words, but Pierre, hearing their echo, heard Johnny's in their trek up the hill, blaming Semple, hanging the whole cathedral of the town's evil, the angel-gargoyle framework of any town anywhere, or all good-and-evil, on him. This was the human mind, simple or profound, unable to face the matrix of causation, gagging at the sight of the crisscrossed inflections covering what should, must be the central absolute, hunting down some Judas to bear the monotheistic blame. It was *she . . . he . . . they;* curse *him.* And when all else failed, then came that last cry from the depths, from the dark workings before priests were heard of: *mea culpa,* curse me. Poor Johnny, poor uncle — poor Rollins, who must every day be confronted with blame to assign. Where his own mother might assign it — whom she would choose — he must hold himself in readiness to bear.

So he came home, heeding those streets for whose pattern he had been preparing himself all the long train ride down. The street leading to their own was dark as they approached the long line of houses, but as they turned left, a yellow neon sign, far down to the right, imprinted itself as it flared backward: the Bantam Café. Not as he had dreamed it, the return, never as one dreams it — the wild image treasured or feared. But it had come to be. He was home.

One house was widely lit — theirs. "You have awnings?" he said, incredulous, even with a jealous twinge of resentment because the house he had been so reluctant to see no longer jibed with his memory of it.

"She asked for them this spring," muttered his uncle, then, as they drew up, gave one of the exclamations, half resigned, half impatient, with which the tenders of the sick meet the vagaries of the ill one. His mother was standing in the door. Above her the awnings, striped mascara and white, one to a window, projected the house forward with a tropic falseness; beneath them, around the door, a trellis had been erected, in the center of which his mother's figure, tiny in its usual dark habit, one hand resting on the latticework, the vine shadows clambering over her face, seemed that of a soubrette about to sing. As he came up the steps, the porch light was on his face, the trumpet-shaped shadows quivering on hers, but one glance at her dress, upright almost of its own stiffness, told him all he needed. Plain as her clothes were, each of them had always fitted her to the quarter-inch; it was her one vanity. Now her collar, once round and tight, slumped on her breast and fell inward; the cuffs of her sleeves, doubled in circumference, enclosed wrists that dangled within them like a child's. Glancing down without meaning to, he saw stockings hopelessly girdling legs like canes, and quickly averted his eyes. Two steps above him, she bent her head toward his, chin thrust forward, mouth turned down at the corners.

"Yes, yes," she breathed, "yes"; as if he must mourn with her the worst — the terrible collapse of her neatness. Gazing up, he held his own breath, thinking that he must never again for one second let her see him flinch from the sight of her — the hooded eyelids swollen to casques, lips the color of veal. One step up and he had enclosed her, and circling almost nothing, still sought her. Under his nostrils he smelled an odor that no orris could cover, never met before, instantly known to the full in an animal opening of all his senses. He knew what he held — he held mortality in his arms.

There was no scene; what it came to was that, still upright, every faculty erect, she had faded too far back for one. She had no more perspective, or only one; therefore all was clear. The great fact, for her, was the general scene; she could scorn, or perhaps had even forgotten, those fragmentary intensifications of it with which others tried to thrash themselves free of the dull prospect before them. Every day, as she diminished, she knew more incontrovertibly where she was. And what dignity spread from her because of it; one could almost under-stand from the sight of it why a man might spend his life walking this way, that, around the question of where was he. "This was the mercy," Pierre told himself later, "that we had read of, had heard accounts of as descending, in their last days, upon the dying, but its heights, if such they were, were too sore for us. In the aphasia of living that was our own daily mercy, we gathered dimness warmly around us, and told ourselves that she was 'fading.' "

That evening she gave them one flash of it — one strike of the match to show them in their darkness where she was, then no more. It was after dinner, after they had eaten all they could, watching her not eat, had listened to her find questions for them when they could speak no further.

"Let's not pretend," she said suddenly, and put her hands forth on the white dinner cloth, then withdrew them, perhaps because of what they now were. He could have told her, had there been any way to say it, that he had already grown used to them, that because of the in-finitely adjustable lens he had just discovered we all carried inside us, even the mask she now wore was once more his mother. His uncle, sitting stiffened in his chair, made him hear her words, delayed.

"Let's not pretend," she said. "It's too much for us. Each of us not knowing for sure what the other knows. A waste, too." She leaned forward. "George . . . you know. They told you." She paused. His uncle sat motionless. "And *he* knows. I wrote him. To New York. That's why he's here."

Would she never name him? But she was gesturing to herself,

drawing a hand down the whole length of her from shrunken bodice to ankle, forcing them to survey her. She looked at them both with pity. "And *I* know," she said.

In the silence that followed, a great embarrassment stretched between them, as if the three of them were a childish gang caught out by authority in a joint misdeed. Then his uncle, that strange man of actions so few, reached out for her hands and put them back on the table. They lay there like the purest drawings, anatomized by life. The very cloth whitened beneath them, as if it had a piece of truth lying upon it. Then he covered them with his own. "When did you know?" he said.

She smiled, grinned rather, for in the way of people who die of attrition, the contracting flesh of her upper jaw was daily starving the skull into sight. Looking at that impish, still delicate protrusion, all their triangular pretense, every pretense could fall away, even into a kind of rest, as if health were only a long lapse of memory, now repaired, behind which she was showing them the one certainty that gave life — even joy — its character. "When I asked for the awnings," she said. "They had them in France, when I was a girl. In hot summer, there's nothing makes one feel so cool, so rich. I always wanted them. So, when I asked them at the hospital how much time I had, and they told me, I thought — 'I'll have the awnings.'"

And in the weeks after, it seemed to Pierre that it was objects she clung to, not in the way of a person who could not bear to leave her hoard behind, but as if their positive presence were a help in delaying hers. The house had never been so polished, so serene, so stopped in every crevice. The servant Lucine, a quiet yellow woman with convent manners, came daily, and between them they restocked the household linen, rivers of it flowing beneath their hands, as if his mother meant to leave behind her a trousseau of all the things men would never think of, enough to last them forever. In the evenings after dinner, Pierre sometimes caught her scrutinizing the room, almost chairbound as she now was, in the thoughtful way that women did in the springtime, and one of those evenings, his uncle being absent at the "pub," kept to that habit at her insistence, she made Pierre rearrange all the furniture in the parlor, saying exhaustedly when it was over, "There. That will be a better light for your uncle. Yes. There."

Otherwise, except for what could not be helped, everything was encouraged to remain the same; it sometimes seemed to Pierre that his mother was passionately trying to teach them how to live in the present. Never a gossip, always formal, even in private, with the facts of other people's lives, now she was energized by every account of the daily scene that his uncle could bring her as evidence that the warm, quotidian current of living still lapped their beleaguered household round. Of Pierre's doings in the years of his absence she never asked, if only because this would have admitted the possibility of his return to them, and the future was the inadmissible danger now. He had no stories that could beguile her in the way she wished to be, that were safe. Meanwhile few people came to the house, few had ever done, and the weight of any fresh, real contact was more than she could sustain. Even the phone, across which one or two correspondents sent what communiqués they could, was literally too heavy for her. Interest, daily more disembodied, was all she had. And the burden of feeding it fell therefore, with heaviest irony, on the one who would be assumed to be the most unsuited to the task — his uncle — a man who all his life long had breasted conversation, tempered judgment, with a cough.

What he did with that task was a marvel, equal, Pierre thought as he was forced to watch it each evening, to the feat of a man with some hidden ear for music perhaps but no performance, who, required by the ogre to sit down night after night at the stiff instrument of his own imagination, finds that for the sake of another, if in this way the castle door can be opened to her, he can. It was the worst of summer heat now, and only his mother throve on it, muffling herself in scarves the color of the dead air and the moths that flitted it, waiting on the porch that Pierre carried her to each dusk at this hour, raising her skeletal head as a blind person might, minutes before he himself heard his uncle's reviving step.

Each day he came earlier. As he came up the steps, his face, lifted toward them in the peculiar, refulgent light, showed the black-ash daubs under the eyes like a child's play of spectacles, and although he came quietly, putting down the paper with the air of a man who has done this a thousand times and expects to go on so for a thousand more, he always seemed like a man who had been running. And once Lucine had left them with the tea, his uncle began, opening his day to them like a pedlar's pack from which he drew one item after the other, watching her face the meanwhile, as if he had done nothing at the mill, the café, the street corner, other than buttonhole people for something to add to his stock for home. As perhaps he had, for what he accumulated each day was almost a columnist's lore. But the lore with which he fitted each item to its saga and kept a dozen such going, the power with which he brought her into places where she had never been or would never be again — from pub to church meeting, to the new golf club at Denoyeville and the shower talk of the red-faced men there — must have been served by a lifetime of behind-the-scenes silence, of that deep, judging flow of comment which his cough must always have forestalled. It was the way a stutterer might have spoken, finding himself suddenly, for a great stake, able to spill. And his reward was to see her face, that had faded so far back, slowly transfuse forward again, as if he had brought it blood.

Tea would decline toward supper; the awnings were drawn up against the dew, and the three of them came inside, his uncle carrying her now. Inside, the three of them sat in their old triangle, but Lucine now moved softly behind them, and the windows had long since opened and closed to the rhythm of a real, not a remembered weather. The years had melded his mother and uncle with the town, and even he, brought here by the gloved hand that arrested all knife-play, had been returned to the trinity. Any envious passer-by, croucher at sills, would have thought them a true family. His mother, if she knew the limits of her triumph, gave no sign of it, as, her face almost a face again, turned toward his uncle, she warmed to the business of interpreting what he had brought her.

"They'll send the Denny girl to Martindale, you'll see," she would say. "Poor thing."

His uncle would nod, his eyes on the lips that said "poor thing."

She would go on, briskly. "Mrs. Emerson, the one who used to keep boarders on F Street, she'd have let her stay there. But I expect she's moved on across the hill." This was Tuscana's euphemism for the dam site. "She'd no scruples about getting on in the world, but she was kind."

Martindale was the girls' reformatory, and Mrs. Emerson, a former client, was a woman in the full-blown tradition of those whose male boarders often went beyond that status, but his mother's interest ranged wide, and was never scabrous, foraging equally between happiness and its crops, tragedy and its portents, probing restlessly beneath even the mere drama of what happened to people, to the continuity that lay below. It was this continuity, blind as it was, that reassured her. And no one could have understood this better than his uncle, sitting there white-knuckled, spending all his breath to keep her where she was.

"That Mrs. Emerson, you know," he would be sure to say, putting down his paper the next day, or the next. "She's taken over the old Davis place in Charlotte. And you were right about the Denny girl — they've sent her to Martindale." Nothing ever foundered in his memory these days; Pierre, listening, reminded of that bedside litany of his the day she was brought home, sometimes wondered now if anything ever had.

Meanwhile for Pierre the town was being repeopled, all the old names and characters coming out of lodging again, not on the scrawny scale of childhood revisited — for staying so close to home, he encountered none of them — but with all their legendary thickness retained. In a way this was better so; the work of the past three years was not to be undone then, only suspended. So things went on for two weeks, three, and he was beginning to believe that, with luck, painful as that luck would be, the two halves of his life would remain unjoined. And so they might have done, had his uncle's name not been drawn, just at that time, for the grand jury.

All three of them were grave at the prospect. The real history of the world is made by the snailed-in, private lives of millions, a current occasionally muddied by the supposed plenipotentiaries at the top. Historians, biographers tying the world's way to Alexander's crupper or Hitler's, know this and ignore it, for they too must work. But the dullest private citizen knows enough to equate any public action required of him with disaster, rightly measuring it by the immemorial occasions when he has been most forced to it, in time of war, of political storm, of plague. Thus, even the most minor prod from the public weal — a notice to register, a tax bill — can make him uneasy out of all proportion to its weight, if proud.

"I'll beg off, of course," said his uncle, then coughed — not quickly enough to hide that unguarded "of course."

Pierre was silent, as mostly these days, under the childish superstition that the less he said or did in Tuscana, allowing the Fates the least possible thread with which to reweave him in here, the easier it would be to retain his status as a visitor from elsewhere. But his uncle's cough had remanded him back to the old, hated evenings of their threesome, a safety for which now, looking at his mother, he found he could even sicken. He got up and turned his back, trying to deny that he was implicated in this scene, unable to deny a twinge of what life held in wait for him — that he had just been dealt one "It is so!" out of a great store of implacables against which the most arrogant "I!" might be powerless.

"That you will not!" said his mother, just as she had done when his uncle had proposed to give up the café. "I shall be wanting to hear!" Her grin, meant to be gleeful, could look only rapacious on that starveling jaw, reminding them that it was she who, lightly as she could, with the least trace of assumed heroine, now held the reins. It was she, most imminently mortal of their three, who would keep them toeing toward health, on their frail, cliff-perched *status quo*. Death was remaking her, at a time which all but a few early Christians — to whom neither Pierre nor the rest of his world now belonged — would deem too late. If we might all remember our own deaths, he thought, then none would be villains, and he idled for a moment — the one that sense allows the young — over a vision of such a world: wars melted, lies cleared, everyone walking abroad in that immediate element, every

274

medley solving under that pure-struck, personal tone. Meanwhile his uncle, doing just as she bade him, was to be the unwitting means of bringing back into her eyrie the final thrust from the world as it un- regenerately was.

On July eleventh, then, 1939, at the current term of the supreme court for the trial of criminal actions, a grand jury was empaneled in the county (as known here) of Banks, Alabama. It is presumed that the names of all those summoned had been drawn under the usual pro- cedure — from the annual list of persons qualified to serve as trial jurors, as submitted by the county clerks to their respective county juries, after the removal from the list of any whose records contained convictions either for felony or misdemeanors involving moral turpi- tude. It is true that, as may well often happen in a small community, several of the names were of those who had reassuringly seen service before. But as afterwards recalled, the judge was not local, the district attorney only half so. Nothing had leaked to the county at large — or rather to those who considered themselves to be this — of any extraor- dinary matters to be proposed. It was slack midsummer, in a slack place. Like all small places threatened by growth from outside, it could remember this fact only intermittently. And like such places every- where — where influence has ancestry, authority is always married to somebody's cousin — it still had its contempt for the laws that are written.

In any event, no juror, before being sworn, had been challenged on the grounds either that he was insane or that he could not act impar- tially and without prejudice to either party. None of the persons cur- rently held on various charges in the county jail, for instance, would have been ignorant enough to wish to challenge a roster of such good names as Charlson Evans (minister of the First Baptist), Ian Frazer (railroad watchman, retired), Miles Blankenship (Rhine's — retired), E. V. Semple (factor of same), Treacher Nellis (formerly of same, now member inspection crew Dam Number Three and federal employee), the Jack Lemons, father and son (horses, and allied arts), Robert Rollins (youngest son, already called "Doc," though still a student),

Hannibal Fourchette, Jr. (also of course the son and associate of justice), and others of the like — all names ringing like the alphabet on any local ear. Whether or not from the same kind of ignorance, the district attorney also acceded to all names without challenge. Perhaps he was counting on, or at least encouraged by, the presence on the panel of some dozen foreigners. These were citizens, resident within the last ten years or so, who had been brought in by the dam in various capacities, members of a group now too prominent and too pushing to be overlooked without trouble. Citizens they were of course, of the nation if not of the region, some from the East, more from the West and Far West — all, in local eyes, from the "North." All twenty-three of the jurors were male, for although women possessed the right to be called, in this neighborhood they were both unlikely to be called and disinclined to it — often a matter for comfortable courthouse laughter. Of those special foreigners of the place who would never be called there was never any mention — this being a matter buried too deep for laughter. From this group of twenty-three, George Higby (born in Birmingham, England, grandnephew of Luddite rioter, now naturalized and presumably neutralized citizen, foreman at Rhine's) was — by lazy analogy, compromise, or accident — appointed foreman by the court.

A grand juror performs an important duty to the public. He is selected with care, and is a member of a body of men who stand between the people of the State and one accused of crime. No person can be put on trial for a crime of any magnitude until after a grand jury has found a bill of indictment. Its deliberations are secret. It usually hears but one side of a case, and that the people's side. The accused, who is called the defendant, has no opportunity to appear by counsel, nor ordinarily, even in person.

Bender's *Grand Juror's Manual*

Early on the morning of George Higby's first day of service as juror, the doctor was called to attend his wife, who sometime before dawn had had what appeared to be a slight hemorrhage of the bowel. Even then, still dictator, she had refused to let the doctor be summoned until a more reasonable hour, with the remark that young Lee Rollins, since taking over the practice after his father's retirement, often looked tired enough himself to stumble into the nearest grave. Besides, what more could he do than "make her comfortable," which, due to her "leeching" — she called it this — she now was? Lucine, however, must be called at once to make her tidy; she had had some nurse's training with the Sisters, and being a woman was used to the sight of blood.

"Eh, isn't that so?" she said, as the doctor was leaving. "We women are blooded early." She caught sight of Pierre through the half-open door. "Mind you remember that!" she called. "Any young priss says she can't stand it, she's the bloody liar!" She was sitting up, elated, consciously heroic now for the benefit of the doctor, who must be made to see her as still strong. Until her illness, her language had always minced away from the bodily, in the limbs-for-legs euphemisms of her class, but recently she had seemed to be returning to an earlier speech, perhaps her father's, before she had been genteelly instructed away from it, and sometimes now she even relished the simpler "functional" jokes that sweet old ladies take glee in at their dotage — as if her sickness must replace her aging. "Only a lady could afford to say 'bloody,'" Pierre as a child had often heard her decree. Now death, along with its other purifications, had at least given her leave to be one.

"Mind you tell George there's to be no change," she said, pushing her chin out, monkey-sharp, at the doctor. "You go on, George, it's nothing new," she called out before the doctor could speak. "I'll be waiting to hear; you go on downtown!"

Outside, the doctor warned them that her final trip to the hospital ought not to be delayed.

"She wants no change," said his uncle. "We'll manage things here." Feet planted wide, his stance reminded Pierre of the day he had scooped her dead weight from the two men returning her, and arms all at the wrong angle, had for his own moment upheld her.

Young Rollins shook his head, obviously used to the plea. Only in the city where he had received his training, his sad shrug seemed to say, had people learned to go quietly, even to hurry toward the snagless last rites of the hospital; everywhere in this backward place one still met the primitive suspicion that the hospital, ciphering a man to one bed among many, was itself on death's side, being so used to it — that at home, earthbound to the dirtily personal, clumsily upheld by amateurs, one might still hang on. No, he said, the terminal stage might be long-drawn; her amazing constitution was against her here.

"Against!" His uncle's eyes stared from their lampblack. "A day is a day!"

But the young man, still so far from his own terminus, could not agree. Morphine. He let the syllable drop gently. Perhaps to be administered in such quantity that only a professional — otherwise he could not be responsible.

"Your father — is responsible."

Rollins flushed. Third doctor-son of a father who, bred in some raw, homeopathic college of the nineties, had had a tough-tender, mid-wife competence with birth but should never have blundered near disease, he was also the only son who had been willing to stay on here, to inherit, it was rumored, more than one such of his father's mistakes.

It was settled that Lucine, with some instruction, would sleep in, the patient to be moved from home only if an oxygen tent, other like impedimenta, were required.

Walking out to the sidewalk, the doctor hesitated, remained leaning on his car door. Not long down from the classroom, perhaps he still dreamed of some discovery made by a young backwater practitioner, some digitalis out of old wives' foxglove. "Really . . . her staying power's remarkable . . . our man at the clinic says he's never seen anything like . . . what do you feed her?"

"Nothing out of the ordinary." The answer was uninflected. His uncle, already dressed in his dark suit at her insistence, stepped back from the curb. Turning, he surveyed his house with the householder's ratifying glance, appraisal of tasks to be done there come evening. He turned back to the doctor's car. "You might drop me at the court-house, you going on downtown."

And that evening, carried to her chair on the porch, she was waiting as usual. "Foreman!" she said. "Foreman! And who else is on?"

He told her. She chuckled, thinking. "That lazy crowd. Not many of them with brains enough for the job — Charlson maybe. How is it they didn't . . . ? But I suppose they thought a foreman once might as well be foreman twice."

He explained that in this case the foreman was appointed by the judge.

"Oh." Let animation fail her for a second and the skull seamed forward, papier-mâché with its candle removed.

No, said his uncle, gently avoiding the name, not *him,* he was away — a stranger, from another county. And launching quickly into as many details as he could muster, he described their swearing in, the charge by the court, their retirement to a room in the rear, too small for them — but the court was sitting in the other. He did not know why he had been tapped for the job. Accident — or perhaps the older hands had got bored with it; some, he understood, would not turn up regularly; others, like old Frazer, were only there for their six dollars per. A good lot of them were pensioners; old Clarence Whitlock had naturally been chosen clerk. For — he rattled on — once they'd been left to themselves, it had been like a club rather, at least on one side of the room. The jury had spent most of the afternoon fixing the hours of session and adjournment. The first case would be heard tomorrow.

"Quite clear — you make me see everything. I wonder what the case will be." She was smiling, almost a visible line between their gazes, as if when he respired, she drew in.

He reddened. Perhaps he decried his talent, would otherwise never have revealed it. But this was not the reason now. "Dora . . . the proceedings are secret . . . we each of us had to swear." His voice was weak, asking to be overridden.

At once she helped him, bringing to bear all the advantage she had forsworn. Delicately she rested her hands forward on the tea cloth. "I shan't be telling."

Leaving the porch, Pierre at first heard nothing behind him. Then, through the thin door as he closed it, the voice of the petitioner came, still powerful. "George . . . tell me the oath."

The following oath must be administered to the foreman and acting foreman of the grand jury:

"You, as foreman and acting foreman of this grand jury, shall diligently inquire and true presentment make, of all such matters and things as shall be given you in charge; the counsel of the people of this state, your fellows' and your own you shall keep secret; you shall present no person from envy, hatred or malice; nor shall you leave any one unpresented through fear, favor, affection or reward, or hope thereof; but you shall present all things truly as they come to your knowledge, according to the best of your understanding. So help you God!"

Code Cr. Proc. Section 238

The scrupulous man, when he breaks a pledge, often makes a wider sweep at it than the careless.

"Oh, come out of there," said his uncle the next evening, opening the door on Pierre hanging back in the stifling parlor. "You've to get your tea somewhere!" And his uncle, who had never been comfortable enough to arrest conversation in Lucine's presence in the high manner of those born to servants, did not do so now. It is probable, therefore, that among the twenty-three or so families who must surely now and then have heard scraps from the people's counsel, none could have had such full account of any one matter as was given here on this porch — each cramped summer evening — of all.

An indictment is an accusation in writing presented by a grand jury to a competent court, charging a person with a crime.

Section 247

That evening they heard the charges against Mary Jo Denny, accused of infanticide. Evidence connecting the exhumed remains of a newborn infant with the defendant was found to be insufficient, malicious and not corroborated — certainly not by several jurors known to have been acquainted with the defendant, who chose rather to be guided by the minister, Charlson Evans, in his role of merciful doubter, and by the reflection that the girl was already at Martindale. No indictment found.

The grand jury ought to find an indictment when all evidence before them, taken together, is such as in their judgment would, if unexplained or uncontradicted, warrant a conviction by the trial jury.

Section 251

So the daily parade went on, trailing minor swindles, obscure rapings, small crimes, single and eternal, unaccompliced except by the nature and history of men.

On this evening, however, they heard the case of the people of the county of Banks, Alabama, against Arthur Bean, of Tuscana in that county, defendant, former member of Inspection Crew Dam Number Three, dismissed, after two warnings for drunkenness while on duty, April fourteenth last. On the night of May tenth, it was alleged, defendant had been seen on the farm of Henderson Presson, Negro, which farm, including tenant house and several outbuildings, had that same evening burned to the ground. Witness to this, including members of the Presson family, could not be found. Defendant, however, it was further alleged, had on two occasions publicly boasted of setting this fire in retaliation for the hiring in his place of Presson's son Wesley, the first of these occasions being in front of witnesses in a local café that same evening, the second occurring the following morning, in the federal employment office at the dam site. No witnesses of the café incident came forward. Two federal clerks, however, both recent transfers from an out-of-state district, did so testify. In the proceedings, it was also revealed that the farm, of which Presson had been tenant only, had been federal property at the time of the burning, having been acquired from the bank, its actual owner, by the dam authority, some weeks before.

"So there you have it, d' ya see," said his uncle, almost expansive, in the manner brought home with him, these past evenings, from the professional colloquies of the day.

Gazing at their view and through it, through the clutter of moths batting at the screen, beyond the line of porches semivisible in the late, astral light, his audience of two thought they did see. They saw the room in which the jury sat daily, the rows of seats — five

281

to either side of the aisle, one step up between each of the rows, the flanking tables for the use of district attorneys, the witness's focal chair. Clearest of all, allotting their own bias in spite of his uncle's modest disclaimer, they saw the jury — a central cloud of importance, with George Higby, foreman, at its core. Old Clarence Whitlock, retired clerk of the court, sat at his right, once more exercising well-known powers of transcription. On the foreman's left sat the acting foreman, name unfamiliar, quantity unknown and to remain so, excepting as he belonged with others from across the hill, with — in town parlance — the "new" men from "the other side." They saw too how the jury had ranged itself, by subtle adhesion, into "old" and "new," each on its own side of the aisle, and how this separation, having to do neither with the age of a member or the immediate geography of the county, persisted even in the informal hobnobbings at recess, in the obliquity of a glance, the lowering of a voice, in who at times unobtrusively clasped hands with whom.

This, however, they saw almost without knowing in passing that they did so, would have assumed it even if his uncle had not accurately limned it for them. For, in the sudden craters in the farmland, long since forgotten in the sight of the large one, in the steady tinkle of money on small bourses, the silent tribune without flags between state and nation, the change had come to Tuscana, up to now without guns. Under such besiegement man's life is still daily; power shifts quietly, seen only intermittently even by those with hands at their holsters — of the twenty-three men likely to have been sitting on such a county jury a decade before, almost all would have been born in the county. Now there were but ten, and they felt the need to sit together, on one side.

"So there you have it," his uncle repeated. "Federal property. Not even the bank's." He did not bother to say "Not Presson's," his auditors taking for granted that in that event there would have been no case.

And, said his uncle, this was not all. Hesitant at first, he now showed the amateur's willingness to expound his own growing relish at the discovery that the law, when one had a good look at it, fitted together in all its parts not unlike a machine. The grand jury, he told them, was not bound to hear evidence for the defendant, but under certain circumstances the defendant might appear in his own behalf. And this, as per request filed with him that day, was the intent of Arthur Bean. Rumor further had it that Bean intended full confession, along with the names of certain persons he claimed as accomplices — members of a confraternity not unknown either to the community or to burning, but never before publicly named. Rumor had it this way at least on the left side of the room. The right side sat mum.

"This is why Neil Dobbin's been hanging about, chaps say," said his uncle. His audience, good pupils, nodded. In the absence of the district attorney or assistant, the foreman usually conducts the examination of witnesses, but his uncle, to his mother's regret, had been required to do so only twice. Dobbin had been in almost constant attendance, to the surprise of some.

"Rum thing," said his uncle, taking a sip of his tea, now cold. Lucine came around to replenish it, while his mother watched, squinting her eyes away from the sight of a prerogative now taken from her, unable to stop monitoring Lucine's handling of the pot, too heavy for herself to lift, that she had taken to using only recently — a monster of a pot of some thick Irish ware come down to her from her father, big as a hearth in the orange woolen cozy it wore even in this weather.

"Rum thing . . ." Arthur Bean's act, he said, was known to be one of personal vengeance. Because of drunkenness, he had been read out of a certain membership sometime before. Pariah from such, he would have been hard put to it to find any accomplices, least of all those he claimed. But it would be odd if these, never before having had to account for what they had done, were to be brought to reckoning on what they hadn't. "Rum."

Justice, however, was not required to be so specious. On the Monday that Arthur Bean, having waived immunity, was scheduled to appear, he did not do so, nor could he be found in any of his haunts on that or any subsequent day. The members of the jury appeared as usual, indeed, as had seldom occurred during their tenure so far, in almost full number — every one being in attendance on the right-hand side. All of these concurring, a true bill was found against Arthur Bean on charges of arson. No one might say either that they had been afraid to appear, or, having done so, had failed to perform their duty to the people's side.

In towns such as Tuscana had once been, where not only God had marked the sparrow, the disappearance of even a bachelor of low habits like Bean would have left a gap that could not be ignored — lack of gossip alone would have been telltale. Tuscana, snubbed as it had been by the dam, by the preferential rebuilding of the two towns destroyed when the earthworks had given, had kept its character far longer than most. But now, in the daily spillover to and from Denoyeville and Charlotte, strange cars, piloted by strange faces, pullulated in the streets like jack rabbits. There were thirty thousand people now in the three towns. In the matter of cars and people both, it was no longer humanly possible even to keep the bloodlines clear in the mind. Only the Negroes, encysted in the body politic, could still do this, sometimes for others, always at least for themselves. But from the advantage of a fixed position in life, they would know better than anybody how to save their breath, when to hold it.

In the meantime, his uncle's legal education was suddenly expanded, his own with it. On this evening, two nights after the verdict on Bean, his uncle came up the steps, slowly as usual, but without his paper, his face red and abstracted, for once outside their trinity, and told them that he'd been made a fool of.

"For fair," he said, sitting down, his air still angrily distant but already more judicial, now that he was telling. "For fair!" Repetition had grown on him, carryover from his new work maybe, or perhaps as it grows on the aging — a recognition of the sameness of what life has to teach.

"About Bean?" His mother's face was shrewd, live, in the way that his uncle would normally have rejoiced to see it. Whatever he had to tell her, life was lapping her round. "No doubt we've all been made fools of there."

"Bean? That's the least of it. Or only the beginning."

"Beginning of what? Come now, George." His mother stretched her lips in what once would have been a smile. She knew he was no fool.

"Of why Dobbin's hanging so close. And all of them knowing it, I'll wager, except yours truly." He paused, then put his fist against his forehead, not distracted but grave, as Pierre had once seen him do long ago. "Of course. Of why yours truly has been let be foreman at all."

"But you said . . . the judge appointed . . ."

"Before this, the judge was always Fourchette. Or another one of that — of the like. A closed corporation, as they say, for judge and jury both. Why, not one of that crowd but's been on it a dozen times. A fiddle for the foreman it must have been usually — any one of them who could read." He looked up from his twirling of the cup that Lucine had just set before him. "Frazer can't, you know, for one. But he's sitting there."

"Surely all that's nothing new. Not for here."

Pierre, in his corner, started. He had never heard her speak of Tuscana from such disloyal distance — from any — or not for years. *Frost. Are there frosts here?* Not since then.

"No, that's not."

"George . . ." Impossible for her to shrink further, into a smaller space, one would have said, but now she seemed to. "Then it's you. With that crowd. Some danger. Because you never —" She broke off, glancing sidewise at the servant. Because he never had joined them, she had been going to say. Up to now, Pierre had never thought of this as remarkable. Their reticence — his mother's and his uncle's — had always left so much submerged, unremarked.

"No, Dolly, of course not," he said, intent on the cup. "I don't like to be the last to know, though." His words came more measured even than usual. "I like to know. I like to know beforehand what's going on. One doesn't like to be used." Then he looked up and saw her. "There's no danger," he said quickly. Gulping his tea at a draught, he set the cup down and leaned astride of her, a hand on either arm of her chair.

To be a good liar one must have more self-deception, thought Pierre, remembering them seen once through the bedroom door, just so posed. To lie well, especially to those one loves, one must join one's own self-deception to theirs — and he has none.

"There's no danger!" his uncle repeated.

At once his mother sat back, knowing at once that there was. "From where?" she said.

His uncle sat down again. "It's naught . . . naught." One of his hands went out, hovered over the tight knot of hers, and withdrew, as if this could not be lied to.

What queerly constricted gestures the old made, they made, Pierre thought. He had never seen them kiss. But in times of stress, they always made for each other's hands. Then he remembered, with a shock because he had forgotten, *he* had forgotten, the time of stress when this had been their only means of communication.

"When the towns went under," said his uncle. "They're looking into it — you might say."

"When the dam burned . . ." She was quiet for what seemed long. Then she spoke crisply. "Arson. Is that it? And they meant to hang it on Bean."

"No," said his uncle, "not on Bean. And not arson."

"Six years ago." Her voice dimmed momentarily, to the one people kept for the past — the good past.

"Seven," said Pierre. His voice was hoarse from silence. "September, nineteen thirty-two."

"We were in Memphis," she said, and Pierre wondered how even on the night of his homecoming, he could ever have thought the three of them, under their evening light, a trinity — for here she was, dreaming back on her wedding trip, he of the boy who had been left behind, and meanwhile his uncle, catching his eye, was trying to exchange with him the glance that two men, in the presence of an infinitely wounded woman, will give one another. Only the watcher outside sees a unity, he told himself, and still felt his chest fill with longing.

"Almost seven." She came out of her dream. "But that's so far back. So long ago . . . what are they? . . . and not arson . . . and not . . ." Her needle-finger moved back and forth on her thumb. Soon she would have it, whatever it was, and if time were allowed her, the outcome too. ("They'll send the girl to Martindale.")

"Long enough," said his uncle. He reached for his newspaper, and not finding it, held his cup sideways to be refilled. When it had been, he sat without drinking. "Long enough. But they've ways of getting what they're after. That thing they call 'statute of limitations.'" He pronounced it carefully. "It doesn't hold. Not against — murder." A cheek muscle twitched, as if his mouth begrudged the word it had made.

Neither of his auditors repeated it, but the word went round the table, joining the three of them like an alerting whisper.

Finally his mother spoke. "Whose?"

Pierre held his breath, so sure of the name that would come like a face seen at a window pane and summoned from within, the name of another boy whom by now no one should have remembered.

"I doubt if they know for certain — or care. But they're inquiring into the disappearance of two brothers, one of them a boy that the hiring office took on a few days before the dam went. Two colored boys — by the name of Perry Brown and Lucius Asher."

A low groan came from behind them — not a sound that anyone would ever forget — a low dove-bubble of woe.

Lucine still held the pot. They saw that when she turned. It was not until they turned on her, a phalanx of three suddenly reminded that they were four, that the old pot slid from her hand. She backed up before them, eyes shifting like an animal that has messed, and hunched herself, still backward, through the house door. Inside, they heard her at the closet that held the brooms. They waited without speaking, but she did not return.

"Curse the habit here," his uncle said then, very low. "Never a second name, like dogs. Is she an Asher . . . or a Brown?"

"Both," his mother whispered. "They were her sons." Her glance was terrible, from eyes stretched wide in sockets worn down at the temples to two thin, pulsing spots like a baby's soft one, the fontanel reborn in the death's head. And her cry, when it came, was terrible, that piercing wail so strangely colonial, so late. "This never would have happened — at home!"

But although her gaze was fixed, they could not tell whom it accused, whether it was for his uncle — over the deed just done, or because now she knew exactly what was his danger, or for her son — because he was a son, or because he too had taken himself from her, or whether it was only for the old smashed pot, lying there with its great shards sticking up awkward as broken bones through wet orange wool and weeping tea leaves.

> *If a member of the grand jury know, or have reason to believe, that a crime has been committed which is triable in the county, he must declare the same to his fellow jurors, who must thereupon investigate the same.*
>
> Code Cr. Proc., Section 252

"There is no statute of limitations against m-memory." All that night the words inserted themselves through his tossing, in the dreamer's blind, timbreless notation — the first phrase coming with exaggerated slowness from around a corner, then the final one appearing, always with the stammer, then the substitution. While it was still dark, he forced himself up from sleep, dressed, shivering with the low physical ebb of the hour, turned on the light over his childhood desk and sat down there, still drugged, to wait for whatever people did wait in such vigils — perhaps the birds. Long before their edgy cries, he heard the call of a train, one out of all that convocation which used to push up the dawn here, a short, stopped plaint from far across the hill, in the new yard miles away. Then he was left to hear what, since his arrival, he had never quite kept himself from hearing: the noiseless current of "no change in spite of change" — as if valved from a venous system shared by all inhabitants here — that had always seemed to him the real sound of this place. No

288

quicklime of leaving, under which his new world had all but vanished, was ever to be proof against it. Across from him was the same window frame at which he had once flung Demuth's chocolate. He had lost the power ever again to see that clearly ahead of him. On the desk at his elbow were two half-finished letters, one, already crumpled days back, to Lovey, the other to Serlin — neither of which he was ever to mail. As he left the room, about to douse the light, he let it stay, for the possible use, maybe, of some crafty presence that must never have left it, his own *Doppelgänger* perhaps that all these years must have remained here holding down the seat reserved for him somewhere between honesty and doom.

There was a dim light on in the parlor too. In direct line down the passage, his uncle sat under it in his own vigil, in the chair so recently arranged for him, his head bowed over his knees. He has fallen asleep under it, Pierre thought, glancing through the door, slightly ajar, of the second bedroom, where, in the blue light of yet another lamp, his mother lay profoundly still under her sedative. Then his uncle's shoulders moved, his head bobbed above hands clasped tightly in front of him, and Pierre, frozen where he was, thought "He is weeping," turned to move away and could not, stayed by the bond in his breast that held him toward the man on the sofa, toward the figure of him seen from the train three years back — figure of a man he could ask, could trust never to ask — and scarcely breathing, he stood there, thinking "He can weep." He himself had not wept since the night he had gone to look for Johnny, and now, with the careful stiffness of one reared by women, he let himself think "A man can weep." As he watched, these thoughts passed through him, not in confusion, under their own lamp, and he took a step, his own eyes hot, across the distance that had always been too great for speech.

"Mind yourself — !"

He had been stopped just short of treading on a line of shards spread on the floor to dry, their edges glistening. Others lay on the table, some grouped on a square of paper. A tube of glue lay beside them. His uncle looked up from the pieces he held gripped together

289

for pressure between his fingers, the undamaged handle protruding. He made the faint, shamed grimace of someone detected at a puzzle not deep enough. After a minute he got up, carrying his hands before him as if he had a cracked egg in them, and leaned over the table, examining the paper.

Behind him, Pierre leaned with him, his eyes returning to focus. Neatly, as in a mechanical drawing, his uncle had outlined the pot, dotted in the shape of the fragments, and numbered them. Very slowly now he shifted the mended pair to the proper spot in the center, imperceptibly released them, and withdrew his hands. He flexed his cramped fingers, uttering a sigh that said nothing distinguishable, cast Pierre the same apologetic grimace, and went out to the scullery, where he could be heard setting the kettle to boil. Bending down, Pierre picked up the fragments from the rug and set them on the table, one by one. Neither will he speak, he thought, neither will he press others to.

On a spindle of a chair nearby, a black oilcloth shopping bag hung slackly by one of its worn straps, the shiny surface rubbed down to the fabric in many old creasings — Lucine's tote-bag, used each night to carry back to her own quarters that tithe of the day's larder which she considered her due. All of the house servants "toted," in anonymous packages or in bags like these, the contents of which must never be questioned and never were, except by those new wives from the North who could not be made to understand the difference between this and stealing, that it was the "squeeze" which still linked servant to household in the old way of owning and being owned — a portion which could never be taken care of (as more than one, to local smirkings, had tried) in the wage. Lucine, by marriage an Asher and a Brown, by color probably a Booker, or one of the Dibbelaises or Bontemps brought here by whites from Louisiana, came of trusted strains; she had been away, but not too far, to the convent — by virtue of all this, not in spite of it, she still toted. To-night the canvas cot she slept on here in the parlor was neatly stacked as usual in the corner in which she replaced it each morning, took it down again after her evening visit to the backs — for this too, even if they slept in, was their unfailing habit, as if the company here drained a strength that only the touch of their own could renew. But now it was nearly morning. The broom closet hung open, bare of the single change of garment and towel she kept there, and she had gone without her tote-bag.

In the hall, the phone, long since muffled by some trick of his uncle, struggled to burr, scarcely doing so before his uncle reached it. He spoke into it at some length, so inaudibly that Pierre could hear the kettle at boil. Mashing the tea, putting the milk in the cups as had been done in his childhood, he peered out the scullery window. All the other houses on the street were dark. To any watcher opposite, theirs, fraily lit at all corners, must seem like some warning craft cradling disaster as carefully as his uncle had his cracked egg, making the watcher think perhaps of how all households ripened toward dispersal, even of how tonight Higby's was the safest, since it rode the dark already knowing where its own disaster lay.

"That was the hospital," said his uncle, returning. "They've no nurse to spare us." He sat down heavily for him, always so neat and median in his ways. The china bits on the table listed faintly, and some of the sugar he was spooning pattered like sand. "We'll have to manage by ourselves."

"She won't come back, then?" Pierre nodded toward the tote-bag.

"They'll want to stay out of it. One can't blame them. Even if she would — the rest won't let her. They'll fold their tents — now that they've heard."

"But you'll be out of it too, then. If you have to stay here."

"Yes," said his uncle. "I s'll have to beg off. I s'll be out of it. Yes."

Pierre drank his tea in silence. The silence of the young, cold with its own fear of compromise, is a bitter courtesy.

"I do not *choose* to," said his uncle.

You chose not to beg off in the beginning.

"Last night, when I said what I did — that I would not be used — I said it in anger. . . ."

Last night, when my mother cried out again and said, "Now send me to hospital!" you refused her. "No," you said, "you'll stay here. And I with you." I saw her grateful look when you said that. You chose.

"One way or t'other," said his uncle, "a man must expect to be used."

You chose to break your oath. You will be.

"But one doesn't always choose for oneself, d'ya see . . . you see that?"

I see that you can speak, in your way.

"For that matter . . . rather by Dobbin . . . than by that crowd —"

And I listen — in mine.

"That man, Dabney Mount — the one who's always hanging about the courthouse — that scrap — you remember?"

I remember. All the characters are coming out of lodging.

"Stopped me yesterday, as I was leaving. Asked after your mother . . . that dirt. Hinted he'd like to sponsor me at the cockfight, down at Semple's. They keep a cock there, you know, match it once in a while, just for show."

I know. Shall I ever tell you — what I know?

"The Lord is my witness I've never been friend to them."

No one is my witness. And the listener is never the friend.

"What's Dobbin after?" said Pierre.

At these words, his uncle leaned back in his chair, his eyelids rising and falling — and Pierre saw that he had been speaking in that communicative trance which comes with exhaustion; not counting other interrupted nights and days, he had been up since six the previous morning. "Jury trial." He spoke thickly. "Get them to a jury trial, no matter the verdict. Get the names down on legal record, sooner or later they're done for." He rested his head back. "Done." He closed his eyes, his lips still moving. " 'Write that kind of cock with two *k*'s, don't you,' I said, 'Mount?' "

"What's in it for Dobbin? Why would he?" The district attorney's name was faintly familiar, surely local.

"Judgeship. Say he wants . . . federal ju'ship." His head moved

292

from side to side. "Do a job, maybe — know whose blood *he* is."
His jaw fell, closed again. "Forty winks. You spell me." His chin
sank to his breast; the stubbled cheeks moving tranquilly out and in.
It had barely rested so, when the whole head snapped back, eyes
wide. "Somebody outside. At the door."

Pierre went to answer it; had his hand on the knob.

"Stand back!" His uncle's whisper warmed his ear; he had been
crept up upon from behind. Silently he was motioned aside, his
uncle's hand, arm outstretched, replacing his on the knob, turning
it fraction by fraction. Suddenly he whipped the door back against
him.

Nothing entered except a little dark, of the same temperature as
the room, yet different, the infinitesimal gap between outdoors and
in, appreciable in the roots of the hair, by the skin on the backs of
the hands. His uncle peered around the door, Pierre after him. Nothing was there. As they stood there, they heard the gathering chip-
chip of the birds.

"Dreaming myself in Ireland — must have —" said his uncle. He
had been a Tommy there from 1916 until the truce, was ashamed of
his part in the war, ordinarily never spoke of it. "That's what they
used to tell us." He spoke close to Pierre's shoulder, eyes on the distance, as an elder huntsman might speak in low-voiced counsel.
"Never stand in a lighted door."

Pierre nodded, as if he too could see Ireland. Eastward, the great
embankments rode like true cloud, their immense counterside as
hidden. At such an hour, or darker, a town enfeoffed here might
still dream it kept its own horizon.

"Uncle —" He spoke without thinking, as men say — or from the seat
in the depths of thought, ever reserved. "Get me to Dobbin. I
know the names."

In the moment he spoke he knew his stumble as an actor does,
foresaw the look on his uncle's face before it turned.

"*You* — ? *You* know?"

The role of the listener is never fully learned.

His uncle swept an arm outward. Against that wide sweep, his

293

whisper seemed small. "D'ya think there's anyone — including Dobbin — who doesn't?"

Still whispering, he pushed Pierre inside. "Including — the jury?"

The door closed safely behind them. "Including — Bean?"

As if in answer, they heard a shuffling, a scraping. It came from outside the back door; an animal, no animal. While they watched, the door opened. A dark hand appeared, set down an old leather satchel roped with clothesline, a corded wood box, a bulging string bag. She came in crabwise, pushing the baggage behind her with one gray, bare heel. Once in, she set down her shoes, rested the small of her back against the door. When she faced round and saw them, she straightened away from the door, hanging her head sideways, arching and lowering it, eyes large on them, cast down and raised again, standing so with her goods beside her — Lucine. Her face was a bad color, but whatever had affrighted it lay behind or ahead of her — not in them. While they watched, she slid out a foot, watching them, slipped the foot into its shoe, then the other, managing in the same movement to edge the satchel further into the room. When they still said nothing, she gave a sudden half-bob, begging permission, in the same instant taking it. Quick as an eel, she stowed the satchel in one corner, the box in another, where they fitted perfectly, in niches the small room never would have been thought to hold, as if all the way here she had been reflecting on her scrub-pail lore of it, saying to herself: the satchel will be out of their way under the sofa, the deal box just fit where the molding ends, behind the chair. When she stood up, her face had returned to its natural ocher, her figure, patted here and there, to its neat calm — a world away from that bare, searching heel. Arms folded, she looked down, expressionless, at the broken stuff on the table. Something, her breath perhaps, dislodged them as she hung over them. As they all watched, the large, mended piece gaped slowly at the jointure, the part with the handle rubbling over on its side. She shook her head, in ownership as well as blame, and went on to the corner where the cot was stacked. Taking it down, she turned, regarding them.

"I'll mek up the cot in t'yere," she said softly. "You go on, get what res' you can on it; t'aint only four. I'll go 'long in there, sit with her." This too must have been reflected. She put out her hand, just short of his uncle's sleeve. "Mek it up good and nice for you, you go on. Less you get your res', you be all tuckered out in the morning." Soft as steel, her voice urged, speaking its owner-ship — they of her, she of them. "You go on, now hear? Less you be all tuckered, time you got to go to the courthouse. You go on."

And so next day — he went on, and all his entourage with him, in that small craft where each hand thought himself alone, rocked between darks and Orions while all thought themselves still, in a great estuary of the same.

There come times in men's lives when any accounts of their inner monologues cannot further explain them. Only their acts can record them then, as later they must record themselves. Such a time had come for Pierre.

On that day his uncle, rising from his cot, left about an hour and a half late for his duty; his mother, awakening early to hers, curling up like a griffon on her pillows, silently let herself be tended by Lucine, saying only when time came to move her: "I'll bide here." He himself, not returning to bed, marked the day only by showering and changing his clothes. Lack of sleep benumbed them all, letting each harbor his shocks and his speech, promising a day without any heroic other than that needed to get through it. Mean-while the weather had "gone in," as people said here of those gray interims, blamed by some on the surrounding masses of water, when the sun went in and took the appearance of heat with it, leaving greens sharper, sounds cooler, people abstracted to shades in a lull like a midweek Sunday or a snow, during which some hastened to sit with their kind over minor husbandries, others sat away from them, paring their nails, hearing time bide. Is there an ecology for all climes perhaps, some balanced pause between a life and the lives around it, when the actionless can act?

Pierre sat in his room as usual that morning, rereading one of the few books he had brought with him. Usually he kept his door closed until Lucine's soft knock apprised him that she was going to shop, when he opened it in order to hear his mother's bell. Today he did not close it. Around midmorning his mother suddenly asked for something to sew, a request not easy to satisfy now that the linens had been mended, and all the paraphernalia of her trade cleared away. Finally, at her direction, a packet of silk squares, their edges still raw, was found for her, where it had been lodged with others in one drawer of the old treadle sewing machine now stored in his room. He had glimpsed enough — edges of photographs, letters thin enough to be foreign, envelopes thick enough to be documentary, to know that he had come upon the hoarding-place for which as a boy he had sometimes pried, but now he did not pry. Scattered among the books on the shelf above his desk were certain ones any meddler might have assumed to be his own private mementos: the largest, a German dictionary with an inscription on the flyleaf, the oldest (faded to curiosa long before it could have been his) a bookseller's trinket marked *Affection's Gift for 1845*, the smallest, so insignificant that it must have been saved for a reason, a dime-store address book with one leaf gone. They were ranged above his head as brashly as the silver cups of the oarsman, as plainly as the purloined letter — the book he had been given, the one he had pinched, the one, first of his life, that he had bought — but any watcher might have seen as plainly that today he did not look at them.

All that day he comported himself with awkward honesty, an especial openness, for what great eye at the transom? Watch a second-story man on his way to work at dusk, as he drops his quarter in the beggar's cup, see how far from the cup his fingers are, spread wide at the root as a child's. Follow tomorrow's headline bogeyman today, on his way not to keep his black appointment, as he sees the movie twice, yawns at the marquee, trembles into conversation at the coffee counter, cedes his place in the bus queue, and still arrives on time. And Pierre too managed it so that some twenty years later his most inflexible arbiter, eager informer, might say here, "He was honest as the day — that day. As far as I know — he premeditated nothing."

That afternoon he had an errand which took him directly into Tuscana. He was to call at a house across town, pick up a wheel chair relinquished by the death of a woman there, and trundle it back home. Actually the chair was one of a scarce few circulated to chronic outpatients by the new hospital in Denoyeville, but since, as it happened, the woman had been a Mrs. Jebb, their former neighbor, politeness had delayed the exchange until after the funeral, which had been yesterday. Better not wait for the hospital delivery, Mr. Jebb had kindly informed them by telephone; better pick it up by hand, since it was no shape for car transport, and wheel it to its new destination. In the routine of respectable loss, the Jebbs would be "at home" today at four.

Other afternoons, setting out for the daily walk without which his stint here would have been intolerable, he always paused below the porch steps for a minute, looking westerly down the few blocks that led to the center of town, then turned east, always on the same route, down the state road and along the three-and-a-half-mile bypass to Denoyeville, breaking into an easy track-pace on the way there, going at an amble on the way back. Denoyeville had been rebuilt on a single idea; in the middle distance of its dams, as he approached it, that idea still presided and was noble. Otherwise, once he got to its main street, walking between its seven-year brick antiquity and six-month shoddy, he was in the useful limbo of the quick, ledger-built American city, after-image of others even as one stood in it, lost to the closed eye quicker than one could say Ozymandias. Nothing in Denoyeville was ever likely to be older than its name. He was of the generation not yet repelled by this, but comforted. Usually he sat for a while, sweat-soaked and air-cooled, behind the plate glass of the big new Whelan chain drug, at a counter where, except for the hominy on the club breakfast, he might be anywhere south-of-winter, north-of-summer. Sitting there, for an hour or so he was once again on his own.

This afternoon, in the way of things filial, he would have no time for that. He had an errand not his own. So, in the nature of things, after a pause below the porch steps, in which he seemed only to be looking into the general lull, he turned on his heel and walked west. So, late downbeat after the measure, we follow him.

He came near the café, where he had never been inside. There would have been time and enough to stop and meditate there. But it had too much past — or not enough of one — for him to want to enter it now. He went by it.

He came to the church where his mother was to marry his uncle. Had. A church is a proper place to meditate. But he remembered it too well with the light out over its door, and went on.

There is a ring game that children play, with an "it" in the center, the rest in a ring, hidden. Thicket is needed. "Ring" may not move. "It" has three tries for the gaps in the circle. Here a boy confronts him in a bush. Another bars his way in the bramble. Between those trees is a third.

Such a trio confronted him now, unseen by anyone but him, at three doors. One at the courthouse, one at the school, one at the store.

Let the school come first, as it does for most. Its yard was null with summer, the door sealed. The boy there was no more distinct for him than for most men. He passed him quite easily.

Next came the store, far down the baseline of his triangle, beneath its old scribble of neon blue. No Semple lounged under it now, creasing and recreasing his duck trousers to an ingoing line of creditors, allotting leeway to some with a nod or odd crook of his thumbs, refusing others with a stillness, a stare. Credit was being arranged for him elsewhere. As a stranger in town, Pierre himself would not know this, must not know it, think only, as he approaches the door with the hung sign which like others on the way will say CLOSED NOON WEDNESDAY, that this is the only reason the street is so empty, folk retreated somewhere behind their gray weather and their Wednesday. As a stranger, therefore, he approached the store. Half a yard from it he bent his head, sauntered by without looking. Perhaps he saw that it had a small annex or lumber-room; things catch on the periphery of sight that the eye does not will. The door to this was on the other side of it, hidden. So, if a boy stood there, he passed him.

Now he faced the apex, the courthouse. Its steps lay directly across a square of park, behind two sentinel trees. A paved path circled the park and the courthouse walls.

Politely as any outsider, he took the path. Just as he did so, a figure standing at the top of the high steps, boy or man, its features screened by the trees, turned and went inside. Judgment was always in session; this had nothing to do with him. He examined the face of the building like any tourist who would not bother to go inside to view its staple of flag and lectern, gloom-light that fluttered in women's breastpins — who had no uncles there. Portcullis 1870, inscription above it too worn to read. *"Nomen mutabilia sunt"* perhaps — names are mutable — as would do for any court in the land. *"Res autem immobilis."* "Ring" may not move. He drew a finger along the cornerstone, where there was an old watermark, flood mark, three feet or so above the foundation line. A few pariah dogs were always slumped there, for god-knows-what-all, not for warmth surely, perhaps fraternity. One of them, muzzle stretched on its paws, rolled up its eyes at him and measuredly thumped its tail. He shook his head at it, at the door up above. Once entered there — judges, Dobbins of whatever blood and petitioners alike — one was already in the dock.

"Got me wrong," he said aloud to the dog. "I'm a stranger here." At once, not ten yards from him, he saw the gap in the circle — the mud alley where the farmers set their stalls on Fridays, that had been here always — as if the hypnotist had at last slapped him, stung himself awake. He ran toward it. Behind him, the dog, its brow wrinkled, again thumped its tail.

Once in the alley he went at a brisk pace, just short of the one he kept for Denoyeville, otherwise he would get to the Jebbs before expected. Going along, he hummed. Down here, he opened his mouth so seldom that his voice had been rusty when it addressed the dog, but now he was up and about again in the jigtime, daytime world. "Do, act, speak, laugh!" he chanted to himself, as he sometimes did in that other world, where personality could be multiple. Here, between the iron bands of family, he had only one — perhaps everyone lost courage for alternatives there. This alley was grim now with the general Ash Wednesday, but he meant to visit it on its bright bourse-Friday, if only to remind himself, like an Alger hero at the scene of his first dollar, of the great bourse to which he had escaped. He stopped now, to look back at the obstacle race just run. There were no planes in the sky, not one since he had been here, to remind him that to some, Tuscana was invisible, not swinging alone as Arcturus, not holding all that there was to the human condition in its sphere. To the new men at the dam it was already bypassed. Those who revisit the buildings of childhood, it was said, always find them shrunken — the chandeliers to rushlight, to wickets all the imperial gates. It was the fault of his "familiar," then, that cartographer of the condemned and accurate eyes, if the three buildings he had just passed, surely so small in the sight of some, seemed to him as large as they had ever been. Unless he was careful to keep chanting, they might yet appear — golden architraves floating on shadow — as seen once through other eyes, from the height of a hill long fallen, whose scale could never now be known.

He was walking slower now, checking the house numbers where there were any. The Jebbs must have gone down the ladder since leaving the high estate of the Higbys; this street petered out just ahead of him, almost at the railroad line. Yonder, where there had once been fields of weed that moved like wheat in the evening breath of the trains, now only one short one kept the divide. The opposite edge of the backs had crept nearer. A rim of shacks lined it, already harum-scarum with the rows of plants they potted in tins, unmatched curtains flying their savage motley, but the porches and chimneys were straight, not yet tumbledown, and the tar-paper covering, stamped to look like brick, slickly new. Here on this side the seedy houses, some derelict, all pale as Methodists gone far in drink, still had the indefinable look of the white dwelling. He found numbers nine and thirteen, no eleven, none marked Jebb. Eagerly he retraced his steps, looking for the special signs of life that marked the house of death on its post-interment day here — a concourse of women mostly, walking in with prepared faces, coming out, wry or pleased, with a bit of jet or a cookpot, trophy of agility as well as grief. The chair would be ceded to him in somewhat the same rhythm, in progression from sideline to sideboard, from random elegy to calculated bottle and cake: he knew how people were here, and not only here. He was half reluctant to miss this diversion, not scorning it, as usual with the young. Already he had begun to understand old people who attended funerals with which they had no earthly connection, patient ghouls hurried by age toward the gossip that might be eternal, old voyeurs after the single story (whose?), old humanists — all bending over the casket to look at the cut gem. And of course he must have the chair.

"You come about the chair, h'aint you?" The question, echo, came from a man hurrying around the corner of number nine, on legs so short that he toddled. "Saw you from the window. Cain't see this place from the road." He led the way, the dumpy seat of his sawed-off pants grimaced this way, that, by his gait, toward a shambles of a cottage not much larger than its outhouse. On the porch, he stamped his boots long and virtuously, looking up at Pierre with soft, brown-bulb eyes. "Doggone if she warnt right! She held all along nobody'd come but you!" He was a compact gargoyle of a man, whose outline came to points at several places, at the high shoulder blades and the ears, between which an oval cranium rose like a darning egg, protected by a cap made out of the top of a woman's stocking. Pierre remembered the deceased, the huge slattern in slippers, neighborhood fence-leaner, who had eased herself into their household the day his mother had been carried home. He had never seen Jebb until now — if this was Jebb. The mailbox, clamped to the porch post, showed another name. It said *Bean*.

"She says to come on in and have something first." The man swallowed shyly. "Won't be no snap, lugging that thing all the way back to Rhine Street."

So they surely knew him then; he was in the right place, or the wrong one. "No thanks, I won't trouble you." He stole another look at the mailbox. "I'll just get the chair and go on."

"*She* says to." The brown eyes shone trustfully up at him. Oracle, whoever "She" is, says to.

"Come on!" a voice boomed from within, deep, but a woman's. "Enough for a feast here." Stooping to get under the door frame, the first thing he saw was the expected: humble table substituted for sideboard, pop bottles for liquor, food in a stiff array not yet broached except by the energetically breeding flies, to one side of all this a large box. "He would do it," the voice added. "Told him only one to count on was you."

He followed the voice to its origin — the chair. "Chair," as it might have been addressed, was prodigious — a high, oaken affair, pedaled, chained and levered, on tandem-size wheels — and chair was filled. An immense bulk of a woman sat in it, trunk-legs planted on the footrest, baby-shaped hands at the wheels. In the elephant-hide dimness she filled the chair without jointure, like one of those balloons that rode carnival carts, Buddha head lolling in a fixed, aerated smile. His first wild thought was that this was the waxwork exhibit itself, the deceased Mrs. Jebb, set up natural as life — that he had come a day too early after all. Then "She" rolled forward, saying "Howdy"; the short man urged a chair under his knees from behind, and there he was, wedged between them, tender focus of their inch-close solicitude, feeling extraordinarily like a dummy himself.

"Here you are, now." A loaded plate was thrust on his lap from the right — potato chips, grocer's ham, cake indefinable, curdled slaw. "Eat hearty now." Stocking-cap nodded at him pleasedly, over-extending it, like a child playing house. "She'd have liked that." From Pierre's left, the woman snorted, at the same time pushing into his grasp a pop bottle.

"Thank you, thank you!" Pierre turned his head to each. "Mr.

Jebb, isn't it?" The woman would be the dead wife's mother, that was it. "Mrs. . . . Bean?"

"Jebb!" both chorused at him, one to an ear. Both sat back, not far, regarding him, their simpleton, between them.

"Marcus Jebb," the man said. "And this is Mother." The woman blinked, accepting. Her son clasped his hands primly, sat up straighter. "Bean . . . he took off somewhere couple weeks ago, ain't been heard of since. Leaving her all swole up and helpless, right there in that chair." He swallowed again, eyes bulging with the accompanying emotion, whatever it was, virtue perhaps, and its own modest pleasure in same.

Pierre, unsure of where to allot his sympathy, looked back and forth between them. "Oh, then you'll still need it," he murmured. "I mean, the chair."

Both exploded in laughter, Mr. Jebb slightly behind his mother, like two straight men over the sally of the comedian between them.

"Not *her*," said Mr. Jebb when he had recovered, nodding toward his mother. "Her," he said with almost equal reverence, nodding vaguely at Pierre's plate, as if it were there, hovering over this honor done her, that the departed might still be found. "Didn't wait till she passed on. Bean and my old missus, I mean. He just took off."

"She took off first!" the woman said harshly. "And don't you ever forget it!" With sudden violence, she gave the chair a shove, sending herself past Pierre's knees to the table, where the wheels wedged, bringing her to rest just over the food. Slowly she hoisted herself up, a job for block and tackle, or for what already glutted her eyes, expanded her doll-shaped nostrils. Seeing her upright, it was already improbable to imagine this diva of the flesh as ever sitting, ever moved from where she was except by some fluxion of gas within or ground beneath, then as suddenly she kicked the chair behind her with a foot that came from beneath her skirt like a kitten and disappeared again. "Works right good," she said, "but I ain't yet ready for it." She applied herself to the food, at first without benefit of plate, then turning back to them over a loaded one, her voice coming ventriloquially, as if thought were only a secondary chewing. "Mar-

cus' lawful wife she was. Always taking off with that Bean. Two years
back, when Bean got the dam job, she took off for good. Then when
he takes off, leaving her sick, she puts the health service on to us.
Next of kin, they say, and you know who come running." She paused,
munching in the direction of her son.

Mr. Jebb gave Pierre a gentle poke. "Eat hearty now," he said.
"You ain't hardly had nothing." Swallowing, he reclasped his hands.

"Two weeks he waits on her, hand and foot, night and day. It
ain't decent, Marcus, I said, not after what she told the whole town
last time. Bury her decent. But the rest ain't."

"First-class burial," said Mr. Jebb.

"I'll say. Last carriage empty, you know, for respect. That's all
right too, she was his children's mamma. I won't say otherwise, Bean
or no Bean. But surely, I said, you ain't going on with that second-
day business!" Mrs. Jebb paused, this time in Pierre's direction. "That
cake come all the way from the Jew dellycadessen in Denoyeville,"
she commented, lowering at his full plate. "Don't nobody make better
funeral cake than the Jews." Under her frown, he broke into the
cake.

Fondant cheeks pursed, she watched him work backwards across the
plate, free himself as best he could of the sin of nongluttony. Mr.
Jebb sat poised alert, on the edge of his chair. Catching Pierre's eye
on him, he swallowed again, not, as now could be seen, from present
sentiment only, but from a kind of permanent tic of it, as if Mr.
Jebb's heart constantly rode so near the surface that every now and
then he was put to the trouble of gulping it back down.

"Delicious . . ." said Pierre into the silence, once, twice, and again
when he had finished. More than this was expected of him, he
knew; he was their only hope of audience, of elegy; how else was
Mr. Jebb to divest himself of his feelings, his mother divulge what
she yearned to, unless he knew his role? Once more he repeated himself, this time, with a sudden hiccough of remembrance, in the town's
own idiom. "Very tasty."

"He would do it." Hope gleamed again in her eel-jelly eye. "Who'd
come after those pickings out there, I said. No more and you'd get

from a hen in molt." The hand resting on her bosom flicked toward the relic box and lay flat again. "Next of kin, that's all he'd say. Next of kin is the children, I said — eight of them they had, four living and working — and when they come to choose wasn't so much as a pinky-ring to go round. You'll see, I said. Only thing in that place ain't trash is the chair."

"Sorry to bother you about it." Pierre stood up and took hold of the chair. "On such a sad day!" he heard himself add. Why, it was easy; the extra word, phrase, had popped out of him like a belch, half hypocrisy, half Coke. This then was what "condolences," empty as the last carriage in a first-class burial, were for. We help each other round the bend, improvisers all. For Mr. Jebb, set off at last, as if by the turning of a proper key in his back, had begun a slight, steady rocking. What with his size and his cap, it gave him an unfortunate resemblance to a child needing to go to the bathroom, but under the circumstances was still recognizable as that formal palsy with which mourners, greeting each other, say nothing, say all.

Somberly his mother regarded him. "More'n one way to make a man remember you, ain't there?" she said to the air. "I say for shame."

"Give him something of Zella's from the box, carry it on back to his folks," said Mr. Jebb, aloof. "Her and them was neighbors."

"Oh, no no. Thanks, I'll just take along this."

Mrs. Jebb held the screen door for him. The chair, too high for the jamb, had to be laid over on its side. It went out with a grudging noise, a catafalque dragging its chains. Mr. Jebb winced when it passed him.

"Oh you there, hush!" said Mrs. Jebb, from the door. "Bean give you the laugh, he could see how you take on."

Her son closed his eyes to her.

Mrs. Jebb gave the chair a push over the threshold. Hand knocking her bosom, still great with her story, she leaned over Pierre, her whisper hot in his ear, loud as the Trojan women. "Eight children they had, then she took off, saying he wasn't *big* enough for her."

Legs adangle, the mourner once more gulped down what troubled him, bulging his eyes open, their indefensible smile.

305

"I buried her," said Mr. Jebb.

They paid no attention when Pierre closed the door. Outside, he bent double over the laughter that had been mounting in him since he entered. Seeing the outhouse handy, and needing it, he went in. Its slatted window was almost up against the house. From the clinking of plates, the Jebbs must have returned to the feast.

"Told you," he heard her say. "Nobody come but him."

There was no answer except the hiss of a pop bottle.

"Know your kidneys better'n your own mother? Take some milk. Know well as I do, that stuff gives you gas."

Whether Mr. Jebb did as bade could not be seen, was never heard. After a pause, his mother spoke again. "See how you take on when *I* go!" said Mrs. Jebb.

On the way back the chair went hardily, broken in as any hired nag whose attendant was nodding, or laughing for all to see, like a fool. In the center of town, Rhine's was just coming off shift; the chair walked him through these noisy ranks, oblique glances, affording him something of the quick, uneasy rapport extended a cripple; along quieter streets it freed him to listen, trotting him along behind with the high dignity of a Seeing Eye dog. After a while he bent over it with the trust one gave a talisman. It had its own silent repertoire, offering up such humoresques as Marcus Jebb, morsel, still alive and kicking between those two stern judges of anatomy, his *She's*. Why should he always feel that laughter was somehow contraband in Tuscana? He had a proper errand, had met diversion by way of it, was returning. Once more humming, he followed the chair.

On the edge of niggertown it faltered, then went on. Quiet those streets seemed, in the low-keyed weather, but surely only in order to rise refreshed for the rich, brown evening, grackled with voices. He himself was sweating. If the demi-company here had folded its tents, in this fishbowl weather so had much of the town.

But, nearing Pridden Street, the chair ambled, and he let it. Here were the horse troughs, never wetted in his time except with rainwater, each with its pilastered house behind it — a row of abdicated queens, Corinthian-curled. Natural ghosts, in the subaqueous light they looked more alive than the streets through which he had come, the habit of stillness on them not for an afternoon but for years. Three of the latter had not much changed their color, all of them the gloomy off-white of smudged conscience, except one. There at the end was Miss Pridden's, still the ward of Montgomery, still white. Affection rose in him as he neared it, seeing it as neatly espaliered on reality here as it had remained in his mind. Here it was, pretty and pallid as a harmless reminiscence should be, bloodless that battlement, absurdly prinked against the sky. The glassed-in card on the door no doubt still gave the same hours, ten to twelve, two to five. He stood back on the path to look at the place. It made him happy, token of what memory could do when it was kind. A smile quirked his cheek. He must have been happy there in spite of himself; now, with graceful precision, it told him so. It had done as a proper memory should — it had kept itself up. And it had shrunk.

He parked the chair at the side, in the shrubs where, with one of its quick changes, it fitted in at once, born to rosebay, waiting for a dowager of the same high-backed incarnation as itself. Then he opened the jalousied door as if he had just done so yesterday, and stood inside. Was that the smell of benné seed cakes, the sound, just ceased, of a voice like Palmer script speaking? No, the air had a hollow, glassed-in quiet — museum air, best in the world for reverie, when one had the museum all to oneself. But there on the ceiling were the molded garlands, just as he recalled them. He had not yet opened his eyes.

When he did so, they were there. His watch told him that it was past five, but visitors had always been precious here, the rules only for form. A latecomer would still be welcomed by whoever was curator now. Quiet as an epitaph he felt the presentiment that Miss Pridden was no longer alive, if only because he had not ever been urged to go and see her; in the daily anthology at home she had not once reappeared. For memory's sake perhaps this too was as it should be; people kept up better when they did not. He smiled in passing at the thought of Miss P. intruding on her own image, she who had so timidly held it back from greater personages' mirrors. But it was the library that had been his love, still must be, for at the thought of standing again under that clerestory light, fingering the books there, he was filled with the most foolish emotion. He listened to it a moment, for its quality, then, still wondering, opened the low door under the stairs, and entered.

It was the same, three shafts of light shining faintly even on this gray day. Still smiling, he moved to let one of them center on his face, a bit of sun long preserved for his coming. It was so foolish to feel as he did, such a welling of comfort as if he were some prodigal returning, at an age when he was still to do much of anything, good or bad. There was the famous table, and it was not the same, piled now with papers, heavy books that even in the dimness he could see were not native here. The new curator perhaps was a scholar, or perhaps some other boy, silent catechumen, came here, as once he. He liked the thought of that, turning to the shelves, a collection shrunken indeed now that he saw it, fingering one or two of those quaint incunabula that at a touch once again were real. Gazing down at *The Voyage of Commodore Perry*, he felt himself once more a stylite on his pillar, knew his emotion for that delicate levitation of the heart when it looks down from the burden of new innocences, on the old. Sweet room in amber, may heaven and Montgomery preserve thee — to return to even when one plans never to come back. He put the Commodore in his place again.

A light was snapped on behind him. "Oh, sorry!" said the man there. "Thought Miss Minnie'd shut up shop for the day and gone home."

Later, Pierre's eye would never erase its early impression of him there in the orange nimbus of the first lamp, and there was no reason to — a head that kept its blunts and shadows firmly aligned in any light, like a good medal, whose outline, a breadth too small for the shoulders, at second glance had the same perfected, equivocal balance with the body beneath as the old plaster casts of classical statues that were kept in a long gallery to themselves, demoted but not quite shelved, in the basement of the Metropolitan. There was no other resemblance — this face had eyes that were anything but blind.

"I expect she has. I'm afraid I took the liberty of letting myself in. I used to know this place quite well when — when I was a boy. Miss Pridden used to let me come in and read."

The man smiled slightly, from his height of the late thirties, early forties perhaps, at the word "boy." "Oh, you knew my aunt, then. You knew — she died about six months ago?"

"Yes, I knew."

"Well — do go on and have a look at whatever you want to. I shan't be settling down for some hours yet."

"Thanks, I was just going."

"You're sure now? Actually, I just came in for a wash." He stretched his arms in a jacket, crushed but not slack, that like his speech, his manner, had not been tailored here, yet he had said "Miss Minnie" in the slurred way that had. "Been a rough day."

"Thanks, I should do." He heard his own suddenly Anglicized inflection with embarrassment. It was one that rarely came over him even in answer to its like, but sometimes took him without warning, a secret obeisance, telling him that he was in the presence of his betters. "Nice place to work though, isn't it."

The man nodded. "Matter of fact, I'm baching it here, while they build my place in Denoyeville. Right now, of course, it's very handy." He sauntered to the table, moved some papers, revealing a tantalus back of them, as if in dismissal, then turned, his head cocking, "You're not — British? Yet — you're not from these parts?"

"I was born there. Brought up here." Pierre hesitated. "Neither are you, are you? I mean — from here."

"Went to school over there. Born in Boston." There was the slightest intonation, as if from more reserve than would want to add "of course" — yet had. "Spent a good many summers here. Before your time, though." His smile was friendly, not assumed but economical, quick and purposive toward decent intimacy, no further — it too learned in a good school. His hand hovered over the tantalus. "Hold on a minute . . ." He came forward. "You wouldn't by any chance be — you're George Higby's boy, aren't you? Stepson, or nephew?" He leaned back. "Wait a minute now . . . you're the one . . ." Don't tell me yet, his gesture said, this is my forte, my business. These were eyes that indeed took no dismissal, sunk back on the trail of some evasive knowledge that when it came would seem to do so not from them, but from those they were looking into.

Summers here. Who? It almost came to him, in the thin Palmer script of those mild confidences. The nephew from Boston . . . you're the one who. Who are you?

"Paul . . . isn't it? . . . Peter . . . Goodman! That's it. And you've been away to college, up North." He mentioned the name of it, in triumph.

"That's right." Who? "You know my uncle?"

"Well, rather!" He bent over the decanter, pouring. "Like it up there?" From his posture, one would not have thought that he could see Pierre's nod, but he had already flexed his brows in answer. "Shouldn't wonder," he murmured. He turned. "Join me? Won't you?"

"Thanks, sir. Don't mind if I do."

Both laughed. Whoever he was, there had already sprung between them the nimbleness between two intelligences who can speak to one another, the easier perhaps in a foreign land.

"Here you are." His manner toward a younger man was perfect, Pierre thought — nothing of the *pater*, no spurious youth. Few of his own professors did as well. And yet there was about him what a few of the very best of these had — some superiority that shot its rays from several corners or one center, a nexus of talent not too forceful for manners, of some noblesse of ideas that did not disdain to clothe itself either in good jackets or poor ones, of men who roughed up both admiration and jealousy because born so clearly to the purple, no matter where. Well, the man himself had told him where. Now — who?

"Drink up."

They were types to be wary of — just because he so admired them. They had the listener's subtle frankness, and they were keen. And because, hungry as he was for his own level, this man's smile, address, came to him like a breath from the North.

"Funny old place, isn't it?"

Pierre nodded. "Yes it is. Or — you mean Tuscana?"

"No." A frown turned down the corners of the mouth, thinning it. "No. There's nothing funny about Tuscana."

He was almost on the edge of it. Why could he not remember! "You know, I have to confess something," he said. "I don't know your name."

"Why . . . I am sorry!" A light of amusement broke on the man's face, turned on himself. "It's that job of mine . . . I get to thinking that everybody . . ." He thrust a hand forward. "I'm Neil Dobbin."

Chapter IV. The Proceedings. Jurors Are Seen.

HE WALKED into the courthouse like a naked emperor. Order had not yet been called in the main room; no one noticed him standing there in his peculiar clothing. For him, his nakedness lay in what he had told Dobbin; the jury would see it otherwise. His power lay in what he had not told. This no one would see at all. Yesterday's lull was over; outside the window the court attendant fished for a high shutter with his pronged pole and closed them in from the dazzle. It was the afternoon of the next day.

He and Dobbin had been up a good part of the night, talking. The color of Dobbin's eyes by night was gray-green; he was forever after prepared to attest to that — to the special pattern that flecked them — in a court anywhere. And he still admired him — as one ranks those of one's superiors who can be deceived. If Dobbin wanted a judgeship, then it was not that only he wanted, or rather, he could pursue it only along certain lines, deeper than principles, *his* "themes" perhaps, that flecked all his tissues in a pattern as specifically mapped as his irises, as similarly inborn. He was clearly incapable of wanting the judgeship above all, and this was admirable. Even as a listener, last night, he had had his subtleties, not to be deceived by the frank, transparent cornea, the sunny, reciprocal stare of youth alone. Confidences were his business too, and like the best of lawyers he knew the pace for them, sharing a dinner brought in downstairs by a manservant, risking the half-bottle of wine but not pressing it, shaking out a few metropolitan feathers for this hungry young man but never preening them, careful of this instrument that the gods had sent him, that of itself was so keen. At seven, the chair, glimpsed by accident through the dining-room window, was at once sent on its way with the servant, with Pierre's message by hand, that he would dine late with a friend. By about eight, it would have been, Dobbin had heard of the Jebbs. No audience could have been more appreciative of them. It would have been about ten that he had heard all, had made his proposal. He too knew how to manipulate his brothers, listening with advocacy, like the best. It was not Dobbin's fault if, lacking the ultimate imagination, he had assumed last night that he was joining truth to complete truth. His limitation was that of those born to the purple of never having felt alien in the world, born too rich to suspect the keenness that comes from poverty of spirit. Dobbin was blind to it. Unless, of course, his eyes changed color, saw better by day.

By another nightfall this too might be known. Dobbin was in there now, in the smaller room where the grand jury was sitting. It was to have sat this morning also, by now must be acquainted with the nature of the evidence to be heard this afternoon. "We shall present a witness . . . certain events on the night of September 19, 1932. You have already heard . . . concerning the alleged abduction of Lucius Asher and Perry Brown. . . . Evidence we shall hear . . . identification of persons allegedly involved in willful destruction of property belonging to the United States Government on that same date. . . ." Or however it would be — far less formal, Dobbin had cautioned, than what he might expect to find. He understood, did he, that they were not trying a case here, only inquiring into the grounds for one. And if necessary, Dobbin had said, circling a wineglass in its small orbit, "the people" might shift its grounds. Murder, property under federal jurisdiction, misconduct of public officers, even, since they were in a corner of the state here, abduction across a state line. Federal grand jury. Dobbin put his glass down, not bothering to explain further, not even seeing the need, treading so sure-footedly across the spokes of this invisible network which surrounded the common man that even Pierre could see it: the small county jury moving across the field of justice like a company of moles with a lantern. And here, there, a face, a mask — a company of them — suddenly illumined in that swinging, polyhedral light. He had put down his own glass, his hand trembling, only seeing the full extent of things now. What if — small towns being what they were — some of both companies, mole and man, were the same? What then? Dobbin and he had not mentioned it between them, Dobbin only smiling — when he heard the names — a smile not learned in school. But out of the quorum of at least sixteen sitting inside there now, how many, on learning of the line of testimony to come, had bent their nude cheekbones, looking into their laps for cover? Now, suddenly, it was beyond his belief that any of them were in there, about to be seen in the proportions that six years or more had made them, not as he still saw them, all head, bodies no bigger than the unit men on graphs — a row of tiny figurants, each holding forward a face as large as a shield.

But here he was, Dobbin — the same man who last night had stopped him short at a certain point, saying, "That's enough, I guess. Let the rest of it come out before them" — cutting through the throng of idlers, petitioners, would-be licensees, politicos with a power range of one tobacco chew, cracker-barrel well-wishers, his passage across the room starred here, there with hands that reached and fell back, as if the touch of him held the king's cure. Here he was, saying, "Good. You're here. Good," once more thrusting out his own hand.

He drew Pierre aside, nodding as the judge passed them, coming out of chambers, a short, bald man with a pug jaw, two cranky dewlaps that promised benevolence to nobody — the new judge.

"Come in here a moment," said Dobbin, and drew Pierre inside the chamber. Later he had no memory of its looks, whether it had stayed itself with its fan and its flies, at the time not even reminding himself that it was, had been, the Fourchettes' office. All that afternoon things went on as if he had never been here before, or indeed anywhere, had no history up to or beyond each moment as he spellbound himself to it; later, the act of that afternoon seemed the purest thrust from the void — an obelisk emerged from the depths, to no sound of waters dividing — as those acts must seem which rise from the total sea bottom of ourselves.

"Recess," said Dobbin. "Ten minutes or so. Then we're ready for you." Last night he had said "they." He was smoking a cigarette whose stub he kept concealed in the hollow of one hand, occasionally peering in on it. "Didn't know until last night that Lucine Brown worked for you people."

"Last night?" Asleep until an hour ago, he felt stupid, his own mask not gathered.

"The old man who served us. He's her father."

Was it all to be as simple as this? Or was this too simple, even for Dobbins?

"Lucine came to me night before last. They've a sixth sense, you know." Dobbin was not looking at him. "Wanted to testify. I shut her up of course. For her own good. And no use to us."

Generally, Dobbin had said last night, looking hard at him, eager — *one witness to one fact, or one set of facts, is enough for a grand jury. Very often the complainant himself.* But this one is no use to us. Who now were "us"?

"But the old man was terrified. Poor old devil, he feels guilty on his own part. And what he told me fits. That night every Negro who had a phone received the same anonymous call — 'Stay inside!' Louie, the older boy, never came home — they would have got him as he came off the job. The old man tried to keep Lucine from going out after him, but she went. And while she was gone, Perry, the young kid, slipped out after his brother. She ran back in when the cars came. Went through without stopping, the old man said. For show. To show they had him. The flood cut niggertown off for two days. And Perry — he was only thirteen — never came back at all." Dobbin's voice was dry.

"They wouldn't have — !"

Dobbin raised an eyebrow.

He felt his own softness, against men out for judgeships, out for other men.

"Who knows? Of course, quite a few were lost in the flood at the time. But we don't know for sure, do we?"

His head flung back in sudden reflex.

"What?" said Dobbin.

"Nothing. I just remembered . . ." He was awake now, enough to switch names, even marvel at his own sudden resource. "Perry. Didn't he used to carry for Miss Pridden?"

"Mmm, well . . . yes. Matter of fact, he did." Distance was suddenly put between them, between Dobbin and his job. This was not the issue. Silence — a false note of it. "They've their own underground dynasties. That's their real sixth sense, of course, nothing odd about it. My aunt used to say" — he said "awnt" now — " 'Just whisper to yourself in the mawnin'; bah nee-un-tahm int a dawky in nigguhtay-un don't say to himself *"Do tell!"* ' " His imitation was just a little bit out, careful not to mock too much. It was not hard to see how he would ingratiate himself here, how much he could imply, with no more self-incrimination than any man who was used to being liked.

"Time," said Dobbin. With an exclamation, he dropped the cigarette, down to a mere coal, onto the floor, spat forth a bit of the paper that had clung to his lip. He rubbed his hands together. His whole manner had coarsened, in the way of a man who puts on shabbier clothes to keep himself out of notice in a low neighborhood. "All right now. Remember what I've told you. You'll be under oath of course, but there's nothing else too formal about it, certainly not here. You'll be able to tell your story. I'll be examining you. Right?" Thumbs in armpits, he regarded Pierre with satisfaction, as brought by the passage between them to a certain routine point that Dobbin recognized — as both softened and primed, shaken into that state of precipitation where Dobbin might look through him and let others do, to the goal beyond. "Right? Let's go." Hand on Pierre's shoulder, he guided him down a corridor back of the main courtroom, leading to the door of the smaller one, outside which the attendant stood guard.

"Dobbin," said Pierre. There, that was better. If he said "sir" he would feel it. "You kept your promise?"

"Mmm?" They had halted a few yards from the attendant.

"My uncle."

"Oh yes. Took him aside early this morning. He knows you're to be the witness." Dobbin seemed already abstracted, shoulders hunched, hands in pockets, one softly clanking his change.

"Nothing more?"

"No." The curt tone reminded him that he had been advised last night that it would be preferable if his uncle were to be no more prepared for Pierre's appearance than the rest. ("Hadn't you better be on your own in this, Goodman?") Pierre's insistence had been put down to filial delicacy, making it clear that either Dobbin knew less about the town than he himself thought, or else that the Higby day in court had already dropped from its annals.

"What did my uncle say?"

Dobbin shook his head. "Not one for surprises, is he? Just — was it still in order, then, for him to administer the oath?" Dobbin made a vague, impatient gesture of dismissal. "Anyone may, of course. Juror, that is. Come along now. We must." Then, in the very act of going, he turned, slipped his hands into his pockets again, leaned back as if he had all the time in the world. This was his mettle, his smiling stance said; the pace, fast or slow, always remained his.

"Tangled webs, these small principalities. Families . . . servants . . . childhoods." The two of them might have been still at dinner. "But we'll keep what order we can, shall we?" His voice had hardened; they were not at dinner. "The law doesn't anticipate, you know. The law sets forth. It's not for a district attorney to anticipate any disorder that may occur from such — in there, for instance." He indicated the door of the room ahead of them. "Nor is it for anyone else to. Remember that!"

"I — "

But Dobbin, seizing his arm, gave him no chance, so that his answer, whatever it would have been, true or false, was lost — to himself as well.

"Listen to me —" said Dobbin. A phrase not as wise as it is common. "You were born Armistice, 1918, right?" Did his lip have a twist of *pater* to it after all? "That night you were . . . not quite fourteen then — a mere child; if there were not a chance of that other corroboration I would not even put you on the stand. As the bright young man you are now, full of the customary moral hair-splittings — oh, quite honorable ones — that come with majority, I've no present use for you at all. *But I do have a use for that child.* Now listen to me!" His voice gentled. "Remember, how it was for us at fourteen? How simple things were for us then? How we saw certain things, without understanding them? Did them, not even knowing there were consequences? 'When I was a child, I spoke as a child'—" The phrase moved him. It was a measure of his gifts that he remained unashamed of this, not lowering those steady irises by a fraction. "That's all you have to do," he said softly, gripping Pierre's biceps with a consolatory squeeze. "Just remember how it was for that boy back there. Tell his story, just as he might of, then."

No, Dobbin had never been an alien.

The attendant nodded as they approached him. His lofty nose and brow, meanly deserted by recessiveness beneath, gave him a tribal resemblance to Mount, the courthouse lounger, in the way an indoor replica of civic virtue, barbered and salaried, might recall an outside one eroded by pigeon dung and rain. " 'Lo, Mr. Dobbin."

" 'Lo, Felix," said Dobbin out of the side of his mouth, like a password. Once more his glance traversed Pierre — old stager checking novice for unlucky signs of green in the breeches, in the gills — then the door shut behind them with a silky *t-lick* and they were in.

At first, following Dobbin, sitting down in the chair indicated, he kept his eyes lowered, engaging with himself in a kind of blindman's buff that restricted his impressions to peripheral images, to the murmurous confusion of a room which numerous figures were still crisscrossing on their natural tangents, in which twenty or so individual men were only slowly settling down to their duty as a "body" of the same. The room, perhaps fifteen by thirty feet, its ceiling as high as the main room but not domed, had a backstairs feel to it after the seedy, armorial space of the other. To his right, one tall, low-silled window obliquely flashed daylight and grass. At his left, the long table almost bisected the length of the room, leaving behind it a waste space through which Dobbin and he had brushed past a small table of Cokes and empties, a couple of choked spittoons, and in a corner the care-taker's bucket, its stiff, gray mop hanging down to a point, like a sub-stitute flag. Facing him, a curved dais held rows of auditorium chairs, their iron stanchions fixed to the floor. Feet shuffled past these, to the hollow, lecture-hall sound of seats successively snapped down. He might be in a classroom on a campus a thousand miles away; yet every pair of feet passing knew this place as intimately as he. This was the public room where men collectively tried those ideas of learning, pun-ishment, prayer that they fled from in private, and it was always the same. In it, humanity always stank resentfully, ghostly transactors, reminded that their parts were animal by the toilets that were always somewhere down the line. Each man sitting down to serve his time here already knew how, as the day waned, the one window opening on a grosser reality would come to seem like a mirror at the end of a burrow, and each, as he left the place, would draw the same deep in-take of breath, whether what had been done here were good or bad. They would be at close range when he looked up at them. Was each sitting there as he did now, an animal transfixed in the smell of man?

Dobbin touched his arm, sat at attention, stared forward. "Okay now," he whispered. "Every son of 'em's there." The room fell silent. Pierre stood up.

They were men. They were both larger and smaller than memory had bred them. Each face made its own crotchet of space, as his own must, fear undomesticated, looking across at fear. In the center of the first row, one head remained bent — his uncle's. Now it raised.

The clerk muttered his identificatory questions; Pierre answered. Here in this room, a name, that device under which a man labored so hard toward identity, meant nothing even to himself — a number answered to from a prison band, a patched patch between the shoul-der blades. But the space between himself and his uncle, who by now had risen, had compressed; once again they were in the narrow hallway, under the light that no one had ever bothered to shade. Nearer and nearer it came, the face that could not be surprised, and it knew him, saying *You*.

"You do swear . . ." it said, "you do swear, in the presence of the ever-living . . . that the evidence you shall give to the grand jury upon this complaint . . . shall be the . . . the whole . . . nothing but . . ." The truth. "So help you God!"

He strove for the great "Om" that must be proper to this question; heard the voice of the mole that answered. Dobbin rose, and touched his arm again; the witness, he said, need not stand, either now — during those remarks with which, since the jury had sought advice, he, Dobbin, must try their patience on such a hot afternoon — nor during witness's own testimony to follow. Meanwhile Dobbin, lounging with a token hand on the table, hip against it, remained standing. But if it please the jury, he said, he'd stay as he was — by now they all knew anyway that the only way to shut him up was to hope that his feet would sooner or later get the message to his tongue.

From down at the far left of the line facing them, an appreciative snicker came, an aged voice assenting. Pierre kept his eyes on the other half of the body of men on the dais, on those who were at the foreman's left — for Dobbin and himself the right-hand side. Except for this switch, the picture was just as he and his mother had been made to see it from the veranda. On his left must be gathered all those whom he had not yet dared scrutinize singly, for on his right, five in the first row, six in the second, all were new citizens, among them not one face he knew. Several of these were smiling slightly, at Dobbin or the snicker. "Otherwise," said Dobbin, his eyes crinkling, "the witness will find things a mite more informal than expected. Coats off or on; we find we can still do our business here." He was drawling now. In this respect, he said, they were perhaps a little luckier than the folks next door. The smiles broadened — then the new judge was a stickler. Again from the left came that slow, cackling "Heh, heh!"

Now at last, under cover of Dobbin's preamble, he turned his head and looked there. Second from the end, the old man who had made the noise was still nodding with the faint, ebbing tremor of the elderly.

He recognized him at once. It was the night watchman — Frazer. He's the only of them, there on that side, who does not seem to be looking at me; therefore it is safe, safest to look at him. Or is it? Here he was, seen through no window frame now. The old man sat there, a senile St. Bernard, behind gold-rimmed glasses (one recalls he cannot read), wearing the white shirt of the pensioner whose days are all special now, the very clean clothes of the workman who once swung his lantern "Oyez" on a clear night's zenith and is worth his six dollars per day emeritus still. Here he is, one of the ones from "down there."

". . . crimes against the elective franchise . . . " Dobbin, at his side, was speaking very rapidly, covering the grounds for indictment in a dull for-the-record tone, coursing through the evidence already heard, using a heavy verbiage that seemed almost designed to obscure it for his hearers.

Charlson has brains enough. Yes, Charlson Evans, his great form seated at the very end of the line as if for ballast, understood what Dobbin was getting at, had shifted his gaze to him. These eunuchoid men are often very quick of brain; how better conceal it? The minister's bulk had always been useful; he kept a convivial pulpit. And he was known to be softhearted — remember how kind he was to the Denny girl? Between what we do and we do not — in his job he would know about judgment. He and I have not seen each other since my aunt's funeral. But I remember, on a clear night's zenith, the minister's car.

And I remember the doctor's. He's not here, Rollins, but he has sent a substitute — the young man on Frazer's left, by the look of his brother Lee on him — Rollins has sent a son. An honorable custom of war hereabouts, to send a substitute, doubly so if one sends the son. This is Robert then, called Bobby, perennial flunkee, commonly called "Doc." He looks sulky — too many brothers? Oh Bobby, does your mother, brother, know you're out? Five or six years older than I am — you could have been there that evening. Depend upon it, your father knows — a doctor's car is his hallmark. Perhaps we should ask my uncle, an expert on Rollinses. He's not one to accept substitutes, even in sons. Or rather, say that, confronted with blame to assign, he can.

You look frightened. But my uncle has his head bowed again. Until he looks up, until we have to look at him, we are both safe.

". . . that murder has been done . . . has been established sufficiently for the charge . . . for a charge, mind you; that is our purpose here." Dobbin's voice dropped again to its monotone. "Secondly . . . we then come to . . ."

The Lemons, father and son (horses and allied arts), see what he's after too, though one can't tell it from their faces. Of the senior I know nothing. But Lemon was always one to see certain things early — even if his reach sometimes exceeded his grasp. A boy to brag as syphilis what was only acne, and come off in the end with no more than the clap. It's thickened him early too; except for his pocks and that Indian hair hanging down just the same, I'd never know him for the string bean I stood up to in the Charlotte gym, doing better than either of us expected. He wasn't afraid. I was. He's looking at Dobbin now, got his answer ready, by the grin on him. ("What if we did? No more'n anybody here would do.") Men who won't accept the nature of man tend to amuse Lemon. He himself suffers proudly all the manly diseases. And is therefore not afraid.

". . . rumors of concerted action by a group . . . purported to be taking the law into . . . on that night . . . Of more recent date . . ." And Dobbin, still leaning negligently, dropped the name, Bean.

Lemon still has traces of a smile, like a trader recalling a good trade. But even he is no longer looking at Dobbin. They are all staring at the back of the room, a class called to attention, pledging its allegiance to the caretaker's mop. All do so except one. In the pause that Dobbin intended perhaps, but not for him alone, Hannibal Fourchette, Jr., his bruin gaze swaying — did he know me once? — is heard to be humming. He too has a disease which, when well tended, keeps him fearless. How incredibly it preserves them; he has changed least of all! The strength of his shirt front still upholds him; in some shell for his ear only he must be hearing the Gulf. Tactfully, the man next him touches his arm and he subsides at once, feeling down the side of the chair, his hip pocket, for — a cigarette. The kind neighbor at once strikes a match for it. Morning's Junior Fourchette's time of course, but he is still happy. What a fine place, club you might say, a grand jury room is. Lawyers must wait outside it. Even Dobbin, gentleman though he is, must leave before vote is taken. And a judge — no matter who — can never come in here at all. He puts a finger to his lips and nods gratefully at his neighbor. Tact. Tact is all that is necessary in this cat's cradle world.

Now. Now I must look at his neighbor. His long chin.

". . . until now, for lack of witnesses, we have been working pretty much in the dark. . . ."

Neighbor Nellis, lamplighter extraordinary, will strike a match for you. At the end of day, his orange light pops out on the dusk, first one. *You know what grace is?* In all public ceremonies, he shall be the Bearer. *Don't say nothin'; just join hands.* Call for me. When the night hawk flies, then housewives place in the window those hooded lights that mean a man will be late from home. There, the lights go out again, one on a street we know. The last one. Nellis's light.

"Of course, until now we have not had the resources of the Federal —" Dobbin bowed almost imperceptibly, no more than a shift in accent, to the new faces on his right, then turned again toward the left, where, it might be assumed from this, his own allegiance lay. "Now, however, Washington promises evidence . . . it may come any time . . . depositions of witnesses formerly connected with this office, concerning Asher, who was buried as a flood victim. Also, from nearby states, transcripts of records impounded. If we refuse . . . a show of airing things here . . . a federal grand jury may not be so persuaded. . . ."

Memory also impounds. Once, Nellis, your heel, slouching past, almost caught on a face raised to look at you from the long grass, next to mine. You don't know me; you've never seen me in your life. I had the matchless invisibility of my age. But you should know well the urge that comes over us when we are in hidden places — toward the enormous joke to be played. You bend now, but only to confer with your neighbor on your other side.

One by one they are all coming out of lodging. One more. Between Nellis and my uncle, a pair of white duck trousers.

And now Dobbin is at last calling his witness. Witness need not stand during testimony. But witness does rise, to face Semple.

For the entire state of Alabama, some say. Or for the world? Strange, how, seeing you here, I no longer trust in the general klandom of evil. Here in this room, we too have no knowledge of how to ascribe evil except singly. It must go by one and one, by face and face. *You.*

So, Dobbin, I obey. Truth bombards us from wherever it can. I speak as that boy.

There *is* a place — filled with the moral fragrance of how people really are. Outside its orange lamp we are all Ishmael, until we enter there. There is a town — above the town — Johnny, Johnny Fortuna, I believe you. I believed you all along.

"I kept watch for them in the grove," I said. "I helped cut the pine and truck it down to the café. I rode lookout for them all that day."

Chapter V. Klanship.

YOU. You. You, you, you, you, you. I. There was not a face there, no matter its guilts or its sympathies, which was not for that one moment my enemy. And for the same reason — beneath all reasons. When the witness speaks, he brings the problem of truth into the room. There was not one man there who, for a moment, did not curl protectively around whatever secret he thought kept him in swinedom, wishing to be left in his sty with it, only not to have to aspire.

And I watched them with joy, thinking I had found the adversary at last.

"Will the witness explain whom he means by 'them'?"

So my preceptors had been correct — there were choices to be made. For the general "they" of the feared, we may choose our surrogates. The lie I told then was greater than any I told later. Much may be done in the name of justice by those avenging their childhoods.

"The Klan," I said.

The word was new to the room. Everybody heard the echoes refuse it. Outside, a bird spoke, *chelo, chelo,* from siesta. I had time to remember exactly what I was doing. I tallied it:

I speak as Johnny would, using what he did, what he knew.

Dobbin does not know this. As far as he knows, I alone was "that boy."

"They," up on the stand there, will know I am lying.

They cannot declare it.

I even had time to note that the clock over the dais was the same as the one in the main courtroom, even to the gilt "Seminole." Then Dobbin, rushing in, allowed no further pauses.

"Will you tell the jury what you mean by 'that day'?"

"The day the dam went."

"According to record, September 19, 1932. If you don't mind — would you tell us how old you are?"

"I'll be twenty-one in November." Lemon was the one who made me feel youngest. He had taken out a small, old-fashioned cigar clipper and was elaborately fooling at fitting the end of one into it.

"Then, on that date, you were just close on to fourteen. Do you ask us to believe that a kid like that would observe all those details I'm going to have you repeat to these gentlemen? And that seven years later, you can still quote scripture on 'em?"

For one second, his hostility dumbfounded me. Then I almost smiled at him. Oh downy Dobbin. He had to be.

"Nothing so scriptural about it." My dander was up, tongue loosened. "It wasn't the kind of day that anybody down here would be likely to forget." But the very next day, they all had claimed to. Their blank faces remanded me. Not a man could be found.

"Excuse me — Mr. Dobbin?" A man on the other side of the room, the new side, had spoken — the first voice from them. Would they speak much? I had not considered. Now I scrutinized them. But scrutiny was not the word for it. White-shirted, dark-tied, most of them, these new men, more stiff-backed than the others and not as colorful, not as easy in the crotch. Not as much at home here, they offered themselves to the eye as a group, like men in an office picture. Time-study clerks, engineers, office managers, as might be, they had that look, drained of the personal dossier, which went with the man of business. And their business here was precisely that — not to be at home in this place.

326

"Yes, Mr. Anderson?"

"Excuse me, but I'd like to clear something up — this witness — isn't he some relation to Mr. Higby, our foreman?"

"Stepson." My uncle's face, raised to look across at Anderson, shocked me, seen now in public perspective. It had the shielded, masked guise I had expected of the others. "He's my wife's son."

So that was how he thought of me. I had sometimes wondered.

"Things like that are bound to happen in a small county, Mr. Anderson. Perhaps you're not yet used to it." Dobbin showed his teeth very slightly. "We may even bump into — other instances — as we go along. Not unusual."

"Oh, no reflections on anybody, of course. It's just that — wasn't the witness involved in a court case sometime ago — something about his name?" Now I recognized him, the heavy white cheek that he was rubbing. He was the second man in court that day, the man who had helped Dabney Mount bring my mother home.

"I understand he changed his name legally. No 'involvement,' as you called it. I believe — a family matter?" Dobbin, addressing me, deflected those probing eyes of his. Probably he too thought me a bastard, if not my uncle's. For testing opinion, the dock had its use.

"Yes," I said. "A family matter."

"Ah," said Dobbin. "That satisfactory, Mr. Anderson?" Polite, excessively so, he no longer lounged, suddenly tall defender of those privacies that some of us here would hold to be still paramount. Covertly he sent them a glance, these parfit knights on his left, that reassured them. Delicately, for Mr. Anderson and other tiresome bumblers, he checked his watch. "Shall we go on then?"

"I'd like to establish something first," I said. "My uncle never knew of my — activities. Doesn't yet."

"Entirely suitable," said Dobbin. "Would Mr. Higby like to, er — ?"

In the pause, my uncle seemed not to be answering. Then he coughed. From the store of honesty that hampered him, what would he choose? Who was that other man who, from a mouth full of pebbles, learned to speak clear? "No," he said. "We did not confide."

"Eh . . . yes . . ." Dobbin pursed his lips, for all fathers. And in the same instant he turned on me, hard-voiced, all procurator. "Explain what you meant by 'the grove'!"

And it was in that moment, with his repetition of the word "grove" — tossed by me, accepted by him — that the full, serious sense of where I was came to me, and its marvel. Once more the owl tapped, showing me the spectacle of what was, the great gamble of what could be, and this time, in this old, professional room, worn and capable as a whore's bed where the pure and venal chased each other through all the odors and malodors of man, I was not afraid. I apprehended my powers, like sportsmen on those charmed days when the shot, not yet sighted along the barrel, already rings true on the limp, glazed target. Like an actor, stretching his limbs to the arena on that sure day for which all the practice of life had prepared him, I understood how a man might elongate himself until he was of a length to hang another, how he might make those long, simian jumps which are made in dream. The word "grove" had done it, magicked by me out of memory not my own, cast like a boomerang and perfectly returned, whang, to my hand again — "Catch!" I understood without mysticism the power that mind might wreak on matter. From then on I did not falter. I used Johnny's words. The use of them was mine.

"Maxon's Grove. If you go through the backs, straight westerly from the whistle stop, you come out to two crossroads on the other side. Take the dirt one, about three quarters of a mile down, and you come to it. I came on it once, exploring, and after that I used to go there the way a kid will when he finds a place that looks secret; used to read there, try and slingshot rabbits, generally hang around. Built myself a kind of cave in the bracken." Johnny had done that, found the place on one of the afternoons his mother had had to turn him out of the house because she had a man there.

"The grove was near enough to the backs, but the Negroes never went there. I was still new enough to the town so I didn't know why. Maxon had been one of the organizers of the first Klan in the old Civil War days. Place had always been used by them. Still was. But of course I didn't know that. Summer nights, I sometimes took my supper there, leaving by sundown, since I had to be home soon after dark."

328

Johnny used to camp there overnight. "One night, though, I fell asleep there. When I woke up it was dark, and they were not ten yards from me, the whole ring of them. They were holding a tribunal, and of course they were wearing the hoodwink. I was too scared to make a noise. But I'd not been brought up to believe in ghosts, and these talked like men — one with a voice I thought I recognized. Upshot of it was, I spied on them several times running, by getting there early. They had a guard of course, the Klexter, but he always watched the road. Then, one night, they caught me at it." Johnny had spied on them for months, only being caught when he wanted to be, when he yearned for it.

"I let slip all I'd seen; I was even fool enough to address that one of the men by name." Even now that scene, as it had come to me through Johnny's lame pauses, still shook me. He'd let himself be brought out, collared and kicked forward in his fowl-stained overalls and boiled-out T shirt, into the center of their cleanly ring. Then he'd gone down on his knees to that seated figure, to the slit eyes in the peaked white hood above him. ("Oh, Exalted Cyclops," he had said, "please let me belong. I could be the mascot." And then, out of his simplicity and his longing, "Please, Mr. Semple, please!")

I paused for breath. Following my double thread, I no longer saw my audience. "They saw I was harmless — and dazzled. Gave me a blood-curdling warning — it only thrilled me the more, though I was scared enough — and turned me loose. But later on, the man I'd recognized tapped me on the shoulder one day in town. Started me out on small errands. Kept me on a string, like." That last was Johnny himself speaking. I must be more careful. "It was supposed to be for him, but I soon knew it wasn't. And as I got older, he — they — let me do more. They — just got used to me." I stopped again, fighting my heart-beat for breath. I had done the first lap, come round the circle. "And that's how it was that day."

Dobbin spoke. "You were a kind of apprentice then. Till you were old enough to be eligible. That how they do it?"

"They may do. I only know my own history. And almost from the beginning I knew I couldn't belong."

"How's that?" Softly he led me, toward what was to both our interests to make clear.

"I got to know their rule book by heart, all seventy-five or so pages of it. You know what parliamentarians boys are." I smiled slightly. They would never believe the other — that I had seen it once. "I knew it as well as the baseball scores. I still do. You have to be native-born to belong to the Order. And I'm not." At times, Johnny's mother would tell him that he was the legal son of a husband in the old country, at others that he had been born a few years after that man's death, in a town somewhere near Shamokin, Pennsylvania. He too had had his choices.

"I'll ask you to quote from that book shortly. Meanwhile — just for my own interest — and no doubt the jury's — what in God's name is the 'hoodwink'?" I had piqued him. For a moment his other world showed itself.

"It's the official regalia of the Klan."

"Question, Mr. Dobbin." The voice, a ringing nasal, was not Anderson's, but came from their side. I found its owner, a small man in their front row, bald as ivory. His heavy lips moved as slowly as if they were.

"Yes, Mr. Hake?" Hake, the general superintendent of the dams. He emanated the chill that came from all the absolutely hairless. A busy man, often in Washington. More chill was to be taken from the fact that he had found time to sit here.

"Of what country is the witness?"

Dobbin let me answer. I did so with impatience. "Great Britain. I came here at the age of ten."

"I take it that his noncitizenship has no bearing on the legality of his testifying at this hearing?"

"None," said Dobbin, grave to this absurdity. "None."

"Thank you. Some of my colleagues here were doubtful." A nucleus of men around Hake nodded. So they too had taken counsel among themselves.

"Tha-at's right!" Lemon spoke without looking up. Cigar in mouth, ever a man for activity, he was now trimming his nails with a pocketknife. He leaned forward, easily flicking one hand, and the tiny, invisible gauntlet fell on the papers on the desk before me, with an almost inaudible *pip*. "What's he down here pimpin' for trouble for, spyin' on us? Him and his uncle."

"I already said — my uncle had nothing —"

"Uh-huh. I heard you." He was trimming the last nail. "How come you here then?"

"The witness was called," said Dobbin. "He is not required to explain why he is here." Did he suspect that I could not? "If he's allowed to go on, no doubt that will appear. Do you wish to question him yourself, Mr. Lemon?"

"Nah-h. I *was* born here, Mister Dobbin. But not yesterday." He looked up for the first time. "And I say — *that* for your witnesses!" In the same instant the knife left his hand with a hard swish and embedded itself, handle up, a perfect mumblety-peg throw, in the desk just in front of me.

I flinched back in reflex, then thrust my hand out for it. Lemon outreached me.

"Boys! Boys!" It was the minister who spoke, a curious reed from that bulk.

"Tha-at's right, Charlson, you tell us." Lemon was standing. His head moved only an inch sideways on its fulcrum. "He'p us separate the me-en from the boys."

Men as fat as Charlson redden clearly; even Dobbin could not help staring for a minute without shame. Lemon lost none of his swagger. Coarseness freed him, allowing hits so low and near that men more tangled in decencies could only be jealous of it. Lemon, born so deft with the knife, had long since learned the uses of words that were unanswerable otherwise. Now he snapped the jackknife shut, balanced it on his palm for a second, then slapped it away in a pocket. "Well, who's for leaving?" There was no doubt of whom he was addressing, although he still half faced Dobbin. Ignoring Charlson, he let his gaze rest on each in turn. "Well? You all going to sit on here, listen to this thing right through to the end? You just going to sit here?" He bent forward, nursing his thigh. "Now. There's twenty-three men present on this jury. If just nine of us leave — no, even eight — there can't be no further business. I say it's time to break things up, maybe talk over our rights and privileges in private." Lowering his voice, he spoke almost as if they were already alone. "Whether this fellow's lyin' or not — that won't make no difference — you know that, don't you?" He swept a fist in front of him. "Come on, what say!" He waited. "Rollins? Only takes two." Hesitated. "Nellis?" One further corner his eye still refused. "Who's to say we can't walk right out if we want to, and not come back? Who's to say we got to sit here?"

Because Lemon was looking at Dobbin now, everyone looked there. Head cocked back, lips parted, Dobbin seemed to be waiting. While we watched, he slipped a cigarette from his pocket — quietly — as if the packet within must not be crackled, held his lighter in abeyance. Turning to the window, he seemed to take a respite from the room. Because he breathed like a man counting his breaths, we breathed with him. The wait, interminable to us, seemed not to bother him. Did he know what would come, or only gamble that something might? It came from behind him.

"Sit down, Lemon," said Semple.

I heard Dobbin sigh.

When Lemon sat down, it was almost as if he sank to his knees.

Over on Hake's side, the men around him stirred for the first time collectively. They had lived all their lives under a dominion of invisibles — governments, powers, subornations they had heard to exist, but never expected to see. But, even up to now, perhaps, they had only idly believed.

Dobbin lit his cigarette. "I think possibly — there might be more interrogation on the part of the jury." He surveyed them, lingered, as if with regret, on Hake, went past the assistant foreman — a stammerer, passed quickly over Charlson, as charity for the moment should, stopped at Nellis — who bent his head, and came to rest as all along intended. "Mr. Semple?"

Semple. I have described him elsewhere — and can do it over and over: brown features, none of prominence, hair cut short, thick white hair, the look of extra energy this often gives a middle-aged man. Or did I err there, only interpret? Hair cut short — I had not said that

332

before. Each time round, a detail adds itself, subtracts, but the whole avoids, like that retinal after-image the scudding eye can catch only by not pursuing, can never hold still and square. Dobbin's head, that good medal, aligned itself at once in any light; Semple's, struck over and over, remained — even when I faced it — blurred. He was a man of the most ordinary description — of that I am persuaded — but like all whom the mind raises to a special niche of good or evil, his description had already been given elsewhere. Even there that day, he sat in its nimbus, seen through the same vibrating haze that surrounds an object of love. He wore the hoodwink still. Only once, at the end, did it raise.

"Would you care to question the witness, Mr. Semple?"

The telling thing was that he had stayed, and not only to quench Lemon. I thought I knew why — each of us drawn in his own way to the scene of the crime. It might be tactic for him to stay; it would be torture to leave our whispering phalanx behind him. The dreadful itch to revisit had come upon him. He longed to comprehend what he had done, as it looked in the eyes of others.

"I could," Semple said. "Along the lines of that day."

"Hold on there." It was Hake again. "Aren't we going to hear from that rule book first?"

Dobbin, as if reluctant, checked his watch. I glanced at the clock up above; I had been here one hour. "Three-thirty," said Dobbin. He raised his eyebrows, shrugged. "The day's yet young." Afternoon sessions ran until five-thirty. But I would have bet anything that Neil Dobbin almost never needed a watch to tell him the time. "Well — we did say, didn't we?" He said. "Not all seventy-five pages, please — and I must ask the jury to restrict its questions as much as possible to what's salient. That telegram from Washington might still get here today. And I'd like for us to get through the heart of the testimony before that."

I heard him with awe. "Whatever we do," he had said the night before, "I want them to hear you reel off from that manual. Christ. It chills the blood, doesn't it. There's a man there, Hake, who may worry at you like a terrier. Let him. He knows what he's doing. Let

333

him take as long as he wants. Those other boys from Charlotte are sober and willing enough — but maybe it's time the iron entered their souls." Drawing the paper ring from his cigar, he had placed it carefully on the cloth. "And from then on," he had said, touching its red and gold coronet with the tip of a finger, "they're not likely to doubt your powers of recollection."

"We can check it later on, I trust, Mr. Dobbin?" said Hake. "By means of a copy?"

"Yes," said Dobbin. "Later on this afternoon, perhaps. I trust." And lifting his chin, he nodded at me to begin.

I could hear my heart beat as if it were across the room from me, the room a cave. I was on my own now, Johnny the mascot. I looked at Semple. Just as one dreams it — the wild image of what could never believably come to be. Once in one's life just as one dreamed it. It had come to be. "Klansman's Manual," I said with dry lips. "Nineteen twenty-four. Knights of the Ku Klux Klan. P. S. Etheridge — Chief of Staff and Imperial Klonsel." I heard the men on Hake's side stir in the small crepitations of the tense; I heard the absolute quiet on the other. My tongue was dry also. "Klonsel," I repeated, and stopped. My tongue clove to my mouth, filling it.

"Go on!" Dobbin spoke sharply.

I could see the white page in front of me, bird-tracked with K's. Down the page they went, like the track of feet, set down one after the other, of a long line of men stalking in secret procession. But I could not see the letters between them. Like underbrush, the gray, long sentences between. "I —" Here and there the fabric of silence gave way — the creak of a chair, a man shifting his knees. "I — just need the first line."

A titter came from the left. Frazer.

Dobbin shielded his eyes with his hand.

My hands were fisted in front of me. I pressed one thumb, bent at the knuckle, against the other straight one — K. What came next? K. I glanced upward.

"The Order." Semple spoke it softly. "The Name."

Had he too been waiting, hoping in spite of himself for what could

334

never — ? How could one tell? His face had not changed. I noted a detail I had forgotten — the sharp fold of the eyelids, like halves of nutshells, that kept the pupils unfringed. These were brown, the color of the cul-de-sac. I saw it again, the annex room, heard the wardrobe door, big as a coffin lid, creaking. Past bladder-shapes of leather, iron and shadow, I walked to where twelve chairs enclosed a circle with exemplary neatness. Once again I leaned over their center, the hairline cross stirring at my breath. The pins came out easily. And now I no longer needed him. I turned to Dobbin, smiling. "The Order," I said, "The Name. Forever hereafter it shall be known as KNIGHTS OF THE KU KLUX KLAN. Its Divisions: There shall be four Kloranic Orders of this Order, namely: The Order of citizenship, or K-UNO (Probationary) . . . Knights Kamellia, or K-DUO (Primary Order of Knighthood). Knights of the great Forrest, or K-TRIO (the Order of American Chivalry). Knights of the Midnight Mystery, or K-QUAD (Superior Order of Knighthood).

"Its Nature: Six outstanding features are . . . are particularized in describing the nature of this Order. Klansmen will do well to fix them in mind . . . so that they will know the kind of an order they have joined." I hesitated, went on.

"*Patriotic.* One of the paramount purposes of this Order . . . is to exemplify a pure patriotism toward our country. Every Klansman is taught from the beginning of his connection with the movement that it is his duty to be patriotic toward our country. And . . . and when he knelt at the Sacred Altar of the Klan, he was solemnly and symbolically dedicated to the holy service of our country.

"In its influence and its . . . its teachings and its principles . . . the Order seeks to generate . . . impart a spirit of loyalty to America . . . consecration to her ideals . . . fealty to her institutions . . . support of her government . . obedience to her laws — and unselfish devotion to her interests." Now I had it, at a clip.

"*Military,*" I said. "This characteristic feature applies to its form of organization and its method of operations. It is so organized on a military plan that the whole power of the whole Order, or of any part of

it, may be used in quick, united action for the execution of the purposes of the Order. There are definite, concrete tasks to be done —"

In the pause I took for breath, Hake cleared his throat, a hoarse
sound from those pale business lips. "Can the clerk get all of this down
verbatim?"

Boldly I answered for Dobbin. "Mr. Whitlock is the retired clerk of
this court, a very experienced man." Old Clarence Whitlock, known to
me as a lightning gabbler of petitions, otherwise as Keeper of the Seal
and recording Kligrapp, raised his great bagged eyes, mournfully
clowned by death but still bypassed, and bent again to his pencil.

And Dobbin's face shone with my mastery, as once Demuth's had
done, hearing me on the terms of the Pacification of Ghent, fourteen
pages from the Wars of the Roses — all once as swarming with blood-
images as this, tracked, one after the other, by processions as alive as
this. Standing there, on the steppingstone that lies, ego and innocence
had built for me, I may even have seen into that unity of history where
all its evils blended, but I had no more time for this than any other
man, and chose one. I turned to the new men on the right.

Nearest the middle, a small, round-headed young clerk, he looked to
be, sat holding up the large nose that had forged ahead of him, its upturned nostrils as open, aspiring toward knowledge, as his mouth. I
spoke to him.

"Pages nineteen to twenty-one," I said, "treat of The Invisible
Empire, its two-fold Significance, Territorial Divisions and Conven-
tions, plus a definition of what is therein termed The Alien World. If
you wish, I can give any of this or the following in detail." But he
only stared at me and I went on, softly. "To page twenty-five: Membership in all its categories — which are Racial, Masculine, National,
Religious, Mental, Character, Reputation, Vocation, Residence, Age,
and How Membership is Attainable." Still he said nothing, and I left
him with that and passed on.

Next him was a man wearing thick glasses, whom I knew by sight
as the pharmacist in the new Walgreen's at Charlotte — a man always to
be heard fuming restlessly back and forth behind his counter while at
his compounds, grumbling at everything — from the weather to the

336

state of the nation — on which his pharmacopoeia could give him no answer. He too was here, perhaps, in default of finding a single prescription. "Pages twenty-five to forty-two," I said to him. "The Emperor of the Invisible Empire, His Responsibilities. The Imperial Klonvokation. The Imperial Kloncilium. Their Powers and Functions. The Imperial Wizard. His Position, Authority and Power." He remained immobile.

"Revenues, Realms and Provinces," I said, pleading to those thick lenses. "How a Realm May be Organized. The Initial Klonverse. The Klorero." I looked up and down their row and I could tell nothing. It must seem to them, as almost now it did to me, that I was reciting the black verse of nightmare, or only the comic thrill of a child's campfire — at best some cabalism of a star too distant for combat.

In desperation, I turned back to Dobbin. And Dobbin, himself barely wrested from dream, shaking his head like a man emerging from water, understood me. "And now the local Klans themselves," he said. "The working units." He brought his fist down, hard, on the table. All along the line, men, lulled in postures of enchantment, awoke.

"Pages forty-two," I said, "to the end."

Dobbin, lips parted, stood very close, as if we were to speak in chorus, match theme to theme. "What are the Requirements of a Klansman?"

"Requirements. And all Klansmen are strictly enjoined to valiantly preserve and persistently practice the principles of pure Patriotism, Honor, Klannishness, and White Supremacy, ever keeping in mind and heart the sacred sentiment, peculiar purpose, manly mission and lofty ideals of this Order . . . loyalty to their Emperor and Imperial Wizard . . . faithful keeping of their Oath of Allegiance . . . constant, unwavering fidelity to every interest of the Invisible Empire . . . the influence of Klankraft to be properly promoted . . . and that they be blameless in preserving the grace, dignity and intent of their Charter forever." I looked at Hake. "That's not verbatim. But it's the gist."

"Can you give the Charge?" said Dobbin. How impeccably he had learned last night's brief lesson! Only now did it occur to me — why it might be he had accepted my story so readily. One man's special recall, so weird to the general, would be no surprise to another of the same. But there was no time to consider this, now.

"The Charge," I said. "I (The Imperial Wizard) solemnly charge you to hold fast to the dauntless faith of our Fathers and to keep their spotless memory secure and unstained, and true to the traditions of our valiant sires, meet every behest of Duty . . . without fault, without fail, without fear and without reproach."

"What are the Offenses against the Order?" He had quickened the pace. I matched it.

"The Major Offenses are treason against the United States of America, support of any foreign power, relinquishment of citizenship. Violating the Oath of Allegiance, Constitution or Laws of the Order. Disrespect of virtuous womanhood. Habitual drunkenness, profanity or vulgarity during a klonklave. Being responsible for the polluting of Caucasian blood through miscegenation, or the commission of any act unworthy of a Klansman. White men must not mix their blood with that of colored or other inferior races."

"How are offenses tried?"

"By tribunal. In organized Realms, by a Grand Tribunal, composed of Hydras, Furies, Exalted Cyclops and similar statewide officials. In Klans, by the same on a local scale."

"Describe the Sitting of the Tribunal. Who are present?"

"Klan officers, and eight Klansmen selected by lot, by a member wearing the hoodwink. A prosecutor. The defendant, represented by a member. Witnesses who are Klansmen."

"What are the Penalties?"

"Reprimand. Suspension. Banishment. Ostracism in all things, by all members of the Order."

A low assent came from the left somewhere, like an "Amen" in church. On my right, the phalanx of heads slowly turned in that direction. I did not need to. Frazer again, quickly hushed by someone.

Dobbin waited. "And — now —" he said, ponderous as he had been quick, his tone a signal that the recital was almost over. "The Oath of Allegiance. Will you oblige us?"

"Obedience," I said. I said it to Lemon, but he was looking else-

338

where. "Secrecy." Rollins also. "Fidelity." And Nellis, long-chinned Nellis, the same. At Semple. "Nishness."

"Nishness!" said Hake. Throughout, he had been sitting arms folded, the polished knob of his head scarcely glinting. Now the word whistled from him, as if escaped through the small hole between the lips that Buddhas sometimes had. He leaned forward, in the pale summer suit that was cut like Dobbin's. The young clerk beside him shifted with uneasy awe — this was the general superintendent. "You sure he isn't dreaming some of this up? Jesus Christ, Dobbin. Nishness!"

"Yes, I'm sure." Dobbin said this over his shoulder, on his way to answer a knocking at the door. "Better if he were." He opened the door on Felix the guard, who managed an inquisitive look round before he handed something over. Dobbin walked back slowly, reading what had been given him. "Better if he were," he repeated absently, and shoved the yellow form into a pocket. He passed in front of me. "Sit down, will you please!" I sat down. When he was sure that he was the center of interest, he nodded in all the requisite directions, let himself slide by degrees into a chair, as a tall man can, and leaned back, hands clasped at his neck behind, long legs stretched before. He had us all where he wanted us. The clock said four.

"Okay, Mr. Semple," he said. "Your witness."

I answered quickly, before Semple could, feeling inordinately nimble, precise. With the recital just done, I thought, my second wind had come; really it was my first — the wind that had been blowing me toward this spot for a long, long time. Upborne in its current, I remembered many things at once — and they were all the same. Once again I felt the hermetic privilege of opening the side door of the Pridden place, the involuntary, peculiar comfort as I stood within the gate, inside. To none of you any longer, I thought, remembering the lesson that was not in German; to all who had asked to be called *du* I had listened, and now I too was speaking. I too entered the world — through a door that no one had expected, and for a brief time I saw that the light of Tuscana could be as brilliant as anywhere on earth.

"There'll be no need for questions," I said. "I'll just tell what happened."

Semple and I sat opposite, not more than a few yards between. For a moment, or so it seemed, the room ceded us our silence — two cocks, before what hoods were slipped? Had he already thought of Johnny? Neither of us could see the other's private vision, but surely for him too the room and its men of either side had dropped away, were of no more account than poor Fourchette there, thralled now in his afternoon sleep — and as far. Who sat opposite Semple? Opposite me — who? The adversary? All the villainy and fright of the world, convenient in one neck for hands to squeeze.

I put mine down quietly on the table between us. "As he knows it did," I said, and I began.

"That day — that day — my mother and stepfather had gone to Memphis for the week, leaving me on my own. It was market day; the stores were supposed to be open till nine. But your store closed early that night, didn't it, Mr. Semple? And the café never opened up at all. But in the café, behind those windows painted green halfway up, there was plenty going on. I knew, because they'd had me coat the upper parts with Bon-Ami the day before. Anyone could tell there was still something going on, though. Maybe they wanted the niggers to know it. They had the wood piled there — early that morning I'd helped them truck it in from the grove — two-by-fours for the bracing pieces and logs both — pitch pine that had been cut a while back and let season — they always kept the grove well thinned. And the café telephone went all day long. I wasn't allowed to do any of the phoning of course; my voice hadn't even changed yet." Johnny's had, but he hadn't been allowed.

"Everyone else took a turn at it. 'Stay in tonight, nigger!' was all they had to say, then hang up on them." Meanwhile, Johnny had done the legwork. "My job kept me running back and forth between the de-pots where the cars were supposed to line up that evening. Market day was a help; even so, isn't the easiest thing to round up fifty, sixty cars in a town this size. Ran my feet off in the morning. I didn't have no — any bike." Careful. "Then when they found I could drive, they let me — wasn't far. Trout's Garage, we used, many private yards as we could, and the M & H Livery." I caught my breath; surely now he would

340

know me, or whom I stood for. I meant him to. "First time I'd ever driven any car but my uncle's; if I didn't remember anything else, I'd never forget that. A sweet job she was — I don't suppose she's around town any more." On the table, my hands moved closer to each other. "Old Packard with a hundred-forty-five-inch wheelbase. Ran like a dream, she did. Came from Montgomery. Built for a man six and a half feet tall."

His eyelids flickered. He'd got it. I waited. "Maybe you do have a question, Mr. Semple?"

If he made any further move, I did not see it. But his eyes must have looked like that at Johnny — through the slits in the hoodwink.

"Of course, we didn't go anywhere near your store," I said. "We had special orders not to. And we didn't."

"Why not?" said Hake. "What store is that?"

Even Nellis, whose long muzzle was always pointed sideways at his master, turned with most of the rest of them there on the left, to look at Hake with amazement. Power shifts so quietly, seen only intermittently, even by those who already feel the need to sit together.

"Mr. Semple is the factor for Rhine's," I said quickly. "Used to be the biggest store in the county. Before they built the bypass."

"Oh, I know that place." It was the clerk with the big nose who spoke up eagerly, in a voice like a young drake's. "That's where they hold the cockfights — at least, I've never been, but I —" His voice trailed off, suddenly recalling whom, by the chances of citizenship, it sat next to. Equality was not enough. Before our eyes, he shriveled. Hake did not even look at him.

"Easier to close up the café, for one thing," I said. "And it was nearer the new state road. Tuscana had itself an entrance to that then, before the dams went. Mr. Semple will recall it."

He said nothing.

"The plan was simple. Cars to line up there at nine o'clock, at the edge of town. Men to dress in them when they got there. Each man had his place in a car, same as a funeral." Same as a funeral, Johnny had said, sliding a look at me, then away again. "Every car had a number. Pace set at eight to ten miles an hour — it was a mile and a half to where the macadam ended, at the base of the dams, where the procession was to stop and watch. Only the lead cars were to go on to the top. Two farm trucks and two eight-cylinder tourers. One for each dam." My fingers laced together. "The Packard was at the head of the line. She was almost new then; had an extra gear could pull her out of a ditch like a tractor. She was to carry the Exalted Cyclops and the Night Hawk up to Number Three Dam, the highest."

"You drove her?" Hake's distaste was plain — the use of such terms lessened the dignity of pursuit. What sensible man could pursue "nishness"?

And now Semple, puzzled, hung on my answer, as if all would be explained by it. Was I "Johnny"? Had I come from that corner? Or had I come from some other still unknown. Would I go on — to the top?

"I was only the runner," I said. "A kid. I was told to go home at nine."

Semple's eyelid flicked again. Johnny had been sent home then. He had his answer. But only part of it. Another puzzlement was beginning. What was my reason?

Silently I sent my answer to him. You. I. There is no other.

"And did you?" asked Hake.

Careful. Take it slow. I forced my hands to lie separate again on the table. Not yet. For now I had come to the part where I must make my jump across the gap between what is and what might be. What had been and what might have been. And this was the part where, last night, Dobbin too had halted, made me repeat. Head sunk on his breast now, his eyes, whatever their change by day, were veiled, but that no longer mattered, and if he cared to look, I should not be afraid of what he saw. I was that boy. He himself had said it.

"No, Mr. Hake." I smiled at him. "At fourteen — would *you* have?"

Everyone on Hake's side burst out laughing, except for the young clerk — too near him, still too abashed. Laughter was precious in that room, and I had provided it; they could not help but like me the better for it. And as they relaxed, stretching in their fixed chairs, one could see more clearly their human differential; they were emerging from the office picture one by one. It was the moment when their group took the ascendant, and I with them. For their own laughter had reassured them; as so often happens when men think collectively, it gave them the confidence to believe in what further I would have them believe.

"You see —" I said. In their receptive faces I could see my own bearing — sunny, boyish, median, image coveted for their sons, resembling or replacing their quondam selves. "You see — I knew they hadn't told me all their plans. I knew they were concealing something. I didn't know what." And this I had seen to be true enough, in its way, in the moment last night when, still unwitting, I had said it to Dobbin. Johnny had told me of the grove, what they did there and had done, of what they had done that day and would do that evening — while we hunted the hiding place, poked about in the room's decaying niches. On and on his words had come, spoken into a bin as we pried there, to a corner as he absently turned to it — a rush of words fascinated with its own release, like that of a boy who in that very moment had learned to read. And even then, following after him, I must have sensed and somewhere recorded it — the something he had not told me, that still for my innocence, or for us both, he had held back.

"What had they told you?" Hake, intent on his memoranda, had let the laugh wash by him.

"What everyone knew — that they were going up to the dams."

"You knew what they were going to do there?"

"Burn a cross on each one — as a warning." I could see Johnny, pushing at the fallen paper with his toe. "Will they be coming back?" I had asked him. Not tonight. They're going up to the dam. Nigger took a job there couple of days ago.

"You knew why?" Hake had to ask me twice.

"A — Negro had taken a job there. A few days before."

"Why — we'd had a whole mess of them for months, on the construction gangs!" This was Anderson.

"Yes, sir." I spoke slowly, from two positions in space. "But not for equal pay. They kicked back to the foreman, and it was redistributed to the others. Everyone knew it."

343

"What was this man's name?" This was Davis, the pharmacist. One by one, there on the right, they were coming to the fore.

"I didn't know. Nobody much did, I guess."

"You mean to say they just went along with it? Let themselves be called out — and didn't even know that!" His glasses shone with pedantic triumph and he turned them from side to side, letting their light shine on all. I knew his type as well as his accent, having encountered both in New York. He would see injustice behind every bush, often where it was not, but any to really interest him must first be humanized by some inside dope that, inaccurate or not, he always had.

"There was nothing personal about it," I said. I had had to go North to see that.

"For the record." Hake, holding up one hand to address the clerk, read from one of his memoranda. "Triplicate of employment record in files U. S. Employment Office, Washington, D.C.; original lost when the Charlotte hiring office was flooded. On September 12, 1932, one Lucius Asher, aged 23, born Tuscana, holder of mechanical draftsman certificate from manual training high school, Philadelphia, taken on assistant inspector on blueprints, attached to Dam Number Three." He glanced briefly at Davis, a ward boss's appraisal of the underfoot liberal, then turned back to Dobbin. "Suppose the existence of such a person here can be further established — no need to go into it now."

"No." Dobbin was fiddling with the yellow paper, folding it, tapping with a nail. "Let's finish with the witness." He leaned back. "Any questions?"

"Where *did* you go?" It came uninflected, a voice to match the eyes.

I had forgotten him for the moment. I was remembering Johnny in the long grass — "Weren't due to pass this way!" Johnny at the door of the annex — "Where else they gonna find him?" Johnny waiting there. "You coming? Or ain't you?"

"Where all the cars did, Mr. Semple." I had been there before the cars came, not with them. But, early or late, a fair of that sort is much the same. "Through the backs."

"Why-eee!" Frazer's aged semiquaver rose to a height and faded. "Sit here," he grumbled. "Sit here, listen to a continental liar. But now we got you." His voice rose again, and one wavering finger. "No-ow we got you. Because I was right there on the job at my signal, all that night. You couldn't a crossed thew there 'thout me seeing you. Not you nor any other bo —" He stopped, finger in mid-air. All but senile as he was, it had got to him too.

"No. You wouldn't have seen me." Once more I felt how it would be, to cover the white face. "But there's no road to the backs, there at the signal light, Mr. Frazer. And I didn't mention that we crossed there. How did you know we went across the tracks?" Mouth open still, he did not answer me.

"Did you — they — meet anybody?" Dobbin no longer lounged. "In the backs."

"No one. There wasn't a sound." One voice calling: Louie-lamb? Louie-lamb?, but they would never hear it. "It was like a fairground, I thought. Like after the fair is gone."

"Did they stop? Pick up anybody?" What was it he wanted?

"Not as far as I knew. They kept the pace. Went through without stopping."

"Go on." I saw by his face that I had given it to him. They already had him.

"Getting out was easier, along the old road that led back to the highway, then the new mile and a half of macadam, to the base of the dam site. They went slow all the way, as if they were on some kind of work operation — from the outside it looked as if the cars were driving themselves. Nowadays there'd be too much traffic, but that night they were all the traffic there was. And when they spread out — it was hard to believe that over a hundred men could be that quiet. From then on, it must have gone according to plan. I don't know how the lead cars got past the gates and the guards, but they got there. It was a clear night. After a while, everyone for miles around could see that they had."

"What did *you* see?"

That image was still on my retina; let Dobbin probe as he wished now, this is what he would find. I answered to the room at large. "The crosses burning. One on the top of each dam."

Hake put his papers aside. Their rustle was the only thing heard. Again I had the sensation that what I said was new to these walls. And almost at the moment of triumph, I wished myself outside them. If I turned my head, the window there on the periphery would flash like a mirror at the end of a burrow. At least let that bird speak again, bearing in its poetry of elsewhere. But the moment remained heft on its pin.

"You're the first person to say that publicly, do you know that?" With his screen of papers down, Hake seemed more threatening. I nodded to his every question. "I was here later," he said, "on the investigation. It turned up nothing — you recall? Dam Number Six wasn't built yet." This was the dam that now blocked off Tuscana. "A clear night, you said? Then Tuscana had a clear view. Eight thousand people, and they saw nothing. You know that?"

"Where were you?" Semple's voice was hoarser. "I asked you that before."

I drew a long breath, took the long jump.

"I was invisible," I said.

I could feel the recoil in the room, the air curled like a lip ready to explode with the nasal rage of the tricked. Here in this public room, a hundred men might be credited their dream of "nishness" and still be found sane; the same tolerance would not be accorded the private fancy of one. It took the simplest sleight of hand — to slip the private dream inside the other. "The Invisible Empire, Mr. Semple. You remember? I had a pass to it for one night."

Then, quickly, I turned away from him to the others, for now drama must be deserted, the manner to be as ordinary, dry, humbly aware of the strange stuff it dealt with as I could make it.

"Believe me, I couldn't do it now. Only a kid that age could have." Did the older ones already begin to smile at my assumed eminence of age, the way Dobbin had at our first meeting? "I was the go-between for all sorts of errands, among them the delivery of the tokens for seats in the cars. By mistake one of these was for a dead man — I found that

346

out when I brought it to his widow." Davis must have his name, I thought, glancing at the pharmacist, and *whang*, in the same instant it was provided me; in the hour of triumph, I thought, arrows fly to the hand. I mentioned the last name on the list, the one scratched out and replaced by Nellis's. "She made me take his hoodwink back with me — that's what gave me the idea. I was tall enough. I knew the proper signs and exchanges, all to be whispered. We were to remain as anonymous as we could. I knew where the car was. I could be already dressed and seated in it when the others arrived." I turned to Dobbin. "I saw what I saw, in privileged company. No account of it can sound more reasonable than it was." I turned to Hake. "I can't prove what I saw. What a whole town said it didn't. But there must be those who saw it from the other side." He knew that as well as I. And finally, I turned to Semple. "There were one hundred eighteen of us who were invisible that night, Mr. Semple. I took the place of a dead man named Victor Miller." I raised my fists with the thumbs aligned so that all could see them. "I was Klansman Two, of the thirty-ninth car."

Outside, the heavy sunlight had dipped beyond the eaves; within, all the faces before me darkened to a platinum with gleaming edges, the daguerre stillness, I thought, that must be asked of life by habitual liars. "Later on, I was scared enough," I said. "On the way back there was drinking in some of the cars, luckily none in mine. But everybody was more careless; most of us were set down still in our rig. I'd asked to be let off at Pridden Street to mislead the driver, but he was from one of the other towns and went past it, instead let me off at headquarters. I was the only one on the street — and the street looked strange. I remember thinking that the town looked inside out." I smiled, in patronage for that boy back there, and they smiled with me at him, at me, their son, their "self," and I saw that I had them now — from now on I might show them the truth as freely as the lies. "The public lights were out," I said. "There was none on this courthouse." I glanced down the line, at Charlson. "The light was out over the church door. It was the houses that were lit, waiting for us to come back. But there would be nobody at home in mine." I hesitated. There was not much truth left.

347

And here I faltered, not just in speech, but deep within. For now, advanced far on my plateau of time shift, fact blend, truth change, I saw opened like a pit before me, that up to here Johnny, either in what he had done or had yearned to, had been with me. All along, in the lies just told, he or his theme had been there. But now, just as I neared that denouement toward which — still innocent — I saw my story to be tending, I was deserted. That line of faces before me — I had meant to bring them, with a great lariat swing, into Semple's lumber-room, there, before their eyes, to let them see me once again hide the pamphlet with its list of names. And in the same moment reveal it, for its practicable uses. After which I could fall silent, Semple and his band struck down by the perfect boomerang of memory, my testimony — ours — done. But Johnny, back there in the lumber-room, evaded me like an after-image, sliding to the door when I fixed on him at the table, back at the wardrobe, the peaked hood over his head, when I strove for him at the door. Now, when I needed him, he hid himself in the unforeseen shadow of memory, behind what he had not told me, whatever it was I did not know. And I knew myself lost without him. "There *is* a town," I said to myself, but that moral dream, magic prop, could not help me; it had always been more his than mine.

"I went back inside headquarters," I said in a weak voice. "To . . . get rid of the rig, of course. I . . . put it in the big wardrobe . . . where they kept the extras." The wardrobe was solid enough, still. I clung to it. "Then . . . I don't know why I did . . . what I did then. There was a rule book there on a table . . . under an arrangement of pins and thread in the shape of a cross . . . they would know when you touched it. Something . . . made me. There was a list inside . . . all the members and officers. I read it. Then . . . I suppose I wanted to play a trick on them. Let them know, in a way, that I'd been there. And there were so many places to hide a thing . . . in that room. So . . . I took it up, pins, list and all . . . and I hid it. Then I ran home."

Surely they must hear how false my tone was, how labored my story and breath. I forced out the remaining bit of truth I had. "I can't explain — why I did it. But they would never look for it there. If the rats haven't eaten it — it's there yet." Surely now, in a great, healthy, hawhaw burst of reality, they were about to put me down. Perhaps, in my way as Semple in his, I wanted the secret to snap like a pod. "I'm sorry." I finished — or thought I had — with a quaver. "I can't explain it . . . any better."

Then I saw the phenomenon that I was never to forget, that taught me the trick of a lifetime to come. I had not yet learned fully what happens when men think in a group, together. Tender, protective, the line of faces on the right was nodding back at me, ready and eager to help me explain.

All were, that is, except Dobbin, who, as would shortly appear, had tricks of his own. At the moment he was intent on watching Lemon, who was trying to sneak to the door. But Lemon was not the man for creeping; an empty chair in his path tipped over and he kicked it away. At the door, he stopped to show his teeth at all of us, in a flexion of hate so pure that once again it must be envied by all less animal, not yet saints. He knew its object. Then he was gone.

"Catch — hold him, somebody!" The young clerk rose from his chair, "Isn't anybody going to —!" Excitement had helped him forget his neighbor, Hake. Even Dobbin's voice, compelling as it was, did not press him back in his seat.

"Let him go," said Dobbin. "Seven years is a long time. Keep him out of mischief, maybe." He was wrong there.

"I recommend we all go." Anderson stood up also. "In a body. Then, if anything's found, there'll be no question." I remembered him better now, the accent kin enough to this place to tolerate Mount's company, the linen too clean to bear it for long.

"Go where, Mr. Anderson?" said Dobbin.

"Why — why down to the café, of course — isn't that where he'll — ?"

"Is it?" Dobbin turned to me.

"No," I said. "He knows where to go, of course — to the real headquarters. If the thing's still there, it'll be where I put it. High up, in one of those old spice drawers." I kept my gaze on the table. On it, my hands moved together, as if not my own — and clasped. "That's where he'll go. To the old storeroom in the rear. The annex. The rear of Mr. Semple's store."

Two voices came almost together. Three.

"Wh-y, d-don't I know you?" said Hannibal Fourchette, waking to the rise of voices. "Change you n-name, but I know you."

"He lies!" The cry came straight at me. It was the first I had ever heard Nellis speak. "He was never —" He choked on it.

From the end of the line at the left, the third voice came, weary. "No he doesn't," said Charlson.

A wave of motion went toward Charlson, heads stretching forward toward him there in his corner. It passed over him; there was nothing to be got from that inward stare. Nor was there need.

Dobbin, ignoring all three, reached in his breast pocket and set a small, white pamphlet on the table.

I recognized it at once. The years had kept it strangely fresh, I thought, but I had been trained earlier than some to the mute survival of objects from one part of life to another. This one still had its power. In its presence Nellis made that move so often seen in the faithful toward the master — ready both to cling and accuse. Semple made none; perhaps this was in part a sign of what had made him master.

Dobbin's hand — he was standing now — picked up the book and held it high. A loose paper fluttered from it. He replaced it and pushed the manual across to Hake. "The copy I promised you." Behind him, Anderson and the young clerk, one after the other, slowly sat down.

Then he turned to me. "While Mr. Hake is checking — just one question." As he stood there, momentarily taller than any of us, did the others hear, as I did, the sudden cooling of accent, like a shabby coat doffed? "Think back to that place — the annex, lumber-room, whatever you call it." I had said lumber-room last night, not today, I thought. Once again his eyes probed mine, as if they would draw all my perceptions together, toward him. He spaced his words. "Did you see any signs of anyone recently having been held prisoner there? Earlier that day, perhaps?"

I knew what he meant at once, of course. The whole jury, heavy

350

breathing, knew also. They would have got him as he came off the job. But there'd been no signs of such, no one but Johnny, who was still there for me, refusing to look straight at me. "There was all sorts of stuff there," I said. "As much as an attic. There might have been — but . . ." In later years I would learn that a revenant's facility may not stretch too far beyond.

"You're sure? Nothing?"

"The big wardrobe was open, that's right. I remember it creaking."

Dobbin had already turned away, with a shrug, to look at the clock. "Ah. Well. A small point. No matter." I realized that he had already made his point. "It's five o'clock, gentlemen, and you've had no recess. But by your indulgence. By — yes, by five-thirty, Felix can open that door and you can all go home." He had drawn the yellow telegram once more from his pocket. No one denied him.

"It's all here." Hake looked over the tops of the glasses he had put on to scan the manual. "Just about as the witness here quoted it. And more."

"Then let's wind it up, get it over with." Dobbin spoke with an anger I at first thought assumed — the clever prosecutor chafing, in proper tempo, at his own delays. But if this was partially so, as he went on, it gathered an anger against history, toward whose evils he might not advance straight on but must stoop — a puritan's anger against himself for being like other men — so mixed. "Let's get on with it." He glanced up at the men on the right. "You'll have all the names you want, Mr. Davis. Mr. Hake, will you kindly read down the list of officers, as set forth categorically there. The witness, if he pleases, to identify each, if he knew him, by function and name." He paused. "But first —" He put a hand on old Clarence Whitlock's shoulder. "You've had no recess either. Now, Mr. Stallman here . . . isn't it? — knows shorthand, I understand. Let him take over." He watched while Whitlock, tremoring to a stop, handed the minutes over to the young clerk. "Careful with those minutes, Stallman. The judge has two federal men outside — to help Felix protect them." He nodded to me. "Ready?"

This was where he had stopped me last night. ("Let the rest of it

351

come out before them.") I was ready — and still dangerously able, as they by now knew. It was the light in the room that had declined — and not the sun only. But I could still see the list, clear as even in my mind's eye. It came to me then, with the names full in my mouth, that the moment of triumph is over a minute before it begins.

"Dobbin — wouldn't you rather — ?" Hake was reading to himself with distaste.

"No, no. A member of the jury."

I rallied myself. "I can do the whole thing, if you like. From memory. Mr. Hake can monitor me."

"Very good," said Dobbin, a little too gravely. He is manipulating me, I felt at once, but there was no time to consider.

I began. "The Klexter," I said. "According to the Manual, the Klexter is the outer guard of a Klan. He shall keep a diligent and faithful watch at the outer door."

Hake was the kind of reader who wetted a forefinger to turn a page. "Check," he said. "Klexter."

I checked too. There he was, second from the end, one of them, this tidy, senile relic, but surely not "they." "According to the list I saw — Alec Frazer." His mouth opened as I said it. I went on.

"The Kligrapp. Recording secretary of the Klan, and custodian of the seal."

"Check."

His shoulder twitched just once, meek as a workhorse. "Clarence Whitlock."

"The Klarogo," I said. "He is the inner guard of the Klan, who shall permit only those to enter the Klavern who are qualified."

"Check — Klarogo."

"Felix Spetmore."

Heads turned to the door, then back again, Dobbin's with them. Rabbits, where there should have been tigers, they were thinking. Was this all?

No. To two sons I could present their absent fathers.

"The Klokard. He is the lecturer or instructor, and the Klan censor or critic." His son was already nodding, to a rhythm I had not set.

352

"Check."

"Hannibal Fourchette," I said. "Senior."

"Klaliff," I said. "On the list combined with the office of Klabee, Treasurer, though not so in the manual. Vice President. 'Who shall preside over the Klonklave, in the absence of the Exalted Cyclops, and in his presence assist him.'" And who in his own absence, much excused by mercy to others, will send a son, a son and a car?

"Check." Hake turned the page.

The clerk held up his hand to stay me — I had gone too fast. Young Rollins, young as he, had already shrunk in his seat before I looked at him. Surely this poor thing, as stunted at one end of life as Frazer at the other, is not "they" either. But I kept my eye on him, in order not to see the face, toward the center of the row, that would raise at the sound of this name. "Robert Rollins," I said. In spite of myself, I had seen it. "Senior."

I went on quickly, to give a father, still present, his son. "The Kladds are the conductors of the Klan. 'Who shall collect the countersign and password at the opening of a Klonklave.' And I think — 'who shall be the custodians of its paraphernalia.'"

"Check. And check," said Hake. He looked up, wondering why I had slowed. Indian hair, face as stolid — except for pocks on one side and age on the other, the two Kladds were very like. "Jack Lemon," I said. "Senior and Junior." But, even taken together, was this pair large enough to be "they"?

Hake turned another page. I followed him, to present a man to himself.

"The Kludd is the Chaplain of the Klan," I said. "'He shall perform the duties of his sacred office. And such other duties as may be required of him by the Kloran and his Exalted Cyclops.'"

And before I could give his name, Charlson Evans gave it, whispering one added word. "Yes."

The silence, chill in the room, came from both sides. According to it, if one could ascribe evil singly, then he was the nearest. But there was one nearer. (And then at the end, at the very last: One.)

"The Night Hawk," I said. The man up at your mother's. The

353

neighbor with the light. " 'He is the special courier of the Cyclops, who shall carry the Fiery Cross in the ceremony, and in all public exhibitions where same is used.' "

"Check."

Back there in memory, Johnny pushed me aside and read the list for himself, his lips moving, his finger going down the page. The twelfth name, of a man who had died recently in the town, had had a line through it.

"Victor Miller's name — the dead member — had been scratched out," I said. "Another name had replaced it." I leaned across the table to Hake. "That's the list you have there, isn't it." I pointed toward the single sheet of paper Dobbin had tucked back in the manual. "You can see where."

Nellis, hunched forward in his chair, had forgotten his master. With a cry, he stretched his long arm for the paper. I was there before him. I held it in my hand without reading it. "The Night Hawk." I never said anything with more satisfaction. "Treacher Nellis."

But Hake, head to one side, hairless brow knitted, had not checked me. I looked down at the paper I held. It was a slip identifying the pamphlet Hake held — bearing its catalogued number in the Library of Congress.

"I thought —" I said. Dobbin's face had a warning lack of any expression whatsoever. "The corroborating evidence," I said. "Without which — you said you wouldn't even put me on the stand." But already I knew what I thought. The law, in its way, fitted together not unlike a machine. This meant that men, in full sight of their fellows, could twist a screw here and there toward their own uses, as Dobbin never by word, only by gesture, had just done with the two pamphlets, one existent perhaps only in memory, one lying here. As I.

"Ah, yes," said Dobbin. He walked around to my side of the table and in one seemingly gentle move slipped the paper from my hand to his, pressed me down into a chair. Turning to address the room, he kept a hand on my shoulder — paternal praise for a good witness. Actually, I could feel each separate finger. "This jury has no further function. That must be clear to all. A new panel? Frankly I don't know myself — we must wait on the judge." He sounded bewildered. From his fingers I knew otherwise. "We're rather the victims of your coincidences, Mr. Anderson." I could hear his smile. "But the law can't — anticipate — them all." Did he mean the witness as well? "And I know of no precedent for this one. No vote is possible, of course. The judge. We must wait on the judge." His hand left my shoulder, came down on it again for emphasis. "Now. Ordinarily it would now be my task to summarize admissible evidence, advise you on whether you have enough for indictment, draw one up if you so ordered. I may tell you that, taking what you have heard here, along with word just received, you do of course have enough for a true bill — or a future jury does — on the most serious charge. But under the circumstances, I recommend that you adjourn." He waited. "There is nothing further to keep you here, gentlemen."

But there was, and it was more than curiosity on the one side, fear on the other. Certainly any man from the left side would have been free to get up and open the door, could have slunk out, like Lemon. Or they might have filed out in a body, to flee thereafter to their separate decisions. Something held them here, more powerful in the end than pamphlets whisked to them by legerdemain, witnesses self-conjured out of shadow. In after years, when despairing of self and kind, I often thought of it. These men on either side had not fled — they had waited to hear. It was the room that held them, old shell of the body politic, holding out to them all the fascinations of judgment by their kind, even that ultimate chance, the last one — that men, thinking in congress, might someday come to do so honestly. If the true church, as one was often told, persisted forever, no matter the venality of its practitioners, then this was the true court, which partook of a wafer that went round the world. Each of us, if able to say what held us, would have given some version of the same answer: this place, where the tongues of angels are still hoped for, this corner, poisoned with the possible and sweetened by it — this room.

"I'll summarize it for you." No one should have been surprised that it was Charlson who broke the silence; perhaps no one was. He rose slowly, in his great bulk a shakiness like Frazer's, although he was not old, a weaving, though he never drank, that recalled Fourchette. Head thrust forward on his chest as if half severed, he stood there, coming to terms with that vibration — his interior monologue. Upright, he showed the full details of his size, the finger ring in diameter like the wrist of a small child.

"Murder," he said. The voice was a reed still, but the manner, dealing every Sunday with like deeds, ennobled it — as did the word. Out of habit, the ring finger pointed, as if accusing, at Dobbin. "You have all the evidence needed to put ten men on trial for the murder of Lucius Asher — to show that he was abducted, held, driven through the backs as hostage and taken up to the dam, in whose rubble his burned body was later found. You lack only one thing." He paused, wheezing, but from habit too — where in that self-apostasizing bulk would one come to the kernel of him; where would he ever come to it? "You lack only the corroboration to two questions. When was he taken? And by whom? And I presume that the wire telling you this is what you have been holding in your hand."

"Yes, it is, Mr. Evans." Dobbin had long since released my shoulder. He was leaning back, one eyebrow scowled high, now at last watching the disorder that might be visited on the law and by it. "It's an affidavit sworn to by two former clerks of the hiring office here, identifying a car and two men in it — one a dam employee, both known to the parties swearing — who picked up Lucius Asher when he came off the three o'clock shift that day. Half the shift saw the struggle, some of them forming an aisle through which Asher, who had been kicked in the groin, was carried to the car. The assailants made no attempt to conceal who they were, and were cheered by some of the crowd by name. Two federal clerks, neither now in Alabama, have so sworn." He coughed. One could see the strain in him now; he was a man who, when tired, stood that much more stiffly. "And you're right, Mr. Evans. That was about all that needed to be filled in. Only we shan't need to put ten men on trial. Two will do."

" 'Evans' is it now, Neil?" the minister said lightly. "It was 'Charlson' years ago, even back as far as when you used to come to summer Sunday school." He looked past Dobbin, past us all. "Years ago."

In that region, the time elegy, more than ordinarily elsewhere, is a part of normal conversation, being the recurrent chime of a place where friendship can revisit, fresh as ever after twenty years, on a street corner, where the talk of men, prowling the network of cousinship dead or alive, ticks away in those old houses of Usher as comfortably as a kitchen clock. No one in that room underestimated its importance. As Charlson began his ponderous move from the dais, everyone took for granted what he was after — to sound that chime in old Neil's ear, to get him to play one of those tricks of fealty which were as common as coinage here — to get him somehow "to keep all this dark." That it could be, in the county of old Fourchette, who would doubt? And if Dobbin did so, all reared here, whether or not in agreement, would understand it — as the final coincidence. So, in the spell of this knowledge, all were quiet as Charlson stepped down, carefully choosing his footing beneath the vast stomach, moving his arms like a prince regent. But it was not Dobbin he went to. He came to me. His great hands, planted down, starred the table in front of me.

I can smell him yet — the odor of revelation — a fat man sweating after his own grace on a hot day. He didn't betray *them*, only himself — from moment to moment. That was his vibration. His chin stretched forward, the pouch under it quivering like a tenor's. "You saw the crosses. Tell us what they looked like."

We had reached the fundament. I knew it at once. The room knew it, as over and over in its chronicle it must have known such. Dobbin knew. His tired face, no longer wary, said it to me. Here's your disorder. Relish it. There's a chance, peered from history and gone again, that it may be divine. And back there in the faceless shadows, Johnny raised his eyes.

"There were four." I spoke from that long-gone hill. Before my eyes and Johnny's the crater line of the dam site crested its tidal wave in an arc that took in half the world. Its four peaks rose like pediments. "One for each dam."

"Yes, yes, go on. *Describe* them." He swung his head at me, fleshy Iaokanann, chestnut-curled.

"It was a clear night. There wasn't much wind — but it was enough." I turned up my palms, almost in supplication. "That's all."

"Is it?" The head swung. Suddenly he stretched his arms wide. "A cross looks like this, doesn't it? And a Christian always sees a man on it!"

I turned my head from that spectacle, that mouth agape. I saw him.

The jury heard his whisper, not a question. "Doesn't he." All bent their heads away. No one wanted his exegesis. Leave us in our sty. All did except one.

"Tell him, my son," said my uncle. "The whole truth. You will remember." He knew I would remember — and more. He knows me, as in his lifetime I was never to know him. He was the listener from behind.

But I, who at twenty-one knew so much, did not recognize him. I was sick with another kind of learning. Back there in the shadows, Johnny stood very still.

"I — I watched them for a long time." Each cross streamed backward, image of a running man, his flesh a yellow mane behind him. "For a long time." And in the end I had held out my arms to that Biblical glory. Here now in front of me, held out in place of mine toward it, were Charlson's, at his side the young clerk's face, lifted like an acolyte, reflecting it. Gathered round them were all who had assisted me, the men from the left as well as the right, Dobbin, my uncle and Semple. The truth had trumped me up to serve it. I had come to the top of the hill.

"One of the crosses — the one on Dam Number Three — it was thicker than the others." I whispered it. The apocalypse hits the eyes — long before it reaches the heart. It had taken seven years to reach mine.

"I watched it," I said. "I watched it until it fell."

Charlson had his face buried in his palms. Dobbin leaned toward him but did not touch him. A fly buzzed once, twice, between them. "Charlson," said Dobbin. "It's nearly six."

358

The great, bleared face lifted. "The two you'll try," it said. "Am I one?" Already it had shifted; petulance dyed it. "No? I should be!"

"That reminds me," said Hake. The words seemed absurd, his aspect no longer chilling; he was merely a man somewhat smaller, balder than the rest. "You realize there's one name we haven't yet on record?" It was typical of the way vengeance shrank as one went toward it — that this little man who wetted a forefinger as he turned each page should have to remind us of the one we had all forgotten. "The Exalted Cyclops."

They turned on him to look at him — all the jury on the left-hand side. Even I had forgotten him. To me he would never be ordinary. But even I must begin to doubt that the man sitting there was the one neck to squeeze, the One to stand *in loco parentis* to all the dread in the world.

"The Exalted Cyclops is the supreme officer of a Klan and its official head," I said. Give him his due; his head did not sink; the crescent eyelids gave me stare for stare. "He is to be a pattern for Klansmen . . . and he shall do such things as may be required of him by the laws of this Order." And he had done them. But try as I might, I could not revive him in his original horror. Vengeance is mine, saith the Lord. I had always taken this to mean that the Lord would avenge. Now I began to see its real meaning. Vengeance is never ours. "E. V. Semple," I said.

Hake's voice came, lagging too. "Check."

And now the room was already dispersing like an audience rustling at the coda, although everyone still remained in his chair. Anderson and Davis, speaking in twinned breath, moved for adjournment; in the low growl of assent, Dobbin went to the door. Everyone scuttled toward it with the strange, ragged seeking of crabs when the box is opened; sidling through it, no one, not even the righteous, seemed to wish to touch his brother. Outside, in tableau, Felix the guard gaped at the young clerk, just reverently giving up the minutes to Dobbin, who handed them in his turn to the pug-jawed man flanked by two unknowns — the judge.

In the room with me, Nellis and his master remained, heads together, conferring. As quickly as anything in life, men sense their separation from the general. I too was once more only the witness. I walked the few steps to the window which had drawn me all the stages of that afternoon. Now that the heat of the day was over, the caretaker was mowing the green space between this wall and his cottage, moving in and out between the lines of his wife's wash — faded nightdresses, child's jumpers, pantaloons. This was all the mirror reflected when one drew near it — once again the world outside one at its passions and completions, once again the inner, monologuing eye. Had I expected that one brilliant burst of light to impose a helium noon here forever, hoped to look up, up — here at six in the evening — to a meridian quiver of larks?

Behind me, those two, murmuring, evidently were finding words enough now. How should I pass them? When I turned they stopped talking. Then Nellis made as if to speak, but Semple, lifting an uncertain hand, stayed him.

The hoodwink had raised. We took each other's measure. Why had I troubled, asked that beaten face? Who was I? Who was he, around whose neck I had twined murder? Was he the accidental man? Was I?

Where then was the adversary? If I gave Semple up, then I reentered the difficult, uncodified world. In that vast indiscriminate of pain wherever a child screamed, a neck or a mind was squeezed, a god or a man was hung — I would never find such another.

"It wasn't *you*," said Semple. "Then — *why?*"

I examined his face like a lover. Silently I answered, and left him. It wasn't *you*. Then — who?

Outside on the steps, I found my uncle waiting for me. Dusk had already spread its webs, through which my uncle's features were tenuous, as mine must be. I was grateful for this, able to feel no other emotion. We fell into step without any exchange. Lights were being turned on for the spectral hour so protracted here at this season; through the open windows supper sounds came, gentled by it, to porches that seemed to drift, waiting. It was the kindest hour of the day. My uncle walked without haste, at a pace consonant with his evening reappearance. As we walked, I felt him to be recharging himself with the burden of my mother, after the day's business. Between that, just done, and what we walked to, words would have fallen idle. A valuable moment was passing forever for both of us; later it did not seem to me that we had made less of it than we would have, had we known.

Two blocks from home, his hand on my arm stopped me where I was. We stood there, while he chose his words. By now I knew from what a granary these came, but I was not dwelling on it in my present state, only expectant of what I thought he meant to tell me: what we were to say, how we were to bring the news to my mother. I had to leave it to him.

"You're not to tell her you were there," he said at last, as if he had heard me thinking. He brooded. "We'll say nothing of this day. *Nothing.*"

"Yes." My mind was suspended, a blank thoroughfare. "What will you say to her? I mean, how will you — ?" Far off, at the other end of exhaustion, I saw the evening before us. There was fear in her interest now. And she was so keen.

We stood there for a fair time, two men pausing naturally on a street corner, while one chose his words. Finally, he found them.

"I can lie," he said in a low voice. The addendum came even more quietly. "Too."

So, in those final moments, we came to our understanding. It is a measure of his power that still, after all these years, I find it enough.

We came almost to our own porch before we could make out the high, eccentric form of the wheel chair, which meant that she was there waiting in the shadows behind the railing, muffled in her scarves. Lucine had not yet lit the lamp. My mother, to spare us the sight of herself, had recently found herself fond of the gloaming. Through it her voice could come still untouched, as it came now.

"You're late. How is it you're together? Is anything wrong?"

We had stopped at the bottom of the steps. He also may have been grateful for the dimness, preparing the face which, expressionless as it seemed to others, was not so to her. But his reply cut the dusk cleanly, deftly explaining all, even preparing for me, its only error in that it came too quick — for him.

"Naught's wrong. Mind, you might find your son a bit tiddly. We had a couple, down to the pub."

A shot from a rifle makes a clean kind of noise also, as any sportsman will tell you. The sound of the reloading, if you are near enough to hear it, is a little like a man clearing his throat. The first of the shots went through the latticework under the porch, into the dirt. With the second shot, or just before it, a broad light illumined us, trained from a porch several houses down on the opposite side. My uncle pulled me down with him; as we dropped, I thought he cried "Ireland." I think neither of us was hit by that shot either. There was a third. The light went out with the last.

Then we were left to the dimness, which, after the light, was almost dark. If "we" might still be said. I was not sure. Hit in the leg somewhere, I crawled to my uncle, but in the curious tie of instinct, it was for my mother, only inches and days away from death, that I was fearing. Then I heard her scream, the long, strong, hopeless cry of the chairbound. None of the shots had hit her then — or all of them.

For he had preceded her. A slug from a gun of a size to hunt squirrels with can be minor, in certain parts of the thigh. But he had received it perfectly, from the hand of a good gamesman, in the chest.

If I leaned forward, holding my smeared thigh, I could just barely make out his features. He was a man without effluence. What he liked, if he suffered, no man knew. Yet, sometimes, he moved. Most honest of men, his last words had been a lie for my mother's sake, if one did not count the scarcely caught "Ireland" that had been meant to warn me. So he died, with all his virtues on him, and such sins as might be.

"Who — who is there? Who?"

I looked up. Tears blinded me, sprung from eyes which had not paused to note they had them. I had forgotten she was there.

"Will no one come?" she said, in the small voice that converses with itself. "Then I must walk — somehow." I heard her struggle. Then I heard her scream again for Lucine.

Holding on to my wet thigh to keep the faint from me, I wondered why she did not speak to me. Then, my eyes clearing, I understood. Darkness had fallen — she could not see me.

Before I could make myself known, she spoke again, from her side of the dark. Over and over it came, that ululation.

"One of them is moving. One is. Oh God, oh God. Speak to me. Who is there? Who?"

I had to answer her somehow, from my side of the dark. Out of the depths, I gave her my lifelong answer.

"I."

PART IV
Entry

For three nights since, I have sat here and written nothing. Confession, one assumes, will be like coming in out of a great wind. Instead, mine blew me on in a continuous circle. Over and over, my mother and I were taken to hospital, where my contemptible wound was dressed, where, toward morning, as soon as the sun affirmed an indifferent world, different to her, she died of hers. With every cell corrupted, she died upright, conscious, grieving. Over and over, I sat by her bedside, watching to what end might come, would come, that power of which I had inherited my dram's worth. And over and over, Dobbin, waiting, my bags in hand, in the anteroom, plucked me from the still room and drove me ninety-five miles through the just glinting countryside, to the safety of a train. There, until it began again, the round ended.

Last night, hoping to stop that haggard marathon, I broke the promise made to myself — not to read back. It did as I hoped. Even a memoir does not stand still. I was not the person who had first sat down.

What have I learned, then. *What have I learned?* That we live between certain arcs, not self-imposed? Looking backward, as commemoration only, is not good enough. Death *is*. Tragedy resides not in the facts of existence, but in the mutations between. Change is the tragedy. Where else can we find hope then, except there?

While I wrote, the telephone rang, at the same odd hour. It's almost four. Ruth is back from London, then, with my letter. She rang at this time, so that I might know it was she. Also, because she too has her struggles, perhaps even her mystery. I've lost enough arrogance now to admit even that. I don't refer to the commonplace that every human unit is a mystery. What if there should be something special which — how else could she have been so knowing, so drawn toward me? "You are so . . ." she said. And I asked "What?" and got my reply. "Honest." The lives of others always look so active, so competent, so lacking in the specious — to ourselves. What if, all the time I have been monologuing here, she in her turn . . . ?

Vade retro. I must keep to my line. Looking backward in itself is nothing. There is still the whole chapter of devices that my life has been since. The phone rang, but I didn't answer it. I wasn't ready for her. Not yet. Not quite.

Chapter I.   A Chapter of Devices.

WHAT I reveal now is indeed a chapter of devices twenty years long — all to be summarized as briefly as possible except the last. From the outside, this second half of my life would certainly be chosen as the important one, bright with all the tangible events of manhood — war service, a career of sorts, a thin chain mail of affiliation with society — all that increasing clutter which we call maturation. Only I came to know, gradually and in secret, how the first half, bulging as the forehead of a fetus over the tentative face beneath, always overhung the other. For a long time I didn't know this fully.

When I returned to a New York still emptied by summer, I went directly to a small, cheap theatrical hotel I knew of in the West Forties, had my trunk transferred from the fraternity house to the hotel basement, and sat down at my narrow window facing the fire shaft, to consider. Life with no goal, in a small hotel room of that kind, on a round from bureau, to closet, to hall toilet, on a circuit of exits and returns for eating, can itself be obsessive. For two weeks, with such intermissions, I sat there, writing no letters, making no phone calls, the room's buzzer never sounding for me except by mistake. No one known to me knew where I was. Against habit, I took no great walks, did not even read. If I had an obsession, it was that I might meet the two in New

York from whom I had absconded — Serlin, even though long since gone to New Hampshire — and Lovey. Therefore, though I knew it was foolish, I kept to the immediate district, avoiding the main library and shops, the garment section where Bijur's was, and one nearby street, devoted to hats and artificial flowers, which Lovey sometimes frequented for bargains. These two had been my sole intimates; graduation and school dispersal had relieved me of most acquaintance. Those other two who had known me best were dead, my need for them numbed forever by the manner of their death, my role in it. Or so it seemed. I was as free of ties now as might fill any man with hope — or despair. No one knew where I was; no one here knew *who* I was. I was free to contemplate, if I wished, my identity. But this interim was the reverse of those three days before I had first left Tuscana, during which I had first dealt with that simple, cosmic drop into space, down whose shaft one falls soundlessly asking, "Who am I?" I'd my identity now, and my glands were choked with the bitter thing, my head split with it. I knew what I was now, and who. Or, in my innocence, so it seemed.

Everything passes, a pendulum statement, neither good, neither bad. In people, this quality is shamefacedly called "contrariness" or worse, since we like to think of ourselves as faithful even to a bad situation, but it is often as much of a spur as ambition, and more often a part of the natural equipment. My scholarship money was almost gone, and jobs were still not to be had for the picking in 1939. Breaking from anonymity just long enough to apply to the college's job bureau for whatever they had in the way of summer leftovers, I was surprised to find a niche that just suited: twenty-five dollars per week as one of a corps of all ages and status, both student and permanent, which was working on various encyclopedias, classical dictionaries, a vast project of all sorts of compendia, under the tutelage of a man as unusual in some ways as his name, one A. B. C. Lasch. Mr. Lasch had no personal monies to expend on omniscience, but was of that breed of devotee whose religious energy attracts backers, one of whom had deeded the large, slightly dilapidated Westchester estate in which the establishment was housed. Over it Mr. Lasch presided year after year — it was rumored that he was now a sixty who looked forty — a testimony of the contentment to be found in the quiet routines of a madness intelligibly pursued. Such a place, staffed inevitably with the "special," who were then isolated morning after morning with the intangible, should have been prey to all the coterie ills — but these either melted away or were banished under Mr. Lasch's arbitrary, impersonal, always light hand. He seemed to have effected some of that harmony whose will-o'-the-wisp certain colonies have pursued by theory; perhaps because, beyond the assemblage of fact for its own sake, he appeared to have no theories whatsoever. He had the advantage, of course, of excesses focused on a kind of norm — dictionaries need no excusing. But fact was king here; one could never get from Mr. Lasch any kind of *a priori* remark, personal or general, that preceded it. Surely he had his own story, but I, already something of a master, could never collect his, even as to whether his initials were the result of his *idée fixe* or its cause — a routine tease that merely drew his smile. It was clear that he spent all his juices of mind, sex, and heart on his compilations. Such a wine-squeezing should have left him *sec* as a centipede; instead one found a man as round and rubicund as some good abbot, genial without prattle, silent but not taciturn — happy.

And of course, such talents as I happened to own suited him mightily; one could have thought, from his pleasure, that all my history had portended my arrival here — as perhaps it had. After a short time, I was invited to leave my furnished room in nearby Mt. Vernon and join the small circle of resident staff. At end of summer, when other student aides left but I did not, he was surprised, then thoughtful. Clearly he was greedy for me to stay. When he heard that I would, he didn't press for my reasons, only saying, "Stick with us, then. You shan't lose by it." Nor, in a way, have I.

That first stint, I stayed for some eight months. My decision not to return to college seemed to me already fixed at the time when I had failed to mail a letter of explanation to Serlin, as absolute as a formal resignation, and one that it never occurred to me was not irreparable. Probably this was the one purely romantic gesture of my life — if one takes romanticism to be, as I do, those lies one tells not to others but to oneself. I told myself that the serene course of my college life to date, the approval which had been slowly accruing, was neither my fate nor my style; not that I felt myself unworthy, rather that real worth ought not to come along so gently, giving no trouble, into that enclosure where so many others already were. Probably that is true, in the large. Actually, I felt relieved to be away from the temptations of that enclosure. I gave up college exactly as I had once tried to discard Demuth's chocolate. I could not bear to be helped.

After a few months, I did communicate with Dobbin, to whom I had given power of attorney, after he had pointed out to me, during the course of that long ride, that my uncle had predeceased my mother, and that I was my mother's heir. More months went by before I had a reply, under the heading of the Boston law firm of which Dobbin was a partner. They were very glad to hear of my whereabouts, since the house had been sold and the estate was shortly due to be settled. With the sale of the house added to my uncle's savings and a small account of my mother's, the total would amount to some fourteen thousand dollars, which, after the proper formalities, they would remit, along with a box of effects that had been held for me. Mr. Dobbin had been overseas since October last, moving from place to place, and was likely to continue so in view of conditions in Europe, but had left word before going that he was to be notified of my address as soon as found, since there were certain matters of which he preferred to write personally. This had been done. Meanwhile, also at his suggestion, they were to consider themselves at my disposal for any future legal services I might require.

Dobbin was overseas. This was what the letter really brought home to me. I have had the luck always to be able to treat money pretty concretely, hanging no extra symbolism on what already had enough effluence as it stood. The sum impressed me, and had its deep, associative pangs, but I went through no "blood money" attitudes about it; almost at once it receded to a certain distance, as something beyond my expectations, that until I had a need for it or found one, would not be quite mine. But Dobbin was overseas, and had been since October.

The sun, where I stood with the letter under one of the horse chestnuts, striped Lasch's dead, yellow lawn with chipmunk black. While I stood there, it went in and out several times with a pale Cheshire smile and finally took itself off altogether behind the gray clouds muddled above the chimneys of the long sham-Tudor house, leaving a fresh cold through which the pure smell of leaf smoke twisted from a few hedgerows away. I had come to like this place mildly for its heavy 1900 virtues of wood, stone, and fumed-oak interior colors blazoned here and there on corners of arranged, fake dark that would not terrify a child. It was comfortable, at my bachelor age, to live among the drabs and absurdities of a bygone taste, released, as in a hotel or boardinghouse, from any exertions of my own. We lived then, Lasch and a few others of quiet persuasion, several physically handicapped, all single, behind mullioned windows, hard to open or repair, whose shared nuisance imparted a light sense of family, in winter lunchtimes (Lasch ran no commissary) appropriately knocking the snow from our boots against the tarnished greaves of several suits of armor which stood about the hall. It was one of those satisfactorily dim places of employment, rapidly vanishing from a world that seemed all "outer," which gave one a sense of being able to stay on in it forever, and more than one drawn here by his own peculiarities had been soothed into that intention. Much the youngest here, I meant to linger in this backwater only until my own intentions declared themselves, not yet awhile perhaps — soon. The letter in my hand, whipped by the wind, flapped like a pinwheel, more active a paper than those dailies which entered the house each morning like tabbies, deposited communiqués already dead, and were gone again at nightfall. I looked up at the horse chestnut waving its branches above me, already dropping new husks on some of last year's satiny brown fruit at my feet — a genus of tree first seen here, but long since mingled for me, in the fast-blotted reference map of my generation, with its forebears on the Bois (Odettes now behind the Maginot Line), with its collateral cousins steadily and impartially growing a fragrance of *wunderschönen Monat Mai* (I knew my Heine now also) as *auf wieder* to men goose-stepping away from Unter den Linden. Where was Dobbin, "moving from place to place," now?

The house, on a rise of land at a squire's distance from its own pillar-

373

box, withdrew in its own Anglophile light, gathered back like a house in an engraving, although I knew that distance also to be slightly faked. Nevertheless, we were farther behind the lines there than even the rest of the country; as many newspapers as entered it did so more to be clipped than to be read, and I already felt a young man's distaste for people who could be so quickly antiquarian with life. Even our one refugee, a Viennese librarian named Schott, was a queer exemplar of martyrdom — a handsome man in his forties who gave us no help in our heavy "sympathizer" discussions, breaking in on them, eyes rimmed with *boulevardier* red, to tickle the nape of our younger female resident (a lame girl named Delphine Smith) with a pointed nail that each time crept toward more meaningful areas. Schott was a professed opportunist, openly amused at our puritan need to see him morally all of a piece with his martyrdom, who meanwhile busily engaged himself in testing the stuff of his new American existence with a trader's thumb. A man eager and didactic on the subject of rich acquaintance, already a weekender in the environs, he kept inviting me to tennis on the courts of his new cronies and had only yesterday proposed a whorehouse, not for information — he was already the patron of a good one — but for the fresher luster of my company, since, as he said, tossing his head with a strawberry-lipped laugh at the drama young men made of these visits here, surely the European custom of going regularly with one or more good companions was more civilized, and on these occasions he disliked the company, rich or not, of the old. I meant to go with him. But meanwhile, the British had declared war in September. The letter blew from my hand and I retrieved it. "Overseas," it said, not the civilian "abroad." The wind that blew it was a March wind. And meanwhile Dobbin, who for all his "theme" saw the law with a politician's squint, who in August I could have sworn to be Ambition walking, must have put his judgeship aside and had been overseas since October.

"Pi-erre! Teatime!" Delphine advanced across the cold lawn, shivering for me to see in her sweater, her dark, high-schoolish masses of hair ruffled back, rocking slowly toward me on the iron-braced leg. We were very English in our habits in that house, nudged both by the architec-

374

ture and the times, and Delphine kept us to it most ardently of all, her sincerity amended by the knowledge that the silver curves of tea-pouring well became a femininity that she had had to express more quaintly than a normal woman, in pinned handkerchiefs, wide skirts, slim, archaic sandals on the wasted foot. A soft-featured, childish thirty above the incongruous spread of hip, reared on all the tender encirclement offered a bright cripple, she had proudly remained unspoiled, gently hoping not to differ. She was in love with me, as I well knew. Schott's recent attentions, so marked and open, had only inclined her more bravely toward me, even to the point of a small, precious confidence, offered tremulously as a bride, that she was not a virgin. Uncomfortably, I wished she would succumb to a man who would make more sophisticated use of her than I felt myself able. I found her attractions much more normal than she would allow, but saw no way of telling her this without coming closer to accepting them — and we lived in the same house. For, well as I knew Montaigne's comment on the special heat in the loves of lame women, I was held back by what he had not mentioned — the heat of the attendant psyche. With Delphine, any "affair" she offered, its end already humbly germinated in the word itself, would have a note of hysteria from its beginning, gratitude twining with fidelity in a lovers'-knot not easily severed even by the experienced — and I meant to leave. Anyone could see what her emotions were, arrested and rarefied to a faëry intensity thin as membrane, and as tough. Only love could match it, or perversity, and I felt neither.

"Any for me?" Embarrassed, knowing I saw her excuse, for I always brought the mail up for tea, she still came on; then, glimpsing the one letter in my hand, went on past me to the box. Surly, I let her, although I knew she hated to have her awkward movement observed from behind.

Opening her own letters, she could not keep her eyes from mine. Everyone knew I got no mail, surely speculating on what ties lay behind me, receiving no help from me other than the name of the college, from which I let them think me a graduate of several years back, Lasch never discussing his staff, most people thinking me older than I was. Delphine, traveled, and a great word-fancier, had discerned, from occasional slips (such as "gum-boots" for the "galoshes" which had been rare in Alabama), my origins, and this too she treasured like an intimacy. I disliked her having it only because it was.

"News?" As soon as said, she flushed at having said it, at my noncommittal silence. And a moment later, could not help herself from going on. "From home?"

I was furious with her, for my having no right to be and no way to express it, for her being the gentle, tumultuous creature she was. And, I suppose, for having that barrier to fury, her leg.

"No."

She would not pry, no not she, a person with feelings so much more bruisable than those who were whole. She wanted to get in, that was all; like anyone in love, she was bedeviled by the thought of it, its proximity, so near, so far. Only one hair of reserve to cross — then to drown together. "But you look so — I hope it's nothing —?"

"Nothing!" It burst from me, as if we had been snarling for hours. "It's just that — one's so far from anything here. From anything important!" I must have crested my head like a peacock.

She bent hers, and started back up the hill, in front of me. As soon as I saw that pathetic gait, which she could not make ordinary if she would, I ran after her. "From the war, I meant, you know what I meant. Delphine."

"*N'importe*," she said foolishly, her mouth bright. "*N'importe!*"

So I begged off tea, and went back to my room — to write Dobbin. In the months since, I had seen nothing in the papers about the events in Alabama, the workings of obscure juries there not being as newsworthy as now. If any notice of my uncle's murder had appeared nationally, it must have done so during the two weeks I had been in my hotel room. I had no wish to exhume it — years later, happening on some AP and UP dispatches for that period, I checked and found nothing. Dobbin's letter, the one he was waiting to write me, would tell me whatever there was to know. Then why did I write him in advance of it? Up to now, my life, school-grooved like most, had cushioned me against the real multiplicity of the world outside, leading me to assume that there as well complexities would present themselves in a lean, single line of progression, to be dealt with one by one. Lasch's had proffered a similar groove, those who stayed on burrowing safely there for that reason. But I had a double citizenship in more ways than one, never knowing when the inner globe of the monologue would pall and I must plunge for the outer. Ducking from school to Lasch's as I had, confusion had still reached me, pulling me with wars, Delphines, my own pendulum, toward the inevitable graduation into it, somewhere along the line.

The letter I wrote Dobbin was as confused, although formal on the surface. Reminding him that I was a national of a country to which I did not wish to return, one engaged however in a war in which I wished to serve, I asked his opinion on how soon "we" would get into it. Unless we would, I did not feel it proper to take out papers here as planned, not wishing to avoid military service, but preferring to cast my lot here, as was natural. Actually it was not at all natural, except in certain small pockets of America, to have feelings ready-made for this sort of thing; thousands of my contemporaries must have been writing just such pretenses to those elders who, neglecting to warn them what heavy thunderclouds of the arbitrary could suddenly loom on a horizon, had taught them to think for themselves. No man really wants to be anonymous. So, in this war, we were to find ourselves running constantly toward the illusion that we had choices, as if this in itself were the white plume. I had rather more anonymity to run from than the average — and this was the real reason I wrote Dobbin, who knew more about me than anyone else now alive. To have someone continue to know. From that deep human itch for which there is no other balm, to be "known." I've no idea whether he ever got the letter.

During the weeks while I waited for his reply, I imagined myself into all sorts of courses. Going to Canada and enlisting there was one — but not being American, would I need a passport? I had none except the old one of my mother's on which I was down at the age of ten. One day, I dropped by the recruiting office in the postal building in White Plains, and casual as anyone, holding my breath as if the bored sergeant there might read "alien" striped on me somewhere, I found out what was needed for enlistment. "Easy as pie," he said. "Getting in, that is. Few little John Hancocks here and there, on the dotted." He handed me some sheets to look over. "You look healthy enough. 'Less you got flat feet." A second man, at a nearby desk, raised his head from a crossword puzzle. There was no one else in the office. "Join the navy then," he said. "See the world." Outside the window, leaf rustled against brick, sun dazed a fruiterer's stall; in the lobby, feet swished on marble. A little boy went out carrying stamps as if they were holy. If ever there was peacetime, it was there. On the way home, my mind went round and round again (if my uncle, being naturalized, had adopted me — but he had not — whether my mother had included me, still under age, in her first papers), winding me in a self-spun court of chancery. There had been too much law in my life already. And like a fish desiring suddenly to live in air, hearing that there were lungs to be acquired for that element, I wished not to lie. Notice came from Boston that the money had been deposited to my name, followed by a large package — the previously mentioned "effects." But Dobbin was still silent.

I carried the box down to Lasch's basement, intending to stow it in my trunk alongside a much smaller one, taken from my mother's side at the hospital, which when opened the next night in my hotel room had disclosed the packets from the sewing machine — old letters, marriage certificates, the passport, a citation from her school in Lyons, a picture of her first wedding — none of which I had scrutinized except the last, finding, at long length, that I did indeed resemble my father. Well I'd never thought myself a bastard; this opera touch at least hadn't been included in my longing, in that peculiar "ambition" which had so worried her. Should I use some of the money to go to London, then, conscript myself there?

The second box was much heavier, still in its Tuscana wrappings. A penciled note fell from them. *Your mama pack away some these things long time back. I done put in what else reckon she want you to keep. Enthing I ken ever do, you write me, care Miss Minnie, the Museum. That the best place. Enthing atall. And God bless you in your troubles. Lucine.* I lifted the cover. Lucine had packed us in by layers, on top

378

all the mementos of my grandfather, taken down from their hallowed places on the wall. Next came a layer devoted to my uncle. I passed over it. Beneath were the books from my shelf, under these, dozens of things, from catcher's mitt to stone collection, that I had forgotten. Objects pursue us, I thought, a detritus we can't shake, and survival makes sneaks of us all. At the bottom, something both hard and soft was wrapped in tissue. The Japanese slippers fell from it, first signal of my arrival in the new world, and a large conch shell. So my mother had brought it there for me after all, but on second thought kept it hidden — I knew why — exactly as she would have burned that copy of the London *Times* in our nonexistent grate, if she could. I did not lift the shell to my ear. Something caught my eye among my uncle's things as I replaced them — the page of legal notices which appeared seasonally in the Denoyeville *Dealer*. I saw almost immediately why he had kept it, my name leaping at me from the required notice of the granting of petition for change. So he'd done that for me too. I wasted no time in gratitude. What a fool I'd been! I came from a town the bulk of whose records for a century back had been lost in the flood. Birth certificates, property attestations — I'd seen their recapitulations paraded on these pages for years. Who was to know that a like loss hadn't occurred with mine?

A month later I had my navy enlistment, the world having beckoned, although my feet were not flat. The sergeant had been right in all his estimates. Just a few John Hancocks here and there on the dotted.

The night before I left Lasch's, as I prowled along the dim upper hallway of its men's quarters, on my way to the bathroom after the late party they had given me, I met Delphine, making her way toward me from the women's side. Since that afternoon, I had had no more of her confidences, although perhaps Schott had, his inquiring hand having been markedly permitted this evening, in the sight of us all. And Delphine, glossy with liquor, proclaiming herself a cork-smeller, had let herself dream audibly of where she would take herself on the competence left her by her grandmother, as soon as the war was over, even letting drop what she had never obtruded on us before, who her father had been, precisely what Smith. She did not tell us of her relationship, on the distaff side, to Lasch's main backer. Perhaps Schott, compiling his *Almanach de Gotha* for America, already knew. As it was, she seemed to be handling things perfectly if she wanted to have him at least for a while. I had reason to know that his other habits had not changed.

As she came toward me, in a high-necked robe that glimmered like pink china, one hand bunched in front of her on the side where the brace was, I imagined with embarrassment that she might be bringing me a farewell gift, for the women never came here. She motioned me to lean down. The hand was empty. "Just think —" she breathed in my ear. There was no liquor on her breath. "Schott —" She let me lean back. "Schott wants me to sleep with him." Her eyes, always shadowed like a tired child's in summer, looked large as a dragonfly's. They were impenetrable, their direction all-inclusive. Did she know that Schott was not in his room tonight? He made no secret of his ways of course, claiming that they made him the more attractive to women, but I thought now that, as with many Europeans of his type, his underestimations of Americans clung to him like a patchouli, obvious to them, in which he did not know he walked.

"And shall you?" It seemed to me that she had made her statement as a man might make it.

She didn't smile back. "No. I'll marry him."

Years later I saw them together, at a party of their own. She still preferred, noticeably in a hostess, not to leave a room, a table, ahead of others, but now she carried it off like a vanity. Schott had faded to solidity, like so many preachers of the butterfly chance, once they alight. It was said that he adored her, that it had always been more his marriage than hers. And he was allowed to walk behind.

Now, she watched me, her eyes glaucous as a seer's. Her mouth twitched, but I couldn't be sure that its mood was the same bright *"n'importe"* of our other encounter. Stretching up, up, she put it on mine, where it warmed, strove.

Inflamed, feeling her brace against my leg, I pulled her closer, growing at once all the perversity I had disclaimed.

"Turn around." She had withdrawn from me, motioning me to face away from her. She was smiling.

I did so. What on earth? Was it that she didn't wish me to see her entering Schott's room? If so, then she'd soon be out again. I could still feel her mouth, round plum wanting me belatedly to know its pulp. At first, I heard no movement from her. Then, waiting, I heard her step going slowly away from me, back to the women's quarters, rock, rock.

In bed, liquor and the hilarity of doom kept me sleepless, like a man after his bachelor dinner. Time's hurrying footstep was at my ear, making me proud. I dreamed with eyes awake of all the shocks and fancies to come in a world even subtler than I had imagined, where the women one did not want ran away, where only to perceive its contradictions proved one old. Finally I fell asleep, to dream that I nodded by the fire, an old man rich with experience and even more wondrous regrets, listening to the silent, Tanagra voices of all the women I had not had. I left for boot camp the next morning.

Toward evening, on December 20, 1946, a tall young lieutenant junior grade, USN, got off the incoming train from Boston to Grand Central, and followed the crowd pushing its way toward the main Forty-second Street entrance. "Haven't seen it since the blackout," said an army captain just in front of him, craning back to look at the dome. "God, how I love this station." His wife, dragging on his arm, looking only at him, answered softly. "We had a brownout too, for a while." Behind them, the lieutenant glanced up also, though he had passed under the same dome only yesterday morning. The lukewarm radiance shed there had always seemed to him too reflective for what went on below. Architect — Claude Bragdon, student of the Vedanta, spiritualist — but no one remembered that now; why should he? He shifted the one piece of luggage he carried, a large cardboard suit box, struck by the consideration that, although he had been "home" here six months, this was his first real return to thought civilian-style. He was not yet separated enough to find anything peculiar in the fact that in order to get processed out, a man stationed at that naval hub, "90 Church," had had to go to Boston. Many had had to go farther.

Hailing a cab was useless. Car lights jostled him, tambourines begged, a searchlight played the chiming heavens, a multicolored rain dampened the city. It was the hour of assignation, and all Christmas was in New York. He boarded a Lexington bus, and for some thirty blocks studied the box — J. Press, Tailor — containing what he could have bought any time these six months, any time. When the bus reached the high Seventies, he got out and walked a block north, a block and a half over, to his own flat, rented on long term by a lucky break through the office, in the first few weeks back. Not many of the horde of his brothers, like him once more at the beginning, could claim his luck — no job as of now, but fourteen thousand and more in the bank, plus a flat worth hanging on to, and no ties. No ties, but an assignation of sorts, with someone he had not seen for a long time. In front of his house, a brownstone, he looked up at his own top floor. A light was burning there. He'd left one for the man he was to meet there, a sentiment surely permissible on this night. Turning, he glanced at the house opposite, no one he knew there, but its façade always pleased him, as much a part of his own flat as the silly sofa, left by the war widow who had preceded him, that never failed to cheer him of a morning. If he'd delayed buying what he now held in the box, he had not failed the man waiting there in the matter of books. A thousand or more, bought but not read, attended him.

The light from above shone down on his upturned face, on his flat hat with its rain protector, on his braid, on his blue. Despite the books and the sofa, he was not smiling. Up the stoop he went, key in hand. At the letter slots inside, he paused for a minute, on his face an obscure expression, then pushed the buzzer for a long, long ring. Nothing whatsoever answered him. But suddenly he nodded gravely, as if someone had. His own key opened the inner door. Swinging his package, he disappeared behind the door, and was never seen again.

An hour or so later, shaved and changed, drink in hand, he stood in front of the long mirror left behind by the widow, and regarded the man there. "J. Press" had sold him a brown herringbone and an Oxford gray "for more formal occasions"; since this was certainly that, he was wearing the gray. Behind him, on top of a trunk exhumed from Lasch's basement, containing among other things the clothes that, twenty pounds heavier, six years older, he would never wear again, lay uniform, flat hat, skivvies, like still another skin he had sloughed. From time to time he circled the booklined shelves, touching a book here and there, never taking one down. Though he had never been much of a one for mirrors, he kept returning to this one. Come time for the second drink, a third, he was still doing so. But since he'd always had a good head for liquor, his mind remained quite clear for his self-set task of remembering — as clear as mine is now, he, I and his image, in our hall of mirrors, all regarding each other. We speak. First I:

Going to war, then, had been my first great device for handling the world's confusion, none the less successful because the idea wasn't wholly mine. I found that out my second day at Great Lakes. One man, solitary in his first grown-up leggings, is Quixote, subject to all the sore trials of broken running; six hundred of the same, standing on a plain — even an asphalt one near Chicago — are St. George. Giving up autonomy is the great prize. Something for everybody in a war, man or woman, and this is what it is. War is noble, being the only mass imitation we have of nobility for its own sake, for which even Christ, if he died for *us,* had no courage. Everyone I knew in the war emerged from it with something, their arms clasped round their deaths, their wounds, their books, the little gas station on disability pay in New Jersey, their livers and religions, their wives. Everybody bore away a piece of the prize. War, for the duration, took the place of providence, and nobody could be blamed. From late 1940 until 1946, then, I was a member of that enclosure, and wearing that best of stripes, I was almost invisible, like the rest. If any Great Confidant, leaning down from his cloud, had suddenly said *"Tell me!"* I could have answered at once, without an ounce of self-recrimination: "Leading a normal life, sir, the normal life of our times. Nothing personal to confess." This was my reward, as it was for my *semblable,* the man next to me. For six years, barring minor details, he and I had the same, single story and knew it. Rocked in that cradle together, we saw the world.

My details being lucky ones, I pay them the bare grace of recording them. They kept me alive. For I still see life as the privilege; this is no suicide's memoir. And I saw no suicides in the service — not enough distinction in it at the time. Life was the distinction — if we had a private romance, public love, it was that. My "details," not always pleasant, required no extraordinary valor. Interest, always my good friend, carried me through them. They follow — from him:

"Out of Great Lakes, I was sent to San Diego as a yeoman striker, serving as clerk to a former bookkeeper, from whom I learned the fine art of posting — in a ledger, not on a horse. There's no telling how high I might have risen as a noncom if I hadn't been suddenly transferred to the navy yard outside San Francisco, to a reception unit for civilian specialists arriving in the first van of ordnance expansion. (We were at war now, the afternoon of December 7, 1941, having caught me, sometime back, on weekend leave, in a bookshop open for Sunday trade in North Beach.) Far as I know, I owe the turn in my affairs to one of these — and Debussy. Chafee his name was; remember that name. Mr. Chafee, chief engineer of an important company in Detroit, not yet in uniform himself or able to distinguish rank below commander, lolled in his chair of a morning as if we still lived in a democracy, reminiscing at large, fresh from his boardinghouse limbo, of the family breakfast table in Palmer Woods. The yard wasn't up to his specifications either; some time-study man had installed a loudspeaker which boomed recorded music, frequently classical, from a tower above the clangor. 'Good God in heaven,' he said one morning. 'It is, isn't it? *La* whadyacall — my daughter plays it.' A few desks down, I hadn't been able to keep from laughing. He caught me at it, in the midst of the stiff office. 'Yes, sir,' I said. 'It is. It's *La Mer.*' He had a son just my age — army, as he himself expected to be. During several dinners at his expense at the Fairmont, he told me what it was like to be at sea, he having just spent eight days on a destroyer, installing the mounts for a delicate bit of business that I might as well know was a thing called radar. Steak every day in the officers' mess. In return, I gave him what confidential information was to be got from where I stood, including the tip that the insignia he was shortly to wear was known among some of the military as 'the whirling douche.' Weeks after he had gone, I was tapped for officer training, and I accepted. From then on, any Gilbertian tinge in my affairs declined — except for one last touch of it. Duly braced, commissioned, seaworthy, I was launched — back to Chicago, to a place called Tower Hall.

"Contrary to general belief, all intelligence officers don't spend their time decoding messages, lurking in mufti at the cheaper waterfront hotels in hope of same. As frequently with me, however, certain lesser talents had been immediately discoverable — in this case a familiarity with the simpler forms of cryptogram and acrostic, a fondness for the mathematics of words. Tower Hall was an oddly dull depot over whose inertia and lack of starch a snooping Congressman would at once have raised an outcry — floor after floor of warehoused salvage, at each silent freight elevator a stalwart seaman wasting his time on guard duty. Two of these floors were sealed with iron plates fore and aft, concealing, the guards agreed, several tons of roller skates, back of which the officers locked themselves in to drink Haig & Haig. At the end of seven months there I finally was sent to sea. During my weeks on the transport, I sometimes tried to invoke the memory of a boy sailing with his mother from Portsmouth to Montreal. I never succeeded. By the time I took up my orders, on a 'supply' ship cruising in various Pacific waters, I had given it up.

"Such a ship as ours, under instructions to avoid action where possible, couldn't always succeed at that either. From time to time we 'saw' it. Who can believe, until he sees it, the shattered liquids, Rorschach shapes a head can make, on its way to becoming what only the clean, desert voice of Ecclesiastes may call 'dust'? Clearest, I remember — against a burning turret falling sideways slow as a paper hat — the tic that appeared like a sign on the perfect, uninjured cheek of the highest ranking officer left to us — a reserve commander, on board as an optics specialist. Name — Eckerman, worked for Bausch & Lomb, Rochester, New York. We sailed safe into port under his command, the tic remaining. After that, I saw some of the world by air.

"From the air, I learned, things often don't look as they are. Along the coast of Okinawa, rock-creamed at the edge of that cruel jade and purple sea, there lay inlets, according to the major in the seat next to me, with beaches as tender for bathing as Malibu — this was now 1945. If we were allowed off limits, he would show me, along with the queer tumuli in which the Okinawans buried their dead. We were, but I never saw them, hearing, instead, the second we touched the strip, of yesterday in Hiroshima.

"My most informative flight — some months later, early 1946, over Cebu. No, said the pilot, those even green cones weren't volcanic, but there were tricky air currents above them; in fact, his plane was a replacement for that other DC-3 went down here couple of months ago with all those bigwigs; I must be new to these parts, or I'd have heard. Overloaded, couldn't pick up altitude. Pilot a friend of his too, just off the European run where they were used to the real heavy craft, big Swede — he'd been on leave with him in Amsterdam once. These little jobs, safe as houses, but on this run — one extra passenger and some-body'd have to ditch his shoes.

" 'Right about here,' said the pilot 'right about here.' We were low enough to see the fuzzed trees. He'd known most of the passengers too, flown some of those generals all over Southeast Asia. He named several, among them one named Dobbin. Yes, he was sure. I asked for the first name. The pilot didn't know that, but he knew the record. In for the war-trials deal, he thought, like the others, but not one of those state-side judge advocates, been through it all the way, starting out, the papers said, with that Quaker outfit even before we got in. And then to get it, after all that, when everything's over. In a little 'Three' too, the safest thing up. Here — he even thought he'd saved the paper, left by a guy just in to Manila from home — but he hadn't. Name of pilot, Herbert C. Tenney, Minneapolis. I asked him if he knew what rank Dobbin had died with. 'Brigadier,' he said, feeling his own shoul-der. 'Yep, I'm pretty sure of it, brigadier.' I don't know why I remem-ber the 'C.'

"So I was alone then, both in that hemisphere and the other, to which I would shortly be returned — 'out.' But the law seemed to wish to hang on to me. *I'm due out*, Eckerman wrote. *At my age they can't really hold me if I squawk. But they're putting the pressure on. Discovered I once had a patents practice, and they have a mess of them to untangle. Means six to eight months more, but at least it's in New York, where you could be looking around.* So I joined him as aide, in that nest of sea lawyers known as '90 Church, New York.' "

He set down his glass next to the bottle and did not take it up again. Properly, he should smash the glass, having made his toast, so to speak, but that too required the audience which after six years he must learn again to do without. Already, like a man feeling his way along newly erected fence posts in the first dark afterward, he was recalling the margins that had to be set for solitariness, if one were prepared to be alone from now on. As it was, he couldn't be sure that he hadn't spoken aloud now and then, in the deadpan Choctaw that was good form for telling such experiences. But even in the telling, these had taken on the faint gilding which meant that they were sealed. And from now on, he would be his own audience. The rest was private, from now on.

He stood up, unaware how long he had been sitting in the room's one easy chair. The absurd sofa, plumped up like the lap of a three-legged woman, he never sat in, reserving it in his mind for such feminine visitors as in the future might fancy themselves Récamiers there from time to time. Meanwhile, his few personal articles, ranged in the familiar two-by-two, were herded together in one corner, as if a sudden sway in the bowels of the old house might dislodge them. *Demuth* he thought, seeing the shoe by the shoe, that paired bachelordom, as for years now in a totally masculine society he had not stopped to see it — Demuth. Except for such minor sparks, he never thought now of that landscape down there — it too was sealed. And the city too, comfortable old sword-swallower of lives, had long since disposed of his former life here. On its streets, shaken like kaleidoscopes even as one trod them, he now felt as anonymous as anyone. Or, in his new clothes, soon would.

Taking down a book at random, he clapped it closed and put it back again, not yet settled enough for that. Most nights, they had worked late on Church Street, burning up their weekends together in restaurants, theaters and bars, speaking loudly when drunk of their yearning for home and family, hiding from each other and themselves, when drunker, their reluctance to return. Treating this place like a hotel room, he had done the same. Soon he would furnish it, hire a cleaning woman, buy a big desk for that corner, get a job, make all the moves. Outside now, it was still raining, colors shimmered into it from all sides, a prettily Yuletide rain. Six years later, it was the season that made him feel like a new graduate, standing, his themes all tangled, on the brink of confusion, ready to move at once, as was expected of him, as he expected of himself — just as soon as told where. It was the season, together with the end of war, an earned sense that all dragons were done with. They had all had the same one — one head it has, one neck, " 'Ware!" and in a single "Pouf!" dreadful as that was — it was done with. Six hundred men — he knew that now — were St. George. Now there was only that village dragon, spice o' the world, death in time.

Behind him, in the dusty trunk, there was a raincoat which would do for wherever he might be going — how could he know where, in a world once more of such scope that, going out for a constitutional, one might find oneself Alexander? It had been years since he had even thought of that private word "themes," his word, he supposed, for that deep, voiceless knowledge he refused to think we were not born with — which could not set us right but only let us know when we went wrong — an invincible ache that could once in a while be touched, for the sore comfort it was, with the timid tongue. On top of the raincoat, he came upon a fedora bought his first summer here, put aside with a blush the first day he'd walked into college. He placed it on his head and found that it still fitted; somewhere he had read that the head and eyes gain full growth out of all proportion early, the reason why in children these often looked so large. His head had not much grown, then, since the first innocences rattled there. In the mirror, he saw that the hat looked ugly on him, but no longer gauche. Giving it a grimace, he reminded himself that the man he expected to see would not reveal himself altogether, so soon. I still want to live, that's all I know, he told the mirror. Turning away, he told himself. I still want to live, he said to himself, and clung to this as if it were holy. An image returned to him, of the small boy he had seen through the door of the enlistment office, crossing the marble floor, carrying his stamps.

An hour or so later, he was still in the chair, hat on head, raincoat in the crook of his arm, telephone book on his knees. Canny rememberer that he was, he would never be able to recall the moment at which he had taken up that book and sat down. We are, at any given moment of our lives, all we are. The problem is how to take stock — with every aside, tangent, kernel duly present and accounted for, for *that* moment — of all we are. In that one blank moment, he had made a journey longer than any from Portsmouth to Montreal.

A minute before it, on his way to the door, he'd been stopped in his tracks by the thought that he ought to call Eckerman — *Eckerman,* who had gone to Los Angeles to be debriefed three days before he himself had left for Boston, who was even now in his plane seat over the central plains on his way home to Rochester, if he wasn't already home. Who, coffee-beer intimate that he had been, tic intimate, up to three days ago, had already been as far from him, when they all said good-by, as next year's Christmas card, farther than any telephone could ever reach. If pressed, each of the men there might have admitted that military life only exaggerated the droppings-off that in peacetime were made every day less openly — else how get through life with such a roster, a telephone book of every hand once clasped, girl slept with, all the names once known? Was that what he was after, with Eckerman? Else, how get through?

A minute after, he was there with the telephone book, fresh and unthumbed, in the chair. First, as was natural, he looked up people like Lovey, who was no longer in it, Serlin, who was — but with no thought of calling, merely for eternal gossip's sake. He knew them already; as was perhaps more guiltily pertinent, they knew him. Second, as was natural also, he riffled through the book's pages, as one idly will. A name caught his eye in the "A's" — Aiello. At once, a picture was presented to his mind, an entire story. "My mother won't send me a snap," Seaman D. Aiello, Jr., had said. "She's sick with the eyes, it ain't fatal. But it makes the eyes lay way out, on the cheek. So she wouldn't give me a snap. But here's everybody else." Here had been everybody else, the family ramifying before him in the bar-restaurant, the tenement house owned, the girl, a little tale of Sicily at the Brooklyn Bridge end of town. There was a column of them in the book, beginning with the father, Dominic, all the uncles and cousins. No Dominic junior, dead of scarlet fever in Chicago. There, at the tip of the bridge, a whole fief and its stories, known to him, did not even know he existed. It was the gothic image of the woman who would not send her son a "snap" that had made him always remember. Musing, he passed on to the "B's," no such fief there. Then, suddenly, not from his navy life but from college — Belden. John Charles Belden, whom he had never seen, never met (except in the story spiraled up from the chair next his in the two o'clock dark of the frat house lounge), about whom he knew so much more than would appear to be safe for J. C. Belden, Major, U.S.A. ret., First World War, member Sons of the American Revolution and the Society of the Forty-eight, on all evenings, for all meetings except those on Thursdays in the rear of his bookshop, owner of a taste for applejack that spanned both. "Applejack Belden," Amos Gillette had said, from the chair beside his. "Alias, of course, 'Chad.' They thrive on aliases." He heard Amos's voice again, Virginia slow, his short, pained laugh, "Even Anzia has one, pore girl. It's 'Betty,'" and his final whisper —"Damned spider." Amos had married his pore girl, poor stupid little fly caught in such a net, and Norfolk money had presumably made her safe from aliases forever. "Amos and Anzia — so pretty," the relatives had said. He had attended the wedding. For curiosity's sake, he looked up both their names separately, but of course they weren't in it, long since out of any acrostic that might interest him. Not so Belden. He could imagine him, if he still had his bookshop, a curdled soldier-scholar in a green eyeshade. The name wasn't there, unlisted of course, but the shop was, such a jaunty spur to memory: Unity Book Shop, University Place.

Jaunty was the word; he'd forgotten the prankishness of a mind left to its solitude. Before the hour was out, he had found several more small clusters, minor worlds one could enter without warning, for a penn'orth of exertion, if one would. For a penny's worth of nothing.

No doubt anyone with a mind to, and an approximate mind, could do the same. The book on his knees was heavy with it. An assemblage of life for the asking. But scarcely anyone in his right mind — and he was sure he was, never holding the pulse of his queerness, like so many nowadays. In the upstairs world he did as well as the next one, nor shivered at what he glimpsed in the down. According to the "quanta" peculiar to this hour and its history — never question the quanta, and you are sane. Accordingly. Meanwhile, there must be many men of such approximate mind. Dobbin, if an old guess had been right, had been one, merely channeling his faculty elsewhere. And his uncle, the unrecognized — what he had done. Do not think of it; do not question. So many words beginning with *q*. Scarcely anyone. So many words beginning with *a*.

Heavy, heavy lay the book, the acrostic. The adventures of anonym. So many names beginning with *A*. He was asleep, could feel himself asleep and unable to rise, the hat still on his head, the crushed raincoat on his arm. He did not rise to greet any newcomer. For a while, even when awake, he would not see him. The man he had come to meet was there.

The rest *was* private — for fifteen years. How to tell the secret of those years? It seems to me that I must already have done that, almost plain. Or am I like a conjurer who doesn't want to show his poor rabbit, who says to himself as well, over and over — "See, how magnificent this sleeve"? The page itself answers me.

Suppose us, then, to be reading an imaginary but possible report, say from the files of the Bureau of Missing Persons of the Police Department of the City of New York, from the year 1946. We of course know the identity of the missing man. Like this:

On a date roughly between Christmas of 1946 and the early New Year, the missing man first made his appearance in Pasquale's Bar, 18½ Cherry Street. Bar owned for past twenty years by Dominic Aiello (aged sixty-nine, infirm), who runs it with the help of goddaughter Stella Agostino (aged twenty-four, fiancée of Aiello's dead son, in this country five years). This pair are parties who have requested search. The Aiellos, several branches of whom own small businesses in the Bridge district, are a respectable family, well known in the precinct. Rest of family would like Dominic to sell the bar, which does a poor trade, mostly with local relief recipients for whom the girl cooks in the back. Building worth nothing, but possible value as part of a parcel. Old man feuding with family re this.

Missing man (descr. below) unusual type for district, first taken to be possible purchaser or scout for same, or relief investigator checking habitués. For six months has visited bar three or four times weekly, afternoons and evenings, eating there, etc. Quiet habits, moderate drinker. Gained confidence of Aiellos and regulars as well. Treated like member family, sometimes tended bar. Apparently unemployed, but not in want of funds. Rest of family tried investigate, on gossip man was after girl or old man's savings, but old man would not let their representative, his own nephew (Jimmy Guardini — son Dem. distr. capt. G. Guardini), in door.

Old Aiello and girl interviewed through interpreter this date. Deny any but friendly connection with man; suspect relatives of frightening man off, or foul play.

Descr.: Age about 30, hgt. well over six ft., wgt. (approx.) 185. Coloring: Fair, hair light brown, brows dark, eyes gray-blue. Features median, no distinguishing marks. Might be Irish. Speaks some Italian, acquired in bar. Some education — always read newspaper cover to cover. Good listener. War service unknown — perhaps 4F, since never spoke of same. Clothing: one good suit, which always wore, from old man's descr. — Brown, some kind tweed, herringbone, label not N.Y. Answered name "Joe."

Period Missing: Six weeks. No communication.

Interested Parties: As above.

Note: To Detective Nicolo Motta.

Nick, no need to run your hide off on this. Checked Guardini, Sr., who says old man been a little off ever since only son died while in service — won't believe dead, etc. Girl brought over to marry son, not very bright, does whatever old man says. As far as the G.'s can tell, savings and girl both O.K., think man some casual, ideas all probably in old man's head.

Report: (30 Days) — No inf. received. Two calls by original parties.

(60 Days) — As above. One call.

(90 Days) — As above. No calls. Case closed.

Or, suppose us to be reading, as in mystery stories of a certain kind, the handwritten notes of the amateur inquirer (himself not without mystery), in which the quarry appears as a shadow behind the recording shadow, and only the reader sees all. Like this:

From the personal notes of J. C. Belden:

He addressed me as "Chad," and let drop the word "applejack." This in itself means nothing, being only what we allow open members, who think they meet here so importantly, to know. Outer contacts must be left open somewhere; he might have got those almost anywhere on Union Square. But it suggests that he has been out of touch — if he has ever been in — for some time, since that word has been out of use here since 1940. Or else that he wished to give that impression? I asked if he had a card of introduction perhaps; his answer: "I carry no card." Meaning, on the simplest level, that he wasn't *yet*? Or that he had long since passed the level where one needed — to the highest? Which would explain the use of old key word. Age — not much past thirty; I judge him one of those who intangibly present themselves as older than they are. Appearance — if it conceals — superb. Eyes as frank as a golfer's, or one of those new-style rookies the police college always sends to check on us, in their off-duty Ivy League gray, which is what he wore. I led him straight for what I call my "duck blind" — the shelves of "progressive literature," Marx, Engels, pamphlets displayed to show them that we are only what they are convinced we are. He went past them, nothing to be deduced from that, that first time. Left without undue haste — but markedly? — when an ordinary customer came in. Himself — an ordinary pleasant young man, to the life. Not even too much to the life. On the simplest level, then, for all but old dogs, wise fools. Except for the one thing which, when sniffed, puts everything else wrong. I smelled the intelligence there, underneath.

The second time, we began with the usual literary discussion — he might have been any customer eager to show himself a bibliophile. The stray ones interested in pornography often begin so, clumsily, with De Sade. He wasn't one of those, nor clumsy, and his range, rising alphabetically as we ambled from shelf to shelf — Burke, Hobbes, Ricardo — was large. I complimented him on it. His reply: "I had an unusual education." Accent peculiar, a ragbag. Used as I am, I couldn't place it, or rather, just as I did, it moved on. Now we were standing in front of the duck blind, "Russia — Lit., Pol., Econ." Bazarov, nihilism, revolutions in general were what he spoke of, the stuff with which a contact might wish to show himself a *parti pris*. But then it came, as we passed on to the travel books. A quote from *Arabia Deserta*. Then from the Marquis de Vogüé. None of the ordinary members can lay claim to that particular marquis. I took his real range then, plus the powerful impression that he had already taken mine.

Since then he's come regularly to our Thursdays, making no overtures beyond them. I'm quite sure he finds them as laughable as I do. I am also quite sure he comes for something, and goes away each time to a point satisfied. To a point, whatever that is. One can only go as deep with a man as he has gone with himself, and how far *he* has is what I don't yet know. If I were reporting on him to the others, I should say 'Honest, in respect to *something*. The appearance of a quite different honesty on top. Between the two — a devious middle ground. For us, as temperaments go, the best combination that exists.' But this is my report to myself. I am both worried — and drawn. The highest level, yes, in himself — no worry there if he also belongs to ours. I'm all but sure that he does. But if he does not, but if he does not — then I am still drawn. And that is terrifying to a man like me. To find a man of equal mind, to whom one is tempted to speak *fully*, and to find it not inside our circle, where I never have, but without. Age makes no difference between us. Or rather, I sometimes feel like a father before a son who has inherited his talents. An odd thing occurred after yesterday's meeting, he already gone. His voice still in my ears together with my own, I suddenly placed his accent. The hair rose on my spine. My accent is its own mixture. And his? It was mine — precisely mine.

I shall find some way of remarking on it, next Thursday.

But the next Thursday, I did not come back.

Now is it clear, the mechanism of what I did, and continued to do? Is it clear that the two accounts above, written last night, though imagined by me, concern true events which happened, which were made to happen by the man who moved, in a double way, through them?

And from above, behind, comes the verdict — from the owl on my shoulder, that ex-human pocket-of-outer-space which makes us human: "So. Still trying your somersaults, even in the confession box. You did better when you spoke *ex tenebris*, 'as a child.' No, it is *not* clear. Your business is not to make it so, but to speak. Speak then. And point the pen a degree nearer the skin."

So, here then is the secret as plainly as I can say it. With the Aiellos and Belden, I first began my practice of visiting, from the mists of pre-knowledge, other people's lives. In each little world I remained for a time, trailing my mists but warmed, always in the end moving on. As I grew more practiced, these excursions formalized themselves, developing their own little habits, easements, even a code of manners, all of which I came to recognize. There were times when I merely "visited" as it were for an evening, dipping into some environment that teased me to know it casually, satisfied to stay there like some tourist with a personal introduction he never disclosed, watching the people there in the light of it, never making himself known. For more complicated excursions, where it seemed likely that my stay would be longer, I rehearsed my disguises more thoroughly, sinking myself well in the role beforehand, like an actor with a two-hour make-up to apply. Such wigs and grease paints as I used were of course always "mental"; as I saw how, when skillfully applied, the barest hints furnished me by memory and predilection could turn into life-size effects, I began to appreciate, in the true spectrum of their possibilities, all the delicately japanned pigments of the mind. That range forever widened as I used it. At its farther end (though to be avoided) are illusions which can become as concrete as the whirling atoms which compose a stone; at its nether point are all the thin, common glazes used every day by the least calculating, the least shrewd. My difference — or so I told myself — was only in degree, and in control, for it was my pride, of course, that I never lost sight of my artifices, precisely because they were more conscious than other people's, more formed. By means of them, I should never step into that web where the artifices become the man. These were to be my tricks of leisure, my avocation, my hobby, kept for myself as others kept more displayable connoisseurships, my trick of defense — beneath it all, the self, that naked contemplative, safe in his grove!

And what then was the general "shape" of these excursions? Essentially, all the elements of those in the long list to come were already present in the two episodes tangentially described above. I have a sentimental fondness for the Aiellos as my *first*, and as the simple sensitives they were. With them, I made all the predictable slips of a novice — telling at one time too little, at another too much. Being simple, their peasant clairvoyance at once apprehended a mystery (making of me more of a one than I had intended), and at once, with peasant practicality, set about making use of it. One of my slips had been to drop the name Serafina. This was the name of old Aiello's wife, the mother, now dead, of the young Dominic I had seen die of scarlet fever. Why did I drop it, not quite unconsciously — partly for its charms (such syllables for a woman with gothicked eyes!), partly for its dangers and curiosities (was there a "snap" of her?) and perhaps partly for a godlike wish to give them, by wires scarcely vibrated, a message from their dead boy. The experience taught me never again to give in to such temptations unless better planned. The old man was certainly far from base, out on a promontory of yearning, the girl not dull but fresh from a land of omens and portents, sprites in the milk and saviors in goatherds, herself one of the swart creatures of which her race once made sibyls — together, what did they make of me to themselves? I dared not stop to see, poor, dear, wretched conspirators that they were, fond as I had grown of them — once I'd got wind of it. Was I Dominic reborn to them, blonde as a Milanese? My flight from that seraglio was an ungainly affair, an impostor just not caught in his closet, all flying pantaloons. I did them no harm, I think, and certainly meant none — this too is an essential part of the "form." But the experience taught me to have well in mind beforehand who I "was" or pretended to be.

The episode with Belden, not so laughable, taught me that complex people, hoist in their own ambiguities, are the more eager to be deceived. Although I rarely recall in color, I always see Belden so. (Normally, black, white, and gray are still the tones of that egocentric composition, tones of voice and posture — and words of course, every word.) But Belden, whom I had anticipated as all vellum veined with ink, a crabbed little counterplot of a man, emerges, as he did that first day from the back of his shop, like a 1910 illustration of Richard Coeur de Lion, a large man, heavy-maned, as rich in tints of gold and red as those apples from which were extracted his brandy and his passwords — a lion in a bookshop, attended always by that persistent antinibble of intellect, his mouse. For a person whose business dealt him men, one after the other, like shadows, I never saw anyone less like a shade. The shop was not only a "front," but, by contortions too ridiculous to trace, a double front; above its base of rococo plots brewed for the acolytes who sneaked, *opéra bouffe* style, into that tiny back basilica every Thursday, there might be sensed, dotted in much thinner air, an austere circle of cardinals' hats. It's possible that, had I lingered long enough, I might even have been brought to meet those, for although Belden was cautious, Belden was brilliant, after forty years among his revolutionary shades, he hungered more than anything in life for a man with whom he might have a "personal" talk. I decamped for both reasons. I wanted no more organizations of any kind; the truth should not trump me up to serve it, in any such guise, ever again. And Belden's monstrous, famished mouse was a warning. Even if Belden refused to see a possible resemblance between us, I did not.

These, then, were two typical "devices" from the long chapter of them which was interrupted — in the midst of one not yet terminated — the night I came home to this desk, from Ruth Mannix's side. Over the years, I had kept to my code. As time went on, my accumulating heap of the histories of others began to hump almost as heavy between my shoulder blades as my own — but I never used my knowledge for conscious harm. Whenever, in a place where I might be sojourning, affections were embroiled on either side, I eventually did us both the brief harm of leaving, but it never seemed to me that anything in us was more scotched by this than if left victim to the undirected processes of life. If change was the tragedy, then it was not one I had invented, any more than I had invented death — the only other unity we could all be sure of. As for love in its various forms — sexual, maternal, fraternal (more than one of which my century seemed to think it had invented) — I had experienced them in their transient beauties, but was not the man to forget that they *were* various, not excluding those vaguer religious diffusions that took in everybody. No one kind of love, it seemed to me, had enough unity to stand in triumvirate with those other two great ones.

So I had reached my forties, that halfway climacteric by which time a man is expected to have settled for a brand of reality at least as conclusively as on his cigars. I seemed not to have done so, still naming myself in private, far better than anyone else could, a vicarious man. But I had my rationale for this also. In the early years of my hobby it had shamed me, brought me periods of guilt during which I abstained. Like a drunkard, I always came back to it, knowing my own strength and in the end glorifying it. My talent was to remember, and in my fashion I had not wrapped it away. This at least was my own. In a world that regimented a public personality from me, meanwhile exhaustively researching the private and demanding that I scramble up enough conscience to serve both, I'd "adapted" as Darwin had predicted I would, thereby gaining an intermittent release from a certain soreness for the absolute with which I still strove — and from which I sometimes feared I would die. In a pluralistic world, as they now told me it was, under all heavens and philosophies exploding, the "real," slipping a pinfeather, flew on. But by means of my devices I was managing very nicely thank you on the teeter-totter, able to be both up and down, in and out, with an endless supply of people and at the same time intractably alone. Voyeur indeed! As I sat at breakfast in convocation with the rest of the air-wave-washed world, all of us at our light repast of picpost agony and joy, could I not quite reassure myself that the world had come round to the brand of reality that was mine? And if our mutual systems showed signs of managing us, I could shrug my shoulders in company. Company was the thing. A teeter-totter takes two.

All lies, public lies. So I told myself them on the one hand, and the next minute *told* myself, this being my curse. I needed no diatonic silence to hear that other voice, *chaste et pur: Each man is responsible for his own chronicle.*

So, you may see me, as for fifteen years I sit in my grove, emerging at intervals, my own ambassador to the uncertain real of other people, like those kings who sat in Venice, sending their Marco Polos in search of Chinas, fearsome but rich, that might or might not be there.

But what we do not do persists, classic and perfect, beneath what we do. The final admixture is the judgment. So now, you may watch me there, naked and sore in my cell, on that day when, bearing their disturbing treasure, all the expeditions came back.

Chapter II. The Last Device.

I'VE called her. As soon as I had written the above, yesterday, I did
so. When I finished, it was about six o'clock of a pre-summer Saturday evening, the side streets advancing tawny toward the avenues,
on one of the longest days, which all the afternoon must have been
gilding toward this perfect, light-blent fall. A day out of my gloss, but
in my own way I had not missed it; the secret had been wrenched onto
the page, the surgery almost done. From the open window the blue
breeze invited itself forward, the sounds strung along its duskiness
softened to bangles on a scarf. While I dialed it brushed me, solicitous.
If she was there, she would be just going out.

Anna answered. Yes, Miss Ruth and her father were home — from
London, that is — but they'd gone down to the country for the week-
end. Anna had opened the place for them the week before. Then that
4 A.M. call a few nights ago, which I had not answered, could have
been she.

"You want the number down dere?" Anna's voice was cool, a reminder of how many weekends I had spent there last summer.

"No thanks, Anna, I have it." It felt strange to speak, healthful to
be reproved. I wanted to prolong the sense of her, firm and starched in
her alcove, theirs, behind her the amalgam I knew so well, chairs flow-
ering silent in their covers, German mantel clock swathed, in the li-

brary the audience of books stiffened primly for the winter concert — the whole old-fashioned sense of a house half closed for the summer, a coffer, mysterious with camphor, which its owners have left ajar. In the shaded library, above the couch, the Chinese horse burned blue-green in his niche, one heavy hoof raised. "Did you — give her my message?"

"Yah. I give it." There was a silence, no invitation to dinner. "Vwah-l," she said, "I go do my packing. Tomorrow I go on holyday." Her "holydays" were always notable, providing sagas for the year, but tonight she would not chat about them. I wished her well. At the last moment she relented. "That Pauli Chavez —" she said. "He's down dere with them along." Then she suavely wished me good-by and rang off.

I sent no smile after her, though I might have. Anna knew as well as I that Paul Chavez was no rival. One of Ruth's cronies from her dance-world days, he was linked also, through her mother's family, who had been music publishers, with their collection of friends from the music world of Fifty-seventh Street. A long, lean exquisite of a man, silver-haired and mustached at only a little past forty, he often put me in mind of his namesake in *Fathers and Sons*, Arcadi's uncle, Pavel, "any of whose nails could have been sent to the Exhibition." Somewhere Chavez kept a small, gouty-voiced Frenchwoman, frog-shaped as retired ballerinas often are, who either would not or could not marry him, and this fact, together with sympathies as delicately articulated as his ankles, gave him the almond-eyed quiet, the sad, silvered aspect of the perfect friend. His was a company ideal for the times in a woman's life when there were no rivals, or he would be the comfort, special but still male, to which she might bring her troubles with another man. As for letters abroad, I thought, some never reached their destinations — I knew of one. Others might reach too many. Is he there with her, hanging over mine, now? I think not. Nor is it Pauli Chavez I fear.

Is. These last days, I seem to be rushing toward the present, head-long.

Late last night, I came up here to Lasch's. No one calls it that any more except old hands like me; it is a foundation now, *in memoriam* Albert Bernhard Chester Lasch — the initials were real. It is also the office of which I am head. He'd been right, in a way; I didn't know that I had lost by coming in. After the war I had tried several things which, by dint of some stretching on my part, I had suited quite well, but had not suited me. Lasch had been after me to return ever since the day I had gone up there, still in uniform, for my trunk. "You belong here," he said solemnly, over the drink we had that day in his office, in front of a coal fire like an English grate, in the smell of cut leather, book paste, the tonic rustle of paper everywhere. "You're not built to serve just anything. I suppose you have to bat around some first; that's it." In the moldy December light, his cheek not as round as once, his upper lip long, he might have been my grandfather taking the liberty of lecturing one of his subalterns, and indeed I felt the deference toward him that one never loses for those with their *fanum,* their standard to serve. This was the very reason why I could not explain my refusal — because his temple seemed to me the epitome of those "side lines" I must stay away from, the very haunt and realm of the *embusqué.*

"You have the talent for it," he said again on the day several years later when, no longer so youthfully sure of where the front lines were, or even enamored of them, I returned. "You suit."

"How's that, sir?" I really wanted to know, and I knew he did not mean mere pliancy with paper and pen.

He put the tips of his fingers, slightly wasted and tremoring now together. "You see the cycle," he said, looking at them, but would not go further, dryly turning to talk of salary, of the place's vast expansion, for which the estate had grown too small. I had attributed the tremor of his hands to age. Not much later I knew better. He had been looking for an heir. During his year and a half in the sanitarium where he retreated with the disease that at the last allowed him to move only the eyes, I saw him almost daily. I do not think of doctors as heroes, as this age does, but rather of those of their unsung charges who round the clock make the least of their dying, and the most. Lasch made the happy end that we are taught all heroes make. He had been a boy from an outlying farm; for him, all his aromatic distances had been achieved. He bequeathed his "place" to me. It was not his fault that this is not a thing which one man can leave to another.

In my own way, though never with his single-mindedness, I filled the job. The war had given enormous impetus to all printed matter, and ours was the kind of matter which held, even for the peace. In supplement to conventional volumes of reference, we now engaged with the future and even compounded it, amassing compendia for sciences still in process, for languages whose full mode waited to be used by those still unborn. Although I was still in my early thirties when I took over, trained men were still scarce, and my appointment was readily ratified by a board of directors, of whom, I found to my surprise, Delphine, also come into her inheritance, made one. Apparently she had voted for me, whether a beneficent "pro" or merely an averted one, I never knew for sure, taking it as more likely to be some deep, ultrafeminine concoction of both. She and Schott live mostly in Europe now, or when in America on the high Alps of the very rich, where, except for that one dinner party, I have never again met them. Meanwhile, like any member of those spheres which revolve vaguely around print, I go to a great many parties myself, my name, in its professional capacity, often appearing modishly engraved on more serious rosters as well. On the surface, then, I wear as much chain mail as anybody. For, far from being on the side lines, our excellent organization, in the glory-jargon of the era, deals with the "frontiers" as their very aide-de-camp, and to the tune of a profit (in wordage *and* money) plural beyond Lasch's dreams. It was not his fault if, with all this variorum at my back, I still favored the deep mystery of the one over the many, and by my poor devices kept lookout on my own. This has been my life, then, almost up to the present.

It was almost dawn when I drove in here. I watched that neglected spectacle, the gradual creation of the universe, then fell asleep here on the couch in front of the dead grate. No one lives here now and it is Sunday-quiet. We keep this building mainly for library purposes now; the main offices are in New York. Ten years ago we bought for "protection" an adjoining tract eighty years ago planted over with pines by a merchant overlord and entailed to his heirs forever as the ultimate luxury to come — uninhabited land. We are his heirs now, and those trees of his are "organizational" trees — almost again, as in the infancy of the earth, belonging to no particular man. I came up here partly to see them, for my bit of "the country" too. Here on this side the grounds show the fresh black humus, clever absence of gardeners, of the impersonal public preserve, but beyond it, at its civilized edge, those trees, rising vast and unpruned, the harsh blue behind them not Cézanne's or any mortal's, have a look of the old terrestrial realm, of that childhood of the earth to which we can no more return than we can to our own. Each of us, unable to shake the flame of consciousness from his head, maintains a green guilt for that green world. We can no more be natural there now than a man can stretch out in a cradle. Perhaps we must no longer try.

On a clear day like this, one can see New York from here, a long gray skyline, bubbled and squared. It seems to me that I can almost see myself there somewhere in its flat center, my old *Doppelgänger*, still working away as he has been these past weeks. I came up here partly too to get away from him. Up here, the present burning quietly in my nostrils, I have never felt more alive. About an hour ago, I reached Ruth, down there with her piece of nature, the sea. They'd been out sailing; she'd just come in. There were people in the room from which she was speaking — perhaps better so, because of all the time that had lapsed between us. Yet even in our few words there was a pressure between us, like that of kind hands gently dooming us toward each other. She will meet me at the flat the day after tomorrow. Will I give her this? She has never been there. It seems to me that when I see her there, then I shall know. Before then, I must affix *her* in the narrative, in her proper place: —

It has not escaped me that, intending all these years, perhaps hoping all along, to give my story to someone, at the breaking point I reached out for her only as the nearest to hand — and in the last defeat of subtlety made her the bogey that required it. One is taught — by its enemies, the hearty boys who never look behind — always to suspect the memoir. Or do I believe, by the Athanasian creed of memory, that however the choice is made one does choose? Out of the tangled scents of my beginnings, haply I think on thee?

Beginnings are not endings. If standing there with her, holding this account in my hand — to be withheld or given — I could arrive at that moment sure for once that I knew *everything* — ?

Herewith, the account of my last device:

With my "entry" into the Mannix household, there came a difference in the scheme, a change in quality of which, like a man alerted to a new thrumming in a motor, I was partially aware. For some time my excursions had been of the mildest, even approaching the shallow level of those social lies, pretenses, charms and cabals aimed at one another now and then by all but the most ingenuous — for a lark, for a "lift" or a climb — for a change. One might have thought my habit almost ready to disappear, or at least merge with the general. I knew otherwise, by the degree of premeditation I still bent on the milieu to be studied, and by the familiar intensity of feeling when I rose there from some spot in its center, like a genie who, pretending to be ordinary, gave nothing — and gave nothing away. Mostly the people I chose to enter upon were still ordinary enough, though less and less often those known to me in my private Morse as "the people down there." It was complication that I craved now, and the warmth once so admired from the window frame, seen now from the intellectual distance, no longer satisfied. I still did no tangible harm to anyone. The alien's drum sounds from farther below. My connection with them — I see it now — was rather the harm I withheld. But I never thought now of Tuscana. I had reached that point of safety where my only emotions were my tastes. So it was. With the Mannixes, I approached my own kind.

Certainly the accident which made me choose them wasn't portentous. About twice a year, until his departure for South Africa, I used to spend an evening with one of our staff, a man of considerable education gone to no seed, whose elaborate after-dinner talk (his term for it "postprandial") had, for the limits of an evening, the attractive bitterness of the disappointed. In my trade I'd known many nonwriting "writers," but Norman Schreiber was the only one who, selecting his nom de plume while still in college, had hung on to it as the "first step" ever since, taking it out from cotton wool on occasion to examine its mint shine. He'd a store of wild, full-blown anecdotes also, each told according to an ancient convention, studded with names and dates, as if it had happened to him, most of them with a fancy pornography that belonged more to literature than life. Since I could never quite recognize their sources, I concluded that Norm was his own fantasist, and it sometimes amused me to think of us together. Despite the heavy circumstantiality of his stories, it had never occurred to me to follow any of them up, until the day, about eighteen months ago, shortly after his arrival in the Union. Gaby & Cohn, Ltd., he wrote, the relatives he had gone out to see on his own, hoping to charm them into taking him into the business, had turned out to be not diamond merchants but tailors. This was not unreasonable, since, with his usual bravura, taking their letterhead on assumption, he had not asked. He would be returning shortly. *Meanwhile,* he wrote, *would you do me a favor? Take a hundred bucks from the pay I have coming and send it to Carleen Jones. She won't be in the book but the madame is, Pontina Sims, a Seventh Avenue address and I don't seem to have it. There's not likely to be more than one as you'll agree, knowing the story. I sort of promised it to little C.* It didn't wholly surprise me that some of Norm's exploits had their poor, faded antecedents in actuality, but of the lot I should never have taken this as the likely one — one of his most far-fetched, containing several classic gambits of sexual adventure — nudes in fur coats on windy street corners, the very young and phthisic, the very grateful prostitute — and over all, like a whiff of anisette from the corner liquor store, a distinct flavor of *The Girl with the Golden Eyes.* The address was in the book well enough, on Sugar Hill in Harlem. Half annoyed with Norm's pretensions — he'd signed the letter with his nom de plume — I checked up on him one afternoon.

The house, its octoroon magnificence just as described, was no great surprise either; such places as I've seen seem to me already to have one foot in bookshop erotica. I was more astounded to find that the embellishments I'd marked down as Norm's were real also, including not only Madame Pontina's staidly excellent collection of paintings and the very circumstantial sister who was a buyer at Macy's, but even the girl, the little tan Mimi herself, out of a One Hundred Thirty-fifth Street *Bohème.* Not until I was back home, about to send off the note she'd given me for him, did the full significance strike me, coming to me over all the seas between us like his breath, choked now with mocking laughter, which had always seemed to me faintly carious with lies. It was all true then — one of his wildest. Then all the stories which, supercilious confidant, I had listened to, might well be. Even poor Norm. Even Norm's excursions were real. The only phoniness about him might be the one thing which still linked us as brothers — that name. A sense, not of sadness, but of the nadir, whelmed me as I looked down at it. "Walter Diabolus." It had always tickled me, this mildly collegiate satyriasis appended, most probably from what I knew of Norm, to the mild tinkler, Walter Pater. Walter was a common enough name still, of course, but in all my wanderings I had only known one. I'd not thought of him for some time, a man whose confidences I had always kept honorably apart from my eccentricities, for reasons which I had not cared to phrase. Standing there in my cell, I re-created all that Walter had told me. I remember how I suddenly spoke aloud — the old paneling giving the warning back to me. "No!" This was how the accident occurred. Not many hours later I was already at my researches, to the strumming, from a deeper register, that said "Yes."

If a physical deformity doesn't sour or sharpen a man, the excess sometimes goes the other way, giving him a goodness, choired by all his friends as "not of this world," which, when it is truly unaffected as it was with Walter Stern, makes him one of the rare seraphs they can bear to tolerate "in it." In 1954, when he and I were among half a dozen patients who took their daily sunning on a porch off the orthopedic wing of Lenox Hill Hospital, it was Walter, then awaiting the operation which would at best lessen the pain he lived with, at worst bring the death it did to his fraily caged heart, who would stand, most attentive of any of us, listening to some disc case tell about his "spasm," his own wastedly aquiline hunchback's face hung like a plaque between his shoulder blades, at the angle of a crow's. Mornings he would go down to the brace shop, chatting with the children there like someone their own size out of Oz, and after my ski-twisted leg had been set in traction, he was forever hopping in and out of the room we shared, busy with the small attentions a man still ambulatory could bring the immobilized. His sympathy was chronic; it was the palely shining aura of his disease. I should have realized that it was somehow involved even with his feeling for David Mannix, had I not been so reverently intent, during our night-light exchanges — and for once with no thought of storing any of this away — on Walter himself. I knew my privilege. I was listening to that goodness which speaks gratuitously, as it can only, to one's own.

Characteristically, it was "Diddy's" goodness of which he was forever speaking, and of course the Mannixes'. In the *Letters of David Mannix* which he was publishing at his own expense, and from which he read to me up to his last preoperative hours, I was never able to find anything more than the tentative, even jejune observations of an amiable, well-placed young man, hearing rather, in the deep intonations of that outsize voice coming unbelievably from the chest scarcely cramping the covers in the bed opposite, only a hunchback's idolization of the ordinary, of the better-favored brother. When I was shown their picture at nineteen, it was not the tall, well-muscled young Harvard boy in bathing trunks, holding his oar, whose slackly good-natured face I lingered on, but Walter, fully dressed, beside him, his eyes already as ringed as they were now, above the specially made suit whose peculiarly vamped vest gave him the look of a goldsmith's apprentice. Walter, though the same age, had gone ahead to Harvard, later acting as doyen and, I suspected, concealed tutor to the boy who had so much else to do besides study and had not even finished, instead edged out imperceptibly into the pleasantly guarded paths open to a young man of his status, of his father's status, into various imprecise capacities of a social welfare order which had terminated in his service with the Friends, ultimately in the death by air crash which, though now so ordinary, remained the most precise thing about him. "I doubt if I'd've dared go to college," said Walter, "if the Mannixes hadn't prodded me, on the excuse that it would mean so much to David. All the things they did for me, and always with that same excuse. And all the things they didn't know they did. Life in that house always seemed to go on in a special way I couldn't define, warmer, sad only for the rest of the world to have to define. When I first went there as a kid, that's what I used to call it to myself, 'the wonderful house.' It seemed to me they had everything, and gave it away daily. When I came, of course, Mrs. Mannix was already ill, though none of us knew — you remember I told you."

Yes, I remembered, all the minutiae he dwelt on so lovingly and more, and I understood his feeling for the Mannixes, walking the corridors of that lavish house better than he knew. When David Mannix had brought him home as a schoolboy, a moneyed boy of much the same background as themselves in everything but fate, his family had already been borne off by catastrophes which had left him, as he must have seemed to the Mannixes, the small, remaining one. I could see how it would have been. He'd become one of those accessory benevolences which all such households have. No doubt, being Walter, he had been its dearest one, but I still knew the flavor of that relationship, fancying sometimes, as he rambled on in the long night watches, that I even knew the house itself in all its savors and modes. The Mannixes, he told me, were German Jews like himself, the name probably Anglicized during the stay of the Judge's father's generation in England, but David had been proudest of his mother's Sephardic ancestry; she had been a Mendès. Walter's voice came through the darkness, amused, and I wondered if he knew how little now, after the first, he spoke of David, how much the letters project was his tribute to them all. "Pereira," I muttered from my bed in answer, and heard him sit up. "That's a branch. You know them?" I was quick to reply. "Damn these wires, would you press the button? Nope, just my penny-in-the-slot mind." That night, the eve of his operation, he talked until the nurse came with his sedatives, and in the morning, until they drugged him again, I kept him in the same strain, so that he might carry them with him even up to the ether's cone. Ruth and her father were abroad for the latter's health, he had told me, and knew nothing of this. Except as a *Backfisch*, Ruth scarcely figured in reminiscences which, that night particularly, were all of the earlier time in that house where the four of them had had everything, where he had been a fifth to such a family as had never existed anywhere else on earth. I pretended with him, always, that there had not.

After he'd gone up, I resolved, staring at my swathed foot all the long hours of that morning, that if he did not come down, anything I knew of them should die with him. For more than five years I kept it — my tribute to him. But a year ago, when at last I walked up the steps and inside his wonderful house, I saw how well I had remembered — and how much I'd forgotten. A New York brownstone is nothing like a house in London which must have been twice as wide, and this one, freshly smartened even in Walter's time, has no trace of Edwardian murkiness, ugly shagreens, is nothing like. I remember only what Walter had, I told myself in the anteroom, looking up at the landing. There was no Knight of Malta in botched glass at the top of the stair. Glancing into a drawing room presided over in the old style by its tribal host of photographs, I remembered *for* Walter, in his boarding-school cubicle, this Phoenician love of the object, this sense in them, scattered everywhere, of the affections preserved. Perhaps, I told myself, as Christian to his Jew, once poor boy to his rich, I recognize even more keenly this racial aura of an Orientalia practicably restrained, this kitchen-palace odor of comfort — this balm. I came here to meet the Judge, I reminded myself — Mr. Goodman will have his little brush with the law. And this is his household, that has never existed elsewhere, which Walter, who will never be mentioned between us, so aptly described. Anna came toward me to take me into him, not Molly. But as I moved away from the banister, my hand, passing over its smoothness, sought for a newel post, shaped like a pineapple, which might once have been there.

Consider the Judge. Consider him as, late of an afternoon, he sits there in his house, ready to receive me, looking the very part under the twinned spotlights of his green tôle-shaded student lamp, his daughter beside him or under the lamp that is "hers," behind them both a good, comfortable century, at the very least, of such arrangements. Between them are the remnants of the day's correspondence, the only disorder; over there is what appears to be a Francophile corner, and everywhere, everywhere as expected, the bibliotheca of a family with nothing to hide. He is awaiting a man known to him through their brief correspondence and by name, of course, who is very kindly bringing the galley proofs of the Judge's article for their encyclopedia, taking the opportunity thereby of meeting the Judge — as who would not? — and awarded it the more readily because of the man's faint linkage, an acquaintanceship just barely pressed, with the Judge's dead son. The kindness, as both are aware, is the Judge's. He understands the duties of the admired, the obligations of the bereaved, and is generous in the performance of both. When the doorbell rings, Anna, at his direction, is just carrying out a bowl of flowers which seem to her still fresh, as she loudly says, but flowers are not allowed to grow mephitic in this house. She has the bowl in her hand when she admits the stranger. Consider him too, though you know him better. The perfect unknown, he enters the house of the perfectly known. Consider them both, and take nothing for granted. (How could I have not seen this — little as Ruth had the chance to say today — until now?) Take nothing for granted on *either* side.

Anna, who does not know that I already know her by name, lets me in. The family expletive, her "my hosh," having been even Walter's, will surely have been David's also, but I shall go slowly. Give the genie time to grow; he is just barely inside. I have decided that I knew David just well enough to call him Diddy as most did, no better.

The stage is set, though it seem to be improvised. Judge Simon Mannix sees me enter, a man of forty-odd, young to his (as stated in this year's issue of *Current Biography*) seventy-one, somewhat fair to his iron-gray, a dispatch case in hand. His own eyes are notably keen, but as a personage, he takes for granted, no doubt, that the young man already knows more about his life than he may ever care to know about the young man. In the full *empressement* of this, he extends his hand.

"You'll excuse my not rising." Most have the impression that since the illness of '53 he has lost the use of his legs entirely, but I know, hearing Walter's tender retrospect, what even few friends do, that the chair to which Ruth, Anna, and a chauffeur are variously tied only garners his strength for those brave morning and evening hours in the bedroom where he refuses to be valeted. His physiognomy, however, is a surprise; in the pictures, the head, the whole man, does not look so small. For a fraction of a second, I saw the type, that Hebraic miniature which, in the recessed eyes, flat, once ebony hair, re-calls the Japanese; I saw the doll-pate (so amazing for that brain), the eyeglass ribbon like the one in Yeats's pictures, felt the hand, smaller at a glance than his own daughter's; then the charm, the reputation, all the *expected* surrounded me and I never saw them that way again — until now.

"My daughter, Mrs. Fenno." She comes forward from behind the lamp a little as if evoked, I think, a little as in that child's game "Simon says," although there is nothing of the Griselda in her looks or in any-thing I have heard. Yet it is there. "Simon says take three steps for-ward." Or perhaps I am thinking of her as Walter first saw her, aged about eleven. She looks in her mid-twenties now, is thirty-one. Oval-faced, and much taller, except in coloring she does not resemble the Judge — the eyes very large. Narrow feet, slender hands, hair high, she is all ovals and narrownesses, with the grisette waist, the aquarelle tints peculiar these days to cultivated young women attached to the arts. The well-bred look of those trained to a performing art they never need use. Of course I know this about her too, as I know that her first name, a little harsh for her, is Ruth. The mark just discernible on her left cheekbone is the toothmark of an Airedale belonging to Diddy's friend Austin Fenno, when the latter was twelve. They make their friends early, these people, sometimes marrying them as the Ptolemies married their brothers and sisters. And Fenno — but I must address myself to the Judge.

He and I spend some token minutes over the galley proof, which I have had our law editor go over, having no wish to immerse myself that deeply in the mazes of its erudition, seeing no need. "Mannix is sure the scholar's scholar in this one," this man had commented. "I had no idea! Sure thrown the book at us!" and reading the manuscript over in the light of Mannix as publicized, as the reputation we had solicited, I saw what he meant. Mannix's career, resting on the delivery of a considerable body of opinions, nothing so homogeneous as Holmes, no single one so memorable as Woolsey's or Hand's, but always sufficiently in the public interest to maintain him in the public eye, did not happen to be a scholar's. It was a sober enough show, and quite honorable, but on reflection, it was a show. That was why and how one knew him. Why had he taken the pains then to throw the book at us, unless for the very reason that in a sense we *were* the book, and it was his nature to take such things under consideration? I put the thought aside, as what we often ran across in our business, the small vanities of otherwise incorruptible men. I didn't stop to wonder whether such heights of "judgeship" as I anticipated in Mannix were rarely envisioned except by men like Dobbin, who had never attained one, or men whose devotional madness ignored the public altogether, like Fourchette. And that night, reading the Judge's manuscript over his shoulder, in the soft, guardian light of all his guerdons around him, I have no mind to see in him any such mannerisms as might remind me of other small men historically dependent on other people's impressions — so eager am I for him to make the impression on me that I crave.

When we are finished, he makes the round of his possessions with me, of his Mannixiana as it were, I taking this to be the courteous method, met before in other personages, by which men who have to be much on display keep their real privacies, meanwhile letting these serve. Corner by corner, by decade, by generation, it is a display to envy now if one had not done that beforehand, if one were not already busy, among *bibelots*, framed faces and family papers all so open to the process, uniting what one knows to what one does not. And all the time, as the three of us go round, we do so on a rising perception of the sympathy of our tastes. I use a light hand, a stroke here and there, never too gross. We pass the corner devoted to the collection of French *objets d'art* (which I know to be her mother's, although she does not tell me so), without any comment on my part except admiration, although I have recently studied a book of plates on some of the same. Before we get to the Judge's study, however, I chance to inform him — and he is confounded to hear — that I have just last week bought a Deming, a small pastel of a Navaho, horsed, on a hill. He hasn't heard a mention of the man in thirty years; in there he has two. I'm interested in Indian stuff, then, as the Judge is? No (lightly,

lightly), it appears that ordinarily I am not. All of which is true. Maartens turned the thing up for me on request, and I like it well enough. I've long since learned the wisdom of having enough background palette and to spare, of being able to choose spontaneously from one's resources, never depending (a weakness of mine) too much on "objects" of this sort, and always keeping one's independence of spirit — how absurd, for a quick effect, to make myself out a china collector! Sometimes, however, there are small jokes that one would like to share. In the study, the Judge offers me a cigar, an Upmann, and the smile with which I let him see I know it for what it is broadens slightly at the thought of two such at that very moment in my breast pocket, bought this morning, which, if it had suited, I might have offered him.

By this time, seated there, we've had our exchange on David, met supposedly in Düsseldorf in 1946, on my Western way home. My plane, lumbering through every stop from Karachi to Lisbon, had as a matter of fact put down there for an hour; in the realities of having been in a place without ever really having been there, the rest of the world, nearing that non-Euclidean point where all places will be intersections of one another, is veering more and more on my side. Careful not to say too much, too eagerly, of David, I do not notice at the time — only now — how little eager the Judge is to hear. I am more engaged in not noticing the wall in front of us, entirely covered with an enormous collection of stamps, oddly but exquisitely mounted. There are always these hazards. Walter received mail from philatelists every morning. Had Diddy shared this interest, of so many others the two of them had? Shall I risk it?

"Some of these were David's," says the Judge, as if he had heard me, and I lean back. He never refers to his son except by the full name. What was the expression which had crossed his face when I used the other? Impatience? I am weighing it.

"But most of the *good* ones were left to me by Walter Stern. Did you know him also?"

One must choose. "I may have. I seem to have heard his name."

"He was there for a while. David's best friend. Matter of fact, it was he who got David into that sort of work." Expelling smoke, he gave a short, dry cough. "As usual."

"I may have met him there."

"You'd have remembered him." A puff on the Upmann. He does not explain.

The room is very quiet, a paneled rear one, dark except for the lamp. Anna has left us with the drinks, Ruth gone up to change. I am elated but nervous, hearing every creak of the chair as the Judge palms restlessly at the wheel, listening to the kind of silence, where people say too much, that I know so well. I wish to hear no confidences in this place. I suddenly realize this. I wish it to be exactly as it appears, and to be here in it. Nothing more.

"Weren't there — letters of his?" I say idly. "I seem to have come across a cataloguing somewhere."

"David's. He edited them." Again that dry cough.

"I must look them up."

"Oh, I — shouldn't bother, if I were you. Walter rather — over-idolized David. They aren't —" The Judge, extending his small hand to a handsome celestial globe on his desk, gives it a spin, the same expression flitting his face as before. But the globe, in perfect order like everything here, revolves and revolves. "One's son, of course. One's son. But Walter — he was the man to be remembered."

I do not wish to examine this eulogy. Eulogies at best so often go awry, and when on persons unknown to one are best received without comment. Besides, Ruth is standing at the door.

She has come there so quietly; has she heard us, him? Bare, her shoulders are fuller than one would have thought, her face, heightened for the evening, less girlish, less — forthright. She is standing so breathlessly still that the minute jewels in her pierced ears catch the light but do not wink.

I am on my feet now, near the stamp wall, ready to leave.

"The rarest is the triangular one, near the center." He speaks in the slightly raised voice of a person resuming casual conversation. "Poor Walter; we were just bringing it home to him. Are you going out, my dear?"

415

"Only with Pauli."

It's permissible to wonder what lies beneath the surface of women. Why *only*?

Meanwhile Anna, rung for, is being consulted by the Judge, under cover of which Ruth addresses me, as it happens, for the first time separately. "I'm happy to meet someone who knew Diddy." She speaks softly, but with emphasis.

"Likewise." It is, I hope, my only stupidity of the evening, and I am relieved that her eyes, frank as a goosegirl's even under their shading, are not on me, but still on her father. The earrings are quivering now, as if in the gentlest anger.

Aloud, I admire the wall, actually a huge, blue-green relief map of the hemispheres, to which some of the unboxed stamps are affixed like butterflies. At first I think she does not hear me. "A beautiful arrangement."

"Yes," she says. She will not deprecate. Set that way, her mouth does a little resemble his; otherwise, she is a graceful but much lesser version of the large, somewhat inhumanly handsome mother of the photograph framed in silver, of the portrait painted à la Sir John Lavery, both in the other room, not here — and now that I think of it, unreferred to in either. "Yes," she says, turning back to me, "we are very beautifully arranged."

Anna's wholesome, blundering voice intervenes. "Sure, I got enough!"

The Judge exchanges a smiling glance with me. People are kept in character by the servants they keep. "I'm informed that if Mr. Goodman can stay to dinner, he will not go unfed."

Unfortunately he cannot. But I too turn to Anna. "Why, you must be Anna," I say. "You must be 'Anna — my hosh'!"

In the general and successful laughter, they escort me as far as the drawing-room door, Ruth wheeling her father. "New dress, my dear?" he says as we go. "Very pretty." Nodding to him, nodding to me as I leave, she stands beside him, one hand on his chair, the long room behind. Modern as the dress is, she looks somewhat old-fashioned standing there, as grown daughters in their father's houses sometimes do. But I have already lost, if I have ever had it, the power to see them as they are, scarcely even hearing Anna's hearty "Come again!" as she shuts the door behind me. Going down their steps, I no longer hear what they have said or what they have not said, all drowned in what I have come for. Behind me it sounds in all its solid C major, the haven-note of the household that was never anywhere else, that was never anywhere. I go back there next week, to show him the Deming.

So I slipped into that household, and if it fitted me like a glove, I took this as a happy instance of the character I expected of it, for just as I had my special footing there, I could count around me quite a train of others who, each in his own way, had theirs. Some were literal pensioners, poor gentlefolk who knew the place as one where they were often welcome to bask in the delicacies of existence; others, abstractly rich, came especially in the holiday seasons, for that seat at a private board for which one could not pay. The Judge himself went out a good deal to public functions but not many private ones; there he preferred to give rather than to be received. Ruth had her own chari-table works, the hospital boards and welfare committees to which these days a woman of leisure might almost professionally belong, but she was ashamed of her leisure, as of some Edwardian vice which kept her behindhand in the world, and never brought these matters home. Good works were never mentioned at the Mannixes' and by their attitude never thought of as such; temperamentally, they had been reared to do what they could, and if their dinner-table talk was as heavily crossed with the sociopolitical anxieties of the day as any other modern one of its class — by virtue of the Judge even more so — the problem of how to be personally good in a vicious world never troubled it, "the way things are" never being confused with "the way we are." Yes, I thought often as I approached the house of an autumn or winter evening, preferably from the opposite side of the street so that I might better savor its serene lamps and stoop, wondering meanwhile whom I would meet behind its curtains, in front of a hearth almost always burning to the convivial tinkle of cup or glass, yes, it was a place to approach in pleasant prospect and at a saunter — an old-fashioned house. Would that long shadow be Pauli's, once celebratedly there with his hostile

Gaby ("Perhaps it would help him with her to bring her here to friends," the Judge had remarked to Ruth, but it hadn't); was that squat one penniless old Miss Augusta Selig, nursery compatriot of the Judge's, whose opinions were of such reactionary vintage that such modernities as old-age assistance (on a pension from which she lived) must never be mentioned before her? And would that more anomalous shadow belong to snub-nosed young Edgar Halecsy, law clerk, whose mother still went to the Judge's maiden sisters' house to do their hair and whose aunt, now dead, had been their milliner? — I had long, long thoughts, sometimes, on the occasions when I met Edgar there. Those several shadows might, on the other hand, belong to personages, or in today's argot, "personalities," bent on shedding at least as much light and dew as was to be received — for one never had the sense that the Mannixes restricted their company either way, the whole "line" of the household, as extended from the Judge, being that it had none, its virtue resting on being in any company the same. "We're middle-class here," I once heard him comment, and thought then of all the grounds on which he could be excused if the statement, with its faintest tinge of *L'état c'est moi!*, sounded rather as if it should have been "We *are* the middle class!"

Once, going up their steps, and passed, as frequently, by the familiar person of unknown quantity going pleasedly down, inside I came upon the Judge emerging from his study with the unmistakable air of a man who has just performed a favor, tucked his pen or his wallet away. "That man, Tom Somers, was one of the U. S. Alien Property Custodians after World War One," he commented. "Son of a rich American colonial in the Philippines. I met him during the depression, when he was down to working as a male nurse. Some men never recover from that kind of drop. Once in a while we chat stamps."

I ventured to joke. "This house — you're really an illegal loan-shark business. Dealing in all kinds of sympathy. No redemption expected, even in heaven. All obligations assumed."

"Do we really appear so?" he asked. "I should hate to think — that we give the appearance —"

I replied warmly that he was the last man to need to think of appearances.

A man in a wheel chair is always a focal point of stillness in a room. The Judge, besides, is very economical of gesture. "Oh — we keep busy," he said after a moment with no particular inflection, and the subject was closed. In conversation he adheres to that older school of courtesy which disclaims the personal; it gives him the air of a generation even prior to his own and makes him the most tolerable of invalids, who, giving no confidences, obtrudes no symptoms either. It's fortunate that he is called Judge; I could never have brought myself to call him Simon. This intimacy I had just dared, first of its kind, showed, now that our acquaintance was six months gone, what my footing was. Something above a retainer (for what did I receive?) and well below a personage, I was that impartial friend with whom one may discuss the others, my allegiance to the members of the household themselves meanwhile being evenly distributed. For evenness is all, here; the Mannix establishment proudly upholds itself in the rich network of its obligations, and if there's a suggestion of tapes and screws in the process, as of it also being upheld by them, I don't see it. After six months without a rift or a change we all retain our original impression of each other.

Anna came in just then. "I give Mr. Somers a box your vitamins. He don't look good."

This time the Judge did throw up his hands. Anna affords him these releases, giving perfect service even to her eccentricities. "You see? It's Anna who sets the tone of this house."

"Enough I set the table." She's very intelligent, Anna. I sometimes think she keeps up her thorniness as a convenience to all.

"It certainly is," I said. "You're quite right. Anna's a compulsive fattener. And if he and I don't give you satisfaction, Anna, it's not from want of trying, at least on my part."

"Him? He don't even try. And you —" She surveyed me. I am interested in how I appear to Anna. I think I know how I appear to the others.

She does not hesitate. A few months later, both of us aware of the direction in which I do not give satisfaction, she would not say it. "Even when you get marrit, you don't get a belly." Leaving, she flaps a hand at me. "You got bachelor bones."

"A token of admiring disapproval," said the Judge. "Past a certain age, she mistrusts all the single. Her own sex, in such case, she finds stupid. Ours — if we're not obvious rejects, then we're too deep." A few months later, he might not say this either.

"Let's hope I'm deep, then." Comfortable, I could say it without a qualm.

"Let's hope you are." Ruth, standing in the same doorway, was no apparition of quietness this time. Breezed in out of the wind, she looked gay and approachable, the way pretty women, pink-nosed and romantically furred, do in the autumn. I had not yet considered what complications might ensue here if I made love to her, not having seriously considered the latter either, although I found her an increasingly winning companion — graceful, responsive. Of late, her conversation with me had become a trifle artificial, for her. "Let's hope you are; you'll need it. Father's Nigerian economist is coming — you remember Mr. Krupong? He's a dear actually, but in front of father he will act the pontiff. Anna was dreadful, last time — I'm sure the poor man thought it was his color. Actually, it was because all those syllables cluttered up his eating."

"Never you mind," said the Judge. "All taken care of. I've invited an extra. Dan Blount just blew in."

Ruth and I burst out laughing; even the Judge just barely smiled. Blount is a journalist who is always blowing in from somewhere; in my short term here he's done so twice before. Crises wreathe his head in an ever-changing trooping of the colors of all nations, and he can take you to six different nations in the course of one of his sentences, all of which — relic of constant interviews with the momentarily great — are couched interrogatively. "Do you think? . . . Would you say? . . . What is your feeling . . . ?" — his intonations were all rising ones. "Dan," the Judge had said last time, "I live for the day when I hear you utter a declarative sentence." He and Krupong would certainly take care of each other.

"Better still," said Ruth. "I've invited someone too." A graceful woman removing her furs is a pretty sight also, until I catch in myself the sudden halt in the rhythm of the plexus, the current in the finger tips, with which we begin the heightened blood-mapping of the movements of another. Too late — once begun, the process is not to be stopped; from now on I shall be aware of wherever she is in a room, how poised and how far — and in the same instant am aware that this is already the case with her. And why not? — I'm no sister-seeker. Yet I wish that the clock could be pushed back to where we all were ten minutes before. Not here, I think. Too late.

"Ah," the Judge said idly, "who's that, m'dear? Another woman, I hope, to even things out."

"Yes." She may have hesitated, but if she did, I, involved with other things, did not notice it then. "I ran into her at the hospital. She's doing volunteer work — with some of the laryngotomies. Alice Cooperman."

The Judge made no immediate response. Then, after a moment, "You've told Anna?"

"Yes," said Ruth. What a straightforward glance, face, she has, I think; the body, with its dancer's control, perhaps less so. "Yes," she repeated in her even way. "It's quite all right with Anna."

Shortly after, the Judge went upstairs, as is his custom before dinner. He has one of those invalid seats which ride, elevator style, up the staircase. At the top, a second wheel chair awaits him. Ruth, Anna, or Charlie the chauffeur, if about, usually help him make the shift at ground level, but at the top of the stairs he always does so himself, as if this marks the transition to a world he willfully keeps private. By custom we don't watch this, but happening to glance up, I see him, already chaired again, watching us; then, with a backward push to his wheel, he disappears.

"Lucky he's still able to do some of that for himself," I said, "else there'd have to be a lot more running back and forth." I was running along myself at the mechanical level one does when one's thoughts are elsewhere, unsure as I was of where these were leading me, not really guarded.

"Lucky?" Poised, she seemed to incline toward me without perceptibly moving. Her brows were raised. Should I have taken this to mean that the Judge, if he wished, could do more? Hung there, her head drooping, she was very near me. "It wouldn't be bearable otherwise," she said. But I was busy interpreting her movements in my terms, in ours, and didn't think to ask, "For whom?"

Anna returned at that moment. "A message come from Miss Cooperman, Miss Ruth. Someone telephone it for her. She send you her love, but she ask you excuse her from dinner."

"Oh. I see." Scarcely seeming to move from me, she has. "Thank you, Anna. Then there'll be just the one extra. Mr. Blount."

But Anna doesn't take her dismissal; stands there, hands pressed against her starched front, the fingers opened toward Ruth, old nurse looking at her grown child. Had she seen us, or even before we have, our status to be? That evening was the turning point, and Anna, in allowing herself this intimacy before me, was the first to show the turn. "Why you bodder?" she said. One would not have thought that Anna, all heavy Czech shrug and cackle, could speak so low. "Miss Ruth, what's a use? Why you bodder him — now?" She glanced up at the stairwell. "Why you bodder yourself!" Recollecting herself, or me, she dropped her hands. Leaving, she flung back a warning more in her usual style. "You want change — that Mr. Ping-pong, he always come early." Before we had a chance to feel the silence she left us with, her head came round the door again. "You look purdy 'nough, that dress," she said with a side look at me, "you don't need change."

I break the silence. "Mr. Ping-pong. Anna knows all our habits to a T, doesn't she?"

Ruth, leaning against the mural of stamps, tracing a finger from one to another, doesn't look up. "Alice was a friend of David's." Six months later now, if she no longer adds "too," I take it to be because I now have my own status here. "He was — thinking of marrying her, just before he was killed." Her finger traces its way toward another

422

stamp. "I'm not sure whether Alice — what Alice was thinking." Again the finger moved on. "She's — she's a deaf-mute, you see. Or rather, she began life as one; she can speak well enough now, in that sort of strange voice they have. And she even works with others. But silence is still more of a habit with her than with — normal people. Not that it doesn't become her. She's exquisite to look at — very blonde, slender. Even after you know why she doesn't speak more, it only makes her seem — enchanted. Natural enough, of course, that David should fall in love with her." The finger stops. If she is waiting for me to say something, she waits in vain. "I don't suppose — he ever spoke of her?"

I am ready enough now. "No," I could say with truth, "I didn't know."

Still she does not look up, but I can feel her concentration. She is watching my every movement; she too is aware. I thought I recognized this moment of stillness, how well I knew it — for now she will confide. *No*. With dismay, I felt myself push against the moment usually so consummately arranged for. If I opened my mouth it would be to warn her. Let's stay as we are. The listener is never the friend.

"Father couldn't bear the idea," said Ruth. "With the way he felt about David, it — it was the last straw. He thought — he thought it was David's way of getting back at him." These last words have come in a rush. I know the familiar pace of that too. I force myself to meet her look. Clear-eyed, frank of feature, she was the danger now — and the mystery — but I refused to see it. "I suppose —" she said, and there was a question in her voice, but I didn't hear it at the time. "I suppose that's understandable enough."

"Yes." I answered from the habit of caution, not really hearing. "Yes, I suppose."

She is at the door now. What is she saying? "Perhaps," she says, her voice hard. "But I don't understand it. I won't!"

After she'd gone up, I traced a finger along the path hers had, past the triangular stamp that, six months ago, the Judge had pointed out as the rarest. She had all but told me what I still did not know about David, even perhaps what she all but knew about me, but I had not heard her. It was the house I had come for, and if I waited I should hear it in all its restless undertones beneath the public one, a cage of wires, naked to the winds as any other, Walter's wonderful house. It was time to leave. How canny a dilettante one had to be, how careful, just in time, to move on. Moving on was not as easy as it had been in the old days; I no longer had the anonymity of youth. Middle age luckily had its own powers and wisdoms; in the social way possible in cities I would manage slowly to detach myself from this world I had grown too fond of, mindful to do its inhabitants no harm for their imperfection's sake.

Anna was just letting in Krupong as I left the library. On his heels, a second ring announced Blount. As Anna took their things, Ruth appeared at the drawing-room door, I opposite, the Judge, slowly descending the stairwell in his movable chair, hand outstretched, between us. To Blount and Krupong, we may well appear already the simulacrum of a family, each member relinquishing some happily unhaunted solo pursuit for the welcome social hour, each punctual at his proper door, and these orange lamps sprung up all about must have appeared to these two, outside on the stoop, quite as an hour earlier they would have seemed to me. I remember Ruth's voice of six months ago, already gilding with memory now that I am leaving. "We are very beautifully arranged."

But, of course, I did not leave.

Once two people are physically conscious of one another, only absence can stop that progression. Progression in some form it is, in whatever terms for the two are inevitable; the sexual clock, like any other worth contemplation, has no *status quo,* cannot be turned back. In the next few weeks I frequented the Mannixes less, but there seemed no immediate way to abscond entirely, my work at the time making it impossible for me to leave the city. Any "break" on emotional grounds was absurd; in the lightly choral tastefulness of our relationship to date there'd been nothing to peg such on. Only a hysteric might have tried to trump such up, and thereby illogically penetrated sooner past the soft diffusion of warmth on the Mannix hearth to what-

424

ever truer cold lay beyond — the careful nonviolence, perhaps, of an establishment whose harmonious planes, liming its coterie birds with so many minor attractions, on closer scrutiny dared offer no handgrips for the heart. All this is retrospect; I no more saw this at the time than I marked Ruth's own attempts to put absence between us for what they were. Firmer than I and actually less free, twice during those same weeks she was off somewhere, the first time (despite a sickness of Anna's which made her own presence even more than customarily ill-spared) on a visit to an old schoolmate now in Chicago, the second, on a visit of much longer duration, to London, where Austin Fenno, her former husband, now remarried, was living.

At the time, I connected neither of these departures with me. Since I'd met the Mannixes in spring and it was now autumn, their summer pattern was better known to me than their winter one, which might have variables natural to people who were not tethered to an occupation. And Ruth's license to move about at will except as she was tethered to her father's needs, which he never appeared to press, seemed to me much broader than most women of her age, and in spite of her own phrase, not at all Edwardian. Had flight still been the woman's part of courtship, vanity might have made me see hers as such, but women no longer said no so elaborately, whether or not they meant it. In any case, I'd come to that point in my affairs — and in our affair, if it was to be one — where I saw her only as the "object." In the most ordinary love affair, normal human solipsism grows beyond all bounds, the opposite person becoming the "object," the "other," whisked into imaginary beds and conversations while at the same time existing in absolute and peculiar stasis, a pawn swollen to power by the mere fact of being where it is, without motive of its own. And our affair, taken from my side alone, could be no ordinary one. The possibility of her side, therefore, passed me by altogether — and the first warning.

As it happened, I saw her both times she returned. In her first absence, by pleading pressure of work, I had already begun my withdrawal, and this particular evening was the first since that I had dined with her father, this time alone with him. The prospect that Ruth, home the day before and out tonight with Pauli, might come in before I took my leave did not trouble me. Balance had been recovered in the interval, and taking further precaution, I had resumed my visits to an old, if casual friend who in her time had used me to similar purpose. Nanette is a proper hard-soft businesswoman of the day, ruthless to the eye and lissome to the touch, stony as any courtesan where her career as vice-president of a department store is concerned, her secret cartilege appearing in the spot where one would expect it — in her cleavage, sticky and interminable, to an indifferent married man. Except for the added fact that we sleep together, I am her Pauli in those periods of lesser agony when, for one or other of all the reasons available in that sort of cat's cradle, she is not seeing her part-time lover. In bed she is lively, matter-of-fact and much the good sport, her long servitude having trained her never to obtrude tears or confessions there, and I never advise her that this perhaps is the reason she cannot win her inamorato. In the morning after such a night, we go off from her flat to our separate jobs like two participants in a humdrum, not unamiable marriage which has never risen to rapture or anger, and never will. We had done so that morning.

To my surprise, Ruth, when met in the entrance hall just as I was leaving, appeared ugly to me for the first time. Her looks, so dependent on tint and grace, haven't the flamboyant regularity or suburban peachiness that weathers all moods — she looked white-faced and rabbity, as some women did after crying, although the availability of Pauli's shoulder (he had just departed) did not occur to me then. We chatted briefly in the nonsensical way one does in halls, the Judge meanwhile behind us, waiting to be able to comply with his strict, self-imposed bedtime. Her responsive, eager manner seemed to have vanished — I felt no thread between us. Absence, even such a short one, had done the trick — and perhaps Nanette. Taken aback at the suddenness of my cure, and apparently of hers, I felt the discomfort one does at the sight of the imagined person who has survived untouched all one's inner dramas of them — or is not even the same. I awkwardly invited her to lunch, which in our early acquaintance we once or twice had done. I both dwelt on her face and avoided it.

"No — no thanks. I'm only here for a few days. I'm — thinking of going to London for a bit." If this was a sudden decision, I was not quick enough in turning to see that on the Judge's face. When I did, he seemed tired, and my knowledge of the rules of the house made me leave the more quickly. It had been a dull evening there otherwise, one of those yawning evenings after sexual satiety — Nanette, being desperate, had been particularly lively — when, nulled in the flesh, still nervously unquelled in the mind, one yearns for some improbable sensation beyond the sexual one, knowing well enough that there is none. Going down their steps, I congratulated myself on the satiety I now felt in that house. A musician could have told me better at what stage I really was — at that anomalous place in the fugue where the bouquet of the unfamiliar is subtly exchanged for a preoccupation with the known.

I walked home. It was spikily clear, under the crude blue heaven of one of the best nights of early winter, when walking in this city is a kind of expensive elation at all the brute energy it still shows, and at the same time a lonely tribute, as from some leftover pioneer, to all that it no longer is. On the way, I mused, with a pang, on her ugliness, and tried to excuse it. Most women had such times, and she was thirty — thirty-one. Two blocks from home I passed the florist — in courtesy I must either call Nanette tomorrow or send her roses. To have such a decision to make, to be able to make it clearly, enlivened me almost as much as the wind on my collar. I slipped an order in the florist's letter slot, and straightway my elation brimmed over into calm. I had seen her. Meanwhile, if it could have done poor Nanette any good, I'd have signed the order for her flowers with the name of the other man, her lover — such bountifulness whelmed me. Going up my own stairs, I told myself that it was not ugliness I had seen in her face but — as in faces long known to one — the sudden, sad prototype of its aging. And having so reconsidered, I went to bed content, and ignorant. There are only two other faces — my mother's and my uncle's — that I have watched with the same generic sadness. When one looks that way at a face newly met, it is not the ending of love.

Two months later, I was again at the Mannixes when Ruth came

427

home unexpectedly, and it was no accident that I was there. In the interim, I'd kept to a few afternoon visits there, until a call from Anna a few days before. She was worried about the Judge's state of health and suggested that I invite myself to dinner and "speak" to him. "He don't look good, and he don't listen to no vwooman."

I could understand his not listening to Anna, to whom people she was fond of so rarely did "look good." And I could not visualize myself being avuncular to the Judge. But Anna's pleas flattered, and the Judge liked to be sought after in just this way.

"Okay, Anna. I'll ask to come, say Thursday." This was Monday.

No, she said, that was her day off. "You ask for Friday." She was insistent. "I make chicken paprikash."

It was as easily arranged. If the Judge had assigned any cause to my recent neglect, he had not shown it on my visits, always proffering unaffectedly neutral news of Ruth. And if he had taken offense, I could hear my request repair it — to be asked for something always affords him a perhaps disproportionate glee. "Miss Augusta is coming too," he added.

"Can I bring her? I know it's Charlie's day off." That pleases him too — to have the routines there remembered. As I hung up I felt oddly young, a rebellious but good boy received back into grace, into a household whose intimate scents settled round me again like the stoppered air of an old amphora, powerful as Pompeii when released. What if the Mannixes, wheeling in a circle of obligations, contredansed by observances of the same on the part of their satellites, reminded me somewhat of a court — why should I pamphleteer against it? Theirs was only a highly refined version of the family stigmata to be found, once one entered that nest, anywhere — the sign of man budded domestic on a wild planet. And why not? Even if it was never as flawless, once one got inside it, this was the way, made Ishmael enough by the elements, men clung to their crag. So, in this mixed state of mind, limed but still struggling, I walked up that familiar stoop again behind old Miss Selig, carrying her ancient dog Chummie, who could no longer take the high steps and could not be left at home because he cried. It was an easy entrance, one that he and I had made before.

Ruth was not there or expected, and any glances exchanged by Anna and me, under the eyes of the Judge and two strangers, were absorbed by the dog, who made one submissive tour of the guests and then settled to his corner like one of those nineteenth-century infants who were reputed to have been seen but not heard, Miss Selig having reared him exactly as she would a child. And he must serve for one here, I thought idly — I had never seen any other.

That night, one of the two other guests was a personage, a vivid young British M.P. named Stukely, whose reputation, somewhat fluidly unsound on his home side of the water, had gained the instant solidity we still extend such exports, once they touch ours. He was an old hand at their game of talking brilliantly wide, and his angular wife, whose painfully brave décolleté, at first blink, made her seem clad only in her excessively heavy earrings, was equally good at seconding him, either by one of those strangulations with which some upper-class British replace the animalities of converse, or, at his best sallies, a sympathetic reddening down to her shoulder blades. I should have found them, in their own word, "amusing," but could not; after all these years they are still the people who make me remember my class, or that I once had one. If Mrs. Stukely, turning, were to ask if we had not met before, again inquiring my name, I was not sure that I would not nod and humbly give her the real one. In the presence of their high-nosed sense of place I was at once their parvenu, beneath what personal flourishes I had added to it, and at the same time, safe on this emigrant shore, more American than I ever felt anywhere else. I could tell myself that both they and I were wrong, that "place" for me was now some moral-emotional position, the echoes of which some repercussion from their "social" one had merely touched off. It made no matter; narrow as they were, there was something solid in them which made us award them more solidity than they had. In its presence, I could feel the terrible moral burden imposed on the single, wandering personality by the American scene. And resting my personal burden on that one, I could better understand my mother's cry, "This would never have happened at home!"

After dinner the Judge, as if my silence had infected him with its cause, began speaking of Edgar Halecsy, who was collaborating with him on a book of essays after the manner of the article he had contributed to our office. All through dinner he had held his end up animatedly, but observing him now, I thought I saw why Anna had called. Diminutive people, offering less surface, often show physical change less than the vapidly large, and the Judge, still as unwrinkled as the Oriental he resembles, did not look ill, but one had a stronger sense now of how small he was, as one sees the constricted figure of a small boy who has just been punished. Who could have been punishing the Judge?

"A milliner's son, mind you, Stukely. Harvard now, and all the rest of it — on his way to being one of the best legal scholars of his generation. Oh, I know that sort of thing happens with you all the time. But Edgar won't have to suffer for it, as you still make yours do, for his rise. He's done it individually; that's our strength. But he was already as good as anybody, right from the beginning."

"Ah yes," said Stukely, tugging his beard. "Poor chap. Oh, right you are, of course. Matter of fact, we're doing our best to imitate you."

"Guy says —" Everyone looked with surprise at Mrs. Stukely, stirred by her husband's modesty to her first clear statement of the evening.

"Yes, my dear? What is it I say?"

"That our way is better. People popping up and down all the time, but inside the class structure. One gets just as much new blood that way. *And* keeps one's standards!" Her blush of allegiance spread down to her sternum, if that was what this declivity of her person should be called.

True enough, I thought, loyal little bitch-rabbit, but the telltale sign was in her use of "one."

"Hairdresser's son, Judge," I said, "the aunt was the milliner," for even though I did not much like the absent Edgar, I wanted to flick them all. By control I had kept my voice dry, but dizzily wondered whether I was going to be ill, feeling the gorge of confession swelling in my throat. In another moment I should tell them who I was and how I had got there, for was I not their rounded pebble, the perfectly public, perfectly private individual man whom they did not really believe in, who had got where he was all on his own? "Let me tell you who *I* am," I should say, only to be struck dumb when, turning, they said, "Who?"

The Judge's stare, baffled, recalled me. It was the first time in my life I had ever felt this hysteria and I knew where to blame it. I should not have come here, to a house where I took things so personally. This was a dangerous house.

"And does he show no signs at all?" asked Stukely. "Of his rise? This Edgar?"

"Well," said the Judge. "Perhaps he has to be a trifle more learned than anybody." He spoke jauntily, like a man who had no need to keep up appearances, but my sense of my own unreality, suddenly after all these years so exacerbated, opened like a nostril, scenting his. Edgar. Edgar wrote that article.

"Nonsense!" said Miss Selig. "Simon, I'm surprised at you. We are what we are, from the cradle." She spoke with the authority of one who had known him from his. "And whatever has made you think that being good enough for anybody is good enough!"

"Bravo!" Stukely, behind her, mouthed this silently, making a face like a horse at his wife.

"Up, down, up, down. It's all nonsense," Miss Selig grumbled. Her thick, gray hands, gripping her brandy glass, trembled from age, anger or greed. "I should know, shouldn't I?" I'd never before heard her refer to her own circumstances, and it struck me now that our delicacy with the subject had been unnecessary. There wasn't a crevice of doubt in her. In her squat, gray mass she reminded me of stone figures I had seen in the East during the war, palace garden ornament now, once ballast in the holds of ships from China. She was far less bruisable than I.

"You've known *me* forever, Augusta," said the Judge, managing a number of avoidances at once.

"Yes." Miss Selig tossed off her brandy and put out a hand to wake the sleeping Chummie. She stroked him. "Oh, yes."

It was then that we heard Anna greeting someone in the hall.

The newcomer came forward, radiant from travel, dropped in on us from the air with eyes still changeling. She had not yet seen me. Behind her, Anna, shunning mine, slunk away.

"Ruth, Ruth, my dear. My dear Ruth!"

She knelt in front of his chair, laying her head down. So much taller than he, she looked improbably near me, like those penitents drawn in the early days of perspective, so much too large for the throne.

He put a small, papal hand upon her. "Why didn't you let us expect you?"

"Anna knew — it was to be a surprise." Her eyes were glistening. "It's your birthday tomorrow. Did you think I would forget your birthday?" Then she saw me, following his glance to where I stood, in my corner. Can a person feel his own face whiten? In her blanched one, I thought I felt it, as I felt myself walk toward her without moving, exactly as she, immobile as I, approached me, and I was half prepared to hear a cry from one of the others, "They are twins!" Then the confusion of introductions, inquiries and answers, intervened.

"What kind of a dog does Austin keep now?" said Miss Selig, when they had all settled again, but on the arms of chairs, as a sign that the evening was breaking.

"Why, I don't know, Aunt Augusta." She had her hand on the back of his wheel chair now, in the familiar, antiquated posture, and the two of them no longer looked out of drawing. His head was down, gazing in his lap; one couldn't tell whether it felt its punishment over. "He probably has one down in the country, but I only saw them in London. The house in Smith Street has no garden. And Ursula has enough on her hands with the children. Plus her own commissions."

"Still, I can't imagine Austin without one. Will you ever forget that Airedale?"

She shook her head, smiling, a finger creeping to the mark on her cheek. I touched it with her.

"Why, that's Ursula Walker, isn't it?" said Mrs. Stukely. "The architect? She and I were at Roedean together!"

Ruth nodded, leaving a smile here, a nod there, in every direction but mine.

"I *heard* that she married an American," said Mrs. Stukely.

"Prue — I think we ought to —" said her husband. I guessed that he knew Fenno's relationship here, or former one.

"You'll have to imagine him with children now, Aunt. Four. The new baby's a darling."

As if in answer, Chummie made his only sound of the evening, a disparaging one. Facing the general laughter, he rose unsteadily, his eyes as obtuse as Anna's when she knows some remark of hers has made her socially useful. Anna herself was nowhere to be seen.

"Chummie," said Miss Selig, "we must go home."

"I'll ride along with you. I bear all kinds of messages." She turned to her father, whose head was still bowed. "Charlie'll bring me right back. I won't be long."

"It's *Friday.*" He spoke in sour triumph, as if her lapse on this canon measured her neglect, past any efforts on birthdays.

"There's plenty of room," said Miss Selig. "I'm sure Mr. Goodman won't mind."

So she was caught, if she had meant to escape. She took up Chummie without a word.

"Oh, he can walk *down,*" said his owner. "Chummie likes to walk when he can. Good night, Simon."

Good night, we all said, in a catching of cabs, closing of doors that put us out again into the fresh, illimitable dark. Good night, we said in a round, snatching at the phrase, wistful even between enemies or bores, which must last us until we were somewhere inside again, good night, good night.

In the silent car, there were no messages forthcoming, and the old woman did not press for them. So many emphases that I had never noticed before had seemed to come from her lips tonight. Like that marble in which one saw the infinitely flattened snails of pre-time, she must be — tough old stone in which the Mannix confidences were embedded. "I'll get a cab back," her companion said when we reached Miss Selig's street. "Don't wait. Good night."

433

The street, not yet sinister but a mean one, was a dead realm to cabs. When she came down, after an interval fair enough for confidences, she hesitated in the doorway, seeing me still there. Slowly she came toward me, a statue warmed down from its niche against its own will, and got into the car. We found nothing idle enough to say to each other. The long rest, borrowable from time, from dissimulation, gathered between us, and at last we touched.

For a short time thereafter we gave ourselves up to a metaphysical delaying — the harmless thumbscrew delights with which a man and woman postpone their arrival at an end of which neither despairs. We were like two people watching, hand in hand, through separate binoculars, the inland tending of the same white sail. And we were like two who, chatting noncommittally the while, hid our locked hands behind us, against the spies in our own breasts. I left off going to her house, and my flat was not mentioned. Instead, powerfully urged into each other's company at least once a day, we met in all the public places, luxury and on the cheap, that a city suddenly seems to offer such preambles, with the air of a great mine opening on treasures that exist for nothing else. We were the engrossed couple on the ferry boat, the two in day clothes (as if this made them incognito) in the opera box, the two met as if by chance in one of the currents of musk or pine sent out by the stores at this season, and fallen at once into an urgent silence which had only the one errand. It was during this period that, when apart, we had those conventionally absurd exchanges on the telephone, and when together, she dropped those bauble confidences which I was as careful to mistake for her simplicity — in which, like any woman shaking out her best attractions, she set up for me the clear sugar-castles of her girlhood, as if she saw that these were what I was best drawn by, and that only they could reassure. I learned why — or several good reasons why — self-apprenticed to the ballet at the age of six, and arduous enough to gain entrance, during a summer tryout years later, to one of the best ballet companies in Europe, she had toured with them for a year, and had as suddenly given it all up, only a week before the troupe reached New York. Oh, she'd been good

434

enough, but if she wasn't to be superb, then, to one of her background, there was no need. Her family, with a musical past of its own, had never opposed her; perhaps she'd have been better spurred that way, like some of her friends shot out into the arts by the bourgeois outcry behind them; but perhaps she'd been a little too subject, at home, to the idea that excellence was all. "And you know how verbal we are there," she said. "For a while I did choreography — there was even a ballet of mine. But the best dancers are stupid, you know, to verbal people. Even the great ones. It's like living in a society of cats busy at watching their own ripplings. It just wasn't my milieu — even if I hadn't another on my own." The family somehow appeared, if benevolently, in all her reasons, as one of those milieus perhaps so binding in its early satisfactions that later on its members needed no other. As such, I admired it — who now, of the two of us, had the guile?

During this period also was when she haltingly gave me those light histories of old love affairs — not many — which are traditionally a woman's sign that she is ready for the new. I learned then why the Mannixes still spoke of Austin Fenno as they might of an absent member of the family or of an associate so close that he could never hope to be really absent, why Ruth could visit him and his wife, and all without the slightest embarrassment. It had been the marriage, lasting for eight months when Ruth and Austin were each twenty-five, which had been the embarrassment — once the unfortunate mistake was over, the waters of friendship could reseal. Could anything be more natural? Even Ursula, the second wife, couldn't summon up any jealousy over that small, submerged shipwreck. Even she could understand the conjunction, so fostered by the well-meaning, of two childhood friends come of age without other lasting preference, who, finally embarking in a crowd of huzzas, found out only then, in their two-in-a-boat darkness, how fatally all that they had married "because of" could keep them disjoined.

"We never would have," she said, "if we each hadn't had a couple of other disappointments, in both cases people our own people never thought too much of. He was always like another brother to me, and now that that's over, he still is. Oh I know, in some cases that childhood sort of thing is supposed to flower, but not with us. Left to ourselves, we would never have made that mistake. Why — Austin is considered extremely handsome, you know — the girls used to sigh at my having him around all the time through David. Even my father could never get over the fact that such a perfect physical specimen should have brains in the bargain. But I never saw him that way. Nor he me." She smoothed a bracelet, one sent her by David from Palestine, that she often wore. "It wasn't even a tragedy," she said gently, "just a mistake," and then went quickly on to something else, lest I notice, perhaps, how precisely she understood the difference. Of my origins and history she knew the sparse, public outline and never tempted my reserve further, seeming to take it for the acceptable male silence. A woman's part was to chatter, on whatever could be made to seem harmless, so she did so, but in a way that almost said to me then as she did much later, "I won't trespass. I will manage — not to." Behind our backs, the neatest paradox was forming. I refused to see that she was a person to be feared; she refused to fear what she had already seen.

For the night I slept with her — the night that also dates the beginning of this memoir — she already knew that I was a pretender. Afterwards, absorbed in my own need, I did not examine her bravery, or if I had, I should have put it down to the congenital bravery of women, Nanettes in some way most of them, bearing within, like a secondary egg, an eager tenderness to be torn. A woman takes up her role of *mater dolorosa* half for humanity's sake, half for personal glory, exactly as her object, the male, goes off to war. And these means, so separate at the start, by which each hopes to find some comet-path out of time and change, are what will drop them both, tired and old, at the same wayside point where, having eaten of those unities, they must die of them. This is the human condition and she was playing the woman's part of it, I'd have said until now — nothing more. But the memoir, dredging up one's own truth, brings up that of others, alongside. If we'd had bystanders that night — our owls gazing down at us from their dimension — what would they have said to one another?

"Look at the two of them lying there in each other's arms. See how she resembles him. She too has something to conceal. They are twins."

For several nights past, I'd brought her home to an empty house but had done nothing about it. Anna was on holiday, for the Judge, taking Charlie the chauffeur with him and, on impulse, Mr. Somers, had finally departed, much later than usual, for his customary cure in Hot Springs. Ruth had not gone with him, as in the past. The word "finally" had hung between us unsaid, until the night before.

"Are you afraid of my father?" she had said, teasing, when I stood up to go.

"A little," I had answered. "Now that he's gone." I had no idea what I meant by that. Coyness and savagery run hard by each other. The next night, standing in the same posture we had for nights past, saying nothing, we sank down. Behind us, the Chinese horse marshaled its shadows. The light burned.

Only a puritan takes the love act for a describable entity; the rest of us know it to be, in its knotting of philosophy with tissue, as ineffable as any other compulsion between creatures who so incurably coexist as we. Like most men, I suspect, I'd devised a few mottoes of inner reference, that was all, and by these I remember it. As it perfected itself in spite of us, there was nothing new under the sun, or needed to be. Afterwards, we lay without grotesquery among the flung clothes. How did I record it before? I look back:

Lying together, palm to palm, after love, is like lying in another country which some Dives had allotted for ten minutes or more. The voices that speak there are already the voices of paradise lost. I remember what I thought when I withdrew my palm. I thought — I could love her, if it were not for myself. We spoke then, or she did, of how we had met, of all the stages that had brought us to this night, in the way women love to do, exactly as children ask again for a story, secure in the fairy-tale end. Her hair was across my forehead. I was only half listening. The moment, with its treble of voices, was over. I watched it as it sped away, pluming into the gathering distance, leaving one of its voices behind.

What a strange disloyalty repeats itself next, as from a split lip. *If it were not for myself, I could love her.* What sex is it, am I, that asks more of sex than love?

Go on. Remember. But this time, watch her also, if you can.

She was speaking of the circumstance that had brought us together, the encyclopedia soliciting her father for an article, the discovery that I had known David. I was thinking of Walter, sitting up in bed with his hump clinging between his shoulders. *I thought of all those whom we leave for dead, either in the grave or in the past, who grow again between our shoulder blades. I thought of the great hump of memory I had made for myself, of such a shape that I could never hope to lay it down. And then I made the accidental slip. I spoke unaware; I was listening, but not to her. And found myself with the enemy lying beside me, in the flesh still quivering in communication with mine. I discovered why I had never looked behind me.*

"You're not listening," she said.

"Yes, I am." For my own ends only. I had kept that vow. "I'm listening." I heard voices black, voices chaste, in a great, impure choiring of all I had not done, all I had.

"And when David left on that plane," she said (as I thought), marveling, "it was just by chance you weren't on it also."

I nodded into the dark. That was how Walter had told it. Delayed at the last minute himself, he had stood on the runway and waved to David.

"And you called out good-by to him. And he turned around and waved."

And again I nodded. "I suppose one shouldn't take these things too mystically," Walter had said. "But of all things, to take it into my head just then to call out to him. He couldn't have heard me. They were already revving up. And besides —" After a long pause he had spoken again. "Yet, he turned."

"Tell me," she said then, her mouth at my breastbone.

"What?" I said, as absently as to a child. "What shall I tell you?"

She raised herself on an elbow and looked down at me, her eyes lustrous and fixed. Delphine in the hallway, I thought — how women at times resemble one another.

"What I already know."

I drew her head down and hid it. She was pleading, I thought, for the three words I had not yet said — so that she might say them. "About what?"

After long silence, her answer came, muffled. "About you."

And mine, after as long. "No, you. No, you do." And when no answer came — "What do you know about me?"

She had so twined herself against me that she was one warm, felt line. Her words came from below, a puff from my own breast. "That — you never knew David."

Her nape was beneath my hand. If I were a murderer. Yes, they are brave. My nakedness shivered with hers; then I sprang from her. Trembling, we faced each other. The real danger walks toward.

She sat up, her arms dangling. Her eyes were tightly closed. "It doesn't matter. If you aren't — who you are supposed to be. Nor am I."

"Cover yourself," I said. "Cover yourself!" Or open your eyes.

She drew something toward her, then opened her eyes to look down at it, my coat. "I have." She replaced it with the blanket we had taken from Anna's room. "Can't we love?" she said. "No matter who we are. Or what?"

If I had not jumped up, would she have known for sure? What does she know?

"What did you mean, about David?"

She didn't answer at once. In the growing light from outside, that had downed the other, her face looked ugly and sad. "I can lie to every-one but myself," she said. "That's what father won't understand." Within the coarse cowl of the blanket she shrugged or shivered again. One hand turned itself up and down, up and down on her bare thigh. "Though I try. Though I try." I thought she wasn't going to answer me further. When she spoke, it was so listlessly that her words were half echo before I heard them. "There was a friend of David's who — who thought he loved my brother. But after David's death he

439

would never mention the one thing that spoiled his dream of him. That David was deaf. Stone-deaf."

My lips were dry over my teeth. We bring ourselves, I thought, we bring ourselves.

"You're just like Walter." She is staring through my neck, I thought, to the hump on the other side. Her hand was at her mouth. She spoke from behind it. "You know nothing about us. Nothing at all."

I'm still at Lasch's. The trees are still there. Behind them, the black is paling before the gradual creation; a lost divinity patiently makes its statement again, today perhaps being the one on which we shall understand it; it will try. Though I try, though I try. My first encounter with the Mannixes held the germ of all the others, then, of the last. But that night, fleeing down their steps like a masked lover in whose silken face the lamp had been thrust, I was still too self-contained to see the germ in its entirety. I had all I could do to carry my bulging sack of terror home with me, drag it inside. She'd said everything, it seemed to me then; she had held the blinding lamp high, looked down. All the three months since, bent at my desk under my own incubus, this had seemed enough. When we spoke yesterday afternoon over the wire stretching from these trees to her sea, she said even less — what did she say? — only a phrase, a catch of breath, and a phrase — but then I began to see the whole of it. I could not have written of them as I have, otherwise. Take nothing for granted, on either side.

I heard what she said through the fly-cries of the people in the room behind her, steady as the climbing tone of the telephone itself, then caught, then righted, then gone. Why she watched me, how she knew me, said to my face in her mirror, You are honest; said to her twin, You are not who you are. "Yes, I'll come," she said. "Day after tomorrow. I — I can't keep it to myself any longer. There's something I must tell you, about us."

Sitting here, I make a different guess as to what it is with every pulse beat. The Judge can walk more than he does. She does not marry. Who is punishing who? The Judge never wrote that article. They speak so little of the mother, whose picture is everywhere except in his study. Who hates there, who loves, who lies? One never sees children there. David did not marry the mute. They married Ruth to Austin, her brother. To what end are they all arranged? She is right. I know nothing about them at all.

It must wait for tomorrow, when I meant to give her this.

Can nothing, not even the memoir, ever be for itself alone, nothing, nothing, nothing? Her explanation does not belong here. And still she approaches, to her own threading of drums. Time is the bystander. Innocent, we approach one another. That murder we seek.

Chapter III. The Distance Between.

I AM in a plane, flying back. Jet flight 119, six and a half hours to London, cruising at an altitude of twenty thousand feet, is carrying me back to my beginnings. Along with me are eighty or ninety others on all the range of human errands. We fly trajectories that once belonged to thought. The small voice of the intercom conscience falls silent. The steppes below us are cirrus. The motto glows: *Unfasten seat belts*. God bless our home.

Today is Wednesday, or when I left still was. Early Monday morning, before the morning wave of secretaries should find me at Lasch's, I drove home dead beat, fell into bed and slept out the day. It was night when I awoke; peering out at the tiered lights, I dropped the curtains again and in an answering exhilaration lit lamps of my own. As I prowled about at my feeding and washing, I felt the hungover, animal restlessness that comes from having disturbed the inner clock. A hangover has its clarity too. Conclusions swarmed toward me as they do to the drugged, and I watched them with a stiff intentness that might be joy. The memoir was gathered up on the desk, not that it was finished, nor that I had moved one millimeter away from what had been enunciated there — only that a shadow, as if from some stagecraft, had fallen upon it. Hers? I knew better than to think that its story could end in that warm, self-congratulatory haze of lovers who feel themselves star-pushed toward one another. We were not such a pair, or ever could be. One by one I watched the truth-bubbles float from the pipe. What sex is it, are we, but that solitary non-sex (once called the soul) which, from the moment it takes up the black dialogue of itself, starts hunting a place to lay it down? A man who has no place — hunts for a person. But we are not star-pushed; we choose our surrogates for the good, for the bad. Standing in the hall of mirrors, before the judges who may be ourselves, we give each other our weaknesses to hold.

In a start of hyper-identity I looked down at my hands. They were locked together. Nothing has changed, I said to myself. Once I chose Semple, on the side of the dark. Now I choose her, on the other. I broke them apart and let them fall to my side. No hand of another would ever feel to me as my right did to my left. Once I had prayed to forget, now I had remembered almost full circle, and I was still in the uncodified world. Youth, the perfect voyeur, had had the knowledge: listen; say nothing; watch the red game. I hid the memoir away, in the desk. And still the shadow bloomed forward upon it. Pretender, approach. Approach the pretender. This is the ordinary thing. Speak. The wildest prayer comes from the lips of those who know that nothing will change. I am not Ruth. I am *other*. I drew the memoir out again from its drawer.

On the mantel, over which Maarten's picture hangs alone, are collected, well tucked back on the wide marble, certain mementos which, as they surfaced in memory these past three months, I had exhumed from their boxes with a hobbyist's tenderness for these objects which persist, scuffed in drawers, kicked about on the foam-edges of a life, eventually to survive it. The three old books are still with me — *Affection's Gift*, Demuth's dictionary with its irritating, schoolboy *Forsan et haec*, and — visitant from the remotest reach of all — the dime-store address book with one leaf gone, which clung adhesive to my fingers every time I tried to throw it away. To these I had added a pair of Japanese slippers thirty years new, a large conch shell of impervious nacre, and my grandfather's picture, that mutton-chopped pensioner whose rainbow array of medals had never faded into dignity, as if he

443

still existed in some meretricious heaven even brighter than Bellini's. Brought out one by one in the midnight hours by their touchingly faithful believer in psychometry, together they were formidable, as if he survived only to maintain the connection between them, in the way that some men are domesticated to their dogs. Beneath the painting which, with the imposed daring of art, gathered itself to a point that it professed to know, they had only the shabbier sincerity of old coevals muttering hopefully together in some park-bench corner, "A life. A life is worth something. A life." My account of mine surely belonged on the mantel with them, having just so much meaning, no more. I raised my arm in order to put it there — and found my arm stayed. Somewhere in this manuscript, I thought, is my paring. Though I can't see it, another might. Put it in the drawer, then; when she comes tomorrow, you needn't give it to her. Put it on the mantel, then; though you cannot see, another might. "That moment when we know everything," said my owl, "never comes." Beneath all came the voice that — if there is any connective in all the disparate events of my life — is most mine. "Time to leave," it said, "before you do." Never as one dreams it, I thought. This is how actionless people thrust themselves toward action — first the wild image of what will never believably come to be, then the plodding, steadfast as a clerk's, to make it come to be. Then, at last, my arm came down and left the folder on the mantel, like a catatonic who, peering for years toward Ararat, at last brings his mouth to the spoon.

The next morning, after my long absence, I went back to the office, in search of that reassurance of my own competence which we all ask of the daytime world. I received it. Removed so long from wherever people congregate under the assumption of acquaintance, I had almost forgotten what it is like with them when they do. On the streets, indeed, one joined with them in that conspiracy of silence whose faces, under the sunset compline, I had found so moving — anonym to anonym, holding himself out of the amnesiac flood of the world only by the power of his destination. But here, where he was gathered under that other priceless assumption, it was the reverse; here the quacking was enormous, each doing his bit to hold together the skin over those private terrors on which we were all afloat, and it seemed to me that nothing in my recent weeks of solitude had taught me as this did, how exquisitely we must be alone. Soft as a polyp from its case, I felt that these animals like myself, for all their cruelties and self-deceptions, were exceedingly brave, so brave in their limbo that even the most stray remark from one of them should be examined with humility and tenderness. It was not a resolve I could keep, but for the span of a flash bulb I saw any room of us as we are — creatures of eternal quiet and the same humble thought within — The Messiah, who is myself, never comes — saying with blind gaze, over and over, "Hello. Hello. Hello."

On the way home from the office, I walked with them. She was coming at six; it was five. The small apocalypses we arrange for ourselves, I thought — so small, in the face of those the unities arrange for us. She and I were doing the best we knew how, in the face of these. As yet I had no inkling of what hers were. As for me, incomplete though the memoir was, it had at least begun to show me the subtle way in which all my life I had despised my own consciousness, taking the gradual thickening of its complexities always for dishonor, leaning back always, as my century had taught me, on the wellsprings of the child. This was all I knew at the moment. Once I had prayed for the intercession of that feeling which wells from a heart that does not pause to know it has it. Now came to me, in a slackening so great it must be happiness, that the heart doomed to watch itself feel is not less worthy. I walked on slowly, waiting for the dusk that we love best perhaps for its ambiguity, when the real can walk toward us with the authority of the dream. It was almost the hour of assignation. I had mine.

Letting myself in with my latchkey, I went by habit to the rear stairs, and was halfway up the first flight when I heard the self-service elevator on its way down. It was she, I thought at once, for most of the other tenants were still out at this time of day, and running down, I was just in time to see someone emerge. From the depths of the hallway I could see in silhouette that it wasn't she, but from the curve of the back, an old woman. As the door was opened by her, a

lustral ray from its fanlight sloped down on a dim hat shaped like a
scuttle, then the heavy door slammed behind her, Tuesday's cleaning
woman surely, my Mrs. Papp. I put down an impulse to run after her
to find out if she was in truth the old woman I had followed on that
day when I had first begun to feel the present, in the way that, a mile
from the coast, one feels, fresh on the face, the limpid restlessness of
the sea. There'd been too many such tangents in my life; that day had
already served me well, showing me, in my vantage on it now, how I
had come almost to a point that some men, even if barely using the
most delicate movements of the mouth, might call happiness.

Halfway up the stairs again I suddenly began to run, in the panic
that comes on us when we have too nearly named the good. What if
Mrs. Papp, in some excess of senility, had thrown the manuscript left
so loosely on the mantel? Or burned it. I had a grate. But from the doorway I could see the folder safe on the mantel, the other objects
grouped as in a crèche around it, all serene. The shades were at severe
half-mark, and from other signs, furniture twitched out of any reasonable composition, the sofa shining as purely as if never touched by
buttock, it was clear that Mrs. Papp, that brown hen who worked
only for gentlemen, had indeed been here. I fixed my mind on her as
she cut her painful swath through the city, imposing on dirty bachelors the standards of Vienna drawing rooms fifty years gone, but I
couldn't keep it up; by nationality and a dozen other ways she led me
back to Anna, to them, to what I would shortly be doing here. I began
moving about the room in a dark, propitiating unease — as if providence tracked me, one panther step behind. But as usual, I recognized
it for my familiar, my own objectivity, the same who had reassured me
years on back, while I sat watching the flies in an old office, that I
would never be George Higby. A man with a secret encounters just
the woman who — ? No. The uncontrollable *coup de main* came down.
Events might strain toward us because of what we were, but once arrived, we always managed to change them, because of what we were.
You'll be unable to give her the manuscript, or she'll recoil from what is
in it. Something will happen. The planned apocalypse never occurs.

I've not come this far, I answered. Whatever happens, I will do something. Passing a mirror, my grimace recalled my old philosophy professor, not Serlin but the other, on the day he had demonstrated the freedom of the will. I shall move this ruler from point *A* in space to point *B*, Phillips had said, and with just such a grimace, as if he were slitting the throat of the absolute, had slowly brought the ruler down. I *shall*, I said, leaning on the mantel, looking down at the objects there. Her telegram, weighed down by the shell, was among them. The room grew dark while I held it. *Sorry, guess I'm funking it. Better off on your own. Both of us. Let it be.*

It was seven o'clock when I snapped on a light. She'd let me off, then. We were both let off, cast back on our own devices, to be what we were. I was what I had been all the time. The relics on the mantel still held my gaze, grouped there as in a crèche with the central infant figure not there. A man who has no person, hunts a place. My hand hovered over them. We are, at any given moment, all we are. I picked up the shell, and this time I held it to my ear.

We're at Shannon now, put down here to wait for weather, in that confusion of bulletins — half savage, half parlor — which is now the way of the world. London airport is fogged. Storms have ruined the flower crop in the Scillies. On the coast, the worst floods since the fifteenth century. A shower of hailstones, big as eggs, in Tunbridge Wells. I sit here in Ireland, who shall never see Ireland the way I never saw Düsseldorf, remembering meanwhile a flight during the war when, somewhere between Seattle and Tokyo, we put down on a strip so small, among waves which moved like houses, that our landing run must surely capsize it — had tea at a fixed parlor-point in the howling wild of the Pacific, and moved on. Shall I never learn the Esperanto of my century? There are no places any more. Sitting here in Shannon, I say to myself, "There is a place," as Johnny once said to himself, "There is a town." Hurry back. I am hurrying. I am trying to imagine — steady-shuddering in the high seas, steady-plowing in the calm — how it feels to sail by freighter from Portsmouth to Montreal.

Day after day, there would be a landscape of white woodwork and water, the squeal of sea birds, the lack of them, and hour after hour, in

447

the core of the ship, the great plunger that pushed us on, vibrating in the food, the voice, the breast, and after a while accepted, like the heaviest heart, down the length of a single, long white day that would never end — was this the voyage? I can't remember. It was the long day that would never end even with land — the day after the last day at home.

That's where I'm going. Journey's end — no lovers' meeting. Destination of passenger in seat 12A, flight 119 — the last day at home. Is that so strange? On the shore I've left, certain sleepers talk by the hour on their mnemonic daytime couches; others prefer to hunt the chronicle only by night, in the paralyzed dream-rooms whose myrmidons, aerially fresh or diseased, can be counted upon never to change or to die. These days we sort our hallucinations as we may. With luck, my plane, riding so fast that it doesn't move, rushes me toward the present by way of the past headlong.

The rememberers ring the world. But remembrance isn't enough for me. It never was. Was this the simplicity toward which all my complex devices strove, and could never bring me? Hurry back?

If so, I'm luckier than most, for if it is in part a physical place one returns to, then the house in which I was born still stands, with certain people still remaining, others clustered near. And for weapon, I have my hump. Heavier now, there is where it began, with all those painful equilibrations I was afraid to call honesty. Also, as an encyclopedist, I have my resources. Yesterday, before leaving, I called the office and had read to me material from a biographic file I hadn't looked into for some years now, though by my instruction kept up more fully than its importance might seem to warrant. Libby, the girl who had once decoded the ants under my sink, read it out to me. Yes, I am luckier than most. Sir Joseph, Fellow of the Royal Society, is of course well documented otherwise, and several of the children have their public notices of one sort or another. Hannah, under a different name, is the distinguished actress known to us here as well as there; Rosalind, after Newnham, Buchmanism, married a Labour peer twice her age. Martin, R.A.F., was killed in the early days of the war. *Requiescat*, Martin, restless dreamer at window sills, boy who pointed out to me,

448

breathing close almost in friendship, how the Knight of Malta bled from the nose; rest, myrmidon, in the peace that cannot change. James is not mentioned, has done nothing then — poor James. Joseph, the next in line, is in Kenya — what may Joseph have not done! Names of several others born later. None named Pierre. No death notice for Rachel, Lady Goodman, but none also for the old lady, Frau Goodman, who must surely be dead by now. Sir Joseph is seventy-seven. Long, sallow, and so grizzled alongside his wife, he seemed old to my childish eyes thirty years ago; perhaps even then he had burdens that a child might feel — or a servant. Included in the file is a *Daily Express* interview with one Mary (Molly) Mulvey, holder of a ticket in the Irish Sweeps, household servant for forty years, who when asked if she would leave her post now, gave a gloriously nonrepublican answer. The Goodmans, like another household here, keep their servants — and their benevolences, dispensed like gold motes on the air, in the end come back to them.

"Going to ask *him* for an article?" said Libby, breaking the silence on the wire. Her question startled me. She is smart, and I know that out of her own humiliations, which I regret, she still watches me — it's not improbable that she's seen me somewhere with Ruth. But smart as she is, even without that other sad, ciliar intelligence, she was not likely to decode this. "No," I answered. "No, of course not." I spoke more brusquely than intended — but we are not able to keep up our flash-bulb sympathies too long. Before I rang off, I asked whether the file gave their London residence. It did. They live in the same house, the same.

"Attention, passengers flight 119." We take off in forty minutes in another plane which will land at a provincial airport from which transport to London will be provided. London airport is still fogged, as is the city. So we limp home. By plane, couch or dream, the woodcutter's son returns to the forest once hung with magic faces, the street urchin to his precious black warren still smelling of the rotted fruit of old hungers, to the same acid voices rising with yesterday's urine from the damp. Haply we think on there.

But the sentimental return has never been enough for me. What I

449

enter for is always the same, inexplicable sensation. The "control that comes from foreknowledge": I have it. I have the family secrets, ornate but with their cud of truth, that the older children sometimes played at toss with; I have the old lady's incessant ranging. Such conversations we had, she and I. And the thousands of conversations intoned back and forth above my head, the *lingua franca* of giants that now, giant myself, I understand — I have those. I remember what Lady Goodman used to hide in the Battersea box; I remember the day Sir Joseph spoke to her about them. With my name, so fortuitously theirs, in how many ways could I not take my specious place among them? And in the possession of all these things, repeat again the familiar, covert sense that, though I do no evil, I strike the blow. For when one is among people on false terms, then no matter what emotion one gives them, one really gives nothing — and I was never on any but false terms there. Above all, I could keep, intensified by a lifetime between, that sense of the utter secrecy of myself which, as others are held to life by work, love or obsession, holds me. For I have not told. The telegram came just in time. As it does.

For I, who do not dream or if ever do not remember, woke yesterday morning to a certainty. It scuttled away from me, but I caught it just in time, and now that I have it, whether I wake or sleep, it will not let go of me. It is — that like children we cannot believe in our own deaths, at best only anticipating them with the interested horror of the voluptuary, always telling ourselves that there is still something more to come. It is — that the only true death for us is that of the past, and whether these are of hate or of love, this is the death that cannot be borne. It is — that we will not assist at the death of the child we were.

For the past is a doll's house. It stands there, finished and clear, centered in the attic of the mind. We stand outside it helpless, swollen with the giant present. Inside, where everything is known, charm, joy and terror chime with the limited pangs of clocks. Outside it we stand, we the enormous children, and there is no little bottle from which to drink, or bit of cake that will shrink us in. At its windows the dustless curtains billow perfectly, and below, the pavements sparkle mica-sharp, in the uneclipsable light of a small but steadfast sun.

Why, then, have I used the word "weapon"? The drum — the alien drum. What one cannot enter, one seeks to destroy. I refuse that. And even as I think it, I recognize it. I see them at their window frame and I, my own *Doppelgänger*, outside it. The listener is not the friend. Pity them, pity him. And deliver them from evil.

Chapter IV. Conversations and Farewells

I SIT in London, who no longer need to see London. Not far from the Museum, near enough to the Tottenham Court Road station for Dick Whittington to feel his way there with the rest of the crowd or be led there as I was yesterday, this hotel, a small one, almost a pension, is, they tell me, on a street called Store. The fog is lifting now, but yesterday was one of the great fog days I had heard talked of as a boy but had never seen, when buses had to be led like bears on a string, the conductor walking the curb with his hand on the hood, a lantern, and no sign of his red juggernaut a foot beside him, when people lost themselves from door to door, and in the most tightly sealed rooms housewives scrubbed for days later at a thin drapery, sliding to the thumb, that had covered everything. By the time I arrived, two days ago, drawn by a cabby who winked out the moment after his hand, palming the fare, left mine, the yellow, dirtyish astral presence had been rolling over the city for twenty-four hours, making a pick-pocket world in which ships rode oyster-still in the estuary, voices on walking sticks tapped the streets under lights which hung a yard from their own corollas, along avenues become a medium's drawing room. But yesterday, when I visited the Goodmans, I saw all that I needed. I saw the real walk toward me with the authority of the dream.

452

That night of my arrival I could not sleep, but not from the common dislocation of flight in which the body is transported while the personality lags behind. Contrarily, all the minor episodes, trial visitations of before, seemed to have been crammed into one whose energy had at last disembodied me, floated me on ahead and dropped me here detached — the perfect visitant. The muffled grandeur that confronted me was as frightening as it was perfect too. Greeted by a newsprint Westminster, a Trafalgar Square sunny with fountains or with hoardings flaring in the eternal filmdom of a rainy evening, with all of which I was as familiar as any tourist from Indiana, it might have been otherwise for me — but all my prevision had not anticipated this. Because I actually recalled nothing of the obvious London, that is what I had expected to see. For the city I remembered in every bone was an interior London, a construction between my boyhood and me, arching between. And now instead this interior city, luminous and echoing, came out to meet me as if it were my own *camera obscura* projected ahead of me, ready for our dialogue.

The effect this had on me wasn't to have been foreseen. Quietly, quietly, the controls seemed to have been taken from me, in the palest civilian version of what happens in war. For a spell of weather, in this mildly beautiful catastrophe of dark-struck streets, we all had a single story. In a city staged for nemesis, all the drama of self-deception could not hide from me that I was at best the small daily one any man is for somebody; in a city of visitants where murderer and victim, thief and Diogenes, all had the same shadow, what was I but another? So the ordinary and I crept near.

This hotel, once the address of a correspondent of ours who survived the blitz in it, draws its clientele mainly from small-time music hall *artistes* who gather nightly in its basement restaurant after their turns, to put on the actor's never-ending show for himself; in the daytime the halls are full of the tap and strain of these devotees at their worship — a rush of grace notes to the telephone, a cockney slap and tickle all in the way of business as a dressing gown slides its way to the bath, and interwoven through all, the steady *galop* of the long, smiling kangaroo of a girl who brings the morning "cuppa" from nine until noon. That evening, sitting on the bed in my room in the weak, European wattage I had forgotten, I prized every human sound, fancying that their makers too, this evening, cherished them in the same way. "Come down again at eleven, do!" the proprietress had said from behind the cash desk at dinner. "That's when the fun begins." But this last night, first, I kept to my ambuscade in the way one spends a quiet, elegiac hour in the house whose furnishings have already been sent on. After eleven, when tags of revel did rise from belowstairs, I could have answered them — aloud if I wished, in this den of rehearsal — with exhilarated tags of my own, for in the extra day it had taken me to reach London, circling the flooded areas by train and charabanc, hearing voices country-thick or those other intonations clear as bouillon, I had remembered more and more, until, still a hundred miles away, I already stood there, in the lost warren I had not hoped to find. I could have rendered them snatch after snatch out of my treasury with its two pawnshop colors — gold and green, Golder's Green — in the way men, fingering a school desk on Old Boys' Day, falter out their Palgrave. But I remained quiet. In the room next mine, some prestidigitator, Svengali of the three-a-days, was practicing his routine. I'd passed him on the way to the w.c., a man with starved cheeks and pointed boots, who looked better able to command the stars than to find his own dinner. Clinks of some apparatus came to me, spurts of falsetto, Stygian growls, and I might have rung my own changes on these also, standing at the transom to declaim murder times three, bending to whisper "Come away, death" at the keyhole. But I remained quiet, with the answer to my letter to Sir Joseph on my knee. If the mood that held me had both epithalamium and knell in it, who was I walking toward, bent on murder, bent on love? — certainly not this old man, neither my father nor a wanted one, living on in the house where, vicarious from the gates of birth, I had been born. His role was at best to be that Merlin who, answering no riddles, might still be able to evoke from me, by powers beyond us both, the nature of the conundrum itself. I had written him from the plane, on a sheet of Lasch stationery over an illegible signature, asking for an appointment without other explanation, and an answer, care of

Cross, at this hotel; the mails had been quicker than I. His secretary, writing that Sir Joseph would be returning from Paris on the weekend, suggested that I ring him then at home if my visit was to be short, or at the Museum on Tuesday, since he was never available on a Monday. Both numbers were given; this was a trusting people and a polite one — even if the secretary had taken the liberty of adding the terminal *e* of gentility to my mother's name, making it Crosse. In a while, the noises in the next room stopped and I heard its occupant go down, after which I imagined an increase in the genial swell from below. He was luckier than I, this *artiste* whose terminal *e* ennobled him no more than mine — he had something to rehearse. Once I went out to the landing, filched one of the heavy volumes of the telephone directory, and brought it all the way back to the room before realizing I did not need it. I sat holding it awhile anyhow, almost regretting the long evening agonies of nonliving which it stood for, having to remind myself that, knowing "where," being almost there, I no longer needed those sickly nostalgias either; the habit of self-abuse, even of the imagination, dies slow. And once I went to the window, opened it and let the fog roll in, opening my mouth to the sea-taste of the present. Downstairs, they were quiet. Outside, I heard no theme, not even silence, only a confused noise like a coda forever propounding. Tomorrow perhaps, when I went there, it would conclude; tomorrow was Sunday. I would go unannounced, on the day for visits. I would go on the chance.

Next morning, the fog had worsened to complete dark; the air was now a brown smut through which occasional bells came like soundings. Joyce, the Aussie girl who ran about with the breakfasts, volunteered to guide me to the Underground when she heard me in the lounge later on asking for directions — she got off at two. We set off shortly after, coughing and hawking when the air hit our throats, despite which Joyce kept up a comfy chatter, through vowels as warping as the damp. Sye wo' yer lah-ik, they'd none o' this in Sydney. 'Ang on now, t'isn't far. Tall as I, she took my arm without coyness, in the jolly way which kept her easy but not too free with the men still on their pillows in the morning, a good sort of girl from a family of brothers maybe, of a plainness which would have made an American girl miserable but did not mar her blunter national confidence; she knew her own worth. Could tell I was an American; more 'er sort we were; 'otel's Con-ti-nen-tals were a nahs lot mostly; some of the nytive lot 'ere give 'er a pyne. The air was so queer that the channel of her breath warmed my ear like the currents one comes upon in lake swimming; the lack of traffic gave a sense of empty width traversed; for a stretch a furniture emporium, or several, followed us like the same, continuous room hunting its occupants. Meeting 'er fella at the Astoria Cinema, tyke me stryte on to Golder's otherwise; been to the 'Ippodrome there once with 'er old auntie in Camden Town. Ask directions at the ticket booth, I should, at a Corner House or the like, some bloke'd show me the wye, sye that for them 'ere. A white squid bulging toward us proved to be a police helmet; any face that bumped us, ruddy from damp or greensick, had the same shy smile on it that I felt on mine; if this was Atlantis, it was snug here. Push on, she said cheerily as a nursemaid, round the cow-ner y'go; 'ere. Her destination was just a few yards down. 'Ere you are, and good luck to you. Shrugging off my thanks, she tightened her tartan head scarf with the first worried look I had seen on her. Ought to go to Camden b' rahts; thought she'd ask him. No day for the flicks. "Sort of weather the old ones *doy* on yer," she said with a shiver; then the permed forelock that made her face even longer waggled jaunty and she was off. A yard away she was gone. Toodle-oo. My arm felt colder without hers. I had a spasm of envy for her fella. Now the last link was gone. Toodle-oo.

Two hours later, I found myself on a street whose conformation, even through the mist, I thought I knew, just as I now was aware, thanks to a half-dozen directives, that the house I wanted was actually nearer to Hendon than to Golder's, which in the days when my mother first took me there must still have been the end of the Underground line. In later years — I could vaguely recall now — our walk had been shorter, along a different approach. But memory, with a fierce fidelity to its earliest counters, to the particolored name with its garden district smells for the boy from Fulham, the maying-in-November sound of the special night on which he had been born, had stubbornly cherished its mistake. There would be others. Such a set piece of the sentiments as Miss Pridden's might remain as it was — not one of us but kept in his cupboard some such antique barcarole — but what lay ahead of me was a more primary cluster. What did I want of it, then, out of that secret cache-pot where the first savageries are confined? I already knew from the Mannixes what it was in itself, apart from me — a cage swung on the strings of its own frailties, organism subject to all the pity the animate can summon for the animate, a live house. Calm yourself, said the elements; calm — we will float you there; swing with the tide. I stopped, felt my way inward from the curb, stooped, warned of a mass by its air displacement as the blind are, and put my hand out — a stone pillar. The fog swirled against my flash. A match, held close, did better. What I touched was a lion's head with a ring in its jaws that dripped fog-tears. Once it had been above my own head. I was two doors down. And here you are. Good luck to you.

The side window held me. The house, made of a brick almost the color of the brown dark, bulked just visible in it, of no shape except comfort's, never a house with a silhouette, only one with a core. It was the window that held, drawing me across a yard of fog that was ocean and years both — a projection-room screen which would be nothing but shadow and canvas if I grasped it — but it held.

The high casement was sealed against the drip, but inside the draperies had been drawn back and a lamp, set on the window seat as if for wayfarers, shone out with a strong yellow gleam. From any distance, the fog baffled the lamp, but if one stood to one side, close against the shutter, one could see in. This was the morning room, side room for the dispensing of benefits, downstairs nursery on rainy days for the older ones, at whose window Martin had mooned over his marbles, to whose games I had sometimes been summoned from the sewing room, at whose doorway, tranced from my backstairs errands, I had sometimes watched. What colors I could see were not the same and long faded; the same fire burned in the grate. Fire and rain had continued, and over there was the old wooden hutch in which they had kept the games. Near it, on a small desk, once gilt, almost child-size, that I had forgotten, a man's dark coat sleeve rested. To see whose it was I would have to step down into the well for a cellar window centered just below the casement. I stepped down. Through the drops sliding along my hat brim, the man's arm was directly in my line of vision on a level just above the sill, its hand rested on the desk while he spoke into the telephone. His back was turned to me, head bent toward the instrument, his words inaudible, but the hand lay under the light in close-up, firming itself with the restless constant of the aged, now clenching, now splayed. Its veins were ropes now, under mushroom skin heavily spotted, and the curled, black mat of hair which would once have been on the level of a boy's eyes was now either whitened or shed, but those long sinews, the fingers still sallowed with tobacco, could only be, in this house, the same. I remembered the scholar's pencil glinting in them, writing in its precise script: *The pig said "Oui."* I remembered how the strong, black hairs seemed to curl and tremble of themselves the day I came upon the two of them, the day I stood behind him, quiet with the bastings, and heard him ask her where she had got what was in the Battersea box he was holding, the day I heard him speak to her about the cachets.

The man inside there finished talking, put down the phone, rose, the hand aiding him, and turned; he was coming toward me, but I had the advantage and was up and away before his shadow intercepted the lamp. While I watched, flattened against the side of the house, the shadow stayed there, waiting for someone perhaps, or just looking out. It could not have seen me. But from that moment, all that I was to do in that house came to me as natural and unpremeditated as if that hand had pressed a fount long dry or never freshened, and that shadow, waiting there long expectant, had seen. When I made a circuit of the house my feet moved surely over the lawn that sucked them, wet flagstone and lawn again, as if they had played at hare-and-hounds here yesterday. I had the advantage over him of youth and memory, my dram's worth of the power only a little less temporary than his, which would be taken from us both in the way that I had seen it wrested from my mother, but I no longer wanted it — any more than I wanted my mother to sit up in her grave to show me, huddled still between her poor bones, my paring, or needed the old monologuist his mother, long since gone to hers with all their rich rubric around her, to read me, from the chance bit of mine she may have harbored, what I had gone down on my knees to beg her that last day. Let her harbor it still, if she had ever had it; let them both. It was the simplest, most impossible question in the world I had asked her, one to which at the end everyone had his answer. I walked up the front path as the real walks toward the dream.

The light was on over the door. Here was the place that I had chosen as the receptacle of my innocence, as Johnny, no less deluded, had chosen the town. Was it in there, that strangling, angel-black presence I came back here to murder? Here you are, and good luck to you. I stared up at the light. Why should I want to break bread with them here as the prodigal breaks bread in the house of his father; this was not my father's house. Nor was it the house of righteousness, only the not impossible house — with a light on over its door. I rang.

I was about to ring again when I heard feet running and the door was opened by a fluttered young maid still tying her apron. "Yes, sir," she said in thick Irish. "Excuse me, sir. Please to come in." As the door closed behind me, a woman's voice rang strongly from above. "Mr. Harley's to be taken in to Sir Joseph at once, Maureen." Before I could explain myself to the little maid, who was nodding over her shoulder and at the same time offering to take my things as shyly as if she had never done this before, the door of the morning room opened.

Stooped as he was, he was still almost as tall as I remembered him, with the same high-shouldered Egyptian narrowness, the head thrust from it like a buttonhook, the talon-nose carried forward to do the honors for the rest of his person which, scholarly reluctant, lagged behind — for these alone I might have known him, nothing else. The head was an old man's enlarged pate now, with the yellowed baldness that comes to men of saturnine complexion; from beneath it the thin, oval face lengthened as if from a hat, an El Greco in oddly dashing eyeglasses, one of whose lenses was dark. He came toward me quavering, arms outstretched.

459

"Harley, how good of you — I scarcely dared hope." One trembling hand grasped my waterproof. "Harley. She's been calling all day — they have instructions not to prevent her from calling, you know — I couldn't stick that. But I shall value your company down there tomorrow, more than I can say." The rushing speech slowed. "I do beg your pardon. You're not even out of the wet." The hand dropped from my sleeve. "Do excuse me." His head retracted in its wing collar, the lowered chin brushing it. "It's the same thing, of course; she wants to come home. Raising his eyes, he stared at me. "You'd think I'd've got used to it in twenty years, wouldn't you. And to those Mondays. But the truth is —" He passed a knuckle over the clearer lens. "The truth is, I'm getting on." Shaking his head, stepping back, he collided with the maid waiting behind him. "Dear me." Again the hand went out, encountering the girl's hair — she was very small, perhaps fifteen. "Ah, m'dear, you'll have to get used to me, too. Harley —" he went on, half turning, his hand still on her hair, "this is our little Maureen, Molly's niece, come just last week to help us, all the way from County Wexford." A flash of his former courtliness straightened him; inside this wavering apparition one saw for a second the ramrod of its youth. "She's going to stay awhile," he said, with a smile that knew itself liked. But tenderness to children had always been able to woo him from his distance, and this blunt-featured girl, not pretty but with babyhood still on her like a deer's velvet, was only a child. I could remember how he had always stooped to them, not sparkled from a safe vantage like that other charmer whose name now was mine. "Lucky it wasn't the Nailsea, eh?" he had said once, stooping down. "And Maureen," he said now, "this gentleman is Mr. Harley, almost one of the family here."

At this last, I remained speechless. I had not yet had a chance to take stock of my surroundings; it had been bemusement enough to be inside here, meet him even under the ordinary rules of exchange. Now, for one dread flash, I even wondered whether I could have constructed a "Harley" to enter here, which personality — in an ironically final stroke of amnesia — I had then forgot. Then from behind him a saving voice came, the one I had heard from above. She must have come quietly down during our interchange, and now she came forward without surprise, sending me one of those faint, telegraphic gestures we make behind the backs of the failing. This woman with the black still in her gray, the kindly face both sharp and blunt, was not Lady Goodman, could never have been, even though there had never been a death notice for Rachel, Lady Goodman, even if the old man, confirming a prescience I must have had ready for him, had not all but told me where his wife was. But this could very well be Molly, servant girl, grown to housekeeper's estate, who had once looked not unlike Maureen here, Molly in dark blue neatness and a breastpin like the one my mother had received here one Christmas. She touched his sleeve. "The gentleman is not Mr. Harley, Sir Joseph." She pressed a switch beside her and the central chandelier came on. "This weather, the lamps do nothing." She turned to me, hands folded. "Yes, sir?"

"Not — not — ?" He peered at me. "Of course not. I do beg your pardon. I was expecting someone, my godson. I'm afraid my eyes are not what they were."

"I'm the one who should apologize. Your secretary wrote saying you'd be here, but I should have telephoned." The matter-of-fact, adult phrases came to my own ears as if they were *lèse-majesté*, a masquerading; this must be a common experience for those who speak as equals, after long absence, to elders who knew them last as a child. But I had never had that experience and now I shrank from it. I could not face his humility and my own advantage. I had left him so proud. It was Molly I turned to. "You're Molly, aren't you? Mary Mulvey. You must be."

"You're not — why you'll be another one of them chaps from the papers, come about the Sweeps, are you, even on such a day. Well, you may leave off. I've said my say." She leaned toward the old man. "Do go on then, sir. Go on in the library, do; the side room's too cold. There's a nice fire in the library. And if she rings again, I'll answer." Whispering this last, she turned back to me. "Yes, I've had the money. And yes, I'm still here. Now that's all now, do you hear?"

"No, I'm not from the newspapers, although I read about your win — and your answer." I must have answered her as slowly as if I were dreaming, for now I was beginning to take stock of my surroundings, and the mention, too, of her windfall had filled me with a dreamer's sudden, lavish benevolence toward all those belowstairs who had been so kind to me in that haven of second breakfasts; I could have wished to have arrived in a whirligig of presents from America for them, and for those abovestairs too, like my namesake long gone. But my presents, couched with the deadly faith of those who remember too well, would have been awkward ones — a sack of immies and those baked-stone marbles from Tuscana, the like of which Martin would never have seen, an air gun for James's excursions on the inflatable raft, and — perhaps the only dateless one — for Cook a bottle of her ruby port. "I shouldn't have burst in on you like this." I was not sorry. "And I'm afraid you'll have forgotten me." But this too was the language of the masque; I did not really believe it. "I'm —" My glance, wandering, greeting this, that, was intercepted at the top of the stairs. "The Knights of Malta — he's gone." In the light of the chandelier, the landing window shone as ever, and clear.

"The — oh yes. Good Lord, the old Templar — he's been gone a long time now. One of the boys broke it, wasn't it, Molly. He wasn't much really, you know, Flemish, but nowhere near first-rate. The house itself isn't at all early, you know; I'd no idea we'd become antique enough for that sort of thing. Trust my secretary didn't raise your hopes." His voice was suddenly as suavely distant, competent as I remembered it, freed of its quaver if a bit breathy, as if he had outrun that — the same voice which had bent, museum professional, over the harlequin-feathered cape. "Maureen will take your things. Do excuse us. I can't think — oh, of course — the dining room. It *is* Morris, and more intact than most, I suppose. We did once have a fellow come photograph that."

"Sir —" Molly's voice had the tremble now, and she had arrested Maureen with a swift hand. "Sir Joseph — James broke that window almost thirty years ago, sir. He couldn't have been ten. With his ball." Turning to me, she held the girl close. "Who *are* you!"

I turned again to Sir Joseph, giant preserved for my coming. Pitilessly straight as a compass needle, innocence turned me toward him.

"Until I was about ten, too, I used to come here with my mother. I'm Dora Cross's son, Sir Joseph."

"Dora . . . Cross. Do — Forgive me if I don't quite —" He passed a hand over the darkened lens, as if this must stand for all his lapses. And indeed it might, I thought, tender for all seventy-seven years of him still preserved, thinking of the thousands of names he must have gone through in those years and have had to put behind him, else how get through such a roster, else how get through? Allowance must be made for that, and for my present appearance, which would have set him searching in the wrong category, among names that belonged abovestairs.

"My mother used to sew for her ladyship." Softened with revelation, I could afford to be modest, even servile, to wait for his "Sew? — why, she was with Rachel when we married. Remember you — tumbling about underfoot with our own children? Why, my dear boy, you may not know it, but you were *born* here!" I trembled on the verge of his smile.

And now, if he delayed, surely it was because he was sifting through another category as numerous, that other long roster of benevolences cast so freely, so casually by such a house, upon the waters — so few of which, persevering as I, would have floated themselves back. I waited, in trust for them all. "For her ladyship?" he said, not infirm, not wavering, but he had slipped off his glasses to stare past me, baring the one empty eye socket already closed, quietly sealed. In it I saw my answer, not only to the favor — of remembrance — that I had just asked of him, but to that other more impossible request to which it was bound. No. To none of us — neither on our deathbeds nor on our childish knees. No, we may not. Not in any house for long, not anywhere. We may not stay. "For her ladyship?" he repeated. "Ah, that must have been a long time ago."

"Dora Cross! Dora Cross — as went to America!" The cry was Molly's, the face thrust up to mine, smiling and tearful, was Molly's, the arms half extended to encircle the boy I had been, drawn up short before the man I had become, were hers; for a moment the hall was filled with all the sounds of welcome that could be made by a

463

chorus of one. Tea was just on the way — if Sir Joseph would be good
enough to go in by the fire ahead of us. He submitted as the old do, with
a humble pleasure at still being part of the bustle of the world; meanwhile, I might just glimpse, peeped out like a fine pocket handkerchief
to the son of a woman whose place here had been well above a kitchenmaid's, how Molly reigned here now. "Lost an eye in the blitz," she
whispered after him, "and now Doctor thinks the other is going." She
stood off and regarded me. "Crossie's son. And how is — ?" My hesitation told her; before I said more she had collected its meaning without
a hitch, like the commonest of passwords, as indeed it must be by now
in this house. "Cook and I wondered, many's the time. Your mother
always wrote to *her,* so likely we never knew when it stopped." So my
mother had remembered. To all I had not known about her, to the
great pile of secrets of the dead which must form somewhere in space-
time their Everest, I added this leaf.

"*She's* — you know —" Now it was Molly who hesitated and I who
nodded, collecting the password as smoothly. "In a — nursing home,
in Worthing. Has been, these twenty years." She clapped her hands
together. "But what am I thinking, to keep you standing here. And
without your tea." She turned, and I thought she meant to lead me
to her own quarters, where the prodigal had after all been remembered,
and perhaps she did. Midway, she swiveled round again to have a look
at me, at first with unease, but when she spoke, her tone had a certain
old-fashioned distance, satisfied, even triumphant. From it, I might read
if I wished, if after all these years I was still able, how far I had
risen. "Maureen! Take the gentleman's things."

He was already seated on one side of the fire when I entered, and
motioned me into the chair opposite. While we drank our tea, Molly
hovered; I had the feeling that on his deathbed, if he came to it with
none of his family about as there seemed to be none now, she would
grip his hand with the most natural fealty, but in any situation short
of it she would never sit down. When he was not using his cup, he
himself sat with his long hands alternately hanging or upturned on the
arms of his chair. "And your mother," he said, "is she — ?"

"Dead for many years. More than twenty."

464

He nodded. After an interval he spoke again. "My wife would have been so happy to see you, no doubt. But she has been ill, you know. For many years." I could not tell whether or not he had echoed by accident the phrase that seemed to equate her illness with death, or whether he had remembered me by now; here his gentility did have the advantage, for if he would not pretend on first sight, he would not clumsily repair on second, taking for granted that my own good manners would not press it, and so awarding me them in his way exactly as Molly had awarded me my rise. Meanwhile I sat on with them in that suspended room.

Of all the rooms in the house other than his fourth-floor study, this one, often containing an overflow of materia belonging to the Museum, and therefore kept locked against that race of children which had reigned everywhere else, was the only one unfamiliar to me. It was a faded enough room that had perhaps achieved its character only very late in life. Fire had persisted here, and rain, and a few furnishings of the sort kicked about on the foam-edges — it was a room where only people mattered now. If this was limbo, it was one that was new to me, for I found that if I thought of the two older ones sitting here with me in the portion of their real existence which for the moment I was sharing, they had nothing to do with the legend I had made of them, although the legend was still there. Here in this fogbound room the three of us were together in some middle distance, middle darkness, where, with the same ichor in our veins, we were all three of us shades.

"Cook died three years ago," said Molly, energetically refilling both our cups. "You remember her, don't you — Mrs. Holland?"

I nodded without comment, risking the charge of coldness rather than embark on all I remembered here. They would never understand what I had made of them. Here in *the* place — if such there was — was the last place in the world to unburden it. In a few minutes, with only that knowledge to brood on later, as was my way, having done nothing, nothing — as was my way — I could take my leave.

At Molly's remark, Sir Joseph's long hands had again made their slow reversal, as if to say "Enough of that side of the medal. Enough." He leaned forward now, shoulders tensing away from some deep, and again I saw the ramrod, heard the sudden, alternative youth. "So you're an American now, eh? Then I may ask you that very American question, 'What do you do?' "

I told him about Lasch's, keeping back only that I was its head. He knew of it, of course, and leaped eagerly to the subject, rapping out pertinent inquiries on our publications in fields allied to his own, going on from there to recent work, not his own but important, at the Museum where he kept a token office, even ranging on, with that proprietary passion Englishmen have for the social order — he was Labour, he told me — to sharply dubious queries on ours. I listened to him as I would listen to any in this house, from the sheer marvel of being in it as I was, my own *Doppelgänger*, whirled through thirty years at a stroke, to be addressed as I was being now. But what I saw, with the half of me which for the moment had regained the gift of that purer, still-life vision before words complicate, was his terrible struggle for liveliness. Once it faltered, when the telephone rang, and until Molly returned from answering, he dropped the thread of what he had been saying. "Ah," he said when she gave him the message that Mr. Harley would arrive tomorrow in time to go with him — only "Ah." There was a pause. I could better have understood dread — at that other expected phone call, or satisfaction at Harley's — indeed any other emotion. But this was the blankness of a man utterly lost — "Ah," he repeated, and on the same note again, "Ah" — of a man who had lost the thread not only of me, of Molly who had gone out leaving us together, but of Harley and even of "her."

Sort of weather the old ones die in, I thought, but his color had not changed and he was sitting very straight in his chair. His lips moved, bit themselves, said to themselves what I thought was "I must do better. I must do," and as I caught their drift I could have groaned with him, for I began to understand what I was seeing. What I had written off as the mild alternations of senility was the exceptional struggle of a man to keep himself complete, summon himself back from the ordinary deeps of decay. The one clear eye looked at me, utterly lost — yet it had not been blessed with complete loss — it still knew. None are so brave as the old, I thought, and could not help him. What I had

466

mistaken for an effort toward liveliness was the mortal struggle of a man to keep that vital intelligence which to him was life. "Ah-h-h," he said, this time in a growl from depths that were scarcely human, but above, the lone eye maintained itself, and as I watched it, grew not merely human again, for it was already bitterly that, but more so, as if I could all but see behind it the resumption of that ticktock flame. "Stukely," he suddenly said in the most natural way, picking up the thread where we had left it. "So you've met him, eh? Hmm. Stukely. One of our better lightweights, of course, but still — Hmmm. Stukely."

I scarcely had time to accept this irony — that of all the names, recognitions, I had hoped to exchange in this house, this one should be the one to appear — when the door opened to Maureen, shyly bearing a tray which she set down between us. Just then, Sir Joseph spoke again, stretching a hand to me across the tray.

"Armistice Day!" he said, with a great widening of the voice. "The first one. Martin was three. You know — about our Martin? He would have been just a bit older than you are. It was the wine that reminded me. We drank to it. Armistice Day. You were born on it. Here."

Never as one dreams it. I barely heard him, never answered him, hearing instead Maureen's "I'm to ask if you'll have some, sir, before I take it up to her," seeing instead, centered in the light of the fire, a phoenix glowing from its ashes, the slim Spanish bottle of Madeira, and beside it, an old image broken now into three, the thin, up-standing glass.

Three. I knew on the instant who the third must be, and not Molly. Could it be? — that old Cybele of the upstairs, still fending off death then with her *sabacthani*, still proffering as hostage to the absolute her point lace and her goblets, *für die Familie, für die Familie,* with that grim Hebraic faith in the object which I had got here, from her. Not to Molly yet, the third glass. It was all too possible. Romance of a lesser sort would have had her die, but this was the world, where the sadder of the unities can sometimes be not death but change. Frau Goodman had been preserved then (that old historian whom even thirty years ago only one person had called "Franziska") for the fate she had wanted — to see the rubric, the formal design of life, of theirs. And in so occurring, it had happened that she was still here to revise whatever fake history her young apprentice had given them in his — kept on for her confidant, her by-blow — me. "It can't be," I murmured, in the stupid way we protect ourselves from giving away how well we know it can.

"What?" said Sir Joseph, with a trace of pride. "That I remember?"

"That — that *she* is still alive."

"Who?" He said it with a sternness which melted into doubt. I saw with pity how unsure he would be of his own alternations — I had forgotten whom *she* meant first of all in this house.

I looked at him, this old child whom I seemed never to have seen before, before I answered. "Your mother."

He bent his head at that. "Oh, I'm a very old party, getting on for seventy-eight. But not my mother. She's only ninety-five. You remember her, then?"

Such inquiries usually faze me. What can someone like me reply? But here it seemed as natural as the honesty with which I answered; looking back, I see that I told no lies in that house. "We — used to have conversations," I said. "I used to —" I gestured toward Maureen, who was still waiting, hung on our words, for the tray.

"Did you indeed. She always has someone. Never one of us, I might add — none of my brood. Not that she fabricates. Just that we'd be too close to — see the glory of it all, I suppose." He smiled at this last.

"The general glory?" An odd question from one shade to another, or perhaps possible only between those who meet as such. I did not expect him to answer unguardedly, and it was as I thought. Struggle as we may, we do not like to admit to more than interest.

"Oh," he said carefully, "I'm afraid she manages to make it pretty much ours." He arose, and I with him — time to leave. But what he said was, "Let me take you to her."

"She won't remember." I discovered that I did not want her to. All were dead now who could have had any real inkling of me early on — Dobbin, my uncle, my mother; even all those who had been supernumeraries in that life were either dead too or far strayed down their own lost paths. I did not want her to be alive, this old woman who had

468

started me down mine. It was the last stand of my childhood. We do not like our monitors to survive.

"On the contrary. Sometimes she's a bit shaky on the present — she has so little of it. But very rarely on the past." He had already pressed me forward, motioned to Maureen to follow behind with the tray.

The two flights up are long ones and not directly above one another, but accessible through a small passage, with several landings on the way. We took them with a slowness which his stiff bearing made majestic — like the old dog, Chummie, he preferred to walk when he could. On the way, he told me that his mother, though she could still walk, no longer got about much; an old hip injury, from which she must have been recovering when I knew her, had been renewed during the blitz. He said nothing of his eye. I thought briefly of Mannix back there, of whatever it was that the Judge in his own way might be struggling to keep, but I put it aside, as only the traveler can. They were in abeyance back there, I thought, passing a fog-bleared window; that is what distance is. They are in abeyance, pending this. "Yes," Sir Joseph answered as we climbed, his mother had gone with them to Japan, even taking up painting while she was there; later, after the second war, when his work had taken him to Paris, she had spent almost every day as a copyist in the Louvre. She had lost interest since, since coming back home really, but one could not say that she was failing, though she of course was frail. "But she shows no signs of failing," he said, squaring his shoulders as we reached the last landing.

From where we stood, briefly resting, I could see, down the hall, those other steep, narrower stairs, the back ones, down which I had cast the tray and myself after it, that last day. "One of the Eyetalian glasses!" Cook had been the first to cry when she and Molly got to me where I lay, in a welter of shards aromatic with wine and a small amount of blood, the cruelly jagged neck of the bottle pursed like a smashed mouth too close to mine. None of the others had reproached me, from Sir Joseph himself, straggling from the floor above this one to join the circle of children looking down at me as if I were down a well; not even my mother, joining us last of all from the muffled room where she had been closeted with Lady Goodman, had said anything. I had been picked up, washed, bound and tended, even coddled, without another word. In the general leavetaking, no one had appeared to notice whether I had suffered any other wound beyond a few scratches about forehead and shins, or that my mouth, though not smashed, was closed. But as I looked at those empty stairs now and repeopled them, it struck me for the first time that my mother, that strict connoisseur of relationships, might have gone to America not only for need of money or in retreat from my father's humiliating history, but also, having watched her young bird in his paradise, for me — but we cannot really add to the secrets of the dead, only discover them. The old woman, still there on the other side of the door facing us, had been the most realistic of all. No. You cannot stay. I no longer looked back at that boy, her apprentice, with the same single-minded pity.

We had stopped just short of the door. "Go in ahead of us, my dear, will you?" he said to the young girl who had trailed us with her load. "Tell my mother I'm bringing in a guest. Just in case Molly's not with her." As she awkwardly shifted the tray in order to knock, I reached out to take it from her, but casting me a cool look from those deep child's eyes, as if to say "This is mine!" she managed it, and almost immediately the door opened; Molly was there. So I entered that room with my hands at my sides.

"You've told her we have a guest?" he said softly.

"Only that you were bringing someone to see her," Molly said, stepping aside for us. The sliding doors which divided the suite had been pushed back, revealing the whole ugly, comfortable, grandiose room, still heavily curtained to appear windowless, boxed to the ceiling with the monstrous and the elegant, from Sèvres urns to Bohemian beer steins, spotted down its length by curio cabinets in which the *bijouterie* of a lifetime lurked and gleamed. Two grates burned the air to stuffiness; stewing on the hob of one of them the old benzoin inhaler sent up a thin, camphorous column of snuff-steam; everything which could keep the elements at bay here had been done. Frau Goodman was at the far end of the room. We approached her through its unmistakable attar, the smell of age. Chin on her breast, she regarded us.

She was more nearly the same than any of us. Old to me when I left, now she was age's very conception, sparrow where she had been eagle, all of her contracted to a minimum, occupying a space almost too small for an enumeration of its parts, and there was no need to, the years having done this for us; she was ninety-five. Only the forehead had gained and was now of a breadth that would have made her sexless, had it not been for the atmospheric dainties with which she was still surrounded. Beneath it, sharpened by many skin-folds, unblinking, the eyes held us, drew us on and stopped us a few feet from her, while Maureen came round the side and knelt to set the tray down between. Sir Joseph let himself down into one of the chairs arranged on either side of her for audience.

"Mother. Mother, here's someone who knew us a long time ago. He's going back to America tomorrow, but he came all the way down here on a day like this — just to see us." His eyes watered with sentiment; it was true — next to her he was an old party. He was an old man; she was age.

"Dora Cross, you remember her. You remember her, him. This is her son." He had not raised his voice; she was not deaf, then. But she said nothing. He tried again. "Dora Cross's son, Mother. The boy who used to come here with her, must be thirty years ago. This is he." She was regarding me now, unmoving. For what seemed endless minutes, she looked at me. Finally he spoke again, in an even lower tone. "You can't have forgotten. *Rachel's* Dora."

A beardlike puff of lace between breast and chin played in her breath. She was breathing heavily. There was a slight, all-over wince of the body as her lips opened. "Amayrika," she said.

He stared at her, petulant. "No, no. He used to come upstairs in the afternoons — you used to have conversations, he says." Already he had adopted me. He pointed a shaky forefinger. "He used to bring up your tray."

"*Hald dein Mund.*" It should have brought me down to earth, that swift, guttural phrase, the raised, perfectly steady hand, but I was still acting from sentiment. I reached for the tray. It was my last impersonation, as it had been my first, but I could not know this; we do not lightly assist at the death of the child we were. Even if I had been listening with all my talent I would not have heard his exit preparing, or at what point during that afternoon the sound came, no more than the squeak of a windpipe garroted with its own undersized collar, his final sound. One expects so much more of murder. I even smiled condescendingly down on the two of them, as I lifted the tray in that sudden flamboyance with which the middle-aged act young to the old. "*Guten Tag, gnädige Frau,*" I said.

She did not smile back at me, but when she took up the cue it came in a whisper as light as a girl's. "*Da bist du.*" Still, she scrutinized me, the corners of her seamed lips turned down. "*Ach,* such *ton* he had, *nicht?*" she nodded. "*Das kleine Herrgöttle von Bieberach.*" Lips working, until the cry came she appeared to be smiling, until the cry came. "Pierre!" Eyes closed, she rocked with it, in the dying fall for the departed. "Ai, ai, Pierre!" Her eyes open, she whispered it, "Pierre, *selig.* Pierre."

Only my grasp on the tray upheld me. The exorcised must stand that way, rigid before the worn syllable that is the curse, that is the blessing, while the inner bulwarks slide. Then his muttered aside — "Why should she take you for *him,* of all people?" — released me, and bending carefully, knees, back, arms, as if I were of an age with them, I handed the tray to Maureen and sat down. For they had forgotten me. Gabbling, they were exchanging the ritual insults with which members of a real family relieve one another in their imprisonment. "*She!*" I heard her say. "I am not 'she'; I am your mother, and I still know what I am doing. Who anyway makes here the mistakes nowadays, does not know himself from one day to the next one?" — his low, answering "I did not mean —" and her overriding "*Gott sei dank,* the women in our family hold on to their minds!" — his rising "Can't you ever forgive me for her, you devil, leave that poor thing out there alone after all these years! Or me!" — and in the sudden, shocked silence, his "Forgive me, it's true — I don't always know, these days," and her quick, agonized "My son, my son, I did not mean —" They had forgotten themselves. With less than twenty years between them, both cornered now in the far end of the enclosure, they might have been not son and mother but in turn a variation of couples — spouse to spouse, sister to unfavorite brother, father to intemperate child — hand over hand, over hand. Age, the far corner, was the relationship that now made them most near to one another, most dear. As I watched, waiting for them to remember themselves and me again, they receded to it, not as far as their obscure legend, but to the more intimate distance of two old ones of indeterminate years, even sex, of certain human smells and lapses, a little ahead of me in the human stockade. The sound of a door closing, Maureen going out, reminded them of me.

"He was here," she told him, pointing at me. "On Pierre's last visit. That's why I said it, *du alte Dümmling,* you old fool. What else do you think!" She turned to me. "He will remember. Der Onkel Pierre, my little brother. Every child he ever met fell in love with him."

Sir Joseph lowered his eyes, in truce for the time being. Not every mistake need be corrected.

"The pig said *Oui,*" I said to him. "You were the one to interpret that for me." Whether or not he got the reference, my absurd post-mortem gratitude, but was being careful because of his alternations, I could not tell.

"He died four years later, in Brazil," he answered. "Got married there, leaving us a parcel of cousins we've lost track of. Never got back." Then his lip twitched, and together, in our separate ways, we stifled the smile one reserves for those who have after all not escaped.

"And of course I know who you are, then," she said to me, "what do you think! So-o. So." She marveled at me. "So, Dora's boy. *You* got back." She leaned back, shrugging off marvels as easily as she had once dispensed them; in her firm grasp they were natural, even when she added, "Well, handsome waiter, pour the wine." As we drank, she turned to him again. "*Deine Grosmutter, my* mother, used to play that game with him — my brother. You never met her. But last time he was here, I recalled it to him. 'What a memory you have, Franziska!' he said, that last time."

"My mother," she was still saying at ninety-five. "Your grandmother," she was saying to this rheumy-eyed man. We were all being equally absurd, equally sentimental. Eternity makes us so, leaving us to make what we can of it. What Lasch had once said of me, in his old age and too soon for me, was now becoming true. I saw the cycle, or began to, even imagining that outside the door Maureen, whom Molly would never think of letting listen at doors, had her ear pressed against this one, yearning toward the epic company of this house.

"Look there," said Frau Goodman, pointing to some shelves I knew well. "Everything he ever gave me is there. Maureen has just been dusting them." What mind-readers, she and I, I might have thought formerly, but saw it now for merely the heavy repetition of the way things are. "And you know what?" she continued. "I would give them all up for just one little thing." She stopped, to wipe a drop from the corner of her eye, nose, mouth — not tears, but that general ichor toward which we all slowly refine. I thought she was going to name the "one" thing for me, give me the nonagenarian's secret, impart to me, just before leaving, a hint of what it is our end to know. "What I would not give for it!" she said. "That little stickpin he wore always in his tie. His horse."

Because she was pleading with me to remember, I nodded back to her. And since hearing another person describe it would bring it nearer for her, I did so, but with no other reverence — recoiling now from any such storehouse of the dead for myself. At the point where she was, had already been when I first knew her, at the point where this brave man opposite would refuse until death to admit that he was, there might be an almost permanent place from which one might look backward only — to the vast, frozen rearguard of the happened — with honor. But I was still in the middle of life, where one needed only enough remembrance to walk toward.

"I'm looking at your pictures," I said, hoping to coax her a little nearer me, closer in limbo. "The ones you painted." Lined up on a wall devoted solely to them, they were a queer lot such as would never be shown in any gallery but might be seen any day, though seldom in such number, in a house. Copies all of them, of modest Dutch interiors, mild Holy Families, they were in themselves too mild to be bad, but taken together possessed an elusive congruity, of domestic subject perhaps, or of that vague diffusion of comfort to be derived from the second-rate — for there did not seem to be a known original among them. Surely, however, the originals could not all have been — that was it. She had made them all exactly the same size. What unity she had tried to bring them all down to, I could only surmise. Around us were those other objects she had massed against change all through her life, just as my mother — each of them in her way the domestic repository — had tried to do so much later, at the very end of hers. Looking at their dim serial, I might even begin to understand the nature of the enclosure which my mother had tried to push me toward too soon.

"Those?" she said. "*Ach* — embroideries. I had never the patience to sew. Any more, I don't do them. I have on my hands too much else."

Sir Joseph moved impatiently. In his opinion, I was reminded, she had no present. In hers, I suspected, she had him, and more. But his manners prevailed. "She ought to write down the family history, I tell her. But she won't."

"A box to talk into, once he brought me from the Museum. When I tried it — such a *schmier!*" A flush had come over her, from several glasses of the wine. "No. Not for me, *boxes!*" I agreed with her. A box doesn't listen, from deep, receiving eyes. " 'Then let Harley do it, be your secretary. He knows anyway all your stories,' he says. 'Harley knows the end of them?' I said." She held out her glass and I refilled it. Sir Joseph, not drinking, was occupying himself by moving and removing the brass weights, no bigger than dice, from the platforms of a miniature letter scale on an end table near his chair. She drained the glass halfway. "What isn't yet finished, I tell him, how can you write down?" She muttered into her glass. "It ends not so quick, such a family."

"Joseph's children come to see us very faithfully," he said. "When they're in town. The others have none; odd, isn't it." Under his long fingers, the letter scale wavered to perfect balance and was still.

"Claire! You forget Claire is expecting!"

"Oh yes, my youngest daughter. Who lives in France. And is always expecting. We're all pretty much scattered, now."

They were talking to themselves through me, as she had done from the beginning, as all that early list, Miss Pridden, Demuth, had done. I listened with less rancor now.

She drained her glass and set it down. "We were *always* scattered," she said fiercely.

He was silent. "My mother takes the Diaspora quite personally," he said then. "As she does everything else." His forefinger poised over the scale. "Oh, I grant you, nothing ever concludes," he said, sweeping the brass weights from side to side so that we heard their miniature plunk, plunk, out of Haydn. "Except the power to go on." He took things no less personally, I thought. As did I.

At his last remark, there was a moment's deference. For all the room's protection, we heard the current.

But when I rose to go, he was charming. "If the history is ever done, he'll be in it, won't he, Mother? After all, he was born in this house."

She appeared to be quite drunk now. *"Wer kommt?"* she muttered. *"Wie heisst er?"* Who comes. And what is his name.

He mistook her meaning, not unreasonably, for she must never have played that trick with him. He had never been king of Beeberock. "Why, don't you remember? I do, very distinctly. He was a posthumous child, named for his father. I was thinking of it only a moment ago." He was triumphant. "Hold on. Hold on." Then, before our eyes, he faded. "No — don't tell me," he said, turning to me. "I'll get it directly. Hold on."

I held on. Let it come, the name of that dead innocent who meant so little to me now. Mine, which I had begun earning ever since my uncle had been the first to say it aloud, was Pierre Goodman. Not a name to be used here, but I had never really expected to, half hoping to get by here as anonymously as up to now I had. Let the other one come from him, then, fitting end to an expedition I was beginning to find as oversweet to me now as the Madeira, which, like my years of innocence, no longer tasted of justice but of sentiment.

"*I never knew it. His name.*" Drunken or sibylline, she spoke in triumph over him, his hands clasped in painful search, lips moving in that soundless "Ah." "To me he was always just Dora's boy. Isn't that so, Dora's boy?"

He came timidly close to me, even searching out my lapel. All his yellowed, grandee dignity gone again, his face was splotched with flushes that worked and faded like the visible dilation of the dying brain inside it. "Wait — was it not —" He bit his lips, and I waited, even prayed for that strong, growled "Ahr-r" which would mean that he had once more recovered himself. Instead, I saw him forced one notch farther back in his struggle. He took off his glasses, but the serenity of that sealed-off eye could not uplift the dreadful softening around it. "For your father —" he said "— surely?"— but the meaning of his own words was already lost on him. His face, nearing me in trust, found itself only inches from mine. Some kernel in it still presided over its own horror. "I — b-beg your pardon, sir." The expletives forced through; he was using speech like a cane, to lead him back. And he was succeeding. "No. I don't know your name." Seeking the arm of the chair behind him, he wavered, almost fell.

My hand and hers went out to him at the same instant — she was standing now — but he had already straightened. He was back. Then it was I who was cornered between them, in as close a trinity as I had ever been in my life, on one side her redoubtable, sexless mask, still suffering with intelligence, on the other his broken, underwater face, one notch less human now. They had not receded. I had to answer to them.

"Yes —" I had stopped, but only to put a hand on his arm, stretch the other toward hers. I'd meant to say it, buzz-buzz, the old name I'd begun with. But quietly, by whomever or however, the controls were taken from me. Or perhaps, in the answer to an old prayer, I was allowed for one unique moment to forget, made to, in the kind of forgetfulness that is a part of truth. Here in this room, where I had managed a crude physical jointure of the past and the present, I could speak the truth to those who were only shades, as I was, being only a

477

little behind them — the truth which was all the tenses at once. "Yes,"
I said. "I was named for my father. My name is George," I said, in
requiem. "George Higby."

We do not *know* the truth, ever. We know merely how it feels to
speak it. The feeling is clinically describable. I felt as if I pulled from
my breast a thorn which, a moment after it was drawn, I yearned to replace. Looking at the two of them here — he was settling her in her
chair again — looking back to those I could no longer break bread
with, ahead to those with whom I still could, it seemed to me that
though I said nothing more, I should never end speaking, and although they could not hear me, in my breast I spoke and spoke and
spoke.

I bent to say good-by, but when I turned to him, he was gone. She
must have seen him go, perhaps knew too well where he was going.
Eyes glinting, she beckoned me to bend down again. "What do you
think!" she whispered. "What do you think! I have heard from them; I
have had a letter. *He* doesn't know it yet, but I have had Pinkerton's
on it for years."

"Oh what? From whom?" Had I been wrong then — in her own way
was she as far gone as he? No — for once I had been right. She was
more the same than any of us. She giggled, the light sound I remembered, ending in a laugh deep in her throat, almost a croon. "From
whom do you think, *Dümmling!*" Counting on her fingers, she crooned
it. "There are two of them, *ein Bruder und eine Schwester.*" Her eyes
fixed on them, obsessive as history's. In her mind she had already annexed them, named them. "From whom — what do you think! From
the *Brazilians!*"

Downstairs, I managed to let myself out without anyone seeing me.
As I passed through the hallway, spiriting my hat and coat from the
hook where they should be and were, I glimpsed him in the morning
room, once more at the telephone. *Her* call had summoned him, perhaps. Or it was possible to imagine that nowadays he called her, in her
madhouse, as much as she called him. But I was no longer that interested in their secondary mysteries. Age had refined the two of them,
making of them that Biblical word "vessels," through which one

478

might see time and change at their work and the mystery beyond which is not ours, is ours. As I made my way to Hendon station, I thought of my luck, and this time was not afraid to name it. The necessary murder had come to me late, but it had come, and they had been preserved to help me, as I, who also had a place in their history, had been preserved for them. This was my luck, and if the crime was not a perfect one, as the extirpation of the innocents can never be, at least I could begin to believe in my own death, to live in the light of it — for it is a light — while there was still time. Intermittently, in those flashes when I could forget the particular, I might even know who I was and where, for I had seen the nature of the enclosure. I had seen what happens to a live house.

And now home. London airport is being altered; this temporary wing where I have been waiting for a delayed plane is deserted except for an occasional guard, a bare sweep of counter, unmanned at this hour, and opposite me, one telephone stall. I could still call Austin Fenno. Since leaving New York it has been in the back of my mind to do so. He knows their secrets, surely. Alternatives for presenting myself occur to me, with the usual versatility. So far, I have managed not to. But shall I ever be able to look at that slim, body-width oratory and see it unsurrounded by the multitude of its echoes; temple of self-abuse, saving synagogue of the air? About an hour ago, just before midnight, I tried to reach New York, it being only dinnertime there, and was informed, through a scratchy chorale of operators, one saying "Double-oh, double-oh" in monody, the other answering a soothing "Dial nine-nine-nine," that transatlantic calls were running far behind the hour I had to spare. We are rescheduled to leave at 2 A.M., arriving in what will still be early morning there. I sent her a cablegram instead. Under the polite avoidance of the attendant, who for all his sense of the proper cannot keep his wistful eye from the only human thing that is moving here, I can put down the gist of it — it was not long. *No, not better off on our own. I have news from London.* That was the gist. I added the probable hour of my arrival, and that I would telephone her at once, as soon as I got home.

No further plea. I'm taking a cruel advantage; I meant to. She'll think I have spoken to Austin. But I want her to come. And — this to be said with the most tentative movements of the mouth — not for myself only. Or not entirely. No memoir is wide enough to examine that double-faced motive, no life that long. There will be other cruelties between us, hand over hand, over hand. But if she comes — and I think she will — let it rest on the grounds that we have each found a secondary mystery which interests us, which seems to us as recondite, perhaps even as worthy — as our own. For I meant what I said in the cable. That is the news from London.

The flight call has finally come, after two postponements. We're leaving, a small crowd of us, on all our Jack-be-nimble daytime errands. Inside each is that other night-blooming one, slow as the self. But this time — no more talk of distance, in cities, in people, in time. We shall never know what it is, only feel it in transit, a void that except as we assuage it in others can never be appeased in ourselves.

And now home — which is anywhere.

I am in abeyance. The room and I wait for her together. The phone was ringing as I unlocked the door. I went to it and answered direct, as if to the god in the machine, "Yes, it's I."

She and I have a strange intimacy over the phone, always instant; one would think, if one did not know better, that we were people who did not like to touch otherwise. At these times I never visualize her. The conversation resumes, stripped to the essential, half of it unvoiced but heard. I knew that she was unable to speak as yet, but there. Then, softly — my name. Then, as if the voice gathered itself to admit, set the tone, not admit: "So?" — the keep-things-light New York "so" — "I'm here."

I drew a deep breath. That fierce angina, absence, is over. Here. "But not *here*. Will you come?" Unless I was direct, she would get away with it. Unless I held fast now, we would both get away with it, back to nowhere.

A long pause. "But — you did go — To see Austin, I take it."

"Oh." My turn to be silent. "No, I didn't. I went — for other reasons.

It's true, I thought of seeing him. For he knows, doesn't he, what you have to tell me."

No answer.

"I was badly tempted to call him," I said. "But I didn't. For me it was — a special triumph, that I didn't. You won't understand why until I — until you come. I could have found out that way. But I — managed not to." An echo came to me, of almost the same words she had once said to me. And she had called me honest then. "For once I was honest," I said. There was a small sound, so faint that I wasn't sure that it was not in the wire. I waited. "You can tell me or not, as you choose," I said.

Another sound — of breath. Not the wire. A loop of meaning, yearning that I had almost failed to catch. How could I have failed to, shut up with such a burden as I have been these weeks — these years! But the role of the confidant is never fully learned.

"Then —" That one note was high. The rest came in monotone. "Then — we are — as we were. You did let it be."

"No —" But I had let it be — for her. Below me on the desk lay all the pages of the chronicler, bits of paper dropped in the woods, useful only to him. In the telephone at my ear, dark as a crater, a void not mine. She was not able.

I understood then. She was not able, but she had hoped. She had hoped that I would go to Austin — and that he would tell me. You poor, poor — I thought, looking down into the crater, and at last I reached out. "Listen —" I said, "only listen." Then I told her — about this memoir.

It happened then, as I spoke, that I began to see her. She looked: not quite as I had first seen her, never to be that again — although she had something of the stillness with which she had overheard her father speaking to me, when only an earring had quivered and shone. She was what a person is in memory, a composite of the facets and obliques of all the moments which could not be recovered until I was once more in her presence. If she resembled any one of them more than another, it was that moment when we had met unexpectedly in the hallway, when, mulling it afterwards, I had seen how she would look

481

when she was old. In that image, her eyes had been cast down, but now they were wide, dry with the hiatus that is not clinically describable — hope. I could see in them the lineaments of the person she was staring at, as I was at her — at the Messiah who was not ourselves.

"Hello. Hello," I said. "Are you there?"

"I'm here." For a minute the voice was richer. You poor, did it say, you poor? Then it was hers again, and it failed her. "I *can* tell you, someday. Just — give me time."

"No," I said. Not in the light of our death. Had I said that aloud? I glanced down at the phone, as if it could tell me, and in the staining blue I saw it for what it was, still bridled if I willed it, still the subject machine. "Are you phoning from your room?" I said.

"I — have none there. Father's is the only — upstairs." A prescience swept me, of all I did not yet know about her. "I'm in the downstairs hall." She was in Anna's niche then. "It was four when I began calling you. I didn't want the phone to ring here." She spoke in a whisper. "I don't want anyone to —"

"No one will hear you then. It's barely light." Suddenly I remembered our early interchanges on this island, when all we had listened for was the glowing mournfulness of the boats, and I felt the shiver that comes as we descend knowingly into a relationship, even into one we crave.

"Except Anna," I said. "And Anna won't mind."

"No, Anna won't mind." The dry tone surprised me, the next words even more. "You treat me as if I were a child." Of course, of course, I thought. I shudder now to think of it, of how my tender patronage must have fallen on that ear.

"Tell me now," I said. "On the phone. It's easier. When it's not face to face. Then when we meet — you'll have told me. Get it over with. Try." I couldn't see her any longer. There was no answer. "Hang on," I said. "Take your time — but now. I'll stay, it doesn't matter how long. I'll stay." I'll stay. I heard its echo, while I waited. Time to stay, I heard, and it came to me in a treble of voices — we change. The voices we hear in this place are the voices of paradise lost, regained and lost again. Death is only the other unity. For we change. And after an interval I heard that actual voice, whispered. "O.K."

It came in pauses, but with dignity, that simple story, and the voice that told it was not a child's. She was so far ahead of me there, and had been for years — as her quiet burden came to my ear I thought it the least innocent voice I had ever heard. From time to time it halted, then went on. To trust the listener is an act of the greatest daring; she had reason to know that even better than I. Perhaps it took less time than it seemed. Neither of us wept. I had not wept since that day in the privy, but from what I remembered of weeping it wasn't enough for this. I listened, and I did the best I could for her. I listened — and I was the friend. She did the best she could for me. I listened, and I was the friend.

When it was over, we were each of us as rough and quick as we knew how, for we must meet soon now, bound as we were, and each of us knows how little of what is said face to face avails. "Come here now," I said. "To stay. Pack a bag and get out of that house. And don't look back." She promised, though there was no need. "And if there's anything you'd miss later —" I was looking at the array on my mantel. "You won't be going back there. Bring it now."

It would take her a couple of hours, she said. Not for the bag. It would take her that long to leave very carefully, to leave as if she were not going — she who had always stayed. "But Anna will help?" I said.

"Oh yes," her last words were. *"I've* not been that alone," she said, and again I shivered. "Anna will help."

So I am here, making my own farewells. I leave, I leave myself. I leave this account, as nearly myself as I was able to bring it to be against the consciousness that nothing which is written down is ever equal to the weight, in life, of the simplest man. If she reads it, when she reads, she will see what I have always really known, the identity of the follower — who pretended himself the quarry — and what he followed after people for, along that gravest journey where, as part of its condition, we must both leave and stay.

As the morning advances, now and then I hear the slam of a car door from below, and I go to the open window, thinking to allow myself one last spell of the voyeur. I should like to see her once again unaware, before we begin to change. And I should like to see the look on the face of one who is making his formal entry into the enclosure, taking up his bag along that journey into what depths, to what altitudes of non-air, alongside him all those others with that bit of misplaced red in the brain which makes them human — knights errant, Knights of the Midnight Mystery, Knights of Malta — all bleeding mortality from the nose. Meanwhile, along our own minor journey, we shall give each other such absolution as we can. Happiness is for younger worlds than she and I were born to, for those green places where we can no longer lay ourselves down; the consciousness that destroyed them is our substitute glory. She knew, so much sooner than I, why we are still born to ours with more innocence than we can ever hold. It is so that we may have enough left over for absolution. Absolution, for people like us, is no longer a heavenly forgiveness of sins. It is to be loved here, for our innocence, by those who know we are guilty. The look on her face should be identical with mine.

More than two hours now, almost three. More than time.

Here we are. A car door has just slammed. Is it she? I thought I heard someone's voice saying over and over Good-by, good-by, God pity you and bless you, my darling. Anna's. No, I shan't go to the window. Hang on, by the pen if need be. This is the silence; this is the theme. Stay here.

Pity us, for we are pitiable. But we dare. The city of tribulation is bedouin, is everywhere. Like a host of Atlases we hold each other up, who cannot hold. The sin is not to try; the illusion — to exalt what we can do. Deliver us to one another — to ourselves.

The bell rings. It is she. I walk toward her, bringing her my paring. This is the entry. Nothing concludes but the power to go on. We walk toward. The ordinary, advancing like lichen, covers us all.

ABOUT THE AUTHOR

Hortense Calisher is the author of seventeen works of fiction and an auto-biography, *Herself*. Her most recent novel, *Age*, was published in 1987 by Weidenfeld & Nicolson. A former president of P.E.N., she is the president of the American Academy of Arts and Letters. She lives in Manhattan and upstate New York.